DETROIT PUBLIC LIBRARY

3 5674 05210905 6

W9-CMO-289

CHASING
Bliss

RELEASE DETROIT PUBLIC LIBRARY

Sabrina A. Eubanks

CONELY BRANCH LIBRARY
4600 MARTIN
DETROIT, MI 48210
(313) 224-6461

DEC 0 2011

Copyright © 2011 Sabrina A. Eubanks

Published by:

G Street Chronicles
P.O. Box 490082
College Park, GA 30349
www.gstreetchronicles.com
fans@gstreetchronicles.com

All rights reserved. Without limiting the rights under copyright reserved above. No part of this book may be reproduced, stored in or introduced into a retrieval system, or transmitted, in any form, or by any means (electronic, mechanical, photocopying, recording, or otherwise), without prior written consent from both the author, and publisher G Street Chronicles, except brief quotes used in reviews.

This is a work of fiction. It is not meant to depict, portray or represent any particular real person. All the characters, incidents, and dialogues are the products of the author's imagination and are not to be construed as real. Any references or similarities to actual events, entities, real people, living or dead, or to real locales are intended to give the novel a sense of reality. Any similarity in other names, characters, entities, places, and incidents is entirely coincidental.

Cover Design: Hot Book Covers
                  www.hotbookcovers.com

Typesetting: G&S Typesetting & Ebook Conversions
                  info@gstypesetting.com

ISBN: 978-0-9834311-7-6
LCCN: 2011938354

Join us on Facebook, G Street Chronicles Fan Page
Follow us on Twitter, @gstrtchroni

DEC - 2011

Acknowledgments

God is great. He is first, foremost, and all things. God is always there. He is our one constant, never changing and always loving us. God is our non-judgmental very best friend. If you call to Him, He will answer. God brings water from the rock. He gets His very own paragraph in this. I love Him and I'm grateful way past this lifetime. Thank you, Father, for this wonderful journey.

Undying love and respect to my parents, Mary and Julius Sr., I miss you and wish you guys could have seen this—but I'm sure you do. Thank you for my foundation. Love always to my brother, Jay. You'll probably never be able to wrap you mind around how much I care. Thank you. Thanks also to my wonderful, much loved son. Mommy loves you, D.J...you make me smile in the rain. You are my sunshine. Jayson and Joli, you are more light in my life. Auntie loves you. Stay on your grind.

Thank you to my small, intimate, circle of friends and family that hold me down and always have my back: Vera, Vickie, Brenda, Desiree, Karyn, Millie, Kim, Elias, and Levone. Love you all so much, it almost hurts to look at you. Thank you all for loving me.

Thank you to my publisher Mr. George Sherman Hudson and G Street Chronicles for putting me out there and seeing something special in me. Let's get it! To Shawna Grundy, my VP, for doing such a great job, and for listening to me bitch and moan even when I say I'm not bitchin' and moanin. Thanks, girl.

As always, I saved my last acknowledgment for all my readers. I wish you guys nothing but good things in life. Thanks for all the love and support. Mad love from me always. Okay, I'm takin' a deep breath for your shout out… get ready…

GOD BLESS THE READERS!!!!!!!

Wow! That was loud… did you hear me?

Dedication

For everyone who ever had my back in my darkest hours

… and for D.J.

G STREET CHRONICLES
A NEW URBAN DYNASTY
WWW.GSTREETCHRONICLES.COM

Prologue

*C*hase Brown had never been moved much by the power of prayer, but he was sure as hell praying now. There, in what were apparently the last moments of his life, he discovered the truth: You really *do* see your life flash before your eyes. His life story did not unwind like one of those grand and glorious old epic movies; rather, it was a jarring assault, just starkly vivid sparks of random memory. He saw hundreds of bits and snatches of everything he'd done: things he'd done right, things he'd done wrong, and things he should have done differently. Then there were the things he never should have done at all.

What should have happened in the blink of an eye, though, seemed to stretch out unnaturally in some sort of strange, revised measure of time. Chase wondered why his thoughts were so scattered, why he couldn't think straight. Everything was flying around in his head with such swirling, blurring speed that it was impossible to get his thoughts to gel. He felt dizzy, and his heart hammered in his chest.

Violence had always been an abstract to him, and he always associated it with his older brother, Cyrus. That's not to say he was a stranger to it himself. Chase had grown up around violence, had seen friends and family fall prey to it, and had inflicted a generous amount of it himself; though rarely had he been on the receiving end, unless it was from Cyrus. And, the violence he doled out himself was for

Cyrus. The shit he did for Cyrus had niggas scared to death…but obviously not *this* nigga.

Objectively speaking, there really was no reason for the guy to be afraid of Chase. After all, the man holding the .45 on Cyrus Brown's little brothers was Herc Mercer. He and his boys went back a long way with Cyrus, but as of late, most of their history was far from pleasant. They'd started out as friends and business partners when Chase was still in junior high. Chase knew Herc, Rome, and Khalid—knew them niggas well. He knew things were turning sour between them, but he never in his life did he think he'd find himself looking down the barrel of Herc's infamous .45.

Herc waved the gun in front of his face a bit. "Stop daydreamin' and answer the damn question. I swear, I ain't never seen a man drift off with a gun in his face. Where's Cyrus, Chase? Is that muthafucker hiding from us?"

Chase narrowed his eyes and licked his lips. He looked Herc straight in the eye when he lied to him. "I don't know."

They stared at each other, neither wavering for a second, and Chase felt sweat trickle between his shoulder blades.

Herc looked at him dubiously. "What did you just say?"

Chase squared his shoulders and held his gaze. He was scared, but there was no way he was about to let Herc see that. If he was going to shoot him, he wasn't going to let him punk him first. "I said I don't know," Chase repeated, careful to keep his voice even. Raising up had no place here. He knew Herc, and he didn't doubt for a minute he'd blow his brains out. His best bet was to try and smooth this dude out by keeping it even.

Herc was glaring at him with murder in his eye, but he spoke to him gently. "I don't believe you, son. You know, a man can get in a whole lot of trouble lying to me. Come on, now. Tell me where Cyrus is, and y'all can walk away like this never happened. See what I'm sayin'? Be good, baby. Tell me where he is."

"Fuck you, Herc!"

Chase and Herc both turned in surprise to see Corey standing there, bristling with outrage at the indignity. His sixteen-year-old manhood was offended, and he was full of piss and vinegar.

"How you gonna pull a gun on us, Herc? What the fuck is wrong with you, man?"

Chase put his hand on his brother's arm. Things were about to get crazy; he could feel it.

Herc smiled grimly and turned his gun from Chase to Corey.

"Shut up, Corey. Don't say nothin'," Chase ordered in that same even voice.

Corey shrugged his hand away. "Naw, man! Fuck this nigga, Chase!" He turned his head and scowled at Herc, his young, handsome face glowing with indignation; his eyes were ablaze with it—with bright anger and naiveté.

Chase stepped in front of him to try to diffuse the already out-of-control situation, hoping he was not too late to change the ending of this story. He could understand Corey's anger, but he also understood the fact that if Herc had the audacity to pull a gun on them in the first place, he most definitely had the nerve to follow through.

Herc grinned and spoke through his teeth. "Who you talkin' to, boy?"

Corey pushed against Chase. He foolishly feared neither Herc's size nor his weapon. "I'm talkin' to you, you big, stupid, motherfucker! How you gonna pull a gun on us, Herc?" he demanded again.

Chase pushed him right back. Corey's fast temper and big mouth were finally about to get him into something neither one of his brother's could fix. "Shut up, Corey! Stop talkin'! Just shut the hell up!"

Herc reached past Chase and snatched Corey up by the front of his T-shirt.

"Let him go, Herc!" Chase yelled, pushing his weight against the big man who outweighed him by fifty pounds, easy.

Herc knocked him out of the way like he was swatting a fly and hit Corey in the face with his .45.

Corey yelped in pain, but it didn't take the fight out of him; instead, it only made him angry.

Chase knew his brother well. He knew what Corey was going

to do even before his hand went under his shirt. Corey might have only been sixteen, but he *never* left the house without his trusty .32. Chase's brow furrowed in resignation. He was resentful about the unfortunate turn of events. All he wanted to do was go to the park with his brother and get in a simple pick-up game of basketball, but this fool had come out of nowhere with his flexing and his questions. He'd even felt brave enough to come alone, thinking he'd intimidate two teenagers. Chase smiled a sad smile as he watched Herc turn his gun to point at Corey's head. He couldn't just stand there and let that murderous fool kill his little brother. Just like everyone else, Herc had slept on Chase, paying him no mind,

Because Herc had his back to Chase, he didn't see him slip his hand into his back pocket and pull out his own weapon of choice. Chase quietly put his foot between Herc's feet and put his left hand on his forehead, pulling his head back to his shoulder in an oddly intimate embrace. By the time the look of surprise fully registered on Herc's face, he was already wearing a broad smile across his neck. Chase wiped the blade of his silver-handled razor on Herc's pants and stepped away.

Corey, who'd been down this road before, wrested himself away from Herc before the blood could touch him.

Herc didn't care that Corey got away from his grip, because he had more important matters to consider at that moment. He instinctively clutched at his throat and unleashed the torrent. He watched in shocked dismay as his warm crimson life force jetted between his fingers, coloring the air with its spray and soaking the pavement. "Shit . . ." he gurgled.

Chase shook his head. "You got a couple seconds to find God, Herc. Maybe you should pray."

Herc gurgled something unintelligible—maybe it *was* a prayer—and then he fell on his side in a growing pool of his own blood.

Corey leaned down and looked him in his dying eyes. "That's what you get when you pull a gun on us, Herc. Don't *nobody* pull no guns on us. Oh, and don't worry…we'll make sure we tell Cyrus you were lookin' for him."

Chase tapped his brother on the shoulder. "It's not right to mock a dyin' man, Corey. Let's get the hell outta here and leave this nigga to his last breath."

Out of the crooked timber of humanity,
nothing entirely straight can ever be built.
~ Immanuel Kant

G STREET CHRONICLES
ᴧA NEW URBAN DYNASTYᴧ

WWW.GSTREETCHRONICLES.COM

Chapter 1

It had been ten years since the death of Herc Mercer. A lot had changed in that decade, but a lot had stayed the same. Cyrus had done a short bid on a gun charge—and lucky for him, that's all it was for—leaving his two younger brothers to look after his interests while he was gone. There was a lot of in-fighting between Cyrus, Khalid, and Rome.

Herc turning up dead did nothing to smooth feathers. Khalid had accused Chase, right to his face, of killing Herc. He'd said he didn't know of no other niggas walking around slitting throats instead of popping them with a pistol, other than Chase. He also said he didn't know of anyone else who had big enough balls to kill Herc, except Chase. They had a meeting and decided to be decent, since they went back so far. Khalid and Rome gave up a third of their ill-gotten gains to Chase and Corey, for Cyrus, and they severed business ties.

Rome had gotten knocked by the Feds for transporting eight kilos of cocaine and four of heroin across state lines, concealed in a Benz with secret compartments. When he got busted for that load, fun time was over for him, and he'd likely be behind bars until he was a middle-aged man. So, Khalid took over as "head nigga in charge" of his own drug empire, ever expanding and always popular.

Cyrus had reclaimed the reins of his own narcotic kingdom, and he and Khalid had managed to keep their uneasy truce until very recently. Cyrus found new suppliers, stepped his game up, and started outshining Khalid. Slowly but surely, Cyrus began to erase the line they'd drawn in the sand, creeping into Khalid's territory and turning many of Khalid's loyal customers into big fans of his own product. While he didn't speak of it often, though, Chase had the underlying sneaky suspicion that everything was not how it really seemed—like things weren't going as smoothly under the surface as he thought.

Cyrus was a big fan of deception and window dressing. He had never been one to play things straight down the middle and had always leaned to the left. Chase sometimes thought the only people Cyrus was even halfway loyal to were Corey and him. Most times, even that was questionable, but they were brothers, and everybody knows that shit's thicker than water.

Chase and Corey had grown into manhood, taking their lumps and bruises and holding things down until Cyrus got back. They were wet behind the ears when Cyrus got sent up, but he advised them well from upstate, and they were hungry, apt pupils. By the time Cyrus finished his bid, he was three times as successful as he had been going in.

Corey had channeled all his energy into being Cyrus's right-hand man, a job Cyrus had originally intended for Chase. While he'd been doing his bid, Cyrus had groomed Chase for that spot. He'd taught him everything he knew, and Chase had natural business acumen. Unfortunately, Chase had proven to be too volatile and unpredictable, and his temperament was way too uneven for Cyrus's liking. Though Corey was a hot-head himself, he was much more even than Chase and less prone to argumentative opposition. Corey didn't have all Chase's business skills, but he made a much better yes-man.

When Chase turned twenty-three, he'd gone to Cyrus and told him he wanted out of the family business. Cyrus had flipped on him, cussing him out and calling him all kinds of traitors; and he simply *refused* to let him go. At the time, Cyrus wanted to edge out a small-time guy in Bushwick by the name of Dante Taylor. Dante was giving him problems and wouldn't go without a fight. He'd even sent some boys to shake down a few of Cyrus's dealers. When Cyrus got

Chase on the phone and told him how he needed it all to go down, Chase only agreed because he was sure it would be the last job he would pull for Cyrus.

Chase waited patiently, for three hours, for Dante to stop his Denali at the corner of Bushwick and Gates. It was August, so Dante had his windows down and his music thumping. His girl was in the seat next to him. Chase walked up to the truck, as calm as could be, and pushed an ice pick—old-school gangster style—right through Dante's left ear. He did it so fast; Chase was in his car driving away before Dante's girl even started screaming. Chase was done—or so he thought.

"Not so fast," Cyrus said. After all, they were bound together by blood and money. "I ain't never gon' let you just walk away," he explained.

When Chase asked him what he meant by that, Cyrus just smiled slow and gave him a benevolent look. Cyrus had taken care of his two brothers every since their mother was killed when Corey was only ten. Chase thought maybe he said that shit because he thought Chase owed him. Cyrus had a side to him that was as black as midnight. For all Chase knew, it could have been a threat to kill his ass if he tried to walk away. Whatever he meant, it didn't make a damn difference to Chase anyway. He told his brother he wanted out, and he damn well meant it.

"On one condition . . ." Cyrus said. Chase was, hands down, the best man he had for handling dirty jobs and wet work. He told Chase he'd finance anything he wanted to do and set him up nice, but Chase had to take care of whoever he thought needed taking care of—certain people he couldn't trust to his regular boys. Chase was quiet, efficient, and never left a discernible trail. He was like a ghost, *like smoke,* there one minute and gone the next. Except for the corpse, people had to wonder if he'd even been there at all. Cyrus grinned at him and slapped him on the back. "Shit, Chase…when I need small-time niggas checked, I'll use small-time killers. When I need a significant nigga gone, I gotta use you. You're a goddamned assassin."

Chase took the deal. He'd never had a real taste for the day-to-day of the drug business, but there was no question he was good at it. He was good at killing people, too, but that didn't mean he was happy about it. Chase was a smart guy. He knew the deal. He realized that drug shit could only lead to one of two places: jail or the cemetery. He'd seen enough people go to jail and put enough in the cemetery himself, and he didn't want to reserve a spot for himself in either one.

In the meantime, he took the money and played hit man for his brother Cyrus. Chase then went on to become a successful entrepreneur. He owned a supper club in Harlem, a club in Chelsea, and his most successful club, Cream, in the meatpacking district. Cream had become a major hotspot with a large celebrity fan base. It was hugely popular and profitable. Cream's success only made his other two ventures, Delight and Shelter, bigger moneymakers.

Chase spent more time with Corey, but he always saw Cyrus at least twice a week. He usually showed up at Cream an hour or two before closing, accusing Chase of avoiding him and trying to sidestep his family. Chase typically shrugged off the accusations and changed the subject. *Fuck it,* he thought. *Let Cyrus think whatever the hell he wants.*

Chase had tried on more than one occasion to tell Cyrus he no longer wanted any part of his drug-dealing empire, but every time he talked to him, it either landed on deaf ears, or Cyrus got angry and reminded Chase how that drug dealing had financed Chase's businesses. Cyrus let Chase know, point blank, that he owed him.

Chase had gotten used to Cyrus and his bullshit though. After all, he'd taken shit off his big brother since he'd come into the world. It stopped bothering him long ago that Cyrus thought Chase was chained to him, his financier. Chase had paid Cyrus back his initial investment before he opened Cream, so he knew he really didn't owe him shit.

What Chase couldn't stand about Cyrus was the way he always insinuated that Chase could never completely sever ties with him and his criminal activities. Chase could fill a nice-sized corner in any cemetery with the people he'd knocked off under his brother's orders. Every conversation they had about it always ended that way. Cyrus left it hanging over his head like a black cloud. At least once a year, he came calling with another mad request, and Chase always complied.

He had his reasons. On one level, he felt he really *did* owe Cyrus. If he hadn't taken them in when their mother died, there was no telling what would have become of him and Corey. Corey, incidentally, was another reason. Chase didn't want Cyrus using Corey the same way he used him. Corey always walked with his gun; he always had. But Corey was more of a shoot-a-man-in-the-leg type. As far as Chase knew, Corey had never killed anybody, and if anybody had to go to hell for Cyrus, Chase would rather be the one. Corey was who he was, but he wasn't a straight-up killer, and if it was left up to Chase, he never would be. Chase loved Corey more than anyone in his world. After all, the boy was his little brother…and always would be.

The last reason Chase always toed the line for Cyrus was because, lately, Cyrus had been making him feel an unspoken *"or else."* He'd make his request, Chase would tell him he didn't want to do it, and Cyrus would sigh and spread his hands with a sad smile, and then chuckle and say, "Well, you have to, Chase."

Lately, Chase had been glaring at Cyrus like he was looking at him through one of those special lights that showed you shit you couldn't see with the naked eye. When he looked at his brother like that, Chase would look at him and see *"or else"* written all over him. *What the hell does that mean? Does he mean I better do it, or he'll make sure the law comes down on me? Does he mean he'll make sure one of his rivals knows I did away with somebody they held in high regard? Would my own brother rat me out like that? Wait…maybe it's much simpler than that. Maybe he means if I don't do his damn dirty work, he'll kill me himself.* The idea didn't seem so farfetched to Chase. They were brothers and they loved each other, but neither of them had ever been the other one's favorite. They were both a lot closer to Corey than they would ever be to each other.

It was hard to say why they both loved Corey best. Maybe it was because Corey was the youngest. Chase couldn't speak for Cyrus, but brother or not, he didn't much care for the man. That had pretty much always been true, but since Cyrus's return from prison, Chase found that he'd lost just about all of his tolerance for his big brother. To him, it was like Cyrus had come home without his clothes, and he saw him like he really was: a bossy, vengeful, tyrant, with no distinct feelings of loyalty.

In spite of all that, Cyrus put up a good front. It was fairly easy to interpret that Cyrus's occasional generosity and benevolence was for the good of those close to him, but when it got down to brass tacks, Cyrus cared about…well, Cyrus. Everything he did was ultimately for his own benefit, and he was the most selfish person Chase had ever met in his life. Cyrus was a genius at manipulation, and he had no problem using people like tools. He lived for the taste of control, and he pulled the strings of the people around him like a damn puppet master.

Chase and Cyrus played a silent game of tug-of-war with Corey. Cyrus held tremendous sway over their younger brother, and while Corey idolized both of them, it seemed to Chase that Corey held everything that fell out of Cyrus's mouth to his ear, like it was a lump of gold. Cyrus spread around a lot more coal than gold, though, and Chase always made it his business to make the easily-influenced Corey see whatever Cyrus had to say in a starker light.

Most of the time, Corey listened to him. Sometimes, though, he'd wave him off and point out Chase's own shortcomings. If he looked all the way to the end of the road, Chase could see how this story was going to play out, and he didn't like it one bit. However, Chase chose to live his life day by day, and *today,* he was still captain of his own destiny.

Chase slouched in the large leather chair behind his fancy teak wood desk in his office at Cream, with his eyes closed. He was brooding hard at this chain of thought.

The door was thrown open unceremoniously, and Delia Montgomery sashayed into the room, yelling at him and smelling like flowers. "Chase, what the hell is wrong with you, sittin' up in here in the dark in the middle of the day?"

Chase opened his eyes and watched her as she did her sexy, slinky, strut across the room in four-inch heels. Delia was wearing a white dress with tiny red flowers; it looked like she'd been poured into it. The straps that held it up were pretty gathers of wispy cloth, but it dipped low in the back to show off her sexy, well-formed shoulders.

Delia went to the window and let up the wooden blinds, and sunlight flooded the room. "I can't believe you! It's two in the afternoon. You ain't a vampire. Now get your ass up!" Delia wasn't a large woman, but she had a great big voice—a raspy whiskey voice that Chase found very appealing.

Chase squinted at the light and shielded his eyes with his hand. He sat up in his chair and looked at the view. Delia was standing with her back to him, twirling the rod that opened the blinds.

Chase smiled to himself. He liked to watch Delia when she thought he wasn't paying her any mind. Dee was a good-looking woman. Chase eyed her now, standing with her legs apart, twirling that stick. Her ass and her full breasts jiggled enticingly. Her calves and thighs were firm and inviting.

She turned and faced him, putting her hands on her shapely hips. The sunlight washed across her face and lit up her tawny skin. She had a light dusting of freckles across her nose and light brown eyes. Her rich auburn hair was done up in a purposely messy upsweep, and the sun glinted off its subtle hints of gold. Any way you cut it, Delia Montgomery was fine as hell, even if she was fifteen years older than Chase.

"When are you gonna learn how to knock, Dee?" Chase asked, a slow smile creeping across his lips.

She gave him a sultry smile of her own and sat on the corner of his desk, very near his right elbow. The warm, flowery scent of her filled his nostrils in a seductively pleasant way. Chase sat back in his seat and folded his arms across his chest to keep from reaching out and touching her, though his fingers itched to do it.

Dee crossed her legs and looked down at his crotch like she was taking a picture. She looked back up at his face and batted her eyelashes at him. "What am I knocking for? You in here gettin' to know yourself a little better?"

Chase laughed as his eyes ran the length of her smooth brown legs. "I bet you'd love to see *that*."

She touched his knee with her ankle and then took it away. Chase licked his lips as she leaned forward and gave him a generous view of her cleavage. "I sure would, honey. Are you gonna get started right now?"

They stared at each other for a moment, and then Chase frowned and laughed. "Damn, Dee. If I didn't know you better, I'd think you wanted me."

She laughed her throaty laugh. "I do, but you won't let me have you. You must have something against older ladies."

Chase stood and laughed again, walking to the window. "Keep it up, Dee, and I *will* have something against an old lady."

Delia chuckled softly. "You talk big, Chase, but you never back it up."

He grinned at her charmingly. "You know I love you, Dee."

Dee had been Chase's "Girl Friday" since he'd been in business, and he would have been lost without her. She handled his affairs above and beyond the call of duty, always with an iron fist. She put a lot of effort into keeping him successful. Chase adored her in more ways than one. It was a mutual feeling that they never acted on, no matter how much or how hard they flirted with each other. Chase refused to see what he'd worked so hard to build crumble to the ground because of someone's fickle feelings—hers or his own.

That was why he was so loath to touch her or stay too close. Too much contact, and they'd both be smoking cigarettes and basking in the afterglow. He knew it was a tried and true way to end a beautiful friendship and a lovely and profitable working relationship.

Delia got up and walked over to him, her hands on her hips and her eyes looking at him with mild concern. "Yeah, I know you love me, honey. I love you too. It's not like you to be sitting here in the dark like that unless something's bothering you. Come on, baby. Tell Mama what's the matter."

Chase rubbed his temples, feeling a headache coming on. "I'd lie to you, Dee, but you'd know it. I was just thinkin' about my brother."

Her eyebrow shot up in a curious arch. "Which one?"

Chase laughed without a great deal of humor. "Both of 'em...but mostly Cyrus."

Dee made a face. "You have my sympathies, baby."

Chase smiled at her. "Don't like Cyrus much, do you?"

Delia shrugged and looked totally unconcerned. "There's no love lost between me and that man. He doesn't like me, and I don't like him...and I know you ain't crazy about him either, brother or not."

Chase looked at her carefully, but he didn't lose his smile. "I feel you, Dee, but Cyrus is still my flesh and blood."

Dee pursed her lips and went into I-don't-give-a-shit mode. "So what? Being your brother does not entitle him to come around here and put his foot on your neck, and it doesn't mean you have to let him just because he is. Come on, Chase. This is me. I know your business, and I know his no-good ass is the reason people call you Smoke."

Chase's smile evaporated. She was absolutely right. People called him that because everybody knew he'd smoke someone's ass. He wasn't particularly fond of the nickname, but it was true.

The look on her face softened, and she laid a hand on his arm. "Stop letting him control you, sugar. You're worth much more than what he reduces you to."

Chase was well aware that Delia knew what role he played for his big brother. She made it her business to know just about everything that went on in his life, and she protected him fiercely. Even if she wasn't aware of it, she was about the only person on Earth whom he trusted that much. He always thought that if his fate were ever hanging in the balance, he'd rather Dee be at the controls than Cyrus...or even Corey. "Maybe I'm not worth as much as you think," he said.

Dee smiled and patted his bicep. "Yes you are. Look around. Look how successful you are on your own, without that fool. You don't need Cyrus, Chase."

He looked at the floor and sighed deeply. "Yeah, but he's my brother, Dee."

"Like I said before, so what? What are you trying so hard to stay in his favor for?"

Chase looked at his watch and was startled to see how much time had gotten away from him. He had to meet Cyrus, and he was going to be late. "We gotta have this conversation later, Dee."

She frowned and then gave him a knowing smile. "Where are going, Chase? You planning on giving some of my sugar away?"

He smiled at her and headed for the door. "I wish. Gotta meet Cyrus."

Dee frowned again. "Chase, don't let him—"

Chase laughed and walked out the door. "Bye, Dee."

He and Corey were supposed to meet Cyrus at a café down on Little West Twelfth Street. Chase really wasn't in a hurry, so he took his time getting there, just because he knew it would piss Cyrus off. He wondered what Cyrus wanted; he hoped it wasn't what he thought it was.

Chapter 2

When Chase walked into the café, Cyrus and Corey were already there, laughing and talking over drinks. Chase joined them, glad to see Corey—glad to see them both, really—but he remained guarded with Cyrus. "What's good?" he asked and sat opposite Cyrus with Corey between them.

Cyrus grinned and put his drink down. "What's up, Smoke? You got no love for your brothers?"

Chase stood and gave them the expected one-shoulder hug.

"That was a little weak. You feelin' all right, Chase?"

Before Chase could answer, Corey did it for him. "He thinks you want a favor. Can't you tell? He's all tight and quiet and shit."

Cyrus signaled for the waiter and looked at both his brothers with a gracious smile. "You would think I ask for one all the time. That's not what we're here for today, so relax, Smoke."

Chase slumped in his seat so Cyrus and Corey wouldn't notice his shoulders dropping in relief. *Whew.* Now he could actually sit back and enjoy their company and have a meal with them without getting a serious case of heartburn.

The waiter stopped at Cyrus's elbow, and Cyrus looked at Chase. "You drinkin', Smoke?"

"Yeah. Give me a *Rémy* straight up," he said to the waiter and then turned his attention back to Cyrus. "So what's up, Cyrus? It's been a minute since I saw your ass in broad daylight." Cyrus laughed amiably, and Corey followed suit.

"You know Cyrus is a night owl, Smoke. Negro's like a goddamn vampire."

Chase smiled and shrugged, mentally noting that they'd both called him Smoke, so something *had* to be up, even though Cyrus said otherwise. He nodded in Corey's direction. "Yeah? Well, you must be one, too, Corey, 'cause I ain't seen your ass either."

Corey looked at him sideways. "I would've hollered sooner, but me and Cyrus been workin' on somethin'."

The waiter dropped off Chase's drink, and Chase picked it up and took a sip. "Something like what? Y'all plannin' a takeover? Need somebody greased?"

Cyrus rolled his eyes in exasperation and then looked at him impatiently. "See? This is what I mean, Corey. You never know who you're gonna get with this nigga. His ass is always irritated. If he ain't in straight-up bitch mode, he's pissin' and moanin' about shit in the past. Why can't he just leave all that snide shit at home and have a decent dinner with his family?"

Corey laughed and pushed his chair back a little. "Uh-uh, Cyrus. You wanna talk to Chase, talk to him. Don't talk at *him* through me. I ain't fuckin' wit' y'all and your bullshit."

Chase glanced at Corey and then looked at Cyrus. He felt anger building in him, forcing his jaw to clench and his fists to curl, but he held it in. "It ain't *my* bullshit, Corey."

Corey took his cell phone out and stood up. "I got a couple of calls to make. When I get back, it would be nice to see y'all holdin' hands and singin' songs." He walked away, leaving Chase and Cyrus sitting there, just staring at each other.

Cyrus leaned back in his seat and regarded Chase for a long moment before he spoke. "You know, Chase . . ." Cyrus leaned forward with his elbows on the table, talking to him like he was a small, petulant, child. "Sometimes we all gotta do shit we don't want to do. It's kinda like when Mama gave us castor oil. Sometimes it's hard goin' down, but the end result is a beautiful thing. Know what

I mean?"

Chase smiled at his brother but narrowed his eyes. "Beautiful for who, Cyrus?"

Cyrus returned his smile and shrugged. "You know when anything benefits me, it benefits you and Corey too."

"I don't need your damn money. I don't need your protection either. Sometimes I get the feeling that a lot of people are scared of you because they're scared of me. Don't you?"

Cyrus laughed. "I don't really give a shit *why* they're scared, Smoke, as long as they *stay* fucking scared."

Chase sipped his drink and complained, "Got people callin' me Smoke and shit? That's fucked up, Cyrus."

"They've been callin' you that for years, little brother. They probably don't even know why it's your name."

Chase frowned. "It's not my fuckin' name. It's some shit you started callin' me. You ain't right, Cyrus. You should do your shit yourself instead of handing me your dirty work."

"I can't do work like that, Chase. I'd be in jail in two days. I'm nowhere near as neat as you." He paused and chuckled. "Picture that. That's some real funny shit, Chase."

Chase narrowed his eyes and finished his drink. "What if *I* get caught, Cyrus? What then? Or do you even care?"

Cyrus gave him his best big-brother look. "Course I do. If that ever happens—which I seriously doubt—you don't got no worries. You know I got your back, *Smoke*."

Chase looked at him with undiluted skepticism. "You *got* me, Cyrus? What? You gonna do my bid for me?"

Cyrus attempted to brush him off like he was tripping. "Why are you always going this route with me, Smoke? Why are you stuck on the subject? It's like it's all you ever think about?"

Chase looked at him coldly. "It takes up a decent part of my day. Look, Cyrus, I got a lot to lose. I'm a businessman. I shook all that illegal shit off a long time ago."

Cyrus gave him a dark, satisfied smile. "Not quite, Smoke."

Chase's mouth dropped open just a bit, and he looked away from

Cyrus. He wanted very badly to just ask him, right out, what he really had planned for him if he decided he wasn't going to be his own personal assassin anymore, but something kept him from asking the question. He suspected he was just afraid of the answer he might get.

Cyrus reached across the table and grabbed his wrist. "You're my brother, Chase. You and Corey and me gotta stick together. You understand me?"

Chase pulled his hand away. "I heard what you said."

Cyrus smiled. "Yeah, but do you *understand* me?"

Chase didn't look at him. "I said I heard you."

Corey returned and sat down. He looked first at Chase, then at Cyrus. "I don't hear no singin'. Y'all still fightin'?"

"There's no fighting—just a difference of opinion. Smoke is stubborn as hell," Cyrus said.

"Did you tell him yet?" Corey asked.

"Tell me what?" Chase really wasn't interested in whatever Cyrus had to say. He'd shown up like he was supposed to, and now he just wanted to be gone.

"I was thinking of starting a legitimate business," Cyrus said.

This piqued Chase's interest. "Legit? For real? You gettin' out of the game?"

Cyrus laughed. "Come on, Chase. You know me. I'll probably never get all the way out of the game. There's too much money to be made in it. I'm just thinking of branching out, that's all."

"What kind of business?" Chase asked, wondering what all of it had to do with him.

"A club—something like your Cream maybe."

"Yeah. And we already got the property," Corey added. Chase smiled and shook his head. Cyrus wasn't a complete idiot, but the idea that he would try to make a serious attempt at running a place like that was laughable to him. It would probably go under in six months.

"What's funny?" Cyrus asked.

"Nothing. Good luck with your, uh, business."

Cyrus smiled himself and fixed his eyes on him. "I don't need luck, Chase. I need you."

Chase laughed. "Me? What for?"

"You got experience running something like this. I don't."

Chase's smile became wry. "So why try?"

Something glittered in Cyrus's eyes. "Why not?"

The waiter came and took their orders, but Chase declined.

"You're not eatin' with us?" Corey asked.

Chase looked at Cyrus. "No. I don't have much of an appetite."

Cyrus stared at him for a moment and then sighed heavily. "All right, Chase. All right already! I got resentment comin' off you in waves. Forget I asked you to help me and Corey. I understand."

Chase looked away, feeling the heavy hands of guilt and loyalty settling down on his shoulders.

Cyrus turned to Corey. "Well, we already committed to the lease. We might as well get started. I mean, I was hoping we'd get some help from Smoke, but it looks like we got his ass to kiss." He glanced at Chase, and Chase's mouth turned down like he suddenly tasted something sour. "But that's all right. If he wants to forget his family… it's all good. We'll still love him, right?"

Corey looked from him to Chase and shook his head. "You know what, Cyrus? Maybe we can go another way. Maybe we can hire somebody to get this thing off the ground, you know? It ain't no big deal."

Cyrus blew breath between his teeth. "Yeah, at least not to Chase."

"Come on, Cyrus. Ease the fuck up. If he don't wanna do it, ain't no use tryina force him. Just leave him alone."

Chase weighed the pros and cons in his head. If he helped Cyrus with his new little business venture, which at least sounded legit, at the very least, he wouldn't have to go through both of their bullshit. For all he knew, maybe Cyrus's club would have a chance at succeeding; if that happened, Cyrus might stop hanging out at Cream, trying to sling his shit in Chase's spot. Maybe, just maybe, Cyrus and Corey would get so involved in running their own club that they'd turn over a new leaf. It was farfetched, but it was a possibility—especially for Corey, because knowing Cyrus, he'd pass off all the problems that came with running a place down to his baby brother. Maybe Chase would finally wrest Corey from Cyrus's influence.

"You want him left alone? Fine, it's done. Smoke never remembers where his loyalties should lie. He'd rather trust his own business to that bitch Delia, a fuckin' stranger, than deal with his own flesh and blood, and—"

Chase had had enough of their judgmental and self-serving bullshit. He picked up his butter knife and threw it at Cyrus. It hit him in the chest and would have stuck if it had been a steak knife.

Corey's mouth dropped open in shock as Cyrus knocked the knife away reflexively, and outrage took over his features. "What the fuck is wrong with you, Chase? *You tryin' to stab me?* Your own fuckin' brother?" He was so upset that he was shaking.

Chase smiled.

His ass was shaking because he was knew Chase had mad skills with just about any kind of blade. All three of them knew that if Chase had meant to hurt him, that little get-together woulda been his last meal, and Chase said as much. "Calm down, Cyrus. If I wanted to hurt you, that knife would be sticking out of your chest. All three of us know it. I just wanted to stop your goddamn whining about my fuckin' loyalties, and since you wouldn't shut the fuck up like I told you, I needed to get your attention."

Cyrus picked up his drink and drained it with a shaky hand. He put it back down and wiped his forehead with his handkerchief. He looked at Chase angrily. "Fine. You fuckin' got it."

Chase leaned forward and put his hands flat on the table. "Good. I'm gonna help you, Cyrus."

Cyrus put his handkerchief away and looked at Chase with sugar-coated venom. "Well, thank you, Chase. Thanks for steppin' down to Earth long enough to help me out. I appreciate it…and I'm humbled."

Chase laughed and shook his head. In spite of the laugh, he had a fleeting wish that the knife had been a steak knife. Cyrus could be a complete asshole at times, and this was one of them. For once, though, Chase was not in the mood. He refused to be baited and talked down to or made to feel obligated. He stood up with his hands still flat on the table. Chase looked Cyrus in the eye, and Cyrus fell back a bit.

Corey stayed silent, still looking from one brother to the other.

"You're a fuckin' bully, Cyrus," Chase said plainly.

Corey looked down at the table and started shaking his head. "Chase, man…please!"

Chase didn't take his eyes off Cyrus as he spoke to his little brother. "Much love, Corey, but you ain't in this right now. I need you to be quiet. No disrespect."

Corey nodded, still looking down at the table, seemingly resigned to obey.

Cyrus, on the other hand, stood up at the other end of the table, perhaps finding comfort in the fact that he was taller than Chase; in his mind at least, he was the bigger man. He looked seriously offended. "You flexin' on me, Smoke? You raisin' up on me?"

The restaurant wasn't overly crowded, but the few people there were starting to stare.

Chase stood his ground and nodded vigorously. He even laughed a little. "Yeah, Cyrus, I guess I am. Depends on how you look at it. Like I said, I'm gonna help you, but only 'cause I see the greater good in it."

It was Cyrus's turn to laugh. "The greater good, huh? Chase, I hate to tell you…but you ain't so high and mighty."

Chase nodded. "Yeah, I know. Ain't nothin' I can do about that though. A lot of it is thanks to you, Cyrus, but maybe most of it's just me. We gotta make some changes, Cyrus. I ain't your fuckin' hand puppet. I'm gettin' sick of jumpin' when you say jump. I'm sick of you guilting me into doing your will. I'm standing up to you, Cyrus. I'm a man. I ain't no kid anymore, and from this day on, I'm not gonna let you *make* me do nothin'."

Cyrus glanced around. "Why don't you sit down, Chase?"

Chase looked around at the other diners, who seemed very

interested in the drama. He smiled and shrugged. "I really don't want *to*, so I'm not going to. I'm gonna do what *I* want to do from now on. If you don't like it, I don't give a shit." He paused as Cyrus sat down, giving him a very black look that Chase didn't particularly care for. *Oh well,* he thought. *Fuck it.* Chase's smile brightened to the point of sarcasm. "What you gonna do, Cyrus? I mean, what's the very worst thing you can do? I love you, man, but you gotta stop treatin' me the way you do. You feel me?"

The black look stayed. "Oh, yeah. Believe me, I feel you, Smoke."

"Good, then I'm out. I'll call you first thing in the morning, and we can start pulling this shit together. Is that good for you?"

Cyrus grinned at him, but that black, deeply offended look still didn't leave his eyes. "Great. Works for me."

Chase put a hand on Corey's shoulder and gave it a firm squeeze. Then he walked out of the restaurant without looking back.

Chapter 3

Bliss was late, and she hated it when she wasn't on time. It seemed like everything that morning was working against her. Her alarm didn't go off, and since they were doing maintenance in her building, there was no hot water. The goddamned train had sat in the tunnel for ten minutes, and she'd just twisted her ankle coming up the subway steps in her high heels. To top everything off, it was pouring rain. She could feel the moisture in the air wilting her pretty gray business suit and drooping her hair. She was almost a half-hour late for the interview, disheveled as hell when she got there, and she was sure she wasn't going to get the job. "Goddammit! Might as well go home," she muttered under her breath. It was all just talk, though, because she needed the job badly, and she had to at least try.

Bliss turned the corner and started looking for the address, walking closer to the street side of the sidewalk so she could see the numbers. She paused in the middle of the block, thinking she'd passed it, but trying to look ahead of her to see if it was up ahead. To make matters worse, a guy on a motorcycle pulled into the curb and sprayed dirty gutter water all over her brand new shoes.

Bliss's first reaction was to scream. No words—just straight screaming, loud and long, until she passed out right there on the sidewalk. She looked down at her shoes, and anger quickly replaced her woe-is-me mindset. Mucky black street water was all over her stockings and flung across the hem of her skirt.

None of the damage would have ever happened if the fool on the bike hadn't driven into the spot like a maniac, trying to beat someone else to it. "What an idiot! A fucking moron!" she screamed, pulling tissues out of her purse and starting to wipe the dirty water off of her; really, though, her attempt was only making it worse.

The asshole got off of his bike—a nice, fiery red Ducati—and walked over to her. "Hey, Miss. You okay?" he asked, tentatively touching her arm.

Bliss snatched her arm away and dropped the leather portfolio that held her *résumé* on the cold, wet ground. The portfolio snapped open, and she watched in horror as her immaculate, beautiful, perfect résumé was instantly ruined by mud and rain, right before her eyes. They both bent to pick it up at the same time, and Bliss's head bounced off his helmet. She saw stars and staggered back as he grabbed her elbow to keep her upright.

"Shit, lady. Are you okay?" he repeated, his voice muffled and tinny through the faceplate of his helmet.

Bliss rubbed her forehead and took a deep breath as she grabbed her portfolio away from him. She looked down at it in quiet anger. "You...you ruined my...God, you ruined it!"

"Sorry. I didn't see you," he said in that Darth Vader voice.

"Maybe you would have if you weren't wearing that dark-ass helmet! Oh wait...I'm sorry. I guess you need it to keep your tiny brain from rolling out your damn ears when you crash!" Bliss yelled at him.

He flicked the faceplate up with one black leather gloved hand and looked at her with sharp, cognac-colored eyes. That was all she could see clearly: those eyes and the bridge of his nose. But still, they were enough to make her heart stutter. "What?" he asked, and his voice, still muffled, sounded like he was daring her to get smart with him again.

Bliss instantly lost her courage. She was angry, but she knew enough not to talk shit to random people in New York City, no matter how cute they may be. She didn't want to invite trouble, so she just turned and walked away. He didn't try to hold her there, but she could feel his eyes on her as she walked away.

After that fiasco, Bliss found the address quicker than she thought she would. A lacquered black art deco door in a stone recess, next to a large plate-glass window with straight black drapes. Bliss rang the buzzer, thinking, *What the hell? How much more could go wrong?* She hoped going through with the interview might be her one bit of luck on such a horrible day.

A handsome guy in his mid-twenties opened the door and smiled at her with even white teeth. "Mornin'. May I help you?"

She smiled back, knowing she probably looked a hot mess. "My name's Bliss Riley. I have a ten-o'clock appointment with Mr. Brown, for the manager position."

He looked her over appreciatively and then looked at his watch. His look turned sympathetic. "It's ten thirty, boo."

Bliss's smile weakened a little. "I know, I know. I'm *really* sorry I'm late, but if you just take one look at me, you'll see I ran into a couple of problems. Please, Mr. . . . ?" She trailed off and extended her hand, hoping he'd take it and give her his name.

"It's Brown. I'm Corey Brown."

Bliss's eyebrows went up, and she regained some of her former wattage. "Oh? Nice to meet you, Mr. Brown. Will you be conducting my interview?"

"Nah. My brother's in charge of that." He looked at her skirt. "Tell you what...he ain't even here yet, but he's on his way. You go try and, uh, fix yourself up, and he won't know you were late unless you tell him yourself. Okay?"

"More than okay. Thank you, Mr. Brown."

"You're welcome. Follow me...and watch your step."

Bliss followed him inside, past the scattered workmen. They walked through an alcove that housed the public restrooms.

Corey pointed at them as he kept moving. "Those aren't ready yet. You gotta use the one by the office."

They went through a door by the kitchen and into a large sitting room. There was an office to the left and a bathroom to the right.

"Here you go. When you finish, wait out here for Chase. He should be here in a minute."

"Thanks, Mr. Brown. I really appreciate it."

He smiled at her. "No problem. If you give me your résumé, I'll leave it on his desk."

Bliss winced and showed him the ruined paperwork.

Corey laughed and lifted it out of the portfolio with two fingers. "Damn, girl! Looks like you've been having a hell of a mornin'."

"I'm sorry about the condition it's in. Some jerk on a motorcycle made me drop it in a damn puddle."

Corey laughed. "A jerk on a motorcycle, huh? *That's* funny. Anyway, I'll clean this up as much as I can and put it on Chase's desk for you."

Bliss went into the bathroom and pulled herself together. She didn't dare take more than five minutes for her mini-makeover, and she thought the end result was pretty good. She walked out of the bathroom and was just about to sit down when Corey popped his head out the office door.

"Come on in, Ms. Riley."

When Bliss walked into the office, the first thing she saw was that damned motorcycle helmet sitting on the corner of the desk. She deflated like a balloon. *Damn!*

"This him? The asshole on the motorcycle?" Corey asked, obviously tickled to death.

Bliss was at a loss for words, and she felt heat flush her face. "I'm pretty sure that's not what I said."

Corey sat on the edge of Chase's desk and laughed at her like he'd known her for years. "Hmm. Well, either way, I'm pretty sure it's what you meant."

Chase was sitting in the big leather chair behind the desk, not quite smiling himself. Bliss just stood there, unsure of her next move. "Should I sit down…or should I leave?"

Chase stood up, still wearing his motorcycle jacket, a sleek black piece with red piping. "Have a seat, Ms. Riley." He turned to Corey as he took his jacket off. "Don't you have somewhere you gotta be?"

Corey's mouth dropped open comically as Bliss took a seat. "Come on, Chase. Why—"

Chase walked over to the coffeemaker and smiled at him. "See you later, Corey. Raise up outta here."

Corey got up, albeit reluctantly. "Damn, Chase."

"Open the door and step outside. See you later, Corey."

Corey looked like he wanted to argue, but he decided against it. Instead, he smiled and winked at Bliss and took his brother's advice.

Chase looked over his shoulder at her. "You want coffee?"

Bliss crossed her legs and watched his back: really a very *nice* back. He was just tall enough to be considered tall, maybe an even six feet. He was dressed, Bliss felt, very inappropriately for an interview, in an Ed Hardy T-shirt and a pair of jeans. "Actually, I'm more of a tea drinker."

He laughed. "That figures. I got tea. How do you take it?"

"Just two sugars…and thank you."

"Don't thank me yet. For all you know, I might fuck it up."

She laughed.

He smiled at her over his shoulder. He fumbled around for a moment, then stepped away and pulled out his cell phone. "Yeah, Corey, do me a favor and run down the block and get me a large coffee and a tea with two sugars."

Bliss put her hand over her mouth and smothered a smile.

Chase sat on the same spot of the desk that Corey had vacated. He was still smiling. "Don't laugh at me. I can admit I'm no good in a kitchen."

Bliss found herself smiling too. "That's not exactly a kitchen, Mr. Brown. It's just a coffeemaker."

He grinned at her. "How about I hire you and you make my coffee… Bliss?"

Bliss shrugged. "I can do coffee, no problem."

He looked at her for a moment, his smile tapering down a bit. It wasn't an I'm-checking-you-out kind of look, coursing shamelessly up and down her body. He looked at her face, and then his eyes hopped briefly to her crossed legs, only to return quickly to her face.

Bliss thought that maybe if she'd been standing, he would have checked her out, but...Bliss couldn't believe herself! She was sitting there half-hoping he'd notice her. She pushed that thought back as he reached behind him and picked up her résumé; that was no easy feat, though, because *she* was checking *him* out. She couldn't help it: Chase Brown was cute as hell.

He lifted the cover sheet and tried to make out what was on it, but it was impossible to read the blurry and smudged ink. He tossed it back on his desk and rubbed his hands on his jeans. "Oh well. I guess that's not gonna work. I *am* sorry, by the way, Bliss. Is it okay to call you by your first name? You seem kind of, uh...formal."

Bliss wanted to tell him, *"You can call me whatever you want, as long as you call me later,"* but she swallowed that corny line back. "Um, sure. Bliss is fine."

Chase folded his arms across his chest. "All right, Bliss. You're gonna have to sell me on hiring you since I can't read your résumé. What're your credentials?"

Bliss sat forward in her seat. "Well, I've got a BA in—"

"Uh-uh. I don't wanna hear about *that*," he said, standing up and rubbing the back of his neck. "Shit like that means nothin' to me. Wait...not *nothing*. It's *something*, but I know a lot of people with big-deal degrees that can't do the job they went to school for. You know what I mean?"

Bliss raised her eyebrows in surprise. "So you don't want to know what kind of degree I have? You don't care where I went to school? That's a first."

"Nah, that crap's irrelevant. I need to know if you can actually run a club. Where was the last place you worked?"

He was looking at her hard with his sparkling brown eyes. They really were almost the exact color of cognac, and his skin was a smooth, creamy brown, like rich coffee ice cream. He was boyishly handsome. His eyes, nose, and mouth were perfectly proportioned to his face—nothing too big and nothing too small. His eyebrows were dark and well defined. His hair was thick and dark with a natural curl to it. He wore it short and neat, like he'd just gotten out of the barber's chair. The hair on his face wasn't heavy: It looked soft and downy, and his moustache was separate from the hair on his chin.

As cute as he was, though, he wasn't perfect. He had an old, thin, scar that extended a good two inches along his jaw line. If it had been a quarter-inch lower, it would have been unnoticeable. It didn't take away from his looks. It just made him imperfect.

"Solstice, over on Fourteenth Street," she answered. "It closed about a month ago."

He smiled at her. "Yeah, I know. You have anything to do with that?"

Bliss was about to give him an indignant answer when Corey returned with their coffee and tea. He put the beverages on the desk and stuck his hand out to Chase. "That was like ten bucks, man. I went to Starbucks."

Chase opened his coffee and handed Bliss her tea. He eyed Corey over his cup. "Put it on my tab, lil bro'."

Corey studied his empty palm for a second before putting it back in his pocket. He looked at Bliss. "How's it goin'? Okay?"

"Bye, Corey. See you later," Chase hinted, pointing to the door.

Corey shrugged and left.

Chase looked at his interviewee with a sunny expression. "As you might have gathered, that's my little brother. I think he likes you."

"He was nice to me when I got here."

"He better have been. Anyway, about Solstice, I was just joking. I know they had to shut it down because Danny found out what was on the other side, so to speak."

Danny Grant, the former owner of Solstice and Bliss's former boss, had two weaknesses: heroin and kinky homosexual sex. They'd found him in his bedroom, dead of an overdose, wearing a bondage bra and wrapped in bloody sheets.

Bliss recalled Danny fondly, for he was a good boss. "Danny was a nice guy. I liked him."

Chase nodded. "Yeah, he was. Sorry to see him go. How long did you work for him?"

"Three years, going on four."

He sipped more coffee, and Bliss drank her tea. "Where were you before that?"

"The Lounge on Fourth. That was the first job I had out of college."

He nodded. "Nice gig. Why'd you leave that place?"

Bliss looked at her shoes. "I just...well, I never really liked it there."

"Why not?"

She looked over at Chase. He was drinking his coffee, but there was an amused, knowing look in his eyes, like he already knew the answer. "My boss had a problem keeping his hands to himself."

Chase looked like he wanted to say something, but he stopped himself. Instead, he sat behind his desk and started writing on a yellow legal pad. "Bliss Riley," he said aloud. Chase ripped the top page off and handed her the legal pad. "I need all your information. You can fill out your tax stuff on Monday. If I change my mind, I'll give you a call, so I need a number."

Bliss stared at him carefully. "You mean...wait, are you telling me I've got the job?"

He grinned at her. "Unless you don't want it."

"Oh, I definitely want it, Mr. Brown. I promise I won't disappoint you."

He leaned back in his chair and laughed. "I don't think you will. I got great instincts, Bliss, and I think you're the right person to run my brother's club."

She frowned, having assumed she'd be working for him. "This is Corey's club? I thought it was yours."

"Nah. This is my Brother Cyrus's club."

Bliss blew her bangs out of her eyes and tried not to look disheartened. "Oh."

Chase came back around to her side of the desk. "What's up? You look disappointed."

She looked up at him, not wanting to mess up her new opportunity. "Nothing. I just thought I'd be working for you."

His right eyebrow lifted a little, and he tilted his head. "I'll be around—at least until Cyrus is up and running. Probably a couple of months, and then I gotta concentrate on my own stuff. I got my own clubs to run."

"Yeah? Which ones?"

"Shelter, down in Chelsea and Delight, up in Harlem. Delight is more of a supper club, though. And I also own Cream."

Bliss's eyes went wide. *He has to be kidding! Those are three of the hottest spots in New York City.* She was duly impressed. "Not doing too bad for yourself, are you, Mr. Brown?"

He grinned his charmingly boyish grin. "Not bad at all…and you can call me Chase. I ain't your boss. Call Cyrus Mr. Brown. He loves that shit."

Chase was still smiling, but Bliss picked up a note of distaste from him when he made his quip about Cyrus. She didn't comment, but she caught it.

He put his jacket back on and picked up his helmet.

"Are you leaving?"

He nodded. "Yeah, I'm out, but I'll wait for you. Take your time."

Bliss finished writing and stood, too, handing him the legal pad. "Here you go. That was the fastest interview I've ever been on that ended well."

Chase took his cell phone out and put her number in his phone. "Well, I don't believe in wastin' a lot of time. Life's too short."

Bliss's cell phone rang, and she started searching for it.

"That's just me. Now you can get in touch with me when Cyrus makes you want to scream…and he *will*."

She looked at him with a wrinkled brow.

"Don't look at me like that. You'll see. He makes me want to scream all the time."

Bliss smiled cautiously. "You're kidding, right?"

He shook his head. "Not a bit. He might take it easy on you, though, 'cause you're really pretty." He paused and let his eyes drift over her. "*Very* pretty. Maybe you can bat your eyelashes at him or something to smooth him out when he starts curlin' up around the edges."

"Is he that bad?"

"Not all the time, but I promise he can get on anyone's damn nerves."

Chase gestured toward the door, and Bliss started walking. She turned abruptly to say something, and Chase's eyes bounced back up to her face. Bliss couldn't keep the smirk off her face if she tried.

Chase smiled. "Sorry about your skirt, Bliss. Send me the bill, and I'll take care of it." He looked her in the eye like he wanted her to know he'd just had a less-than-pure thought about her. "It's a really *nice* skirt."

Bliss bit her bottom lip. *Oh shit, he's feeling me.* "I might just take you up on that."

He moved a little closer to her. "Do it. I want you to."

There was nothing bold about what he said. It was the *way* he said it and the fact that Bliss liked it. That was what struck the match. They stared at each other a second longer than they should have, and then Chase held the door open.

When they walked out, Chase was a little closer than he should have been. He stopped her in the alcove by the kitchen. "Bliss?"

"Yes?"

"What are you doing later? You free?"

She nodded, feeling her heart beat a little faster. *Is he about to ask me out?* "I'm free. Yeah."

"Why don't you meet me at Delight around eight thirty?"

Bliss tucked her portfolio under her arm and gave him a look. "Are you sure you should be meeting me at your club like that? Your new hire? After hours?"

Chase laughed, put his helmet on, and flipped the visor up. "I didn't hire you for me. I hired you for Cyrus. You ain't *my* employee. If you don't want to, just say so. I'm a big boy. I can handle it," he said in an offhanded way, like it wouldn't faze him at all if she turned him down, but he took a step closer to her.

Bliss looked up at him. She wanted to touch his arm or something, but she didn't. He was so close she could smell his cologne and the leather from his jacket. There was no way she wasn't meeting him. "You know…Chase…I didn't say I didn't want to."

He pulled his gloves on, and she noticed he had another scar. It looked old. It was long and thin and ran across the back of his first three fingers, between the first and second joints. She wondered what had happened to him, but she was sure she'd eventually find out. She couldn't see his mouth, but his eyes were smiling.

"Good. Then I'll see you later." He flipped his visor down and walked away from her.

Bliss took a deep breath and let it out. She would have bet money that her day would have ended the same frustrating way it had begun, but things had taken a dramatic upswing. She smiled to herself as she walked out of the building, not surprised to find the sun peeking through the clouds.

G STREET CHRONICLES
~A NEW URBAN DYNASTY~

WWW.GSTREETCHRONICLES.COM

Chapter 4

Cyrus sat at Khalid's dining room table with him, counting money and drinking Hennessey.

"Damn, Cy. Them kids had more money than I woulda guessed hidin' up in that building. Let's take a break. My thumbs hurt."

Cyrus agreed. He pushed his chair back and sipped his drink. He looked at his old pal Khalid and then back down to the many tall towers of money stacks on the table. "You ain't lyin'. There's gotta be almost $200,000 here. That's some sweet shit for a half-hour of work."

Khalid nodded and took a small silver box out of a drawer in the highboy. "Yeah, but I kinda regret losin' Carter. He was a fuckin' soulja, do or die." He took a joint out of the box and blazed it up.

Cyrus picked up the Hennessey. "Well, shit! If you feel that bad about it, let's pour a little liquor out for his ass."

Khalid blew smoke out and laughed. "Nigga, if you pour that shit on my carpet, I will personally fuck your ass up."

They laughed, and Cyrus freshened their drinks. All in all, it had been a good day.

A long time ago, a kid named Warren Jenkins—who everybody knew as Wolf, even though Cyrus had long ago forgotten why—had started selling rocks on Howard Avenue. Khalid and Cyrus had already been selling for years by then, and they weren't really concerned about the young upstart. Time went by, and they all did what they had to do in the limits of their own space. They wouldn't have been bothered by him anyway, because at the time, Wolf was only selling rock and herb. About six months ago, though, Wolf started selling a ton of heroin and ecstasy, resulting in a constant drift of white folks wandering through the 'hood—so many it looked like they were trying to gentrify it. Cyrus had mentioned it to Chase a couple of times, but all that nigga did was shrug his shoulders.

Cyrus smiled to himself at that. Chase didn't feel like he needed to know what was going down on the home front no more. He'd even moved himself up to Harlem to put distance between them. Cyrus wondered when it was, exactly, that Chase had started feeling himself so hard. *Fuck him and his shitty attitude. Chase was so busy trying to elevate himself above what he actually was, that he often forgot the facts. He didn't realize that he no matter how hard he tried, he'd never be shit, 'cause he didn't come from shit. No matter how hard he worked at washing it off, he'd still reek of where he came from..* Cyrus was a bit more than willing to keep his little brother humble.

Cyrus's thoughts wandered back to the events of the day. Cops got suspicious when there were a lot of white folks hanging around the 'hood because they had to have a reason to go there. Cyrus and Khalid leaned on Wolf to move his shit over to another location, a place in Brooklyn where it wasn't abnormal to see a bunch of white people roaming around. Wolf told them to kiss his ass, so Cyrus and Khalid planned a takeover. They swore they'd empty him out and shut him down, and that was exactly what happened. They took all his money and most of his drugs, a fairly easy mission since they waited until Wolf was out of town. While he was in Aruba fucking his girl on a white, sandy beach, Cyrus and Khalid's boys were robbing his ass blind. *That'll teach that nigga to thumb his nose at us,* Cyrus thought.

"When Wolf gets back, his ass is gonna be screamin' mad, Cy. We need to get ready to take care of that nigga. I think you should holler at Smoke and let him know what's up."

Cyrus remained silent and took a sip of his Hennessey. He felt

Khalid on that one. Unless they wanted a flat-out war—which they clearly didn't—they needed to cut the head off the monster. Wolf needed to be dispatched as soon as possible, and Chase was the man for the job. When Khalid passed him the joint, Cyrus took it and inhaled deeply. He knew Chase wouldn't want to do it, but he would play the game, just like he always did. Cyrus would find a way to make him. *Fuck all that high and mighty shit. That nigga's heart's just as black as mine—maybe even blacker—it's gotta be to do the shit as fucking well as he does.* Chase trying to remove himself from Cyrus and his dealings was laughable. Nobody left Cyrus unless he wanted them gone. *I won't be done with his arrogant ass until I've used him up.* He took another toke and passed the joint back to Khalid.

Khalid inhaled and blew the smoke out. He looked at Cyrus thoughtfully. "Let me ask you something, Cyrus. When you gonna tell Chase that me and you are doing business again?"

Cyrus laughed. "Shit, Khalid, we never stopped. Chase doesn't need to know everything. My brother is a lot of things, but stupid ain't never been one of them."

Khalid hit the joint again and put it out. "Maybe you're right…we done a lot of shit together, Cyrus," he picked up his drink and sipped it, still looking thoughtfully at Cyrus as he put his glass down. "You know what, Cy?"

Cyrus raised an eyebrow and reached for a stack of money. "What?"

"We're two dirty, dark-hearted motherfuckers," he said, looking at him seriously. "We goin' to hell when we die."

They looked at each other for a moment and then burst out laughing.

"The devil doesn't want us, Khalid. We'd put his fuckin' fire out!"

They laughed hard until it slowly petered away, and then they lit another joint and prepared to start counting money again.

"How do you manage to keep Corey's mouth shut?" Khalid asked.

Cyrus was quick to answer. "Simple. He doesn't want us fightin', so he don't say nothing to start shit between me and Chase."

They lapsed into silence as they resumed counting the money.

After a while, Khalid picked the thread of conversation back up. "What's goin' on with that club you tryin' to open?"

Cyrus looked at him in open irritation. "I ain't *tryin'*. I got Chase runnin' the show, and it's gonna happen."

Khalid shook his head slowly. "I don't know why you want the hassle of that type of shit, Cyrus. When you gonna find the time to run it?"

Cyrus shrugged. "I probably won't. It'll give Corey something to do—keep him from nippin' at my heels all the time. Maybe Chase will run it himself, if I'm lucky. In any case, it will be a real good place to make some of this money look clean."

Khalid looked at him sideways. "Okay, great, but whatever you do, make sure you holler at that nigga and let him know we need him to take care of Wolf. *Today*, Cyrus. Okay?"

Cyrus nodded as his mind replayed Chase hitting him in the chest with the butter knife and making his little speech. Of course he'd make his plea, but he knew that stubborn-ass nigga might need more than a little convincing. *It's all good, though. He'll do it like he always does and he'll be earnin' his spot in Hell right along with me and Khalid.*

Chapter 5

When Bliss got to her apartment, she was playing another game of beat-the-clock. She spent the rest of the morning getting her hair done. Now her long brown hair hung sleek, straight—and hopefully rain proof—with fresh highlights. Then she spent the next two hours getting her nails done, and of course that meant all twenty of them. You can't get a mani without a pedi.

She spent more time that she didn't have at the perfume counter at Macy's, and then she went upstairs and spent money she shouldn't have on a cute little lilac dress and a pair of strappy sandals in the same color. Bliss felt guilty dipping into her savings to doll herself up, but thanks to Chase, help was on the way. She refused to meet him looking like a 'hood rat.

When she got back to her apartment, she ran a hot bath and got into the tub. She used some of her roommate's bath salts, hoping Tasha wouldn't mind. Tasha was usually pretty good about sharing stuff, but she drew the line at what she called her "relaxation therapy." She said she needed it to help her unwind after a long day in the ER, and Bliss couldn't blame her. Natasha Lowery was doing her first year of residency at New York Presbyterian, and Bliss was extremely proud of her best friend. She was a neurologist, and Bliss was impressed—big time, even if Tasha was something of a pothead in her downtime. Bliss was just getting out of the tub when she heard Tasha come in.

"Bliss? You home?"

"I'm just stepping out of the tub!"

"Well, hurry up. I gotta tell somebody about the day I had."

"Good, 'cause I gotta tell you about mine." Bliss toweled off and put her robe on.

Tasha startled her when she banged on the door. "Bliss, you better get your little ass outta that bathroom and quit using up my damn bath salts! You used so much I can smell them through the door!"

Bliss opened the door with a sheepish grin. "I'm sorry, Tasha. I'll buy you some more...promise."

Tasha looked at her dubiously. "Oh yeah? With what? Your ass ain't worked in a month."

Bliss looked at her loftily. "I got a job," she said and stuck her tongue out at Tasha.

Tasha laughed out loud and did a little dance. "Hallelujah and thank you, Jesus!" She grabbed Bliss's hands, and they did the happy dance together until they were reduced to girlish giggles.

"I gotta get dressed, Tasha, or I'm gonna be late."

Tasha frowned. "What? You start working tonight, Bliss?"

Bliss shook her head dreamily. "No...I have a date—or at least I think it's a date."

"*Stop playin'!* Your ass ain't had a date in 2,000 years."

Bliss gave her a dark look and started spraying on perfume. "Later for you, Tasha."

"Who is it?" Tasha asked, sitting on Bliss's bed and lighting a joint.

"His name is Chase Brown. He gave me the job this morning."

Tasha frowned through her reefer smoke. "You dating your boss, Bliss?"

Bliss put her panties on and started rubbing lotion all over herself. "No. My boss's brother."

Tasha nodded, looking confused. "Oh...all right. Well, you go girl and all that good shit. Is he cute?"

Bliss slipped her dress over her head and grinned lewdly. "*Hell, yes!*" She sat down and put on her sandals, then stood back up, taking the pins out of her hair. "Can you zip me up?"

Tasha obliged, with the joint still stuck in her mouth.

Bliss made a face and waved the smoke away. "Come on, Tasha! Don't blow that stuff in my hair. I don't want him to think I smoke that shit."

"Spray some more of that perfume on, and he'll never know."

Bliss sucked her teeth. "You make me sick. Tell me about your day while I do my hair."

Tasha told her about the horrors of the ER while Bliss combed her hair and did her makeup.

When Bliss was finished, Bliss picked up the small purse she'd be carrying and shrugged into a short black trench coat. "I gotta go, Tash. I'll see you later. Wish me luck."

Tasha got up and followed her to the door. "Later for luck. I wish you sex—and plenty of it!"

Bliss smiled at her. "From your lips to God's ear, girl. See ya later."

******

Bliss didn't bother with the subway; she had no intention of showing up late twice in one day. She hopped into a cab and took it a little farther downtown to Delight. When she got out of the cab, she saw Chase's Ducati sitting right out in front. Delight was a supper club, so there was no velvet rope or outdoor line waiting to get in.

Bliss opened the door and stepped inside. The place was vibrant and colorful. A live band was playing somewhere off to the left, and the bar ran along the back wall, an area was crowded with people. There was another room to her right that looked like it held a dance floor, and it seemed to just be coming to life. Bliss walked over to the hostess and smiled. "Hi. My name is Bliss Riley, and—"

The hostess smiled at her brightly. "Come with me," she said. "Chase is in his office, but he wanted to know the minute you came through the door." She glanced at Bliss like she had a million questions for her, but she stayed quiet while she walked and smiled.

She knocked on the door. "Chase, Ms. Riley is here."

"Send her in."

It was funny, but Bliss wasn't nervous until that very second. She had sudden and total recall of his face, and her knees went a little wobbly.

The hostess pushed the door open and smiled at her.

Chase was on his cell phone, leaning back in his chair, and he didn't look pleased. Bliss caught the tail end of his conversation: "I ain't gonna talk to you about this right now, Cyrus. *No!* I'm busy. Bye, Cyrus." He ended the call and threw his phone on the desk. Chase stared at Bliss for a moment, then stood without taking his eyes off her. "Oh shit," he said. "I think my heart just stopped."

Bliss smiled at him coyly. He'd said exactly the right thing. She felt the first stirrings of something special. "Well, then how do you suggest we get it started again?"

Chase smiled at her and came around the desk. He walked up on her and ran the lapel of her coat between his fingers. "*Bliss*. Where'd you get a name like that?"

She was very aware of his fingers sliding down her lapel. Her lips parted to say something, but she couldn't find her voice.

Chase dipped his head like he was going to kiss her, but he didn't. "You're not gonna answer me?"

Bliss blinked and realized she was breathing hard. She wanted to throw her arms around him, but she didn't. "My dad named me. He was happy to have me, I guess—you know...blissful."

Chase's hand left her lapel, and he put his lips close to her ear. "So am I. You gonna make me happy...Bliss?" He was so close she could see the weave of the fibers that made up the royal blue shirt he was wearing, untucked, with black jeans.

Bliss licked her lips. "Are you gonna make *me* happy?" she countered.

Chase smiled and whispered in her ear, "Don't answer a question with a question, Bliss."

"You're going to kiss me, aren't you?"

He grinned a bit lasciviously. "I was thinkin' about it, but I don't want you to slap me," Chase said, pulling back to look at her.

Bliss felt dizzy, as if nothing else mattered in the world except for what was going on right there in that small patch of space. "I might slap you if you don't," she said in a voice that didn't quite feel like her own. It wasn't, for Bliss would have never said a thing like that. But the words had come from her own lips, and she didn't care how it sounded.

Chase stepped away from her, but he took both of her hands in his and pulled her forward. When his lips touched hers, Bliss felt like she stepped outside of herself and was watching all this go down. Chase put his lips against hers, slightly apart. Their mouths touched, and they savored the feel of their collision. He kissed her again, and she caught the teasingly, tantalizing, taste of his tongue. He let her go and moved away from her, but not too far. "Maybe I shouldn't have done that."

Bliss looked surprised. "Are you sorry?"

He smiled. "Nah."

She smiled back. "Me neither."

Chase nodded. "Well, all right then." He took his jacket off the back of the chair. "Let's go."

"We're leaving? I thought we were staying here."

Chase slipped his jacket on. "Nope. I gotta bounce up outta here. Cyrus is on some shit, and I don't want him showin' up here and fuckin' up my night." Chase picked up his helmet and was about to put it on when he stopped suddenly and looked at Bliss. "I shoulda drove. I can't put you on the back of my bike in that dress."

Bliss looked down at herself and had second thoughts about the dress too. It might have been an error in wardrobe choice, but she was glad she'd worn it. She was also game enough to get on his bike anyway. She didn't want to pass up a chance to be that close to him. "If you've got another helmet, I'll be okay."

He went to the closet and got a midnight-blue helmet off the shelf. He looked at it like it was suspect and handed it to her. "It's Corey's. I'd look it over before I put it on my head."

Bliss checked it out. "Looks okay to me."

Chase put his helmet on and flipped up the faceplate. "It's gonna mess your hair up," he warned.

Bliss smiled. "I don't care, Chase…if you don't."

His eyes twinkled. "Just want to be with me, huh?"

She nodded. "Yeah. Let's go."

He took her hand, and they left his office.

They walked past the hostess, who noticed Chase was holding her hand and gave Bliss a subdued look of hating. Chase turned his head her way. "Goodnight, Maya. If Cyrus shows up, send him to Jayson, okay?"

"Not a problem, Chase. Goodnight. Goodnight, Ms. Riley."

Bliss smiled at her and wiggled her fingers in her direction. "'Night," she said, wondering if that woman had been with Chase or just had a crush. She felt Maya's eye daggers in her back as they headed for the door.

Chase paused by a good-looking, chocolaty, diesel brother by the door. "Hey, J.T. What's good?" They dapped each other, and Chase put his hand low on Bliss's back. "This is Bliss Riley. Bliss, this is Jayson Taylor. You need to know him, 'cause you'll be seeing him a lot."

"Hey, Bliss. I hear Chase has you workin' for Cyrus?"

She smiled. "Yeah. I start Monday."

Jayson wasn't shy about noting Chase's hand on her back and Corey's helmet in her hand. He laughed and hit Chase on the back. "Looks to me like you started already—just not for Cyrus."

Chase smirked. "If Cyrus comes by lookin' for me, tell him I went to Shelter."

Jayson's face got serious. "All right. Where you really gonna be?"

Chase smiled. "Not at Shelter."

"Don't worry. I got you, Chase."

"Thanks. Bye, J.T."

They went out to his bike, and Bliss put the helmet on her head. "He seems nice, " she said, tucking her hair out of her eyes.

"Yeah, he's my best friend," Chase said absently. "I'm gonna get on and lean my bike for you. When you get on, put your feet here," he said, pointing to a short bar. Chase got on and leaned.

Bliss got on behind him, trying not to give anybody a nice view of her panties. She was scared because she'd never been on a bike before, but not as terrified as she would have been if someone else were driving. As Chase righted the bike, Bliss slipped her hands around his waist and interlocked her fingers to hold on tight; it wasn't lost on her how hard and tight he was.

He looked over his shoulder at her and smiled. "You okay?"

Bliss nodded. "I think so."

"You gotta hold onto me as tight as you can, okay? Put your faceplate down and don't let go, all right?"

"Don't worry, Chase. I'm not trying to let you go."

They stared at each other for a second, smiling, and then Chase flipped his faceplate down and they buzzed away.

******

Chase took her to a nice restaurant on the Upper West Side. It was a little crowded, but when they walked in, the owner called Chase by name and greeted him warmly. The round booth he sat them in was made to seat six people, but they squeezed together in the middle.

"You know the owner?" Bliss asked, fluffing her hair out with her fingers.

"It ain't hard to know the owner if you're in the business. Hell, *you* know *me.*" He turned in his seat to face her, placing his arm along the back of the booth, and watched her fix her hair. "Sorry I didn't bring my car. Time kind of got away from me, and I didn't go back home."

Bliss laughed, tucked her dress under for modesty, and turned to face him. "It's okay. Really. I was terrified at first, but I enjoyed the ride. It was nice."

The waiter popped over with an ice bucket that held a frosty bottle of Dom.

Chase raised his eyebrows at him.

"Mr. Mulroney wants you to enjoy this, courtesy of the house, Mr. Brown." The waiter popped the cork and poured the champagne. Chase scanned to room until he met the eyes of the owner and raised his glass, took a sip, and sat it back down.

"Wow," Bliss said, sipping her champagne. "I'm impressed."

Chase shrugged. "It's a nice gesture. He owes me money, and I don't ride him about it."

"That's sweet of you. Are you really as nice as you seem, Chase?"

He rubbed at the scar that ran along the back of his fingers. "Depends on who you ask."

She put her glass down, too, and ran her fingers through her hair. "I'm glad you asked me to meet you."

"I'm glad too." He leaned toward her and put his hand on her thigh.

Bliss was a little shocked, but his hand wasn't unwelcome.

"I like your dress," he said.

His eyes were mesmerizing her. They weren't light brown, but they weren't exactly dark brown either. They were more like the color of dark whiskey. Between him having his hand on her thigh like that and looking at her with his clear, beautiful eyes, Bliss was having a problem keeping her hands off him. The scent of Chase's cologne was also killing her; he smelled delicious. She wanted to climb into his lap and kiss him until her lips hurt. "Thank you," she said finally.

"Did you wear it for me?"

"Yes. Yes, I did."

"Well, I appreciate it."

"I hoped you would, even though I *did* have second thoughts about meeting you. I mean, you *did* hire me to work for your brother Cyrus. Isn't that supposed to be unethical or something?"

Chase laughed and raised an eyebrow. "Who cares, Bliss? Life goes by too fast to spend it worryin' about shit like that. Sure, you got the job, and I think you can do it, but to tell you the truth, I don't care if you *ever* work for Cyrus. I just want you to make sure you got time for me."

Bliss smiled slow. *Damn! This one certainly doesn't beat around the bush. He gives it to you straight, with no chaser.* She found she didn't have the willpower to debate with herself about what she should or shouldn't do. She didn't want to think about what was proper and what wasn't. She liked him a lot. "You feeling me like that, Chase?"

He smiled. "You had me when I flipped my visor up and saw you standin' there in that dirty little gray skirt."

Bliss sucked her teeth, but she smiled when she did it. "It's your fault my skirt was dirty in the first place."

"All right, already! I'll make it up to you, I promise."

Bliss laughed and leaned away from him. "Okay. I'm gonna hold you to that, Chase."

He moved right up on her and put his lips very close to her neck. "What else are you gonna hold me to?"

Bliss put her hands on his chest and pushed him back a little. Again, how he felt beneath her hands was not lost on her. She was certain that if Chase suddenly decided to take his shirt off, she wouldn't be disappointed. Bliss felt more than a little overwhelmed by him. She wanted him, and he knew it. Bliss pushed against him a bit harder. She didn't want to get swept up in the moment and end up making a seriously bad judgment call. "Hey, Chase…wait a minute."

He pulled back and looked at her patiently, with his hand still on her thigh. "What's up?"

"You know…we just met each other, and—"

He laughed. "I didn't *just* meet you. I met you this morning."

The waiter appeared, trying to be discreet. "Do you need more time, Mr. Brown, or are you ready to order?"

Chase didn't even turn around to look at him. He was still looking at Bliss like she'd just stepped straight down from Heaven. "Bring me the veal."

"And you, Miss?"

Bliss couldn't take her eyes off him. "I'll have the same." She wasn't looking at the waiter, either, but she could hear the smile in his voice.

"Very good." He disappeared just as discreetly as he'd come.

Bliss realized with a start that her hands were still on Chase's chest. She tried to pretend she was smoothing the fabric of his shirt. "I'm just saying that you don't even know me, yet you're sitting here all hugged up on me."

Chase grinned at her. "So? Since you put it that way, you don't know me either, and you're feelin' me up. That's okay, though, 'cause I don't mind a bit."

Bliss took her hands off him like he was hot.

Chase laughed.

She frowned. "What's so funny?"

"You…you're scared of me."

Bliss frowned harder. "I am not!"

He gave her an indulgent look. "Okay, let me rephrase that…you might not be *scared* of me, but you're scared of yourself *with* me."

Bliss stared at him.

"You feel like, if you don't rein my ass in, you'll do something you think you might regret, right?"

Bliss sighed; he was right. "Yeah." She looked him in the eye. "I hope you know I'm not sleeping with you tonight, Chase. Let's get that straight, okay?" She expected him to fall back, but Chase was tenacious and stayed right where he was.

"Am I makin' you *that* uncomfortable, sittin' here with my hand on your thigh?"

No, he wasn't. That was the problem. He was making her *want* him. He'd already kissed her without giving her enough time to think it through. She didn't even know him well enough to know his romantic background. He could very well have a wife and kids hidden somewhere—or hell, looking as good as he did, at least a girlfriend. Bliss put her hand on his and forcibly removed it from her thigh.

He smiled at her, and his eyes sparkled with amusement.

"Stop smiling at me like that, Chase. If we're gonna go one step further, we need to get to know each other. For all you know, I could have a real jealous boyfriend waiting around the corner to shoot you in the forehead."

Chase laughed. "I ain't hardly worried about nobody cappin' me, Bliss. Does this real jealous boyfriend exist?"

"No. What about you? Any real jealous girlfriends I should know about?"

"Not until now."

"Huh?"

"You just took me off the market."

Oh shit! Bliss blushed, watching his face for telltale signs of lying; she couldn't find any. "What about kids? Are you a daddy?" she asked, narrowing her eyes. Kids were fine, but she knew sometimes baby mamas could be deal-breaking spawns from Hell—especially if they were still hung up on their baby daddy.

"No. Do you?"

Bliss shook her head. "Nope."

Chase tilted his head, and his wandering hand returned; this time, it settled on her knee. His smile was gone, and the look on his face told her he was dead serious. "Do you want some? 'Cause I really wouldn't mind helpin' you out with that."

Bliss opened her mouth to say something, but her heart was beating so hard that she found it difficult to catch her breath or gather her thoughts. *Damn! Where did he come from with that shit?* "You're messing with my…with my blood pressure or something," Bliss mumbled.

He leaned toward her and licked his lips, and his hand reclaimed its place on her thigh. It was the sexiest thing, but not as sexy as what he said. "For real? 'Cause I feel like you hit me in the head with a hammer, Bliss—right between the eyes. I know you want me to back up off you, but it's the *hardest thing,* 'cause, right now, all I want to do is get as close to you as I can. I want to make sure you're real."

It was sexy, but it was also one of the sweetest things Bliss had ever heard in her life. She touched his face. "I'm real, Chase."

"I don't believe you. Let me see." He went in for a kiss.

Bliss giggled and pushed him back. "This is crazy! Don't you think it's crazy?"

"Crazy? Says who? *Who* makes the rules to this shit? Not me. I told you, I don't care about stuff like that. I can only tell you how I feel."

She tried a very weak argument. "Yeah, but Chase—"

He shut her up by putting his lips on hers. It wasn't like that first kiss, soft and chaste. His arms went around her like he'd been dying to put them there. Bliss's hands went around his waist and up his back, luxuriating in the manly feel of his tight muscles until each one was on one of his shoulder blades. She drew him in as close as he could get.

When Chase's tongue slid over hers, Bliss could have sworn she heard the fire he'd started in her when it ignited. It popped her ears and curled her toes. His kiss was hot and passionate, delicious and thorough. He kissed her like he was enjoying the way she tasted, and it was blowing Bliss's mind. *Where did this man come from?*

She kissed him back with just as much heat and abandon. *To hell with it.* Her back arched when he ran his teeth over her tongue. Bliss shivered and pushed her breasts into his chest. Chase's lips left hers and left a blazing trail along her jaw and down to her neck. He kissed the hollow of her throat as his hand slid up her side. Chase's thumb grazed the bottom of her breast as he kissed her collarbone.

Bliss hands slipped under his shirt, and *he* shivered, too, as her fingers found the six-pack she knew was there. She ran her fingertips over his muscles as Chase kissed her high over her left breast.

He sat straight up suddenly and pulled Bliss up with him, looking a little surprised. "Damn, baby. I think we forgot where we were."

Bliss sat in stunned silence, blushing furiously. The whole thing was rather embarrassing. She wondered how many people had seen that public display of affection. She'd never completely forgotten herself like that. *What got into me?* she wondered. *Hell, Chase almost did!*

"Bliss, you okay?"

She was sitting there with her mouth open, mortified. *What must he think of me?* But she had loved every minute of it. It thrilled her, letting Chase kiss on her like that. *I like him.* Bliss was conflicted. One part of her wanted Chase to rip her pretty new dress off and break her down until she couldn't walk. The other part of her—a much smaller part—wanted to jump up, slap his handsome face, and get the hell outta there.

She looked at him. He was watching her with his eyebrows slightly raised, not like he thought she was loose. Instead, he looked concerned.

Chase took her hand. "Look, I'm sorry, Bliss...well, not really, 'cause I *really* wanted to feel you like that, but I guess I got carried away, and I'm sorry for that. Do you want me to take you home?"

"That's probably the smart thing to do—to get out of here, anyway." She hadn't even finished her champagne, but she felt tipsy, and she knew it wasn't the bubbly that had her feeling that way.

"Okay," Chase said. He took his wallet out and dropped money on the table.

They didn't speak again until they were outside standing by his bike. Bliss stared at the sidewalk. Chase was taking her home, but she didn't want to leave him. It was stupid, and she was beating herself up for things that were pretty much out of her hands. The bottom line was that she didn't want to be good. She wanted to be with Chase. She could sit for hours and listen to him talk and watch him smile. Bliss felt like she could look at him forever, and she thought she'd die if she couldn't feel his mouth and his hands on her again. *Who says that's bad?* When she looked at him, she saw that he was looking back at her patiently, wearing a straight face, but his eyes were saying something different. His eyes were telling her to let go, daring her to take that crazy ride with him. A smile curved the corner of his mouth, and his eyes sparkled. He looked incredibly handsome.

"I *know*, Bliss, but it's what you call a leap of faith. Are you willing to jump off the cliff with me and see where we end up? This is serious, no games. Look how we feel about each other already."

She closed the distance between them and touched his face. "This is really crazy. I'm kind of scared, Chase."

Chase smiled at her. "Don't be. I'll be right here."

Bliss took her hand away. "God, I really shouldn't be doing this."

"Bliss—"

Bliss jumped off the cliff. She threw her arms around his neck and kissed him like she was starving for him. Chase returned her kiss like he could eat her up. They stood by his bike, kissing on the sidewalk, oblivious of the passersby. When they came up for air, they were breathless, smiling, and unwilling to let go of each other.

Chase kissed her again, and Bliss giggled. "I'm still not sleeping with you tonight, Chase. I don't care how *well* you kiss me."

He laughed and kissed her neck. "Damn. How about tomorrow?"

She laughed again. "Let's play it by ear."

He let her go after giving her one last squeeze. "That's fair. I'm gonna take you home now, before I convince you to change your mind."

Bliss put her helmet on and put the visor up, and Chase did the same. "You think you can do that, huh?"

He smiled at her with complete confidence. "I know I can, but I'm not even gonna try. I'll get it when you give it to me. I can wait." Chase got on his Ducati and leaned it over for her.

Bliss was a lot less afraid this time, and she smiled as she settled in behind him. She flipped her faceplate down and wrapped her arms around his body as he gunned the motor. Bliss put her face against his strong back, still smiling as Chase pulled out. She was feeling Chase so hard she couldn't stop grinning. She believed she'd just fallen in love. *Love? Could it be love already?*

Chapter 6

Chase met Corey and J.T. for lunch the next day. He was running late, as usual, but this time it was for a good reason: Bliss Riley. Dee woke him up like an alarm clock, screaming at him and demanding to know why he'd been unreachable for half the night. He didn't tell her any details because she'd meet Bliss soon enough, and for the time being, he wanted to keep what had started between them close to his vest for as long as he could—for a whole lot of reasons.

Chase had the feeling he wouldn't be able to though. Bliss was right: This shit between them was crazy. He'd called her that morning, and they'd stayed on the phone for two hours. Two hours! Chase couldn't remember ever staying on the phone that long with anyone in his life, and even then, he didn't want to hang up. He wanted to be with her right that minute. He could still smell her perfume.

Chase had a flashback as he rode his bike down Lenox Avenue. He saw her clearly in his mind's eye, walking into his office in that little black trench coat and that little purple dress. She'd totally fucked his head up. Bliss might have thought he was joking when he said he thought his heart had stopped, but he was telling the damn truth: His heart literally stuttered in his chest—something that hadn't happened to him since Pandora Sheridan put her hand in his pants in the seventh grade.

The first time he saw Bliss, he started to flip on her because she was making such a big deal over her ruined outfit, but even if she hadn't walked away, his words would have died in his throat. She was the prettiest woman Chase had ever laid eyes on. Bliss just pushed past being truly petite. She was small boned and naturally thin, but she had full, round breasts and an apple booty. Chase hadn't seen a set of legs like that in a long time. Her face was beautiful, too, like someone should paint a picture of her. Her hair, a rich mahogany brown cut into fluffy bangs above her eyes, hung just past her shoulders. Her eyes, which were already large and brown, seemed even larger because her face was so small and finely featured. Her mouth was small, but her lips had that bee-stung look about them, full and ripe. Her skin looked like she'd been dipped in honey—a lovely, even, golden brown.

Chase got off his bike and walked into the café, removing his helmet as he went. He didn't mind meeting Corey and J.T., but he really wanted to be meeting Bliss. Chase smiled as he approached their table.

"Here he comes now, the late motherfucker," J.T. said loudly, waving him over.

Corey laughed and turned his beer up as Chase sat down.

Chase put his helmet on the floor and looked at his brother. "What the hell you laughin' at, knucklehead?" Chase dapped J.T. quick, and J.T. ordered him a beer.

"I'm laughin' at your ass, Smoke, slidin' up in here all late. Couldn't nobody find your ass last night and shit. J.T. says you were with that chick, Bliss. What's up, Chase? Tell us all about it."

Chase drank some of his beer and sat back in his chair. He looked first at Corey, then at J.T., trying to look irritated, but he was having a hard time shaking his smile. A frown wouldn't even get it to move. He made one more attempt to look mean or serious, but it didn't work. His smile won out. "Damn," Chase said in defeat, and the three of them burst out laughing.

Corey shook his head. "I knew you was tappin' that the minute I saw her. I just knew it."

"Naw. I ain't tapping nothin'."

Corey looked shocked. "Get the fuck outta here! I don't believe a damn worda that shit."

Chase drank some more of his beer, aware of J.T.'s eyes on him. "I'm serious, Corey. I ain't getting no skins—swear to God. I didn't even really push up like that."

"Why not? Fuckin' girl is beautiful. What happened? She turn your ass down?"

Chase nodded, and the oddest thing happened: He felt heat creep into his face when he discussed Bliss with those two clowns. Chase tried to bite back his smile and averted his eyes by looking into his beer. "Yeah, Corey. She told me no."

"Oh, shit!" came from J.T. with his loud ass. "Look at this shit, Corey. This negro is sittin' here fuckin' blushing."

Corey's mouth dropped open comically.

"Close your mouth, Corey," Chase said with a laugh.

"What you blushin' for, Chase? What's up with that?"

"I'm not…and ain't nothin' up. I like her, that's all."

Corey shrugged. "Well, hell, I knew you liked when you came in the office talkin' about how fine she was. But I thought you said you didn't think you stood a chance in Hell with her after you wrecked her suit?"

"I didn't think I did, but it turns out she's feelin' me too. Some shit you just can't control, Corey. Believe that."

J.T. hit him in the arm. "Your mack that strong, Chase?"

Chase laughed in spite of himself. "Nah, man. *Her* mack's that strong…and she didn't even do anything."

J.T. smiled. "Damn, son. Looks like your ass is goin' under."

Chase sipped his beer. "Maybe, but I can think of worse things."

Chase looked at his brother, who was staring at him like he was witnessing a miracle. "*What*, Corey?"

Corey laughed. "Nothin', man. Nothin'. I mean, hey, I like Bliss. Maybe she might make your ass less intense. You're my brother, Chase, and I want you to be happy."

"Don't send me off to the chapel just yet."

J.T. leaned forward with his elbows on the table. "I heard, Smoke, and I ain't mad at ya. But what you gon' do when Cyrus finds out you're fuckin' his new manager? He's gonna shit a brick, son."

Chase scowled at him and felt anger start to rise up. "You ain't got no class, man. I ain't sleepin' with Bliss. And don't call me Smoke."

"Yeah, not yet. I mean, not right now at this very moment, at this table, but the day ain't over," Corey said, laughing rakishly.

"Shut up, Corey," Chase replied and finished his beer. He pushed the empty bottle away with a fair amount of insolence. He couldn't understand why Cyrus had to creep his shifty ass into every conversation he had. He couldn't be happy for two seconds without hearing his damn brother's name brought up.

"For what? I saw y'all lookin' at each other. That's a done deal. It's goin' down, and you know J.T. is right, Chase. When Cyrus finds out Bliss is your girlfriend—"

He frowned at Corey. "She's not my girlfriend, Corey."

Corey waved him off. "Okay, Chase, whatever. Like I said, not yet. As we were sayin', Cyrus is gonna be damn straight pissed when he finds out."

Chase sat back in his seat in exasperation. "Why would he even care? Why?"

J.T. folded his arms across his chest and looked at the table. "Because he begrudges you things. We know it and you know it. It's the most horrible, outlandish, over-the-top game of sibling rivalry I have ever witnessed in my entire existence. It's a God-awful shame, if I do say so myself."

They both stared at him, and Corey gawked in disbelief. "Yo, J.T., man, are you for fuckin' real?"

"Very. See?" He reached out and tousled his hair. Corey took it like he was *his* little brother, too, and he may as well have been.

It was kind of funny, but Chase was too busy ruminating to laugh. He signaled for another beer. "Man, fuck Cyrus and his bullshit." Right on cue, his cell phone rang. He pulled it out of his pocket and looked at it reluctantly. *Yep. It's him.* Chase turned it off and put it back in his pocket.

"Ain't gotta ask who that was," J.T. commented.

Corey's cell phone started ringing, and J.T. smiled.

"Don't answer it, Corey," Chase said menacingly.

Corey ignored him and took his cell phone out.

"If you answer it, I'm gonna punch you, you little ass kisser."

Corey rolled his eyes and answered the call. "Hello?"

Holding true to his threat, Chase reached across the table and punched him in the shoulder.

"Ow! Nah, Cyrus, I ain't seen him. Nah, I tried to call him, but that nigga's MIA. Can't find him nowhere. Maybe he's laid up with some bitch."

Chase kicked him in the shin.

"Ow! Nah, it's nothin'. I'm getting somethin' to eat with J.T., and you know how that nigga likes to beat up on me. Yeah, okay. If I see him, I'll tell him to holler at you. See you later, Cyrus." He hung up and turned to Chase. "Man, what the fuck is wrong with you?" Corey rubbed his shin, looking for blood.

J.T. laughed. "You curse too much. I mean, we all curse, but you curse too much. And don't be puttin' me in your family business, little man."

"You are our family, man."

"Why, thank you," he said and ordered another beer.

Corey looked at Chase. "What's wrong with you?"

J.T swallowed the last of his first beer. "I think we pissed him off."

Chase shook his head. "No...Cyrus pissed me off. What's he lookin' for me so hard for?"

Corey looked at the table, but J.T. rubbed his goatee, looking Chase hard in the eye. "I don't know, Chase. Let me think..."

"Shut up, J.T.," Corey mumbled.

"I won't shut up, youngster. You know what that asshole is callin' him for."

Corey shot him an angry look.

"What? You mad 'cause I called Cyrus a name?"

"You curse too much. I'm gonna take a leak," Corey said before he got up and walked away.

J.T. smiled at Chase. "Don't nobody better be sayin' nothin' bad 'bout Master Cyrus now."

Chase smiled back at him. "Leave him alone, J.T."

J.T. drank some of his beer. "All I can say is that I agree with you, Chase. Fuck Cyrus."

Chase sighed and finished his beer. He thought about having another one, but he had his bike with him. He looked down at the empty bottle dejectedly. "I know what he wants, J.T. Whenever Cyrus knocks this hard, I know what that fool wants."

J.T. let out a sigh of his own. "Yeah, ol' Cy ain't exactly the Avon lady."

Chase shook his head. "He damn sure ain't. What do I do, J.T.?"

"If you don't wanna do what he's telling you to do, tell him to go fuck himself, my friend."

Chase mulled it over. He was so tired of Cyrus. If he never saw him again, he'd be okay, even if it hurt for a little while. He'd *told* him he was tired, but it never made any difference to Cyrus, the selfish, manipulative bastard. "I already paid him what I owed him," he said out loud.

J.T. nodded. "This I know."

"Then why is he doin' this shit to me?"

"Because, whether you want to admit it or not, Cyrus is not a nice person, Chase."

Chase frowned and shook his head. "I really don't have time for Cyrus and his nonsense right now."

J.T. smiled slow. "I bet you don't."

Chase looked around and then leaned toward J.T. "I know I can talk to you about this shit, J.T. Corey's still kind of silly. Yo, man, this shit with Bliss is crazy scary. I dreamt about her last night, and she's been on my mind since the moment I met her. When I'm around her, I feel like I can't get close enough to her. I want to be all up on her. The first thing I did this mornin' was call her. I didn't want to hang up just 'cause I like the sound of her voice. I want to see her so bad right now. I…" Chase trailed off when he realized J.T. was smiling at him. "What are you smilin' at?"

"You act like you think there's something wrong with you, but there ain't, Chase. You're falling in love with her, stupid."

Chase blinked. "I guess I knew that. I guess that's what I meant when I asked her to jump off the cliff with me."

J.T. looked at him like his brains were leaking out the side of his head. "Say what?"

"Never mind. It's a long story."

J.T. laughed and clapped him on the back. "I'm sure it's a nice one. Good for you, Chase. You look scared though. Are you?"

Chase smiled. "Yes and no. I want her, J.T."

"Then, shit, don't let anything stand in your way! Get with her and be happy. And just so you don't have to say it, fuck Cyrus, Chase."

"Yeah, you're right. Thanks, man." Chase sat back in his seat, feeling a little better.

Corey came back and sat down.

J.T. leaned forward and sniffed the air. "You were gone a long time. What did you do, take a shit or fall in?"

Chase enjoyed the rest of his time with them, and the only time they brought Cyrus back up was when Chase told them to put him off until Monday. Chase knew he would probably have to see him Monday, because that was the day Bliss started. They both gave him their word, but Chase knew Corey was his weak link, and it wasn't really fair for him. Corey wanted to please them both; he was always caught in the middle.

Although he'd given him his word, Chase knew if Cyrus applied the right kind of pressure, Corey would fold like a bad poker hand. Chase wasn't mad about that, though, for it would at least buy him some time. Chase left Corey and J.T. at the table, drinking beer and eating cheeseburgers, and walked outside to his bike. He took his cell phone out and called Dee. "Go ahead and open Cream up without me. I'll try and stop by later," he said. Dee gave him the business, but in the end, she agreed—and then promptly hung up on him. Then he called Bliss, and she picked up on the second ring.

"Chase?"

"Yeah, it's me."

"I was just thinking about you."

He could hear the smile in her voice, and it made him smile too. "Yeah? What were you thinkin'?"

She laughed, and Chase could feel goose bumps cover his arms. "No way am I telling you that."

"You busy?"

"Not if you want to see me."

Chase looked at his watch and smiled. "I really do. See you in twenty minutes."

******

Ten minutes later, he was ringing her doorbell.

"Who is it?" a female voice that did not belong to Bliss asked.

"Chase."

Tasha opened the door, and they stood there regarding each other. She was a little taller than Bliss, medium brown, with dreads that hung down to her ass. She had cowry shells on some of the locks nearest her face. Tasha was wearing pajamas—burgundy, with a black silk border—and a pair of black Isotoner slippers. The whites of her large brown eyes were an interesting shade of pink.

She looked him over, then put her hand on her hip and made the many bangles on her arm jingle musically. Tasha smiled at him with pretty white teeth that sported a gap in the middle of the two in front. Her eyes went over him appreciatively. "Chase Brown. Okay... yeah, so you're *fuckin' hot*. Come in." After he stepped inside, she walked around him in a slow circle, nodding. "Mm-hmm. Yeah... very nice."

Chase laughed. "You gonna kick my tires?"

She frowned at him but kept smiling. "You've got a smart mouth too. That's very attractive coming from a guy who looks like you. Come on into the living room. Sorry about my books all over the place. Just slide 'em over and have a seat."

Chase followed her into the living room, and she was right: There were books everywhere—big, giant books. Their living room furniture consisted of two very streamlined hot pink leather sofas that faced each other and glass-top tables. She sat down on one of the sofas, and Chase sat on the other and put his helmet on the hardwood floor.

Tasha folded her legs under her like a Native American and waved a lighter at him. "Do you mind?"

He shrugged and smiled, leaning forward with his elbows on his knees, and his hands clasped in front of him. "Nah. It's your house." He was a little surprised when she lit a joint instead of a cigarette. The pungent fragrance of exceptional weed filled the air, and Chase couldn't stop his eyebrow from going up.

"You're not going to be judgmental, are you?"

"Nope. Do what you need to do." Chase looked at the cover of one of the books and then looked back at the joint in her hand and grinned. "You're a *neurologist?*"

She looked slightly offended, but she didn't put her joint out. "Yes, I'm a neurologist. That's a brain doctor."

Chase held onto his smile. He'd made her defensive, but he was not about to argue with Bliss's roommate about what she did in her spare time. "I know what it is."

She took another drag and blew the smoke out slow. "I hear you own a few clubs."

Chase nodded. "Yeah. No big deal."

"Cream is a big deal. So is Shelter. What kind of bike do you ride?"

"A Ducati."

She smiled. "If you managed to get Bliss's little scared ass on a bike, she must really be feeling you. Matter of fact, your name's the only thing I've been hearing for the past two days." She looked at him pointedly. "She's a nice, sweet girl, Chase."

Chase was half-expecting the don't-hurt-my-friend speech, so he wasn't surprised when he got it. "I really like her, too, Tasha. I can't help myself."

"She's like my sister."

"I hear you."

They stared at each other for a second, and then Tasha leaned over and knocked the ash off her joint. "So, Mr. Ducati-riding Club-owning Gangster-swagger Cutie Pie, you know where I can get some good Columbian Gold?"

Chase laughed and let it roll off his back. "I ain't no drug dealer. Sorry."

She smiled and stood up. "Good answer. I'll go get Bliss. She's getting dressed." She paused on her way out of the room. "You're real cute, and you do seem real nice, but don't you dare hurt Bliss, okay? She really is sweet."

Chase smiled, realizing the weed was making her repeat herself. "Okay, Tasha. I heard you the first time."

She gave him a look that said she wasn't sure if he was flexing on her or not, then decided to let it go. "I'm glad you did." She disappeared around the corner and returned five minutes later with Bliss on her heels, whispering at her fiercely.

"I can't believe you're in here smoking reefer with Chase in the house. What's the matter with you, Tasha? You're embarrassing me!"

Chase smiled and stood up.

Tasha looked unperturbed. "Well, shit, he seems liberal enough to me, and he's not a cop. So what?"

They entered the room, and Chase forgot Tasha was there. If Bliss had crossed the room any quicker, she would have been running. She was wearing a pale blue sleeveless blouse and a denim skirt that stopped mid-thigh, with a flat pair of sandals. Her hair was swept back into a low ponytail with her bangs framing her pretty face.

If Chase had been unsure of his feelings before, he wasn't anymore.

Bliss smiled up at him, looking like she wanted to touch him, but she didn't quite dare.

Chase tucked his thumbs into his back pockets to keep from reaching out and grabbing her. They stared at each other, smiling like teenagers. Chase felt a little silly, but he couldn't have wiped that smile off his face if he tried, and the feeling was obviously, genuinely mutual.

"Damn," Tasha said from the hallway. "If we ever run out of electricity, we can just plug right into y'all asses."

"Jealous!" Bliss said over her shoulder.

"Damn, right, but I ain't a hater. Y'all go ahead. Just, please, no romance on the sofas. The stains would never come out."

Bliss turned around, shocked. "Tasha!"

"Sorry. It's the herb. Nice to meet you, Chase." She looked him over one more time and disappeared down the hall.

They waited until they heard the *click* of her bedroom door closing, and then they were all over each other, kissing, groping, and touching.

Bliss caught the giggles, but they slowed down when Chase started tugging her blouse out of her skirt. She laughed and put her hands over his. "Stop, Chase. Wait."

He kissed her neck. "I can't help it, Bliss. I'm sorry." He took his hands off her shirt and slipped them around her waist.

Bliss put her hands on his biceps and gave them a little squeeze. "I know. I can't help it either. Why don't you take me to the park and buy me an ice cream?"

Chase raised an eyebrow. "Ice cream, huh?"

She smiled at him. "Yeah. I think we might have to cool your ass down, Mr. Brown." She licked her top lip with the tip of her tongue.

The small gesture absolutely mesmerized him. "That was cool. Do it again.'

"Maybe later. Let's go."

Chase took off his jacket and tossed it on the sofa. It was almost too warm for it, but it took care of the wind when he was on his bike. Chase followed Bliss out of the apartment and down to the elevator.

When they stepped inside, Bliss slipped her hand in his. She looked up at him sweetly. "You don't mind, do you?"

He grinned at her. "Are you kidding?" he said and kissed the back of her hand.

They walked out of the building and into the late afternoon sunshine of the late May Saturday. Bliss lived right near the edge of Morningside Park, not far from Columbia University. It was a nice day, and a lot of people were outside taking advantage of it. They stopped at the ice cream truck parked outside the park, and Chase bought Bliss a vanilla cone with rainbow sprinkles. They found a vacant bench under a big shady oak tree and sat down.

He fell back into his posture from the previous night, facing her with his arm along the top of the bench. Chase watched her lick her ice cream, turning the cone in her hand like a little kid; it gave him a thrill in the pit of his stomach. She glanced at him and smiled, then gave it another lick. One more lick, and she looked him in the eye and crossed her legs. She was so innocently sexy, and it was killing him. "Would you like a taste?"

He put his hand on her bare knee and moved closer. "I think I'll probably die if you don't let me."

Bliss giggled and slid closer to him, until she was close enough for him to kiss her on the forehead, which he did. His breath ruffled her bangs, and they tickled his nose. Bliss surprised him when she got up suddenly and sat in his lap. She put her arm around his neck and offered him her cone, and Chase took the top off of it.

"Hey, you ate the best part!" Bliss protested.

Chase smiled at her. "No I didn't...not yet," he said, allowing his strong hand to reclaim its proper place on her thigh.

"You are so nasty, Chase," Bliss said and licked her ice cream.

Chase laughed. "Yeah, but you like it. Besides, I'm not as bad as you with that damned ice cream cone. I'm dyin' every time you put it in your mouth."

She gave him a sexy look and licked the cone again. "What's wrong, Chase? Wish it were you?"

"Oh, God yes. You got a little on your lip." He licked the small dot of ice cream off her bottom lip.

Bliss trembled and threw the cone over her shoulder. She put her hand on the back of his head and gave him the sweetest, most tender, kiss he'd ever gotten in his life. It was a flurry of small, hot, little closed-mouth kisses with her lips against his, followed by the invasion of her small pink tongue, sliding and swirling over his like she was claiming her territory. She withdrew and gave him a peck on the lips. "I could kiss you for hours." Bliss said breathlessly.

He smiled. "I wish you would." When his cell phone rang, Chase saw Cyrus's number again. He had thought about just leaving his phone off, but he had to remain reachable in case Dee needed him. He let his brother go to voicemail.

Bliss picked up on it and prepared to swing her legs off his lap, but Chase held her where she was.

"Where you goin', Bliss?"

"Are you screening your calls, Chase?"

Something about the defiant set of her jaw struck him as funny, and he laughed without meaning to.

Bliss frowned. "You think it's funny?"

"Yeah, baby. I do. That was Cyrus, by the way, and not some other woman, okay? Look." He pulled up the last received call in his phone and held it up so she could see it. "See? I told you."

Bliss looked away but seemed mollified. "You didn't have to show me your phone, Chase."

"The hell I didn't."

She smiled. "Okay, so maybe you did. Thank you."

He laughed. "It's nothin'. Just tryin' to establish a little trust." He looked at her seriously for a moment. "You're the only woman I'm involved with, Bliss. No baby mamas, no girlfriends, no drama."

Bliss looked thoughtful. "That girl Maya likes you."

Chase laughed. "A lot of women like me, but that don't mean a thing."

"No? Did you date her?"

He laughed again. "No, and I didn't sleep with her either. I never even stepped to her."

He trailed off, and Bliss frowned. "What?"

"I kind of need to tell you about Dee though."

Bliss didn't exactly develop a stink attitude, but she tried to lean away from him.

Chase went with her and wouldn't let her go.

"So…who is Dee?"

"Her full name is Delia, Delia Montgomery, and she helps me run things. She's not a threat, okay?"

Bliss looked at him like he was lying to her.

"Don't look at me like that. I didn't have to tell you about her at all. Anyway, there's nothing going on there—never has been and never will be. You can't let stuff like that interfere with business."

Bliss looked at him hard. "Are you telling me the truth?"

Chase chuckled and rubbed her thigh. "Baby, *yes*. I volunteered the information. I told you, you're the only woman I'm involved with."

She smiled at him reluctantly. "You consider yourself *involved* with me, already?"

Chase passed his lips over her jaw line and looked comically resigned. "I didn't have much choice, Bliss. I looked at you, and you made my stomach hurt."

"What?" She slapped at him playfully, and he grabbed her hand and kissed her palm. She looked somewhat appeased. "I made your stomach hurt? Damn, Chase. How romantic."

He put his arms around her and nuzzled his face into her neck, inhaling deeply. "I can be romantic. You smell so good, Bliss. What the hell *is* that?"

She giggled. "I'll never tell."

He smelled her again. "No, for real. Is that the stuff with the hormones in it? It's driving me crazy."

Bliss laughed, but it was tinged with a certain degree of her knowing something he didn't. "It's not the perfume, Chase."

He stared at her, wanting nothing more than to be close to her, but being so close to her was intoxicating.

"Chase? You okay?" Bliss asked, touching his face.

Her voice pulled him out of his daydream.

"What were you thinking about just then?" she asked, watching his eyes.

Chase looked into her eyes and ran his hand over her sexy calf. "I was imagining what it would be like to make love to you."

Bliss blushed hard, and Chase kissed her collarbone through her blouse. Bliss sucked in air between her teeth. "God, Chase," she whispered.

"Maybe we should get off this bench before we forget where we are again."

"You know, I think that might be a good idea." Bliss slid off him and stood up.

Chase stood, too, and took her left hand. They started walking back the way they came.

Bliss traced the scar on the back of his fingers with her own. "How did you get this scar, Chase?"

He sighed the way he always did when someone asked him things like that. He knew she would ask about the one under his jaw next. He didn't want to lie to her but wasn't sure he should tell her the truth. His natural instinct was to lie, but he didn't. "I got in a fight with a guy named Bobby Price when I was fifteen. I shouldn't have been fightin' him in the first place, but that's beside the point. Anyway, back then, whenever I was sick of fightin', I'd take the guy and put him in a sleeper hold and put his head out. It was like signing my name on the fight, you know? I had won the fight already, and I had his head lined up perfect to put him out, and he was goin', too, but then he pulled a knife out of nowhere and started slashin' me." He ran his finger along the scar under his jaw before she had a chance to ask. "He got me here too...and here." He lifted his T-shirt, still holding her hand, and showed her a crooked little scar to the left of his navel. "He tried to stick me, but I was a little too fast for him."

Bliss looked up at him with huge eyes, horrified. "Oh my God, Chase! What happened? How did you get out of it?"

"Cyrus's boy Herc pulled him off me. It was the only fight I ever lost." He looked over Bliss's head and back through time. If Herc hadn't pulled Bobby off Chase, Bobby probably would have killed Chase's young ass. Cyrus owed Bobby money for some guns he'd purchased through him. When Cyrus sent Chase with the money to pay him, Bobby claimed it was light by a half-grand. Chase reacted by stubbornly refusing to believe that Cyrus would try to weasel out on what he owed. Being that young—and so obviously naïve—Chase had never even bothered to count it. His trust in Cyrus was strong back then. He spat on the ground between Bobby's feet and called him a liar, then offered to beat his ass. Bobby was two or three years older than Cyrus, and he had no business picking up the gauntlet from a kid like Chase, but his ego wouldn't let him back down. When Chase got the better of him and he felt like he was going to pass out, he just pulled his knife out and started slashing.

Herc had always had a habit of lurking around and just showing up at places he shouldn't have been. He appeared at the top of the alley with his big .45 in his hand. Herc was probably sent by Cyrus to keep the situation under control, but he didn't make a move on Bobby until Chase got that cut under his jaw. Herc probably thought Bobby had cut Chase's goddamned throat. It was poetic justice to Chase when he ran that razor across Herc's neck three years later.

"What happened to this Bobby Price? Did he go to jail for hurting you like that?"

Chase looked down at her. He wanted to tell her, *"No, baby. He went to the fuckin' cemetery for movin' on me like that,"* but this time, he decided to avoid the truth. "It would be a good thing if everybody paid what they owed, I guess." He briefly wondered what his running tab was and how much it would eventually cost him. He hoped like hell it wouldn't cost him Bliss Riley.

Chapter 7

Cyrus didn't catch up with Chase's elusive ass until the following Friday. He was well past just being mad at him for giving him the slip; now he was taking it personally. *Who the fuck does that nigga think he is, making me kiss his black ass?* Cyrus had just left Khalid, and he was leaning on him hard about getting rid of Wolf. Cyrus told Khalid he couldn't find Chase—and hell, he *couldn't*—but Khalid had given him the impression that he didn't think Cyrus was trying hard enough.

He'd looked for his brother's slippery, disloyal ass everywhere. The nigga refused to answer his voicemail. That bitch Dee had her claws out covering for him. J.T. stonewalled him in his snide and obnoxious way. Corey was lying right to his face and getting gone before he could put the screws to him. He decided he'd fix Corey's punk ass later. Cyrus had even gone to Chase's apartment and come up empty. *All this shit is ending today.* Chase probably thought Cyrus was too lackadaisical to show up at his own club to check on the progress, but Cyrus figured it might be the one place he'd be able to snag that fucking defector.

Cyrus pulled his Infiniti up in front of the club with a smile and parked right behind Corey's Lexus, which was parked right behind Chase's Porsche; for once, he wasn't on his bike. Cyrus got out of his car and cracked his knuckles, smiling grimly. He'd caught both of his little pissy brothers together, most likely putting up a united front against him in his own goddamned club. *They must have forgotten who's in charge,* he thought and felt like taking off his belt to remind them. Cyrus pushed on the door, but it was locked. He closed his fist and was about to pound on it, but then he remembered it this was *his* club. He reached into his pocket and brought out his keys.

Cyrus walked into his still-nameless club, and despite the fact that he was extremely annoyed with Chase, he was very pleased at what he saw. He may have been avoiding Cyrus, but he'd been handling his business. Even though the place wasn't finished, he could tell it was in the process of being totally redone. He nodded in approval as he checked out the workers who were bolting the bar into the floor and installing the recessed lighting. The décor was a little dark, but it worked: black, gray, and plum. It was going to look fantastic when it was done.

"I thought I smelled brimstone."

Cyrus turned to find J.T. standing just behind him with a blueprint in one hand and a Red Bull in the other. J.T. had always been a bit of a mystery to Cyrus. He was damn near a genius of an architectural engineer, with his own flourishing company, but he had a serious dark side that never quite let him actually live in the light that could have been shining down upon his brilliant ass. Sure, he kept up appearances and handled the corporate thing quite well, but nothing seemed to give him more glee than to ride shotgun with Chase and watch a nigga get his throat opened up. Lately, though, it seemed J.T. had become the biggest advocate he knew for Chase keeping his hands clean. His theory was that they'd lived the wild style long enough, and he swore a man shouldn't—and couldn't—keep rolling the dice like that and that sooner or later, you'd crap out. Cyrus didn't give a fuck what J.T. thought though. Nobody asked his ass for his opinion. As far as Cyrus was concerned, J.T. needed to be quiet and stay the fuck out of family business. "Ha, ha. Very funny, motherfucker," Cyrus said, looking him over. "Where are my two asshole brothers?"

J.T. laughed, drank some of his Red Bull, and tapped the blueprint against his leg. He smiled at Cyrus pleasantly. "Maybe if they were both holding a wedge of cheese, you could sniff them out."

Cyrus narrowed his eyes at him. "You callin' me a fuckin' rat, J.T.?"

J.T. looked at him like he was one of God's lesser creatures. "If the shoe fits..."

Cyrus didn't really feel like fucking with J.T. Sometimes he made him feel like he thought he was stupid. He probably *did* think he was stupid. Cyrus looked at him caustically. It was one nigga he wouldn't mind killing himself. "So where they at, man?"

J.T. laughed. "You ain't blind. You saw their cars. They gotta be in here somewhere, right? It's *your* club...so go find 'em."

"Get back to work, J.T."

"I don't work for you, Cyrus," he sang, a little like a fuck-you song. He looked at Cyrus like he wasn't afraid of him and walked away.

Cyrus watched him go. *One of these days, I'ma take care of that rude, disrespectful bastard.* Cyrus followed J.T. just in case he tried to give Chase and Corey a heads-up that he was here. He had gone into a large room that was to become a bathroom, and he was at a counter looking over blueprints with a white guy in a hard hat.

J.T. looked up when Cyrus's shadow fell across the doorway. "They're not in here. This is the crapper."

Cyrus's urge to jack him in the jaw had never been stronger. He turned and went back into the biggest room and crossed it. There was an alcove on one side and a door on the other. Cyrus opened it and stepped into a large sitting room. He smiled when he heard Chase's voice coming out of the room to his left.

"Corey, I need you to go see what the hold-up is with the liquor license, the sooner the better. Bliss, we got a bunch of applications here. We gotta start weeding through them and hiring staff."

Cyrus walked into the room, and Chase looked up. He didn't look surprised or even deflated. Instead, he looked like he'd been expecting him. He stood up behind the desk. "Hey, Cyrus. What's good?"

Cyrus moved further into the room. "You tell me. Where the hell you been hidin', Smoke?"

Chase laughed and shrugged, then walked around the desk. "I ain't been nowhere but right here, Cyrus. It's been busy, and time got away from me."

Chase's nonchalance was pissing him off. Cyrus walked up on him and stared him down. "You been playin' games, Smoke, and I need to talk to you."

Chase smiled at him engagingly. "Yeah, I know. It can wait."

The smile Chase wore didn't exactly touch his eyes. He knew why Cyrus was there all right, and he was fucking with him.

Cyrus smiled himself and shook his head. "I say it *can't* wait. I've been waitin' a whole fuckin' week to speak to you, and I'm not lettin' you put me off anymore. We'll talk *now*."

Chase leaned on the desk and folded his arms across his chest. The smile had slid off his face. "No, Cyrus. We'll talk when *I'm* good and damn ready. It'll keep until then. In the meantime, don't be rude and act like we're the only two people in this room. This is your new manager, Bliss Riley."

The girl in the chair stood and smiled at Cyrus. She was so pretty that she looked like a doll. She offered her hand and he took it, temporarily thrown off his A game as he looked her over. She was wearing a pale pink silk dress that hugged her body in all the right places and high-heeled pumps that were the exact color of the dress. She had a string of pearls around her neck, and her hair was caught up in an intricate twist at the nape of her neck, with her bangs softly framing her face. She was beautiful, and Cyrus was instantly very impressed. She looked very classy and a bit retro.

"Hello, Mr. Brown. It's nice to finally meet you."

He smiled back. "The pleasure is mine," he said, and he meant it. "If you're as qualified as you are beautiful, my club will be a success."

Chase stood up. "She is. I'd show you her credentials, but I fucked 'em up, so you gotta trust my judgment." Chase eyed Cyrus with a smirk on his face. *If I had my gun, I'd shoot this nigga right now.*

Bliss looked from one to the other, then picked up a folder from the corner of the desk. "It's about time for the first interview. I'll be out front." She left the room in a hurry, closing the door softly behind her.

Cyrus smiled at Chase. "That's a nice touch, Smoke. She's fine as hell."

Chase didn't smile back. "I know that. Now, what the fuck do you want with me, Cyrus? Spit it out. You've been haunting me like a fuckin' ghost."

Corey had been standing by the window staring at his feet the whole time. "Chase, please man. Don't start Cyrus up."

"Don't start *him* up? He started with me first, fucking stalking me when I've been working my ass off to get *his* club in order. Tell me what you want, Cyrus."

Cyrus ignored Chase and looked at Corey. "And where the fuck you been? I couldn't find your simple ass either."

Corey looked at both of them. "I was around—just tryin' to keep the peace."

Chase laughed bitterly. "Well, you kept it as long as you could, Corey. Now, *fuck* the peace. I said tell me what you want, Cyrus."

Cyrus sat in the seat Bliss had vacated. "All right. Since you don't seem like you're in a social mood, I got a little problem with Warren Jenkins."

Chase frowned. "Wolf?"

"Yeah, Wolf. I didn't know you knew him like that."

"Yeah, well, you don't know everything. What kind of beef you got with Wolf?"

"I told him to move his shit over, and he declined."

Chase grunted like he didn't believe him. "That's your problem with him? He didn't jump when you said so? You gotta present your case a lot stronger than that."

"Look, Smoke, this guy is tryina creep in where I do my business. I told him to fall back, and he didn't. Now he's tryin' to intimidate some of my people, and I'm losin' customers. I need him removed from the picture."

Chase gave him a skeptical look. "That's not enough. What else did he do?"

Cyrus stared at Chase. He knew not to embellish his story too much because Chase still had his ear to the ground enough to separate fact from fiction. He shifted in his seat. "Look, Chase—" he started and was surprised when Chase cut him off.

"No, you look, Cyrus. It's bad enough you come in here wanting what you want, but you got the nerve to sit there and lie to me about it. What? You think I'm stupid? Did you think I wouldn't throw a few questions out there when you started lookin' for me so hard? I want you to tell me the whole story, Cyrus, and don't leave out the part about you and Khalid goin' back into business together. How long has that shit been goin' on? Who's been greased because Khalid said so?"

Cyrus was a little shocked that Chase had found out that Khalid and he were still business partners, and he wondered who leaked the information. He looked over at Corey with a shark-black tint in his eye.

Chase held up a finger. "Uh-uh, Cyrus. Don't you dare look at Corey. Corey ain't tell me *nothin'*. That's my word."

Cyrus frowned. "Then who's been runnin' their damn mouth to you about me?"

"That ain't important, and it really doesn't matter anyway. Hey, maybe I got a crystal ball. You been lyin' to me, haven't you, Cyrus?"

Cyrus laughed and shook his head. The jig was up about Khalid and him. Cyrus had promised Chase a long time ago that he would sever ties with Khalid, because Chase believed Khalid had sent Herc Mercer to *kill* him and Corey—not to ask about Cyrus's whereabouts on the day he died. Chase had never trusted either one of them, especially Khalid, *and* he hadn't trusted him and Rome when they split everything three ways while Cyrus was doing his bid for the gun charge. Maybe he was right, because Cyrus and Khalid had never stopped doing business, and with Herc and Rome out of the way, the money was easier to divide. *Fuck this asshole and his screwed up sense of right and wrong. He'll do what the fuck I tell him to and like it.*

Cyrus looked at Chase. There was no use trying to play the I-don't-know-what-you're-talking-about card with him. His best bet was to own up and let it go, then maybe hope to strong-arm him in a couple of days. He thought he might even be able to twist his arm by threatening to use Corey. *Yeah, that's the ticket.* Cyrus leaned forward and hoped he looked apologetic enough. "You know what? You're right, Smoke. I've been lyin' to you—well, not really *lyin'*…it was an omission. I'm sorry. I should have told you, but I know how you feel about Khalid."

Chase looked over at Corey, whose eyes were staring out the window. "Corey, why don't you go check on that liquor license? You ain't in this."

Corey looked away from the window with troubled eyes. "Yeah. I ain't *ever* in this. Y'all gotta figure out a way to see eye to eye. Shit is always hard between y'all. Work it out, please, 'cause I don't know how much more of this I can take." He left the room without another word, leaving Cyrus and Chase staring at each other.

"Can't you see what you're doin' to Corey, Cyrus? He's always in the middle of me and you. Don't you care?" Chase sat back down in his chair behind the desk. "If you're not gonna tell me the whole story, Cyrus, then I got somethin' to tell *you*. After I finish helpin' you get your club off the ground, I'm gonna step outta your life for a minute and give you some time to decide what you want to do with yourself. I can't keep livin' the way I've been livin' hanging around you. I want more out of life than knockin' people off to help you and Khalid put a strangle-hold on your little piece of the drug trade and waitin' for the cops to catch me. I don't get anything out of it, and I want to be happy. I deserve to be happy." *You'll never be happy, and neither will I. I'll make sure of that, Cyrus thought darkly.*

Cyrus smiled wryly. "Is that what you want, Chase? 'Cause if you want me to *pay you* to erase Wolf, that really ain't a problem."

Chase leaned all the way back in his chair and looked at him like he was a mangy dog. "Pay me? What the hell does that have to do with staying out of lockup and being happy? You just insulted me, Cyrus, but if you want to play around with me like that, I'll tell you what. If you can have a million dollars on my desk by nine o' clock tomorrow morning, Wolf will be pushin' up daisies by sundown."

Cyrus laughed. Chase had just requested the ridiculous, hoping he'd be left alone. Cyrus sat back in his own chair, tapping his steepled fingers together. Chase must have forgotten his infamous ace in the hole. "You got a real good sense of humor, little brother, but I ain't laughin'. Now, I told you, I *need* Wolf gone, so if you want me to play hardball with you, I will."

They stared at each other for a long time. Chase looked away first and stared out the window that had so recently claimed Corey's attention.

Cyrus watched him in silence, reading his face, trying not to smile. *I won!* It had been a simple thing to bend Chase to his will, and he didn't even need to say Corey's name out loud. Cyrus wanted to lean over the desk and stick his face into Chase's and scream, *"Corey! Corey! Corey! That's right, motherfucker! I'll get Corey to do it, and he will if I ask him. You know how Corey hates to disappoint his brothers! He'll do it, and he'll fuck it up and go to jail! Even worse, he might get himself killed in the process! You can't live with Corey's sentencing or blood on your conscience....SO I WIN! Talk your righteous, better-than-me shit now, nigga! If I ain't shit, you ain't shit either! You do what **I** say, and I say **fuck you**! Go kill him!"* But he didn't say all of that. Instead, he sat there and stared at Chase, unmoved by the tears that had started to slide down his face.

Cyrus sat, quietly watching his brother's turmoil. *Should I do it? What if I refuse?*

Chase's internal argument didn't mean a thing to Cyrus, because he knew he was going to get his way. He hadn't seen Chase cry in over ten years. Chase was as tough as they came. He had a good idea what these tears were for, but he'd deal with that when the time came. At the moment, he didn't give a fuck. All he wanted was Wolf gone, and he wanted Chase to do the dirty deed.

Chase sat up in his seat and wiped his eyes with the hem of his Ed Hardy T-shirt. His face was a weird mix of emotions: anger and resentment, sorrow and hurt, and acceptance and resignation. He turned his head and looked at Cyrus; his eyes were like ice. "How soon do you need it done?" he asked, standing.

Cyrus also took to his feet, as he really didn't want Chase standing over him at that point in the conversation. "End of next week at the very latest—but the sooner, the better."

Chase looked at him with his icy eyes and nodded. "All right, Cyrus. I need to let you know a few things right now, if that's all right with you. I mean, these things might not mean *shit* to you, but they mean something to me…and they carry weight. You ready?"

Cyrus shrugged. He wasn't in the mood to hear a lecture, and he wanted to get out of there and tell Khalid the good news that they'd gotten their way, but if Chase felt like he needed to get up on his creaky-ass, crime-laden soapbox and preach one of his hypocritical sermons, then he had a moment to pretend he was listening. Cyrus smiled and said, "Go ahead, Smoke. I'm listening."

Chase's eyes grew even icier when he walked around the desk and stood in front of him. "I just need you to understand what you just did, Cyrus. You're still my brother—I can't change that—but we ain't friends no more. I can't respect you no more, Cyrus, 'cause you won't respect me. You're settin' yourself up so that Khalid will be your only ally. *You're losin' me, Cyrus,* and you best believe if you do, I'm takin' my little brother with me. You need to be *real* careful with me, Cyrus, 'cause you don't know me like you think you do."

"Okay, Chase. Whatever you say."

Chase frowned at him. "Did you hear what I just said to you?"

Cyrus nodded. Of course he had heard, but he really didn't listen or care. It was just a variation of the same nonsensical babble he spewed every time he made a request like this. "Yeah, yeah. I heard you. Okay. All right. Fine, Smoke."

Chase stepped away from him. "What happened to you, Cyrus? I mean, you always had some shit to you, but when did you become this motherfucker I'm lookin' at now?"

What happened to me? You happened to me! Before he thought about it hard, Cyrus had Chase's collar in his hand, and everything else was a blur. Chase tucked in his bottom lip, stuck his foot behind Cyrus, and turned his body. His left arm came up, and his elbow met Cyrus's nose with a *crunch*. Cyrus shut his eyes against the pain and let go of his brother's collar. Chase stepped into him with his shoulder, forcing him backward, as Cyrus stumbled over Chase's shrewdly planted left foot. The small of Cyrus's back hit the desk violently, and Chase was on him in an instant, his left hand circling his neck.

Cyrus was trying hard not to choke on the blood that was threatening to clog the back of his throat. He opened his eyes in time to hear what Chase had in his hand before he saw it. *Click- wick-wick!* Cyrus flinched and blinked. Chase had spun that damned silver-handled straight razor out of his pocket like a gunslinger in a Western. It was open and gleaming right by his nose. Cyrus held his breath. *This nigga crazy,* he thought, realizing all that shit had happened in less than a minute.

Chase's face was close to his, and now he was smiling. "You grab me at your own risk, Cyrus. I think you better think twice before you do it again."

"Let me up, Chase." He wanted it to come out sounding like a command, but it sounded more like a squealing plea. He hated Chase for it.

Chase's smile became a grin. "Say 'please,' Cyrus."

"I'm chokin'! Please."

Chase let him go and went to the door and opened it. "Now get the hell out of here. I don't want to see you again until I'm ready to discuss Wolf. In the meantime, leave Corey alone." Chase returned to his seat behind the desk. "Shut the door on your way out."

Cyrus was in no position to talk shit or even try. He staggered his ass out of the office and to the front door.

"Look at this! Did you take a tumble down the steps, Cyrus?" J.T. asked, laughing.

Cyrus glanced over at Bliss. She was in the middle of an interview, and whatever she was saying, her mouth was a perfect circle. When she glanced over and saw Cyrus, she excused herself and rushed over to him.

"Oh my God! Are you okay, Mr. Brown?"

J.T. clapped him hard on the shoulder. "He's great, Bliss. Continue your interview. I'll walk him to the door." J.T. turned Cyrus toward the door with the hand he had on his shoulder. He threw it open and gave Cyrus a shove. "I'd love to throw you out on your ass, but I'm afraid people will talk."

Cyrus watched the door to his own club slam in his face. It was, in his opinion, completely disrespectful, and whether they knew it or not, they'd just started some shit, and regardless of what Chase thought, Cyrus wasn't afraid of him. *Your ass is gonna pay dearly for that shit you just did. Nobody fucks me over and gets away with it. I shoulda gotten rid of your ass before you took your first breath.*

G STREET CHRONICLES
A NEW URBAN DYNASTY
WWW.GSTREETCHRONICLES.COM

Chapter 8

After five interviews, Bliss had hired a hostess and two bartenders. Her next interview was an hour later, and she was thinking of going back to the office to check on Chase. She hadn't heard a peep out of him since Cyrus left, though she had seen J.T. disappear back there and come back all frowned up. She stood and smoothed her dress as J.T. came out of the unfinished bathroom with a hardhat on his head.

He smiled at her and gave her a non-invasive look of appreciation. "Hey, Bliss. Takin' a break?"

She smiled back. "Yeah. I've got a little free time between interviews, so I thought I'd go pay Chase a little visit and see if he's okay."

J.T. nodded. "Go ahead. If anything out here needs your attention, I'll come get you."

"Thanks, J.T." She folded her arms across her chest and took a step closer, lowering her voice. "Hey, what happened in there this morning? Did I really see Cyrus leaving with a bloody nose? Was it broken?"

J.T. laughed, but in his eyes, he didn't really look amused. "Well, let's hope, for his sake, it wasn't broken, but I really can't say what went down between him and Chase."

Bliss frowned. "You mean you don't know?"

He smiled again. "Of course I know. I just can't say. Go ahead though. Maybe if you sit on his lap for a while, it'll smooth him out."

Bliss took his advice and went down to the office, wondering what the hell kind of violent relationship Chase actually had with his brother. Obviously, it was the kind of brotherhood where breaking somebody's nose was no big deal. *What could Cyrus have done to deserve that from Chase?* she had to wonder. She didn't want to make snap judgments about Cyrus, but Chase *had* spent all the time she'd known him avoiding Cyrus in a very big way. He didn't seem to act the same way about Corey. When she'd met Cyrus earlier, she noticed that he was tall and fine, obviously cut from the same cloth as her Chase from a physical standpoint, but her gut reaction left her feeling like he had all the charm of a snake oil salesman. At the moment, though, she didn't really care about Cyrus or his broken nose; she cared about Chase. "Chase? It's Bliss," she announced, knocking softly since she wasn't sure what kind of mood he was in after his big brother's visit. "Can I come in?"

"Yeah, come in."

She opened the door and stepped inside. Chase was in the big chair behind the desk, slouched in his seat with his fingers laced across his stomach. She stood across the desk from him, studying his face. He looked like he'd been crying, of all things. "Are you okay, Chase?"

He looked so sad, but he smiled a little. "I'll live. Come here, Bliss."

She came around the desk. Chase reached for her and really did pull her into his lap. Bliss put her arms around his neck and hugged him fiercely. His strong arms circled around her and held her close. They sat like that for a while, not speaking and just holding each other, with their faces close and touching.

She'd stepped into his office to comfort him about whatever was happening between Cyrus and him, but sitting there so close to him was making her yearn to be even closer—as close as she could possibly get. Bliss put her fingers on his hair and her lips on his. She kissed him with soft, closed-mouth kisses, loving the feel and taste of his lips against hers. She darted her tongue in his mouth, and Chase moaned, kissing her back with a skilled, but tender passion.

Chase swung his chair around with his feet, placing his back toward the door. He leaned past her and closed the window blinds. He kissed her on the hollow of her throat, and she trembled and kicked off her shoes.

"Oh, Chase! Put your hands on me...*please!* I can't take this anymore."

He kissed her chin, and she could feel him smiling.

She looked down into his beautiful, clear, cognac eyes.

"I've been *dyin'* to. Take your hair down for me, Bliss."

She reached behind her and started taking her hair down as Chase put one hand on the small of her back and used the other to pull down the zipper on her dress. Bliss fluffed her hair out over her shoulders, and Chase pulled the top of her dress down. Bliss took her arms out of the sleeves and reached behind herself again to unhook her lacy bra. She held it in place and smiled down at him, teasingly, even as somewhere in the back of her mind she wondered what the hell she was doing, sitting in that man's office, on his lap, taking her clothes off.

Bliss pushed her doubts back as she looked at his face. There was no doubt that Chase Brown was a strong, virile, dominant male, but there was a very large part of his makeup that she found vibrantly and refreshingly boyish. The way he spoke, his enthusiasm, and the open way he displayed his emotions—hell, even his good looks were boyish—and Bliss found all of these incredibly endearing.

He was looking up at her, his eyes seemingly undecided on whether they should stay on her face or drop to her soon-to-be-bare breasts. His mouth was slightly open, and his breath was a bit rushed, just like hers. Chase's hands drifted up her sides, his thumbs skimming over her ribs; but it was the look in his eyes that floored her: He was looking at her like he couldn't believe he was sitting there with Bliss on his lap, as if he absolutely adored her.

He moved to kiss her, but Bliss put her hand on his chest. She could feel his heart racing. Chase looked surprised, and she laughed softly. "Not so fast. I took my top off, so you have to take yours off too."

Chase reached down and pulled his T-shirt over his head, as he had in so many of her daydreams, and she was just as impressed as she'd been in her fantasies. He was lean, muscular, and well defined. The muscles in his stomach rippled nicely when he threw his shirt over his shoulder.

Chase smiled at her and tugged at her bra. The boy in his face was gone, replaced by the man who wanted to fulfill her request and put his hands on her. "This is pretty, but I'm tired of lookin' at it," he said, pulling at her lingerie. "It's gotta go."

Bliss slipped it off and dropped it on the floor, and Chase's mouth was on her instantly, licking at her like she was the most delicious, delectable dessert in the world. Bliss's back arched with pleasure, and she put her hand on the back of his head. Her breath puffed between her lips as he changed breasts. She squeezed her thighs together and sighed in delight. Chase closed his mouth and did some little swirling, sucking thing that curled her toes.

She ground against him, and he ground back. That bit of highly intimate contact seemed to shock them both. They stared at each other, moving against each other leisurely, like they had all the time in the world to pleasure each other. Chase's hand slipped under her dress and made its way to her panties...

KNOCK! KNOCK!

Chase held Bliss close to his chest, and they both stopped moving like two deer caught in the headlights. "What?" he shouted over his shoulder.

There was a silent pause, and then, "Damn, man. You ain't gotta shout! It's me, Corey. Can I come in or not?"

Chase sighed deeply, and Bliss shivered at the warmth of his breath. Chase smiled and kissed her, holding her a little closer.

"Chase?" Corey called again, but he didn't wait for an answer, and the door burst open unceremoniously.

Chase ran his hand over Bliss's thigh and shook his head. "I'm busy, Corey. Leave."

"Yeah, but Chase—"

Chase lost his patience, but he didn't quite yell at his little brother. "Come on, Corey. Give me a minute, okay?"

"Yeah, but Chase…" he repeated, taking a step further into the room. He caught himself when he realized Chase wasn't alone. "Whoops! I'm sorry, man. I didn't know you were in here with your woman. Hey, Bliss."

Bliss wiggled her fingers around the back of the chair, careful not to reveal anything more of herself to the unexpected visitor. "Uh… hey, Corey."

Chase frowned at her. "Don't answer him, or he'll never leave," he said in a low voice.

Corey retreated to the doorway, snickering. "So…uh…what y'all doin'?"

Chase stuck his head out from behind the chair. "Get outta here, Corey!" He didn't sound entirely pissed off, just irritated.

Bliss kissed his neck to calm him down.

"All right, I'm out. Don't do nothing I wouldn't do."

"Bye, Corey."

Corey laughed. "Bye, Chase. Um…bye, Bliss."

"Bye."

After Corey slammed the door behind him, Chase looked around the chair to make sure he was gone.

Bliss laughed and pulled her dress up, covering her breasts. She hopped off his lap, stuck her feet back into her shoes, and picked up her bra.

Chase stood up, but he didn't make a move to stop her; he just watched her put her bra back on and fix her dress.

Bliss looked at him as she ran her fingers through her hair and licked her lips. She'd thought he looked good sitting down, but on his feet, he looked even better. She turned her back to him to prevent things from going any further. "Would you zip me up please?"

Chase walked up behind her and put his hands on her small waist. He moved his body against hers and spoke into her ear. "Are you *tryin'* to torture me, Bliss? Don't go."

She turned in his arms and put her hands on his biceps. "No, but I'm not going to stay in here with you a second longer. Corey already walked in on us."

He looked past her like he wasn't really trying to hear what she was saying, but he also didn't seem to want to press the issue. A little more, and he'd be sulking. Bliss pursed her lips to keep from giggling, because it was kind of funny.

Chase looked at her with mild annoyance and zipped her up, speaking volumes without saying a word. He stepped back and pulled his T-shirt over his head, covering up his wonderful body.

This time, Bliss *did* laugh. She couldn't help it because he *was* sulking. "Oh man, Chase. That is sooo childish."

He shrugged. There was a hint of a smile on his lips. "Oh well. Sorry."

She took his hand. "No, *I'm* sorry. I'm not trying to tease you, baby...really. Corey made me feel a little uncomfortable, walking in here. You're the only man I want to see me...*like that*."

Chase looked instantly placated. He gave her a peck on the lips and smiled. "I see you stepped me up."

Bliss smiled back. "Well, you stepped me up first, according to Corey."

Chase kissed her again, another one of those soft, lingering, not quite closed-mouthed kisses.

"How many interviews do you have?" he asked, letting her go.

"Two."

"Okay, good. I got a couple things to do, and then I gotta talk to nosy-ass Corey about the liquor license. I gotta talk to J.T. about the progress with the renovation too...and I should give Dee a call."

Bliss looked at him expectantly. "What then?"

Chase smiled at her devilishly. "Well, after that, I'm gonna drop you off at your place so you can change into somethin' real sexy, then I'm gonna pick you up and take you to dinner. Then, I might stop at Cream and dance with you for a little while. *Then*...I'm gonna take you back to my place and talk you out of your clothes. Maybe I can convince you to get naked for me *like that*."

She smiled. "So you think you're sleeping with me *tonight*, huh?"

Chase laughed softly and looked at her cockily. "Sleepin'? That's the last thing on my mind, Bliss. If you need a nap, you better take one now."

Bliss put her arms around his waist and looked up at him warily. "Plan on wearing me out?"

Chase smiled and gave her another one of those sweet kisses. "I plan on seein' if you can live up to your name...*Bliss*." He took her hand and walked her back to the main room of the club. Chase kissed her again and patted her on the ass, then spun her out into the room like he was dancing with her, slipping his hand out of hers.

Bliss watched him walk back down the hallway, loving the set of his shoulders and admiring his easy stride. His swagger was so exhilarating she could have skipped down the street shouting his name. Bliss took a deep breath and closed her eyes; she could still smell his cologne. It had become entwined with her own and created a new and lovely fragrance. She loved it so much that she wanted to lick the feel of him off of her fingers. She wanted to go back into his office and...

"Hey, Bliss! You all right, girl?"

Her eyes flew open and found J.T. looking at her with a knowing smile on his face. Bliss blushed furiously. "Oh! Hey, J.T. I was just—"

J.T. laughed, a bit indulgently. "No need to get flustered around me. I promise not to tease you and Chase. I'm happy for both y'all."

She smiled. She honestly liked J.T., who handed her a clipboard. "Your interview is down front."

"Got it. And thanks, J.T. You're very sweet."

He laughed. "Yeah, okay...just don't say it too loud." He walked away.

When she was sure he was out of sight, Bliss licked her finger and rolled her eyes. *Wow, I've got it bad...and I'm not sure that's good...*

G STREET CHRONICLES
~A NEW URBAN DYNASTY~

WWW.GSTREETCHRONICLES.COM

Chapter 9

After Chase dropped Bliss off, he stopped and got his hair cut, then went straight home to his loft on Riverside Drive. He'd chosen a loft over a brownstone or condo because one of his quirks was that he insisted on being able to see all around him. Chase wasn't fond of places with a lot of hidey-holes. At least there, in his personal space, he would know it if someone was lying in wait for him. He wasn't particularly worried about anyone doing that, though, because he knew most everyone was scared of him—for good reason.

He rode up in the elevator, and it opened up right into his apartment. Chase stepped out and walked to the bedroom and then into the master bath. He took his clothes off and took a rather long shower, running the events of the day through his mind. He hated what was going on between him and Cyrus. Cyrus had threatened him with Corey for years, and their little run-in that afternoon was the last straw. He knew that if Cyrus forced Corey to do it, Corey would… and he would fuck it up and get himself arrested or killed. Chase was a risk-taker to some degree, but he wasn't willing to risk his little brother.

So, he'd get rid of Wolf himself, but he'd also start working on Corey. He hoped he could convince his little brother to leave New York with him so they could live and operate in a place without Cyrus and his bullshit around. That had been his plan all along, and he knew eventually, he'd get Corey to go along with it. He had to get Corey away from Cyrus before Cyrus ruined his life too. Now, though, there was a major knot in Chase's noble plans, and the more he thought about it, the more Gordian that knot became.

Frankly, now he was stuck where he was because he wasn't about to leave Bliss. He laughed at himself: All it took to bring the almighty Chase Brown to his knees was nine days with one sweet little fine-ass woman who'd walked into his office in a dirty gray skirt and shown him a muddy, smeared résumé. He hadn't even slept with her, yet he loved her so much it hurt to look at her. Chase knew she owned his heart already. Even there, in his own hot shower, thoughts of her had him covered in goose bumps.

Chase was not a stupid guy by a long shot. He knew that feeling so completely in love with someone so fast was a rarity. He also knew it was rarer, still, for the object of a man's affection to feel the same way—like Bliss did. He knew it with his entire heart.

Chase thought this over as he stepped out of the shower and toweled off. The very last thing on Earth he wanted to do was hurt Bliss. He had to walk a tight rope to keep everything separate, because if Bliss ever found out the *real* reason people called him Smoke, he was sure she'd walk—no…run—away from him without looking back.

His life had been so full of sadness and darkness, and he just wanted a happy ending. He thought there might be a slim chance of finding that with Bliss. He knew he couldn't let his brother Cyrus even suspect what was going on between them. If Cyrus had any idea, he'd use it to his advantage to keep Chase bound to him.

As he dressed, his brother infected his thoughts again. *Fucking Cyrus. I'm so tired of him—really tired.* There was only one end for Cyrus. He was blazing a path of destruction and ruin, determined to take everyone down with him, just to feed his own greed and have his own way. *Well, fuck that. He's not taking Corey or me with him—not if I have a damn thing to say about it.*

Chase couldn't lie to himself: Greasing someone was thrilling to him in a very dark sort of way. It made him feel powerful and invincible, and he was extremely good at it. He would almost have labeled it fun, except for the inevitable bouts of guilt and self-loathing that always followed. He hadn't killed anybody in a while, and he was seriously hoping those sick feelings were gone, but he doubted it.

Chase was not a psychiatrist, and he didn't try to over-analyze himself; that job usually fell to J.T. Chase's life was what it was. If he wanted to twist it so that Cyrus was the only villain in the whole sordid story, he could have easily said that the first life he'd taken was only to impress Cyrus and make him need him. He could even claim, *"I just wanted my big brother to love me more. After all, I was just young, hurt, and a goddamned orphan."* He was, after all, just misguided and aching for approval from someone he assumed probably hated him from the start. Even then, though, he knew he'd never get much in the way of affection from Cyrus—something Cyrus probably didn't have to give. Cyrus obviously had his own issues, though, and Chase was sure he would die a selfish, hateful, manipulating, greedy bastard.

It was probably the truth, but he wasn't trying to live his days out in Hell on Earth. Chase had never been one to just sit around and wait for shit to happen or to wait and let things fix themselves. He'd always been a man with a plan, and he was about to set one in motion.

Chase put on his pants and stepped into his shoes. Usually when he made an appearance at Cream during club hours, he wore a suit, and the one he'd chosen for the evening was a straight, black Armani-cut so classic it looked like a tux, along with a crisp white shirt. He ran a brush over his hair and thought of Bliss again. He wondered what she would think about working at Shelter or Delight instead of for Cyrus. He'd decided he really didn't want her around his brother because Cyrus was trouble. Also, by getting her away from Cyrus, he hoped if he kept Bliss as close to him as he could until he could pull up stakes, there was a chance she'd never find out about his razor-wielding ways. He hated the deception, but he was only leaving out some parts of the truth that she'd never asked about.

He looked in the mirror again and promised himself that Wolf would be the last of his kills. Bliss was his future—he knew that—and Chase wasn't about to risk her or Corey for Cyrus's sorry ass. *It's time to make my move,* he resolved, checking his reflection one more time.

He walked out of the bedroom as he fastened his watch. He rang for the elevator, and his eyebrow went up when it started to rise from the garage because he was sure he'd left it on his apartment level. Chase stepped back and put his hand in his pocket, instinctively curling his fingers around his straight razor.

The elevator popped open, and out stepped Corey, looking angry.

Chase relaxed and smiled. "Hey, little bro."

Corey looked at him, frowning. "Why the hell did you break Cyrus's nose?"

"Because that fool put his hands on me."

Corey shoved him in the chest, hard enough to move him. "There. So did I. You gonna break my nose too?"

Chase smiled at his younger brother and shook his head. "It's not the same, Corey, and you know it. And don't mess up my suit. I got a date."

Corey smiled. "With Bliss? I really like her."

"Yeah, me too. Listen, Corey, before you ask…yeah, I *meant* to break Cyrus's nose. It wasn't a mistake or an accident. I was fuckin' aimin' for it. He deserved it for disrespectin' me."

"Y'all gotta stop this shit, Chase."

"It's stopped. Everything is beautiful."

"Come on. I'm serious."

"No, *you* come on, Corey. I said everything is cool. I'm gonna do him one last solid, and then I'm gonna step away from his grimy ass for good. I mean it."

"Chase, y'all can fix whatever this—"

Chase turned on Corey with an disbelieving look on his face. "Corey, do you hear yourself? There's no fixing this shit. Don't you fuckin' get it? Cyrus wants me to *kill* people for him! This ain't a fuckin' game. I've been putting people in the ground for him, and I don't want to do it anymore, but he keeps forcin' my hand."

"Can't you just fuckin' say no?"

They stared at each other for a long, drawn-out moment before Chase shook his head, realizing Corey must not know what it was all about. He felt such a sudden wave of love and ferocious protectiveness for his little brother that he almost grabbed him and hugged him. If Corey was clueless that Cyrus would try to use *him* as an ersatz assassin, Chase planned on keeping it that way for as long as possible.

"No, Corey. I *can't* just say no," Chase said, looking away so Corey couldn't read his expression.

"Why not? You still owe him money or somethin'?"

Chase laughed. "I don't owe Cyrus shit, Corey."

"Then why—"

Chase cut him off by throwing a companionable arm over his shoulder. He picked up his keys and rang for the elevator. "Don't worry about it. I'm not rushin' you out, but I'm late. I got some stuff I need to talk to you about, so get with me for lunch on Monday."

"Tomorrow's Saturday. Let's do it tomorrow."

Chase laughed. "I don't plan on leavin' my house this weekend, so Monday's better."

Corey laughed too. "If you plan on lockin' yourself in here with Bliss, I ain't mad at ya, son."

"Yeah, that's the plan."

They rode down together. Chase walked Corey to his Lexus, and then got in his Porsche. He had a million things on his mind, but they all took a backseat to Bliss. He grinned as he pulled his car into traffic. He couldn't wait to see her, and his heart was already racing at the thought of her all dolled up.

G STREET CHRONICLES
~A NEW URBAN DYNASTY~
WWW.GSTREETCHRONICLES.COM

Chapter 10

"Who you goin' out with, Tash? That same guy...Trevor?"

While Bliss got ready for Chase, Tasha sat on her bed, as usual, keeping her company. Tasha was dressed to go out herself. "Yeah. Same ol', same ol'."

Bliss sat down beside her and started pulling on her stockings. "You sound bored with him. Are you?"

Tasha took her foot out of her sandal and inspected her pedicure. "A little. He's *just* a doctor—not some exciting club owner like your fine-ass friend Chase." She stuck her foot back in her sandal, then took the other one out and inspected it. "You like him a lot, don't you?"

Bliss put on her other stocking, pondering whether or not she wanted to let her best friend inside her head. She wanted Chase to be the first person to know how she felt about him.

"Hello? I'm talking to you, Bliss."

She stood up and put on a pretty black lace garter belt and snapped her stockings onto it. Bliss glanced at Tasha with a guarded expression. "Yeah, I like him a lot."

Tasha raised an amused eyebrow. "I see. He gets *real* stockings instead of plain old pantyhose. Very sexy. Are you gonna give him some tonight?"

Bliss looked over her shoulder. "Are you gonna give Trevor

some?"

Tasha sighed expansively. "It looks like it's on the itinerary. So is Chase gettin' lucky or not?"

Bliss slipped on her nicest, slinkiest little black dress. "Yeah, probably." She couldn't help but smile at the thought of him peeling it off of her. "No, make that *definitely*."

Tasha grinned at her and hopped off the bed. She ran out of the room with the heels of her strappy sandals click-clacking noisily on the hardwood floor.

Bliss laughed and shook her head, wondering where she was running off to. She put on her perfume and started to do her hair.

Tasha came back in the room just in time to zip her roommate and best friend up.

"Thanks," Bliss said, still fiddling with her hair.

"Don't thank me for that. Thank me for *these*." She handed Bliss a strip of three condoms. "Just make sure you put 'em in your purse... and use them. Don't stand there looking embarrassed. It ain't always about the monster, though that's always there, but in my humble opinion, Chase looks *potent*. He also looks like he wouldn't mind getting you pregnant. If you need to use them, use them. Please."

Bliss laughed because her mind immediately went back to what he'd said about kids, that he wouldn't mind "helping her out" with that. Tasha was right, and Bliss took the condoms. "Thank you, Tasha, but I'm sure he has his own."

"Never trust a man when it comes to your contraception," she said, sounding like a school nurse or some eight-grade health teacher.

Bliss didn't want to talk about it anymore. She wasn't stupid, and Tasha was coming off a little condescending, like she was talking to someone who was slow. "All right. Okay. I got it!"

Tasha put a hand on her arm. "He looks at you like he loves you, you know, and you look at him the same way. Sometimes when your emotions are that strong, common sense goes out the window. That's *all* I'm saying, Bliss. I don't mean to sound like I'm preaching. You and Chase have some real serious shit going on between you. You'd have to be blind not to see it."

Bliss put on her earrings and was about to say something, but she was interrupted by the doorbell.

Tasha looked at her watch. "That's not mine. Trevor's never on time." She followed Bliss to the front door like a puppy, the shells in her hair clinking, her bracelets jingling, and her heels clacking.

Bliss smiled. Her dear friend could never sneak up on anybody. She made too damned much noise. Bliss looked at her with some amusement. "What are you so excited for?"

"'Cause that dress means suit. I can't wait to see that dude in a suit."

Bliss laughed. "You stupid, Tash." She opened the door, and sure enough, Chase was standing there wearing a very nice one.

He was gorgeous. He smiled at her and, oblivious to Tasha, pulled her into his arms and kissed her firmly on the mouth. "I missed you," he said, letting her go.

Bliss smiled, speechless. *Oh yeah. It's on…tonight!*

"*Damn!*" Tasha said from behind her. "Look at you, all tricked out and spruced up. Showin' up here lookin' like the black James Bond and spittin' lines like that. You give lessons? 'Cause Trevor could use some."

Chase laughed. "It ain't something you learn."

Tasha smiled. "Unfortunately, you're right. Just don't go bringin' my friend back here all knocked up."

Oh no she didn't! Bliss hit her in the arm. "Be quiet, Tasha! Jesus Christ!"

Chase didn't seem upset in the least though. "Okay. I'll try not to, but I can't make you any promises."

They left, and Chase drove Bliss in his very nice car to a very nice restaurant, where they enjoyed a very nice, very expensive meal. They got back in his car, and he drove to Cream and parked his car right in front of the club. Chase took her hand as they walked in. Bliss must have heard his name called out at least fifteen times, and he nodded and stopped to speak to a few people: a guy who played for the Knicks, a guy that played for the Jets, a well-known rapper, a record mogul, and an actress who seemed a little tipsy and tried to kiss him on the mouth. Bliss smiled and let it go, because Chase never let go of *her* and introduced her most graciously to everyone they bumped into. That woman—if she ever mattered—didn't matter anymore. Chase didn't just seem to be drifting aimlessly through the club; he seemed to be looking for someone in particular. He stopped at the bar, and the bartender stopped what he was doing and made his way over to him. Chase reached across the bar and clapped him on the back. "Congratulations, Jimmy! Dee told me you got a little girl now."

The bartender was beaming. "Yeah, day before yesterday. Eight pounds even."

Chase smiled. "She got a name yet?"

"Not yet. We're still working on it."

Chase reached into his jacket and took out a slim white envelope. He handed it to Jimmy. "Here you go, Jimmy. Put it to good use. If you need to take some time off, tell Dee I said it's okay."

"Thanks, Chase. We really appreciate it."

"Speaking of Dee, you seen her?"

Jimmy looked over Chase's shoulder and grinned. "Comin' right at you, boss. Two o'clock."

Chase turned around, and Bliss took a slightly intimidated step behind him. Dee was parting the crowd like Moses in the Red Sea, and people were falling back to make way for her beeline to Chase.

"Uh-oh. I think I might have stayed away too long," Chase muttered under his breath.

Dee was an impressively beautiful woman, somewhere in her forties, with an equally impressive figure. Bliss straightened up and smoothed her dress down as the woman approached the bar like a tidal wave. "Well, well!" she said in a loud, boisterous voice. "If it ain't Chase Brown! I'm a little shocked to see you standing here in *your own* club. I thought you'd abandoned me." She got a little closer to him and kissed him on the cheek. "You're wearin' the hell outta that suit, Chase." She turned her entire body and looked Bliss over from her head to her toes. Dee smiled at her a bit ruefully and then offered Bliss her hand. "Delia Montgomery...and the only person you could possibly be is Bliss Riley. I've heard a lot about you."

"Nice to meet you, Dee. I've heard a lot about you too."

"Don't hold it against me. I'm not as bad as they say. I just like things my way, although his way does work sometimes. Look at you! Aren't you just the prettiest little thing? Oh shit, I'm babbling, and I don't know what for. Shit." Dee never lost her smile through her whole little rant.

Chase was looking at her with his lips tucked in. "You all right, Dee?" he asked.

Dee still had hold of Bliss's hand. She shook it again and then let it go. "Yeah, Chase. I'm great. How about you?"

Bliss looked from one to the other. *Okay. What is this shit?*

"I'm a little shocked, Dee."

She gave him a slightly sour smile. "It's a small thing, Chase. Don't worry about it. I'm good." She touched Bliss's arm. "I'll see you next time, Bliss. We'll get to know each other. Sorry about the theatrics," she said and then walked away before they could say goodbye.

Chase thoughtfully and silently watched her retreat, then turned back to Bliss. "I could say I had no idea what that was all about, but that would be a lie. I just kind of hoped it wasn't true."

Bliss felt bad, but she didn't feel sorry. All is fair in love and war, but she wasn't insensitive. She squeezed his hand. "Let's go, Chase."

He took her out without a word of protest. They got in his car and took Broadway up to Riverside Drive. They rode all the way up to Chase's place, making small talk, with his hand on her thigh. Bliss could tell Dee's reaction bothered him, but he didn't seem to want to talk about it, and having just met the woman, she didn't want to bring it up.

Bliss was slightly upset that it had cast a bit of a pall on their evening, but he'd explained to her beforehand that he wanted to stop by because he had something for Jimmy. Also, he'd wanted her to meet Dee, an important fixture in his life. Bliss looked over at him. He wasn't talking, and he looked like he was lost in thought. Chase had a tendency to brood, she'd noticed. She placed her hand over the one he had on her thigh and laced her fingers with his. "Don't be upset, Chase."

"I'm not. I'm really just a little shocked, like I said. I didn't really think she was feelin' me like *that*. I thought it was a game we always played. Okay, okay…someplace in the back of my mind, maybe I thought she was a lot more serious than I was, but still."

Bliss rubbed the back of his hand. "Let it go, Chase. It'll work itself out."

He didn't answer her as he picked up a gadget and pressed a button. A garage door rolled up on a building that looked like an office space, and he drove in. Chase pressed another button, and the lights came on.

They got out, and Bliss took a quick look around. She saw his Ducati and a black Kawasaki on one side of the room, as well as an old-style muscle-car Charger—not the new, revamped version. It was sleek and black and dangerous looking, and Bliss didn't like it at all. She touched it with her finger and found it to be as cold as it looked. She wrinkled her nose. "What's up with *this* car, Chase?"

He looked at her, but he didn't smile. "You don't like my Charger?"

"Not really."

He laughed. "Well, I only use it to run errands and once in a while, to do an occasional job for Cyrus. You really don't have to worry about riding in it."

She stared at him, and he stared back; a small smile played at the corners of his mouth. "What—" she started, but he interrupted her.

"Ask whatever you want, but let's do it upstairs okay?" He didn't wait for an answer. He rang for the elevator, and it popped open. They stepped inside and rode up in silence.

The door opened back up at the level of his living space. Once again, Bliss was impressed with him. The space was huge, with blond hardwood floors. There was an invitingly plush black sectional, with a huge TV hanging on the wall. The kitchen was to the left; it featured black granite counters and upscale appliances. The dining area was directly ahead, with upholstered chairs and a marble table. Past that was the only wall in the loft, and Bliss was sure it housed the bedroom. There was a full-sized pool table on the other side of the loft, past the living room, along with another sectional.

Bliss smiled. "Wow, Chase. This is nice."

He was watching her with his suit jacket open and his hands in his pants pockets.

She wanted to walk over to him and start pulling his clothes off, but there were a few things her logical mind told her they needed to get out of the way first—like finishing the conversation they'd started in the garage.

"Thanks," he said after an awkward delay. Chase walked over to her, never taking his eyes off hers or his hands out of his pockets.

Bliss put the little purse she was carrying on the arm of the sectional, then put her arms around his waist and looked up at him. "You don't really feel like talking, do you? I know we should, but I don't want to. Do you?"

That hint of a smile reappeared. "No, no, I really don't—not right now. But we will...later. I promise."

Bliss nodded. She had absolutely no desire to talk to Chase about anything at that moment. She didn't want to hear anything she didn't want to know about until after he'd made love to her, because then it would be too late to go back. Then, she'd be in it for the long run. She knew something wasn't right, but she didn't care. She wanted him.

Bliss stood on her toes and held her face up, pulling him down by his tie and unknotting it. She kissed him slow and deep. Chase shrugged out of his jacket as Bliss pulled his tie off his neck. Her hands flew to the buttons on his shirt and started to undo them. Chase unzipped her dress and pulled it forward as she pushed his shirt off his shoulders. Bliss slipped out of her dress, letting it fall to the floor. She kicked the dress away and stepped back from him because she wanted him to see what he was getting ready to get into.

Chase looked her over and licked his lips. He smiled at her with a lewd little glint in his eye. "Come here, Bliss."

She smiled back and patted her thighs. "No...*you* come *here*."

Chase raised an eyebrow but held his smile. "Have it your way." He shocked her when he picked her up like she didn't weigh a thing and carried her into his bedroom. He dropped her in the middle of the bed and put one knee on either side of her body and one hand on either side of her face. Chase lowered his head and kissed her above each breast. Bliss reached down and unsnapped the closure on the front of her bra. Chase thrilled her with a barrage of strategically placed kisses and tweaking, but his real interests lay elsewhere, and he wasn't shy about it. He backed up until he was off the bed, pulling Bliss with him.

When her butt hit the edge of the bed, she rose up on her elbows and moved to kick off her high heels.

Chase put his hands on her ankles to stop her. "Don't, baby. Leave 'em on." In an instant, Chase was on his knees in front of her. His hands slid up her legs, and Bliss trembled. He moved into position between her thighs, and Bliss had to fight the urge to just throw her legs open like a harlot and beg him to take her. Her need for him was like a low, dull ache. He kissed his way up her thighs, and Bliss couldn't help it: She raised her hips, and Chase took the hint and slid her panties off. Bliss watched him looking at her and felt her arousal swelling her up, making her twitch. He put his mouth on her, and she thought she'd died and gone to Heaven. His mouth was carnally hot as he twirled his tongue over her in small circles. In answer to his moans, she offered sweet little squeals of pleasure. Chase wasn't all over the place; he knew exactly what he was doing. He worked on her very precisely, in one spot, spreading her apart with his thumbs.

Bliss felt warm all over, and her legs started to quiver. She ran her hands over her breasts and screamed helplessly as her body began to throb. Chase was on top of his game. His tongue was unrelenting as Bliss's hips came off the bed. He put his hands under her ass and licked her until she was whimpering softly. He stood up suddenly, and Bliss looked up at him in dismay. She wanted him so bad that she was almost panting. "Chase, don't just leave me like this. What are you doing?"

He laughed and removed the rest of his clothes. Bliss watched him, transfixed. No, Chase wasn't just really cute. He was fine as hell, standing there in all his naked glory, and he had the goods too.

Bliss tried not to stare, biting her lip in anticipation.

Chase smiled at her and put one knee back on the bed, and Bliss couldn't stop herself from wrapping her hand around him. She slid her hand back and forth slowly until his breath grew ragged.

Chase closed his eyes for a moment, then put his hand over hers to stop its rhythm. He opened his eyes and looked at her hard. "Move back," he lovingly instructed.

Bliss pushed herself back with her heels, and Chase followed her, forcing her back to the middle of the bed. He was laughing. "You know what, Bliss? It seems like we can never get to where we should be without getting stuff out of the way first."

Bliss giggled because he was right. "I agree."

He laughed again, but it was a shaky laugh. "If I don't get in right now, I think I'm gonna pass out. Let me in, Bliss."

Bliss parted her thighs for him with a smile. "Come on, baby. Stay as long as you like."

Chase took her up on the invitation. He slid into her, looking into her eyes. They both cried out at the slickly thrilling sensation of their bodies joining. Bliss's legs went instinctively around his hips. Chase put his weight on one arm and his hand under her thigh and pulled her closer. He rode her slow, sliding into her long and deep.

Chase put his face close to hers and whispered in her ear. Bliss felt her entire body blush. He wasn't talking dirty to her. Instead, he was telling her how good she felt to him. It was shocking and exhilarating because no one had ever done that before. He was breaking her down slowly and steadily with that long, sure stroke, letting her feel all of him, making her take all of him…and he was taking his time about it.

Bliss ran her hands over his body and let them come to rest firmly on his ass. She pulled him in as far as he could go with every thrust, her hips rising to meet his. She turned her head, and Chase began kissing her and picking up his pace. Bliss could feel it coming like an express train. It was bearing down on her, and she felt like she couldn't get enough air in her lungs. Her hips lunged off the bed and ground against his mercilessly. She was vaguely aware that she'd called his name and that she was whimpering like she was hurt, but she couldn't stop grinding her hips into his.

She felt like she was caught in that strong climax and couldn't get out. That was fine with her because she didn't want to leave. Instead, she pulled Chase into it with her like it was the last thing he was expecting.

He plunged into her with his weight still balanced on one arm. His fingers gripped her thigh, and he tried to go easy on her, not to slam into her, but it was useless. Chase pounded into her, and she loved it, crying out and rising to meet him. He put his hands on her hips and pushed her back down on the bed as the pounding waned into a grind. Bliss could feel him filling her up, and she loved that too. She rocked with him until he was done. They lay there for a moment, spent, happy, and breathless.

Chase got up and took her shoes off. He unsnapped her stockings and peeled them off. He gave her a hand getting up and took off her garter belt and her bra. He looked down at her; Bliss was trying not to straight-up ogle him, and he noticed. He laughed softly and looked her over, not quite ogling *her*. "I know exactly how you feel, and you can get it anytime you want it, Bliss. Ain't this great?"

Bliss got to her knees and ran her hands over his chest. She kissed the scar on his jaw suggestively.

Chase's eyebrow went up. "You want it right now?"

She laughed. "We just finished, silly."

He moved against her, knowing he could be ready again in ten seconds. "So?"

"You're crazy, Chase."

He laughed. "I've heard that before." He let his hands skim up her sides until his thumbs were stroking the sides of her breasts. "I'm supposed to be in bed holding you now, I guess, but can we wait a minute on the afterglow?"

Bliss laughed. "Why? Are you hungry too?"

He laughed. "Yeah. I'm starvin'."

They split a pair of black pajamas and went into the kitchen. Chase opened the refrigerator door with Bliss standing just in front of him.

She was surprised the fridge was so well stocked. She took a cake box off the second shelf. "What's in here?"

He frowned thoughtfully. "Red velvet, I think. It's Corey's. Let's eat it."

Bliss laughed. "That's cold, Chase."

"He shouldn't have left it here if he didn't want me eatin' it. I ain't worried about Corey raisin' up on me over some cake."

Bliss noticed the way Chase talked about Corey with great affection and about Cyrus with a distaste of equal proportions, but she let it go for a moment. She cut the cake, and they sat down at the breakfast bar to eat it.

Bliss nonchalantly looked across the room and caught a glimpse of her little purse lying on the sectional. Her mouth dropped open: She hadn't even thought about the condoms, but she could sure hear Tasha's voice in her head: *"Common sense goes out the window…Never trust a man when it comes to your contraception…You better not bring my friend back all knocked up…"*

Chase looked over his shoulder to see what she was looking at. He looked back at her questioningly. "What's wrong?"

She didn't feel like saying it out loud, so she got up and retrieved her purse. She opened it and put the condoms between them.

Chase almost choked on his cake, but not from surprise. Rather, it was because he was laughing. He managed to swallow his food, then he pointed at the condoms, still laughing. "Where'd you get those?"

Bliss frowned, wondering what the hell was so funny. "From Tasha."

He seemed even more tickled. "Damn! She only gave you three?"

"What's so funny, Chase? I'm not laughing."

He chilled his laughter a little, but it was still there. "Come on, Bliss! Why are you all frowned up? It *is* funny to me. It's funny because you don't get it."

She frowned deeper. "Get *what?*"

"Stop frownin' at me."

Bliss stood up. Real anger was creeping in around the edges. *What the hell am I supposed to get?* She took a step away from him and folded her arms across her chest. "No. Not until you explain yourself—and you need to do it right *now*, Chase. I'm serious."

He looked at her like he didn't believe she *was*. Then he looked a little harder and realized his mistake. "Bliss…are you *really* mad at me?" He asked the question like he couldn't believe he what he was saying.

Bliss looked at her watch. "I wonder if the #1 train is running at this time of night," she said and turned on her heel. She walked over to her dress and picked it up off the floor.

Chase touched her arm, and she jumped. She hadn't even heard him get up. "Wait a minute, Bliss. I'm sorry. I apologize if you took what I said the wrong way. I know you can't read my mind. All I meant by saying you don't get it is that those condoms really don't matter to me one way or the other—not with you."

Bliss looked at him like he was crazy. "What the hell does that mean?"

He smiled and shrugged. "Well, you already think I'm crazy, but I'm not—at least not about this. I can only tell you—or try to, anyway—how I feel about you. They don't mean anything to me because even if you had some terrible disease, I'd rather get it and die than be without you. If you get pregnant, I'll hold you down, Bliss. No, wait…I'll do more than that. I'll marry you and see how many more we can have! If I thought you'd do it, I'd put you in my car right now and drive to the nearest JP or preacher or anybody who could marry us in the middle of the night. That's why I laughed… and that's why those condoms don't matter."

They stared at each other silently. He'd taken her breath away and left her speechless, and she felt like an ass. She was sorry, and she knew the best way to tell him, because they *were* on the same wavelength after all. Bliss reached out and touched his face. "I *love* you, Chase."

He smiled at her and tilted his head. "You sure? 'Cause you were really ready to roll outta here and maybe come back with some of your girls to beat my ass, right?"

"You're wrong about one thing."

"What's that?"

"You *are* crazy."

He kept smiling. "I must be, 'cause you keep tellin' me I am. How crazy can I *really* be, though, Bliss? You just told me you love me, and you've only known me for ten days. I *knew* the first time I kissed you that I'd just stopped lookin'. I need to tell you that I *wasn't* lookin' at the time, but still…there you were. It was as inevitable as rockslides, earthquakes, tsunamis—"

Bliss made a face. "But those are all *disasters*, Chase."

He shook his head. "No, baby. Those are *forces of nature*. I know it seems like this is going really fast—and yeah, maybe it *is*—but don't tell me you've never heard of people gettin' married a month after meeting each other and *staying* married for fifty years. I know you have."

"Yeah, but…" She trailed off, because he was right. *Stuff like that does happen.*

"But what?"

She shook her head. "But nothing. What you're saying is true, but—"

"But what, Bliss? You're basing what's destined to go on between you and me on what other people think. Like I asked you before, who makes the rules to this shit? I said I don't, but you know what? I was wrong. *I* make the rules to this, and so do you. Fuck what everybody says and what they think, Bliss."

She watched his face. Chase was dead serious. Yes, he had an odd way of looking at things, but she couldn't say he was wrong, because he wasn't. "You're right, Chase. I guess I just have to get used to your maverick way of thinking." She paused. "You really would marry me, wouldn't you?"

He laughed. "Would? I'm *gonna* marry you, Bliss. I know you don't think I'm serious, but I am. Just let me know when you're ready."

"Is that supposed to be a proposal?"

Chase shrugged and smiled. "I'm not a real traditional guy, Bliss, so that's more than a proposal. It's a promise."

His phone rang, and Bliss wondered who it could be at one in the morning.

Chase looked at his watch, then at the caller ID, and then he frowned. "I think I should take this," he said, more to himself than to Bliss. Chase picked the phone up, and his entire demeanor changed.

Bliss tried to pretend she wasn't listening. She picked up their plates and took them to the sink, then tuned in to one side of Chase's conversation.

"What are you callin' me for, Khalid? I don't give a shit. You got somethin' you think I should know, you tell Cyrus, and *he'll* let me know. What? Like I said, I don't give a shit. That's your problem. It is what it is, man. Y'all shoulda thought about that." There was a long pause.

Bliss looked at Chase, and he glanced at her and tucked his lips in.

He turned his head and closed his eyes. Then he exploded. "Fuck! Fuck, Khalid! Where the *fuck* is he? Where's Corey? You guys are fuck-ups! No, never mind that! I'll do it my-damn-self. I'll be there as soon as I can." He hung up and speed-dialed someone. "Corey? Are you okay? You sure? All right, Just stay where you are. I'm on my way. Do me a favor and call J.T. Tell him I might need him. Bye." He put the phone back on the base and looked at Bliss. "I'm sorry, baby. Cyrus made a damn mess, and I gotta clean it up.. I need a shower. You comin'?" He didn't wait for an answer but just turned and walked to the bathroom and turned on the shower. Chase's shower was so big it had a seat in it. They took off their pajamas and got in.

"Chase, what's wrong?"

"Cyrus got shot."

"*What*? Oh my God! Is he okay?"

"He's alive. That's all I know."

"What about Corey? Was he with him?"

"Corey's okay. I don't know the details, but I'll get 'em in a minute."

They didn't speak again until they were out of the shower. Bliss

understood that every family has their crises, and they usually find
out about it from one of those dreaded middle-of-the-night calls like
the one Chase had just received. Of course the timing was really
bad, but that wasn't what was eating at her. Usually, those midnight
phone calls are because someone has a heart attack or gets in a car
accident, but this was different. Cyrus had been *shot*. From the little
she'd gleaned about him and what she'd seen herself, Cyrus Brown
left her with some truly uneasy feelings. She'd put off asking before,
but now she felt she had to. She had to know exactly what was going
on with Chase and his two handsome brothers.

She watched Chase as he quickly dressed in a pair of black Levis
and a plain black T-shirt. He sat down and put his feet in a pair of
high-top black Uptowns and then leaned over to tie his shoes.

"Um…Chase, can I ask you something?"

He glanced at her but never stopped what he was doing. "You can
ask me anything, and I'll try my best to answer you."

That was fair enough, and at least he hadn't clammed up or
tightened up on her. She sat next to him and started putting her
stockings back on. "What's up with Cyrus? Is he a…like a drug
dealer or something?"

Chase laughed, but there was no humor behind it. "No, baby.
Cyrus is not *like* a drug dealer. Cyrus *is* a drug dealer."

Her mouth dropped open, but she closed it quickly. Bliss wasn't
naïve. She'd spent her whole life, with the exception of college, in
Harlem. She still lived there, even though they'd gentrified some of
it and had taken to calling it Upper Manhattan. Drug dealers weren't
anything new to her, but still, she had an uneasy feeling about it.
"Chase, you hired me to work for a drug dealer?"

He stopped what he was doing and looked at her patiently. "No,
Bliss. I hired you to manage his club. And about that, now that you
know what Cyrus really is, if you feel uncomfortable workin' in
his club, you can work in one of mine. I could always use another
manager to take some of the weight off Dee."

Bliss looked at him sideways. "Yeah, right, and give her another
reason to hate me?"

Chase rubbed her thigh. "She doesn't hate you, Bliss. How could she hate you when I love you so much?"

She put her hand on top of his. "That's exactly why. Men are so simple when it comes to women."

He looked at *her* sideways for a moment, then smiled. "Whatever. You could always not work at all and spend my money for the rest of your life."

She laughed. "Yeah, I *could* do that, but there're some things we need to talk about."

He laughed and put on his other sneaker. He was wearing black socks, too, Bliss noticed. "Go ahead. Seems like me and you are pretty good at getting things out of the way, like I said."

"Okay. Are *you* a drug dealer?"

Again, he stopped what he was doing and looked her in the eye. "No. I'm no drug dealer. I promise you that."

She wanted to breathe a sigh of relief, but she didn't let it out yet because there was still something else. "All right, I believe you. One more question though."

He stood and ran a brush over his hair as he looked at her expectantly.

"Why are you dressed all in black like that?"

He put his brush down. "Well, Bliss, considering my brother just took a bullet, I might have to kick somebody's ass tonight."

She lifted her eyebrows. "Is that all? You look like a damned ninja."

"Good. You know what they say about the element of surprise."

She stood up, slipped her dress over her head, and turned around so he could zip her up. "I wish you wouldn't go. What if you get hurt?"

Chase winked at her. "Don't worry about me. If you gotta worry about somebody, worry about the shooter." He kissed her forehead and put his hands on her waist. "Why don't you stay here until I get back? I'm not really finished with you."

"Can you promise me you won't kick anybody's ass?"

He shook his head but smiled. "No. I don't make promises I'm not sure I can keep."

She didn't think he would promise, but it didn't hurt to ask. She gave him a peck on the lips. "Then I'm not going to stay."

"All right, but can I come to you when this is over?"

She stared at him. He was a man with his own definite way of seeing things. There was probably nothing she could say that would keep him from doing whatever it was that he was going to do, but she was going to let him know she wasn't happy about it. "Could you zip my dress up, please?"

Chase kissed her bare shoulder before he did, and it was like a little shock of electricity. He spoke in her ear, and it made her dizzy. "Don't be like that, Bliss. If you won't stay, let me come see you, honey." He kissed her neck, and all her resolve dissolved.

She sighed dramatically. "Okay, Chase. How can I tell you no?"

She felt him smile against her skin. "You really shouldn't ever try. You hurt my feelin's every time you do. I love you, Bliss."

"I love you too. Now, drop me off at home, and I'll let you in when you get there later."

Bliss slipped on her shoes, and Chase put on a plain black baseball jacket. He took her hand, and they walked to the elevator like they were taking a casual stroll. He started kissing her when they got inside, walking up on her so her back was against the wall, covering her with lovely, little, intimate kisses that were killing her. She put her hands in the back pockets of his jeans and pulled him against her, standing on her toes. They rubbed against each other, and the friction was beautiful. Chase moaned and started pulling her dress up.

Bliss laughed and started pulling it down. "Chase, don't you have somewhere you need to be?"

He pulled on her dress again, and she pushed it back. "I do, but you're puttin' up a fight."

"So I'll owe you one. Go see about your brother."

He let her go with major reluctance. "Yeah, right. Cyrus. Okay. I'm goin', but there's one more thing you're gonna get mad at me about."

"What's that?"

They stepped out of the elevator and into the garage.

Chase walked past his Porsche, and Bliss frowned. "You're gonna have to ride in my Charger."

Bliss started to argue with him but changed her mind. Chase held the door open for her like a gentleman, and she got in without a word. She didn't care for the car at all. Chase got in and started the engine. It gurgled mightily and then settled into a dull purr.

It was cold in the car even though the night was pleasant. Bliss shivered involuntarily, and Chase looked at her. "You okay?"

"I'm fine. I just don't like this car."

Chase looked at her like she was overreacting. "What's the big deal, Bliss?"

"I just don't like it. There's just something I just can't put my finger on."

Chase reached over and dropped her hand in his lap. "Here. Put your finger on this."

Bliss laughed and pulled her hand away, looking at him like he was a bad boy—which he was. "You've got a little nasty side to you, don't you, Chase?"

He laughed devilishly and backed out of the garage. "I got a *huge* nasty side. You ain't seen nothin'."

She smiled. "I can't wait."

"You won't have to," he said and slid his hand up her thigh.

They drove to the light, and Bliss reached for the radio.

Chase reached for her hand before she touched it and kissed her fingers. "That's not a real radio. It just looks like one."

She frowned. "Chase, how you gonna have a car with no radio? It's already old and ugly and cold. No radio makes it seem like a hearse."

Chase surprised her with a short burst of real laughter. "A hearse? That's really funny, Bliss. You have no idea. You've got a vivid imagination, sweetheart."

"What are you driving this thing for anyway? Why didn't you just take your Porsche?"

He looked over at her patiently. "Because my Porsche seats

two."

Bliss stopped talking and looked out the window. "When you finish seeing about Cyrus, just come to me, okay, Chase?" She glanced at his scars and winced. "I really don't want you fighting. I mean it. I don't want anything to happen to you."

He smiled. "I really ain't lookin' to *fight*, Bliss, okay? I won't let anybody hurt me. I promise."

They rode for a while in silence, while Bliss turned things over in her mind. "How come you were really upset until you found out Corey was okay? Why are you so calm now? Aren't you worried about Cyrus?'

"If I wasn't worried about Cyrus, I wouldn't be drivin' around in the middle of the night. I'd have you in my bed, Bliss, trying to get my point across and make you see things my way."

Bliss smiled. He was already making her see certain things his way, but she kept at him. "Don't you like Cyrus, Chase?"

He glanced at her as he pulled up in front of her building. "I don't really want to talk about my relationship with Cyrus right now. One day soon, I'll tell you all about us, but now's not the time."

Bliss stared at him until he looked back at her. She couldn't read much in his face, and it was clear he'd shut that particular door to her. She let it go. "I'm sure you will. I'll try to wait up for you. Just be careful, Chase. Don't do anything…crazy."

The corners of his mouth turned up. "There's that word again. Give me a kiss."

Bliss kissed him and made sure to make it a good one. "You make sure you hurry up and come back to me. I'm not playing, Chase."

He hugged her and kissed her forehead. "I'll be back as soon as I can."

She got out of the car and leaned back in before she closed the door. "I hope Cyrus is okay."

Chase shrugged. "Whatever. I'm sure he's not dead. I'll be back. Bye, Bliss." He watched her in, then drove away.

Bliss went up to her apartment, wondering what was going on with Chase but loving him anyway.

G STREET CHRONICLES
~A NEW URBAN DYNASTY~
WWW.GSTREETCHRONICLES.COM

Chapter 11

By the time Chase managed to make it to the hospital, he was very pissed off for a lot of reasons. First and foremost, the needles drama involving his hot-headed, controlling-ass brother had cut into his time with Bliss. Secondly, Corey had been with tired-ass Cyrus when all the shit went down and could have gotten killed. And lastly, it just meant more shit he'd have to do for Cyrus. In spite of their differences, he couldn't just let somebody shoot his fucking brother and not answer for it—and they would answer for it that very night.

When he got there, Khalid was sitting next to Corey, who was looking absolutely miserable. J.T. was watching them with his arms folded across his chest, looking at Khalid like he was something nasty. When Chase walked in, everybody looked at him—something he was very weary of. He just wanted to go home and be with his woman, but now he had to deal with that crew of fuck-ups. "All right, Corey. Clue me in on what the fuck's going on here."

Before Corey could answer, Khalid stood up. "They was drivin' down Saratoga, and these niggas in a BMW—"

Chase turned his head slowly and pointed his finger at Khalid. "Is your name Corey? No, so shut the fuck up! I don't want to hear shit from you until I ask you."

Khalid frowned and looked outraged. "Who the fuck you talkin' to, Smoke?"

Chase raised his eyebrows and reached for his back pocket. "You tryin' me, Khalid? Don't press your luck with me, 'cause your shit is already thin."

Khalid fell back and J.T. laughed.

Chase looked at his brother. "Get up, Corey. You okay?"

Corey stood up obediently. "I'm good, Chase. But those fuckers shot Cyrus!"

Chase frowned and nodded, looking everywhere at once, very discreetly.

J.T. moved closer to him and spoke low. "Chill, baby. The cops left about an hour ago. It's cool."

Chase looked at Corey. "Did you give a statement?"

Corey shrugged and continued to look miserable. "Yeah. I *had* to."

"What did you tell 'em?"

Corey shrugged again. "I told 'em we was ridin' down Saratoga, and we stopped at a bodega to get a newspaper. All of a sudden, some niggas in a dark blue BMW rolled up and started sprayin' bullets. Yo, they shot Cyrus, Chase! Shot him right in front of my face. They wasn't even aiming at me."

"I take it you stopped your story at the part where they started sprayin' bullets?"

Corey nodded.

Chase turned to Khalid. "Where the fuck were you at?"

Khalid frowned. "Oh, so *now* you want to hear from me?"

Chase smiled at him maliciously, and his eyes glittered. "One more fucked-up word outta you, and you won't have to worry about nobody hearin' from your stupid ass again. Answer me, motherfucker."

Khalid blinked and looked seriously offended. "Smoke, why you talkin' to me like that? What you disrespectin' me for, man?"

Chase advanced on him, and J.T. stepped between them, trying to keep some order. "'Cause I don't...fuckin'...like...your...sorry... ass. Now, where the hell were you?"

Khalid shook his head. "That's some personal shit you need to work out, Smoke. I was home with my woman. That okay with you?"

Chase stared at him blackly. If there was any living person he hated, it had to be that muthafucker. Besides the fact that Chase thought it was Khalid who sent Herc to murder him and Corey that day long ago, he also felt Khalid had always been a huge and horrible influence on Cyrus, feeding the flames of Cyrus's fucked-up ways. Chase turned away from him and back to Corey. "How bad is Cyrus hurt?"

"Not that bad, thank God."

"They shot him in his *ass*, Chase. Oh…and once in the back, on the right shoulder, high up. Another one got him in the elbow. Chipped some bone in there, I guess," J.T. said.

Chase nodded, somewhat relieved, but also a tiny bit disappointed. "Okay, so them niggas are bad shots. Where's Cyrus at?"

Corey pointed to triage. "Over there. He's got a bed in the middle."

"They're gettin' ready to move him," J.T. added.

Chase nodded again. "Okay. I'll be right back."

He walked through the double doors and scanned the room. Thankfully, it wasn't a busy night at the emergency room. There were people peppered through the room in various stages of physical disarray. A doctor walked from behind an area with the privacy curtain pulled, and Chase instinctively turned his face away. The doctor talked briefly with a nurse and headed down a long corridor to the exit. Chase waited until he was gone, then stepped behind the curtain.

Cyrus was hooked up to several machines. He was on his back, with one arm in a sling and his nose splinted and bandaged. He appeared to be sleeping.

"Wake your ass up, Cyrus," Chase demanded, standing close to him.

Cyrus's eyes opened slowly. "I'm not asleep. Thanks for comin' to see about me, Smoke."

Chase laughed a cold little laugh. "How could I stay away? You're my damn brother, like it or not. You all right?"

"Considering how bad it coulda been, I'm ready to do the Electric Slide," he said with a smile.

Chase ignored his attempt at humor. "Who did it?"

"Two of Wolf's boys, Mooch and Post. I think it was Mooch who did the actual trigger work. You know 'em?"

Chase nodded. "I know Mooch, and I've seen Post around. I know who he is." They looked at each other for a long time before Chase continued, "I'm gonna handle this thing for you, Cyrus. I'm gonna handle Wolf, too, and I'll help you finish your club. After that, I think we should go our separate ways. I'm not gonna be cleanin' shit up for you forever. I meant what I said this mornin'."

Cyrus looked away from him, but Chase recognized the insolence and the smugness in his face. He planned to keep using Corey as a weapon. "Okay, Chase. I appreciate it, and I can't thank you enough."

Chase frowned at his insincerity. "Fuck you, Cyrus. You don't mean that shit."

Cyrus looked surprised at Chase's words and made a superficial attempt to smooth things over. "You shouldn't say things like that, Smoke. You don't mean it. You're just angry."

"No, Cyrus. I'm just tired." He didn't want to be there anymore, and it was time to leave. "You must be tired too. Somebody will let you know how things turn out. Take care of yourself."

"You too, little brother. Watch your back."

Chase looked at him hard. "From the looks of it, maybe you should watch yours. Bye, Cyrus." After Chase returned to the waiting room, he made a beeline for Corey. "I want you to go home. You don't need to be any more mixed up in this shit than you already are, Corey."

Corey was visibly angry at such a suggestion. "Nah, man. Fuck that! He's my brother, too, and I was there when those niggas shot him up. I'm goin' with you."

"No you're not. Go home, Corey. I mean it."

"But, Chase, I—"

Chase wasn't in any mood to argue. "Corey, I told you to go

home. I'll call you before daybreak. This shouldn't take that long."
He put his hand on Corey's shoulder and gently guided him out of
the hospital.

When they got to Khalid's car, Corey turned to face him. "You
treat me like a damn little kid, Chase. I *am* grown, you know."

Chase smiled at him. "You may be grown, but you're still my
little brother, and I love you. I want you safe, Corey, and to stay
that way, you gotta listen to me, grown or not." Chase knew Corey
was pissed at him, but that wasn't important at the moment. It was
more important to him that Corey remained unharmed. He turned
to Khalid. "Take him straight home, no stops, and then go home
yourself. I'll be in touch."

Khalid nodded, but he didn't bother expressing any false gratitude
like Cyrus had.

Chase could envision himself cutting Khalid's throat, and he
almost smiled at the thought as he turned and walked away. "Come
on, J.T. You're drivin'."

They got into the Charger, and J.T. drove to Brooklyn. "Who we
lookin' for?" J.T. asked.

"Mooch and Post."

J.T. shook his head "That's fucked up."

Chase shrugged. "They shoulda thought about that."

"Well, they shouldn't be too hard to find."

"Not at all. Let's get Mooch first. Turn here."

They drove down Bushwick Avenue, and Chase's eyes scanned
the street.

"Here, right?" J.T. asked, pulling up in front of a block of row
houses. It was 3:00am, but it was a warm and early Saturday morning,
so there was still a small smattering of people still out in small social
circles.

Chase opened the glove compartment as J.T. turned on the radio
that wasn't a real radio at all; it was a police scanner. Chase took out
a pair of black gloves, a black baseball cap, and a face visor—the
kind skiers wear in the winter to keep the wind off their faces. He put
the gloves and cap on, then reached back into the glove box and took

out a black nine with the serial numbers rubbed off. He tucked the weapon into his jeans and looked over at J.T. "Meet me two blocks down, by the light."

"Done," J.T. replied in true yes-man fashion.

Chase got out and went up the steps of Mooch's residence. He'd done this all before, so it didn't take him long. He took a small black case out of his pocket and used two metal tools to tumble the lock and get inside. To any onlookers, he would have looked as harmless as a resident who was having a little trouble with his key. He opened the door and stepped soundlessly into the entryway like a man coming home from work.

It was dark and deserted, which made things easier. Apparently, Mooch called an apartment on the second floor home. Chase started up the stairs with liquid grace. The stairway was dimly lit and unoccupied, as was the hallway, but he was glad it wasn't too quiet in the place. Somewhere someone was playing their TV too loud, and a baby was wailing—both helpful, noisy distractions for what was about to take place in the building. He jogged up the rest of the stairs and withdrew his trusty razor from his pocket. He stopped just outside Mooch's apartment door. He was going to put the visor on, but he decided against it. *Fuck it. I want the last thing this trigger-happy Mooch fucker to see is my face.* He was in it now: Chase was gone. Smoke was here.

Chase smiled to himself as he lifted the ring of the brass knocker and let it fall three times. He knew niggas get real stupid when they're in a panic. He tried to squelch the thrill of anticipation that leapt up in him, tried to tell himself that he shouldn't be feeling exhilarated. After all, murder isn't supposed to be fun, like a damn hobby or something. He stepped out of the view of the peephole when he heard footsteps on the other side.

"Who the fuck is this at two in the mornin'?" Mooch demanded.

Chase moved all the way to the left of the door and stayed silent.

"Who the fuck is it?" Mooch bellowed.

Chase didn't answer. As he heard the locks come off, he realized, suddenly, that he'd probably been smiling for the last two minutes.

128 / *G Street Chronicles*

It was awful of him, but he couldn't seem to stop himself. His breath was low and even, and he was eerily calm.

The door opened an inch. There was a pause, and then it opened the length of the security chain.

Chase stayed still.

"What the fuck?" Mooch said under his breath.

The door closed and Chase stopped smiling as he heard the security chain come off. He knew Mooch wouldn't be coming to the door empty handed. His body tensed as he readied himself for whatever arsenal Mooch might unleash on him.

Mooch threw the door open, and Chase stepped in front of it. Mooch was holding a .45 in his right hand, but he seemed to forget it when he saw who his late-night visitor was. His face was a mask of fright. "Oh, God! Jesus," he whispered.

Chase's smile returned. "That's good, Mooch. It's never too late to pray. You got just enough time to repent before I cross your ass out." Chase lunged at him, opening his razor. He swung his arm in an arc and brought it down diagonally across Mooch's face, from the left side of the shooter's forehead to the tip of his chin. Chase never brought his razor down lightly, and this kill was no exception. He felt it hit the bone and slice through the cartilage in Mooch's nose. He felt the gelatinous *pop* as Mooch's eye burst like a too-ripe tomato.

Mooch howled and looked up in shock. His fingers reflexively pulled the trigger of the .45, and the bullet screamed out and thudded into the floor.

Chase pushed Mooch back into the apartment and kicked the gun out of his hand. He raised his arm again and brought the razor down on the other side of the man's face in another diagonal, creating a terrible and gory X in what used to be a relatively handsome face. The skin fell open, revealing layers of muscle, fat, and connective tissue. Blood soaked his shirt in seconds. He was blubbering and begging, blinded in his one remaining good eye by his own blood. He turned to run and tripped over the coffee table, crashing to land on his back on the floor.

Chase grabbed his victim's blood-soaked collar and went right for his neck. Mooch brought his hand up defensively, and Chase's razor split his palm open, causing the man to shriek like a wounded banshee. Chase grunted in irritation and pushed Mooch's chin up with the heel of his hand. He stuck the razor in the soft flesh between Mooch's left ear and his jawbone and dragged it smoothly across his neck. He jumped back to avoid the jetting torrent of blood that shot out of the wound and wiped the blade of the bloody razor on the sofa cushion.

Chase didn't wait to watch Mooch's death throes. He went out the window and down the fire escape and then sprinted the two blocks to meet J.T., staying close to the shadows on the way to his getaway car.

The passenger door swung open for him even before he got to the vehicle. Chase slipped inside, and J.T. pulled out—not screeching away from the curb like in the movies, but calmly and normally, moving right into the light flow of late-night traffic. He glanced at Chase and handed him a Ziploc bag. Chase stripped off his gloves and shoved them in the bag, just like he always did.

J.T. put the bag under his seat like *he* always did. "Everything go okay?" J.T. asked, looking over at him again.

"Yeah. Everything's good," Chase said quietly. Chase began to deflate. The adrenaline was leaving his body, and he was starting to settle down. The feeling was a little like fucking: The deed was done, the rush was over, and now all he wanted to do was go to sleep. He checked his clothes for any sign of Mooch's blood, and his search came up empty, as he couldn't see any evidence of the bloodbath he'd caused. Chase kept two pairs of thin black leather driving gloves in his glove compartment. He reached in and took out the other pair and drew them on. Then he opened and closed his fists for a perfect fit, held his hands up, and looked at them.

"What's the matter?" J.T. asked, concern in his voice. "You hurt?"

Chase slid down in his seat and put his hands in his lap. His mind flashed a picture of the gruesome X he'd made across Mooch's face. He couldn't believe he'd done that sick, psychopathic shit. He never could believe what he did, but he *had* done it. Smoke wasn't a strong enough tag; he felt like Mr. Fucking Hyde.

"Now's not the time for that shit, Chase. Let's go find Post and get this shit over with. Come on, man. Shake it off."

Fuck it, he thought. *We can't leave this shit half done.* Suddenly, an uninvited thought of Bliss popped into his mind, and he pushed her right back out; she didn't have any place in all that violence.

They turned onto Knickerbocker Avenue and almost ran over a small, very dark man who everyone called Baby Hustle because of his short stature and the fact that he was always selling something to support his pathetic crack habit. He jumped out of the way with great exaggeration and started yelling at the car like a lunatic.

"Stop the car, J.T.," Chase said as he rolled the window down. "Hey, Baby!" he yelled.

Baby Hustle looked at him, and his face lit up. He knew Chase might want to hit him up for some information, but Chase paid well. He did a slow bop to the vehicle. "Smoke! What's good, son? If I'da know'd that was you, I woulda stayed my black ass out the damn street!" he said, crowing with laughter.

Chase laughed, too, even though he wasn't even remotely amused. "Come here, Baby."

Baby obeyed and walked up on the car, knowing he could make enough green for a few blasts if he played his loose-tongue cards right. "What you want with me, Smoke?"

Chase smiled at him reassuringly. "Don't want nothing with *you,* Baby."

Baby swallowed hard, but he looked hungry, like he was close to fiending. "You lookin' for Mooch and Post, ain't ya? That's what you gotta be doin' out here so late. Me? I'm out here late, too, but I'm just rummagin' for shit to sell. It's hard to maintain with this goddamn recession. Know what I'm sayin'?" he said in his raspy, but somehow squeaky voice.

Baby was one of Chase's go-to guys to find out the word on the street. He was reliable, and he was so terrified of Chase that Chase seriously doubted he would ever be willing to suffer the consequences of giving him up. To make sure, Chase always broke him off right—enough for him to disappear to Crack Heaven for a week. Chase got out of the car and held the back door open. Baby got in without being told, looking like he'd pretty much been expecting to see Chase sometime that night after what went down.

Chase got in next to him and closed the door. "What you know about Post, Baby?"

A slight frown creased Baby's brow, and he looked at Chase warily. "Post only? Why you ain't askin' about Mooch too?"

Chase looked at him steadily. "I never mentioned Mooch. You did. Mooch ain't my business no more."

Baby looked momentarily confused, but then a look of comprehension settled in his face. "If you already got that nigga, I'm glad. Him, Post, and a nigga named Cicero beat my ass unmerciful once over ten dollars' worth of get-high. Fuckers said I stole that shit."

Chase smiled. "*Did* you steal it, Baby?"

Baby shrugged. "Well, yeah, but that ain't no damn reason to put a man in a coma for three days. Ten dollars ain't shit to them niggas, but they felt the need to beat a man like that."

Chase nodded his head in faux commiseration.

"I hope you got his ass good."

Chase didn't answer him; he just looked at him evenly. "So, you got somethin' to tell me?" he prodded.

"What time is it?"

Chase looked at his watch. "Two thirty. Why?"

Baby scratched his chin and laughed. "You must be one of the luckiest motherfuckers I ever met, Smoke. Post just happens to be one of the people I try to keep on my radar. I ain't willin' to get my head broke like that no mo', so yeah, I got somethin' to tell you."

"I'm listenin'."

"Friday nights, you can usually find that asshole drinkin' at Ricky's Bar on DeKalb. You know where I'm talkin' 'bout?"

Chase nodded. "Yeah, I know Ricky's."

"Okay. If he ain't there, then he's workin', cuttin' product and countin' money at a drug house on Patchen. If he ain't *there*, he's home 'sleep, most likely. That nigga don't get nowhere near the pussy he claim he do. My bet is, though, that asshole's still up at Ricky's, gettin' his drink on. I saw him go in there 'round midnight, and he drink like a damn fish."

Chase smiled at him. "That's a solid, Baby." He took a money clip out of his pocket and handed it to Baby Hustle.

When the crack head counted it with his eyes, he saw $500. Baby's eyes widened, and he tried not to snatch it greedily. "You know I wouldn't take this if I was a regular, cleaned-up man, but I ain't. I is who I is, just like everybody else. Thanks, Smoke."

"It's okay. And Baby, if somebody tries to fuck with you anymore, just holler and I'll come pay 'em a visit, okay?"

Baby nodded. "Okay, Smoke. You always take care of me."

"And I always will."

Baby looked sincerely touched. "I ain't gonna get high till daybreak, just in case you need me. You a damn decent man, Smoke."

Chase had to laugh at that one. "That's a matter of opinion, I think. Be careful, Baby."

"Right. You, too, Smoke." He leaned forward. "And you too, J.T."

J.T. nodded. "See ya, Baby."

Chase got out of the car and let him out.

"Don't forget…if you need me, Smoke, come get me."

Chase smiled at him. "I won't forget. Bye, Baby."

Baby nodded and walked away, pausing briefly to tuck his fresh batch of get-high money in his drawers.

Chase shook his head and hoped he wasn't wearing boxers. He got back into the passenger seat and looked over at J.T. "You heard him. Ricky's Bar on DeKalb."

J.T. looked at him for a long moment. "You, my friend, are truly a multifaceted man. You got a million sides to you, and I believe each one is genuine—the real deal. From kindness and generosity, love and concern, to all the dark shit you do, I think you sincerely mean everything you do."

Chase looked at him. "Yeah, J.T.? You're probably right, but I don't feel like hearin' that shit right now, so go fuck yourself…and I sincerely mean that too."

J.T. chuckled richly. "Your anger's misdirected. It ain't me you're mad at. It's Cyrus."

Chase felt like punching him just because he was right. "I'm mad at your ass, too, with all that Black Yoda shit. Shut the fuck up, J.T., and drive the car."

J.T. sighed heavily. "Forgive you I do, Grasshopper."

"Grasshopper wasn't *in* fuckin' *Star Wars*! Now please shut up so I can get my shit together. I got unfinished business to deal with."

J.T. laughed and pulled a chicken-fried ghetto accent. "I's sorry, homey. I was just tryina help you out, son. That's my word."

Chase smiled in spite of himself. J.T. knew him well, and he was just trying to keep him from falling down the rabbit hole. "Just drive the car, man."

"All right."

They got to Ricky's faster than Chase thought they would, and he sat silently for a moment, watching the people drift in and out. He didn't see anyone he knew personally. There were one or two he'd seen around, and the rest seemed unfamiliar, but that was just on the outside. "All right, J.T., park in the middle of the next block. I might be a minute."

"No problem, boss."

Chase got out of the car and pulled his cap down. He pushed the bar door open and stepped inside. He was instantly grateful for the dim lighting. He sat at the end of the bar and ordered a *Rémy,* straight up. He could see the entire room from that vantage point, and he spotted Post right away. His target was snuggled up in the corner with two hoes Chase wouldn't have touched if they were the last pieces of ass on Earth.

Chase sipped his drink slowly and watched Post go through two rounds of drinks. After a while, the inevitable happened: Post stood, swayed a bit, and headed for the bathroom on his wobbly drunk-ass legs. Chase smiled a little as he realized as piss drunk as Post was, he was about to be stone-cold sober. Chase got up and followed him into the restroom.

Post pushed the door open without ever turning around, and Chase stepped in right behind him, his eyes giving the room the onceover to make sure they were alone. Even though there was no one else in there at the moment, Chase knew he had to move fast; in a place like that, people had to take a piss far too often. Post staggered to a urinal and pulled out his equipment just as Chase reached into his pocket and pulled out his razor. Strangely—and much to his relief—Chase didn't feel any of the thrill he'd felt earlier when he made a butcher block out of Mooch. He just wanted the whole thing to be over, and he silently cursed Cyrus again for getting him mixed up in it in the first place.

He stepped up to Post, stood just behind him, and opened his razor. He never opened his mouth; his razor did all the talking. Chase slid it across Post's throat in one brisk motion. Post's hands flew up as he desperately tried to keep his blood where it belonged, but he failed. Blood jetted and sprayed across the bathroom in bright red splashes, and Chase watched Post collapse to the floor and start dying in earnest. Post was looking at him, clutching his ruined throat, and Chase just stared back at him coldly. "I hope it was worth it," he said plainly and walked out of the bathroom and straight out of the bar.

He didn't run. Instead, he walked to his idling car like he was out for a stroll. He casually removed his jacket and folded it with the inside facing out since he was sure there was some back-spray on the sleeve.

J.T. saw him coming and got out of the car. He had the first pair of gloves that they'd put in the Ziploc in his hand. He opened the trunk and took out a small garbage bag. Chase pulled off the gloves he was wearing and put them in the garbage bag, along with the jacket. J.T. added the first set of gloves and tied the top of the bag into a knot. He reached back into the trunk and took out a roll of duct tape, wearing latex gloves himself. He gave Chase the keys and got into the passenger seat. Chase got in on the driver's side, started the car, and pulled out.

"Everything okay?" J.T. asked, wrapping the garbage bag with the duct tape.

"All smooth, J.T., but I don't really feel like talkin' about it. Sorry."

J.T. nodded and continued wrapping the bag. "It's okay. I understand."

Chase drove down DeKalb to Broadway, then took the Williamsburg Bridge into Manhattan. He turned onto FDR Drive and took it to Avenue C, where J.T. got out and dropped the wrapped package in a garbage can in Stuyvesant Square Park. When J.T. got back in, Chase took the car up Broadway to 91st Street and Central Park West. He stopped a block from J.T.'s posh condo and killed the engine.

"You okay?" J.T. asked.

Chase barely heard him as he threw the door open. He only made it as far as the back tire before he started puking his guts out, barely missing his sneakers. He vaguely heard J.T. get out of the car. He couldn't believe he was tossing his cookies in the street like a little kid, and he couldn't seem to stop. He threw up until there was nothing left but bile, and he coughed and brought that up too. When he was done, he folded his arms on the roof of the car and put his head down. His whole midsection hurt, and he still felt like he might start dry heaving.

"You okay *now*, man?" J.T. asked across the roof.

Chase picked his head up and ran his hand over his face. "I guess. I don't know where the hell that came from."

"Sure you do," J.T. said and rolled a bottle of water to him. "Here…rinse and spit."

Chase did as he was told and when he finished, he felt better.

"Did you get any on you?" J.T. asked.

Chase laughed wryly, without much humor. "Nah. I'm a master at avoiding the splash-back. I make it my business not to get any on me."

J.T. looked at him like he didn't find any of it funny. "You gonna be okay gettin' home?"

"I'm okay. I guess I just needed to sick that shit up."

"I know the shit you *really* need to sick up. His name is Cyrus,"

J.T. said quietly. "Man, you need to change your life while you still can. The brass ring is within your reach, but you'll never be able to grab it long as you keep fuckin' around with Cyrus. You know that as well as I do."

"Yeah, you're right, J.T."

J.T. smiled at him sadly. "I know I am, but me being right won't make you listen to me, will it? Even *now*, you're loyal to Cyrus—even when it doesn't take a rocket scientist to see that he couldn't give a serious fuck less about you and Corey. But I understand. You keep hoping he will. You always have. But I got news for you, Chase... Cyrus will never change. I don't believe it's in him to clean up his act. I'd say he'll die that way, but he's already dead—at least his soul is."

Chase nodded slowly. "I think you may be on to something, J.T."

They got back in the car and drove the block to J.T.'s place. J.T. started to get out but then changed his mind. He turned to look at Chase. "You know, Chase, you and me been ride or die since the third grade. To this day, I'll drop everything to drive your getaway car...but we're not kids anymore. Sooner or later, you stop having kid luck." He paused and touched his shoulder. "I might die for you, but I ain't dyin' for Cyrus. This shit has got to end somewhere, and it may as well end here. You laid these niggas out for shootin' Cyrus, so I think you should let him handle Wolf on his own. Let him and Khalid clean up their own damn messes from now on."

"I hear what you're sayin', J.T., but you know the only reason I do what he says is because of Corey. What about my little brother? I can't just let Cyrus push him into this shit, forcing him to pick up my slack. He'll get himself killed or locked up for good, and you know that."

"Corey's not a little boy anymore, Chase, even though you still treat him like one. You can't protect him from everything. He could get killed walking across the street. You know what I think you should do?"

"What?"

"I think you should flat-out refuse to help Cyrus with Wolf. You've done enough for him. I think you should send Corey away. Maybe you could open another club in Atlanta or somewhere far away from here and send him and Dee down to oversee it. Meanwhile, you got me and Bliss up here to help you with the clubs you already have. When the club in ATL is up and running successfully, you open another one. Keep Corey's ass down there until Wolf takes care of Cyrus or he gets his stupid ass killed by somebody that ain't scared of him...or of you."

Chase rubbed absently at the scar that ran along the back of his fingers and stared out the windshield. It made sense—all kinds of sense. "For what it's worth, I *am* listening to you, J.T."

J.T. nodded. "That's all I ask. Just try it on and see how it fits."

"I will."

J.T. looked at his watch. "It's late, man, and we both had a long day. Why don't you go find that fine-ass woman of yours and let her rub your back and put you to sleep."

"That's the plan."

"Good."

"I'll call you tomorrow. Thanks, J.T."

J.T. looked at him seriously. "You my boy, Chase—ride or die," he said before he got out of the car and disappeared into his building.

Chase drove home with a million things racing through his mind. As he parked the Charger, he thought about Bliss's reaction to it. She was right: It *was* a hearse, of sorts—a fucking death car. He went upstairs and took a hot shower, then redressed quickly. He'd stuffed the clothes he'd been wearing into another garbage bag and hustled his ass downstairs with it.

A private company picked the garbage, and he heard the truck rumbling. He put the garage door up and ran out with the bag. The truck was stopped at a store down the block. Chase left the bag at the curb, then went back into the garage. He peeled out to the street in his Porsche and hit Riverside Drive. Ten minutes later, he was in front of Bliss's building, hitting her on her cell phone.

She picked up on the second ring. "Are you done?" she asked.

"Yeah, I'm here. Can I come up?"

"Of course you can. I've been wonderin' when you'd get here."

When he got off the elevator, Bliss was at the door waiting for him. He had to stop himself from running to her, and he kept his cool, forcing himself to walk a little slower. Bliss was wearing a short pink cotton nightgown with a little ruffle at the bottom. He doubted she knew the light behind her was shining through it the way it was, showing her body in a stark and lovely silhouette. Chase swallowed hard. Her hair was slightly tousled, as if she'd been lying down, but she didn't look sleepy. She simply looked…beautiful.

Bliss held the door open further and let him in. He put his hands on her waist and started kissing her. He couldn't help it and didn't want to. He loved the feel of her lips on his and the taste of her sweet mouth. He loved the tingle that went up his spine when she danced her sexy little tongue over his. Bliss made his knees weak.

She broke the kiss and put her arms around him for a tight hug. "I was worried about you, Chase."

He hugged her back and kissed the corner of her mouth. "I told you I'd be okay, baby."

She touched his face. "I didn't sleep. I waited up for you."

"I'm glad. I needed to see you."

She smiled at him. "I could never turn you away."

He felt a sudden stab at his heart, and he didn't smile back. "Never say never," he said, fearing that maybe—if she knew enough—she could and would shut him out of her life. He didn't expect her to tolerate the things he did for Cyrus. As a matter of fact, he felt that if she ever found out about that shit, she'd kick his ass to the curb in less than ten seconds, rightfully so. J.T. had been right, for the most part, but he hadn't thought it all the way through. Chase needed to relocate too—to start over somewhere far away from Cyrus. He'd just slashed his last throat for Cyrus, and he was ready to disengage.

Bliss was running her hands over his biceps and looking into his eyes. "What's that supposed to mean?"

Chase looked away and shook his head. "Nothin', baby. The last couple hours were hard, that's all."

"How's Cyrus?"

"I don't want to talk about tonight right now. I just want to be with you."

She smiled sweetly and took his hand. "Okay. Come on then." She led him down the hall and around the corner to her room.

Chase wasn't surprised a bit when he saw it. It was very girly, from the lacy fans on the walls, to the flowers in bud vases, to the upholstered headboard. Chase's mind wasn't on her décor, though, and he didn't want his back rubbed either. He grasped the hem of her short nightgown and started pulling it up.

Bliss didn't argue. She only raised her arms and let him whisk it off of her.

Chase took his shirt off and went for her lips again, taking great pleasure in the silky feel of her soft, bare skin against his. His fingers drifted up her body until they found her breasts. He ran his thumbs over her nipples in slow circles until they felt like pearls and gave no resistance.

Bliss's breath was getting short. She moaned and arched her back, reaching for the buckle of his belt. She managed to unbuckle it as Chase traded his thumb for his mouth. Bliss unbuttoned his jeans and pulled the zipper down. She started pushing his clothes off, in a rush to get at him.

Chase kicked his sneakers off and stepped out of his pants. He turned with her so that her back was against the wall. Her hand was on him, holding him tight and gliding up and down with a maddeningly sweet friction. Her thumb swirled over the top, and he sucked in air through his teeth.

Chase put his hands just under her ass and stepped between her thighs. He swung her up from the floor in one easy, smooth move. Bliss's arms went around his neck, and the two of them stared at each other as he lowered her down, sliding in slow, then pumping at her briskly at that crazy angle. She shuddered and made a sound that wasn't quite a scream.

Chase grinned and stepped away from the wall with her. His hands slid up until her ass was in his palms. "Hold on, Bliss." He bounced her right into an orgasm that was so strong, she went through it like she was fighting him, but Chase held on to her. He walked the few steps to the bed with her and sat down. He lay on his back with Bliss on her knees, riding him like he was her very own personal pony. She ran her hands over his body luxuriously, then ran them over her own. Chase found that incredibly sexy and put his hands on her hips, going in a little deeper.

Bliss made that little screamy sound again and put her hands on his abs and started grinding into him hard. She was squeezing herself around him, tightening down on him until he couldn't take it anymore. He flipped her over and drove himself into her, losing control, cummin' (AUTUMN CHANGED THIS SPELLING – SHOULDN'T IT BE CUMMIN') so hard it startled him. He felt her nails trail down his back and her hips rise to meet his.

The pleasure was exquisite, and he simply couldn't stop. He wanted to squeeze every last bit of himself into her. Chase put his hands under her shoulder blades and pulled himself in until his heart was slamming in his chest and he was weak. He kissed her, and she wrapped her arms around him. Chase held her close, and to his surprise, found himself falling rapidly toward sleep. "I love you, Bliss...very, very much."

"I love you, too, Chase."

The lovers slept in each other's arms, happy and satisfied.

G STREET CHRONICLES
~A NEW URBAN DYNASTY~

WWW.GSTREETCHRONICLES.COM

Chapter 12

Cyrus was currently convalescing at the condo of his some-
times-lover, Valerie Durant, in Brooklyn Heights. Valerie
was a CPA in a large and storied midtown firm, five names long. She
currently had her round, shapely ass turned up at him in the downward dog position, going through her yoga moves like he wasn't
even there.

She was real nice to look at, medium height, with milk chocolate
skin without a blemish on it. Her hair was shoulder length, black, and
glossy, but she swept it up in a ponytail to do her workout. Her eyes
were large and so dark that they almost looked black. She was small
on top with a tiny waist, but her bottom half more than made up for
any shortcomings.

Cyrus was admiring it with great interest as she stretched. Cyrus
smiled to himself, remembering when she used to be Chase's woman,
when Chase was only nineteen or twenty. To Cyrus, they seemed a
bit too young to be that involved with each other. He didn't need
Chase getting caught up with his nose open like that, so he made sure
their romance was squashed before he did a bid for his gun charge.
He preyed on Valerie's naiveté and inexperience at the time, knowing
she'd fall for every young girl's dream of being with an older man
and living 'hood fabulous by dating a drug dealer.

He went about crushing their relationship by working it out so

Chase would catch the two of them together. Sure, it had broken Chase's little young-boy heart, but Cyrus slept well at night, secure in the fact that he was doing it for Chase's own good—keeping Chase's chest from puffing out too hard. Chase was an emotional guy, and Cyrus knew he was much more malleable when he was bruised up and crying with his feelings hurt. When he was like that, even though it wasn't simple, it was easier to manipulate him into doing shit. It was when he got cold and standoffish that he was damned near immovable. Chase had always been a problem—*always*. *Oh, well. Enough about Chase*, he scolded himself. That boy had been taking up entirely too much space in his mind lately, and Cyrus smelled a rebellion on the horizon.

He looked at Valerie's ass again. "How much longer you plan on stayin' in that position?"

"Until I'm done. If it's heating you up, you're welcome to jerk off in the shower, 'cause you ain't getting' none of this," she said coldly as she stood straight up and looked him in the eye.

The goodwill fell out of Cyrus's face. "A bitch could get a smack for that."

She raised an elegant eyebrow and patted the sweat off her chest with a towel. "You lay a damn finger on me, and I got the cops on speed-dial…after I finish stabbing your trifling ass, Cyrus. You need to be easy up in here. I don't have to let you stay here, you know."

He laughed. "Then why do you?"

She smiled at him frostily. "Why do you think?"

He laughed with genuine humor. "For Chase?"

"You know it. He's always out saving your ass, even if you are too stupid to realize his influence is what's keeping you and that monkey Khalid's heads above water. He called and asked me to let you stay here, and then he told Corey to put a bug in your ear so your simple-minded ass would have you asking me, thinking you made the decision your-damn-self. You *are not* the genius you think you are, Cyrus, and Chase tries hard not to be the monster you've made him into. *You're* the fucking monster, Cyrus. How could you do that to your own brother?"

Cyrus laughed. "You're the one who left the angel with the busted wings and twisted halo for the devil with the pitchfork. We all got our flaws, Princess. Yours is that you're a whore who broke a guy's heart by fucking his brother. You—"

He was cut off by the wad of warm spit that hit him in his right eye. Rage took over before he had time to realize what he was doing. His hand curled into a fist, and he hit her square in the jaw as hard as he could.

Valerie went down like her legs were made of rubber, knocked out cold.

"Stupid bitch!" Cyrus yelled and spat on *her*. He pulled out his cell phone and called Corey. "Corey, I ain't got my car. Drop whatever useless shit you're doin' and come get me out of this stupid, disrespectful, cunt's house *right now!* Fuck that! *Now, Corey!* I'll be downstairs." He threw his things into the leather valise he'd brought with him and vacated the premises, but not before he turned around and kicked Valerie right in her round, lovely ass with all the force he could muster. Then he slammed out of the apartment. He guessed he'd be hearing from Chase about the whole ordeal, but he didn't give a shit. *Fuck his punk ass.*

When he got to the lobby, Khalid was walking through the doors. He looked first at Cyrus, then at his bag. "What's up, man? Goin' somewhere?"

"Can't stay here. I just knocked Valerie's ass out."

Khalid frowned. "Was she gettin' at you 'bout Chase?"

"I could have lived with that, but that bitch spat on me like she was crazy, and I dropped her ass. She's up there laid out on the living room floor."

"Damn, Cyrus."

"I can't take shorts from no ho, Khalid. You know me." He eyed Khalid warily, "What brings you here so early anyway?"

Khalid looked around. "I can't talk about it in the open like this. Come on…let's take a ride."

"I got Corey comin' to get me."

Khalid shrugged. "So? Let him go up and find that ho sprawled out and cry to Chase. That's what he's gonna do anyway. You can hit him later and let him know you're with me."

They didn't speak again until they were in Khalid's car and on the road.

"So...what's up?" Cyrus asked, settling into his seat.

"What's up? We started a war, I think. Smoke left his callin' card, and Wolf ain't havin' it. He wants to have the last word, so to speak."

Cyrus wasn't sure he wanted to hear whatever else Khalid had to say. "Meaning what?"

"*Meaning*, Smoke might not have done us a favor by takin' out Mooch and Post. From what I understand, he just sliced through Post's throat, but Mooch's ass was barely recognizable. They say he was cut up pretty bad. You know Mooch was Wolf's first cousin, right?"

"Yeah, so?"

"So he ain't takin' that shit light. Don't you watch the news, Cyrus? 'Bout one o'clock this mornin', Wolf got rid of Breeze and Willie—shot 'em in the back of the head while they was sittin' in Willie's car, like somethin' right outta *Gangland,* execution style. I'm tellin' you, it's a fuckin' war, Cyrus. I think Smoke threw gasoline on the shit we started. What's up with him anyway? What's takin' him so long? We need him to take the damn head off the snake. If he takes Wolf out, all the rest a them niggas will fall by the wayside or find their own hustle. You need to light a fire under your boy, Cyrus...and you need to do that shit *today!*"

Cyrus sank down in his seat and stared out the window. He had a problem on his hands, and he knew it. Chase was not being cooperative at all, and his behavior was erratic at best. He was totally wishy-washy and making threats to take his leave. He'd done what he said and got some retribution for Cyrus being shot. He'd even given his word about hitting Wolf, but since he'd taken out Mooch and Post, he'd been dragging his feet about Wolf. No...worse: He'd dug his heels in and wasn't moving at all. Chase was barely speaking to him, and when he did, he was hugely disrespectful and angry.

Ungrateful little bastard.

If it wasn't for Cyrus, Chase and Corey would have been left to fend for themselves after their mother died. Cyrus had taken care of their snot-nosed asses, and the only thing he'd asked in return was compliance, but he was only getting that from Corey, and not all the time from Chase's moody ass. It all depended on what side of the bed he'd woken up on. It seemed if he wanted Chase to do anything for him now, he had to twist his arm up behind his back and scrub his face into the ground. It wasn't winning Chase any points with Cyrus, because Cyrus had harbored anger for Chase since the day the doctor had smacked his ass when he cried into the world.

Cyrus was fifteen years older than Chase. His mother didn't even bother to tell him she was pregnant, even when he saw her belly getting bigger and bigger, growing like there was a fucking tumor in it—and as far as he was concerned, that was just what the fuck Chase was. It wasn't just the circumstances of his brother's birth, but also the fact that when his mother squeezed that baby out into the world, all of Cyrus's sugar dried up. Everything was suddenly split in half, and he had to share everything with him. All her extra money went toward that damn baby. Cyrus wasn't a punk, and he sucked it up, but he was deeply resentful of that little bastard for a whole lot of reasons, and he let him know it.

He did little shit to him while he was growing up, like throwing his toys in the garbage, punching him, bending his fingers back until he screamed, and berating him in front of his friends, calling him a pussy and worse. When Chase really got on his nerves—or sometimes when he didn't—he'd jump on him and beat his ass bloody.

When Corey was born, Cyrus had resented him, too, but not as much as he did Chase and not for the same reasons. Chase had always stood between Cyrus and Corey. He wouldn't let Cyrus run over Corey the way he let him run over him. Chase had gotten a lot of bloody noses on Corey's behalf. Cyrus was a bully and he knew it, but Chase never let him have Corey as a punching bag—at least not without a fight.

He remembered nights when he threatened Corey with serious

bodily harm; Chase would go to sleep with his arms locked around his little brother and their sharpest butcher knife under his pillow. Something sharp had always been Chase's way to go, and he'd even sliced Cyrus once, leaving him with a permanent scar. He'd sliced Cyrus for fucking with Corey.

Cyrus was nineteen when he started dealing. He got tired of always having to go without and having to share shit with those two assholes. He wanted to have his own shit, some nice shit. He started selling rocks for an O.G. named Big Ted. Ted had a partner named Maceo, and they owned shit in Bushwick. There *were* no other dealers back then, so they had it on lock.

Cyrus was happy to sell his rock and drive his nice car, but his mother wasn't stupid, and she knew what he was into. She promptly ordered his dealin' ass out of the house and told him, "Don't you come back up in here till you stop that stupid shit."

Of course, typical for Cyrus, he blew up at her and cussed her out. "You got a lotta nerve judging me after the life you been livin'," he said. "You got three kids with three different daddies, and you can't even take care of your babies. You a ho, and you ain't shit." And then he walked out of his mother's house…for good. The only time he ever came around after that was to put a few dollars in her mailbox once in a blue moon, just so he wouldn't be labeled a complete bastard, and sometimes he'd snatch his brothers up by their collars and slap the backs of their necks if they were around.

When Cyrus was in his twenties, he and some of the other dealers who worked for Ted and Maceo—Khalid, Rome, and Herc—decided it was time for a coup. They knew there was no way Big Ted and Maceo would let them build an empire right alongside theirs, so the plan was to overthrow the government, to commit a mutiny and start a new regime. Cyrus and Khalid put their heads together and planned the battle, and Herc and Rome were their enforcers.

Herc and Rome rolled up on Big Ted when he was a little higher than he should have been, leaving a house party on Hart Street. Rome blasted Elmore, Ted's bodyguard, in the chest with a sawed-off, and Herc put his infamous .45 behind Ted's left ear and pulled the trigger.

Needless to say, it was a closed casket for Ted.

Maceo's revenge was swift and brutal. He wasn't as smart as Ted, and he didn't know who to trust. He had a whole slew of people gunned down at random, grasping at straws and hoping he got Big Ted's killer through the process of elimination. For two weeks, Bushwick was a very bloody place to be. Then somebody put a bug in his ear about them, and Cyrus had yet to find out who that rat was.

They told him Cyrus and Khalid were responsible for Big Ted, and Cyrus and Khalid had to go into hiding once they realized Maceo was gunning hard for them. Herc and Rome, along with a small crew of dedicated soldiers, held Maceo and his vengeful wrath at bay as long as they could. Eventually, though, Maceo got frustrated and started playing dirty: He figured if he couldn't find Khalid and Cyrus, he would start killing the people they loved.

Maceo had Khalid's sister, who was eight months pregnant, gunned down when she was coming out of the supermarket. That was bad—really bad—and Cyrus grieved with him. But then his world changed.

Cyrus's mother and brothers were walking home. She'd just picked them up and had barely left the schoolyard when Maceo himself rolled up on her and shot her in the head. She collapsed to the pavement, and the two boys went hysterical. She took her last breath with her head in Chase's lap; he was screaming, begging her not to go.

Cyrus never wanted the responsibility of looking after his little brothers, but Khalid—whom Chase now despised—worked hard to convince Cyrus not to let the boys become wards of the state. Chase was traumatized, shut down, and sullen when they came to live with Cyrus. He was so sullen that Cyrus's live-in love Sonia just gave up and moved out. Corey was a little different. He was traumatized, too, but he was looking for acceptance and love, something like a mistreated puppy. Cyrus could see it in his eyes. The boy didn't want to be all alone, and at least for a time, it felt like Chase had deserted him. He was vulnerable because his fierce protector was gone.

After their mother's murder, Chase retreated into his own head. He didn't talk to anybody for two months. Cyrus didn't understand him and couldn't reach him, and he finally got fed up with it. He even hit him to try to make him talk, but that only seemed to push Chase further away. He hit him so hard one day that his tooth went through his lip. Cyrus noticed later that night, after the boys had gone to bed, that the cleaver was missing from the knife rack. The next morning, he found it under Chase's pillow.

Cyrus left his crazy ass alone for a long time after that. Then one day, Chase got up and returned to his life, but there was a look in his eye that he didn't lose for quite a while, as if it took a minute for his eyes to get some life back in them.

Chase resumed his life, and he also resumed his role as Corey's protector—to the point that he was knocking niggas out in the schoolyard every week—not fighting, but *knocking niggas out!* By the time he turned fourteen, though he was only average height and size, all the kids in the neighborhood were afraid of him.

Cyrus felt a sudden pride for him, and he found that surprising. All that time, Chase only had one true friend, a kid named Jayson Taylor; Chase called him J.T. Cyrus thought maybe he was the only person Chase talked to during the two months when he wouldn't open his mouth to anybody.

Chase cut Cyrus when he was fifteen, and he caught him totally off guard because it was the last thing he would have expected. Chase would beat a nigga's ass, but Corey would take somebody's shit. Corey was quite an accomplished little pickpocket. Even now, Corey had the lightest fingers Cyrus had ever seen in his life. Back then, if Corey didn't take something he wanted, it was only because you didn't bring it with you.

A man named Tyson ran numbers for some dude uptown. One evening, one of Corey's little friends dared him to lift Tyson's wallet. Of course Corey took the dare, and he did it quite professionally, but one of Corey's so-called friends let Tyson know it was Corey who'd done the lifting. Tyson was a gentleman about the whole thing since Corey was just a kid. He simply came to Cyrus, told him what happened, and asked for his wallet back.

When Cyrus got home, he'd jumped all over Corey. He twisted his arm up behind his back until he heard it snap, and then he stepped back in shock that he'd broken Corey's arm. He honestly didn't mean to do it.

Chase picked that moment to walk in the door. His eyes took in the fact that Corey was screaming on the floor and Cyrus was standing over him. Chase never opened his mouth. He just reached into his pocket and flicked out a silver-handled straight razor. He lunged over the coffee table at Cyrus and knocked him down. He swiped the razor through Cyrus's shirt and cut him right above the heart. "This is how easy it would be. Touch him again and I'll kill you, Cyrus."

At that point, Cyrus abruptly stopped putting his hands on both of them.

The following year, when Chase was sixteen, Cyrus found out just how deadly his younger brother could be. It was one of those times when all three of them were together at once. They both had been cutting up pretty badly at the time, and they were out of control. Chase couldn't seem to stop fighting, and Corey couldn't seem to keep his hands out of other people's pockets. Cyrus figured if he took them out and tried to spend a little time with them, maybe they'd calm down. If they didn't, he was gonna throw them little ungrateful niggas out of his house.

He took them to see some action flick he could no longer remember the name of. They were walking across the parking lot to Cyrus's car. It was late, because he'd taken them to the last showing, and there weren't many people out since it was a weeknight. That didn't much matter, though, because those little niggas only went to school when they felt like it, and Cyrus wasn't much of an overseer.

Halfway to the car, Corey tapped Chase on the arm. "Look, Chase…it's *him*! It's fuckin' Maceo!" he whispered fiercely.

"Where?" Chase whispered back. Corey pointed, and Chase stepped away from them, walking fast and soundlessly across the parking lot in his black Uptowns. "Excuse me, sir?" Chase said when he reached him.

The man turned around, and sure enough, it *was* Maceo. "What do you want, kid?" he asked, gruffly but not impolitely.

Cyrus could see Chase's teeth glint in the darkness, and he saw his razor appear in his right hand like magic. Cyrus's own hands went over his mouth like a bitch when he saw Chase flick the blade out. Everything went down in about twenty seconds.

Chase moved with a terrifying grace, moving behind Maceo and placing his left foot between his legs. He put his hand on Maceo's forehead and pulled his head back. The look in his eyes was dreadful as he brought his blade up. "You owe me a life for killin' my mother, you sack of shit, so I'll take yours." Chase let his razor come down, and it went into Maceo's sideburn. Chase dragged the razor across his throat, severing his carotid artery. Chase grunted with the force of dragging the razor through flesh, but it was lightning quick. Blood was literally *jumping* out of Maceo's neck. It was still so hot in the chilly night air that it looked like smoke was coming off of it. *That* was the reason Cyrus called Chase Smoke—not because he'd most definitely smoke a nigga, though that was true too.

Chase pushed Maceo away from him, and he hit the pavement hard, face first—so hard that Cyrus saw several teeth pop out of his dying mouth. Chase walked away from him and back to his brothers.

Cyrus became aware that Corey was almost chanting, "Oh shit! Oh shit! Oh shit!" His eyes were huge and staring and he was in shock.

When Chase got to them, he didn't have a drop of blood on him. "Stop now, Corey. Everything's gonna be just fine." He paused and looked down. "You pissed yourself, Corey. Come on." He put his arm around his brother and walked him to the car.

Cyrus followed, walking slow, because his asshole was pretty tight. For once in his life, he was horrified...and very afraid.

Cyrus thought about all that shit now, riding shotgun in Khalid's car, with Khalid demanding he *force* Chase to get rid of Wolf. The fact of the matter was that he wasn't exactly sure he *could* force Chase to do *anything*. Chase had been volatile and unpredictable all his life, and Cyrus blamed himself for that, at least to some degree. But then again, maybe a lot of it was just the way Chase was. Chase lived by his own rules. He decided for himself what was right and wrong. Cyrus also knew there would come a day when he couldn't use Corey as a pawn; maybe that day had come. He had to find more than one way to get to Chase. He had to, because time was tight, and sooner or later, Wolf would put a hit out on him and Khalid. They had to strike first. "I'll talk to him," he said to Khalid.

Khalid glanced at him. "Well, hurry the fuck up. If we have to deal with Wolf ourselves, things are gonna get a lot worse before they get better."

Cyrus nodded in agreement. After all, they were just drug dealers. Chase was the killer.

G STREET CHRONICLES

A NEW URBAN DYNASTY

WWW.GSTREETCHRONICLES.COM

Chapter 13

Bliss's curiosity was getting the better of her. She followed Chase into the Waverly Inn, wondering what it was all about. He'd called a meeting with Corey, J.T., and Dee, telling them all he had something important to talk about. When Bliss and Chase arrived at the round table, everyone was already there, enjoying a bottle of wine.

Chase let go of her hand and held her chair out for her. "Damn! Y'all couldn't wait for us? Bunch of drunks," he chided as he smiled and sat down.

J.T. leaned over and poured wine for him and Bliss, and then he shook the bottle to let him know it was empty. "There were only five drinks in this damn bottle. That ain't enough to get me drunk…" He glanced sideways at Corey and Dee. "Or these lushes either."

Dee waved her hand at him. "Be quiet, J.T. Chase knows how we do." She smiled at Bliss. "It's nice to see you again, honey. How are things down at the club? They workin' out okay?"

Bliss nodded. "It's going okay. Everything's on schedule for the opening next Saturday."

Dee picked up her wine and sat back in her seat. "Damn, that's quick, honey." She sipped her wine and turned her eyes to Chase. "Don't you think so? You didn't just throw the shit together, did you?"

Chase gave her a biting little look. "No, I didn't just *throw the shit together*, Dee," he said sarcastically.

"Don't get your drawers in a twist with me. It was just a question."

"Everything's cool, Dee. It's been inspected, it's up to code, and we got the liquor license straightened out. It's all good," J.T. interrupted to avoid an argument.

"Yeah, Dee. Why would Chase want to put a rush on Cyrus's club? They got enough shit goin' on between them already," Corey said, looking at Dee like she was trying to start trouble.

Dee smiled at him and patted his cheek. "Poor Corey. You're so sweet. I know you want Chase and Cyrus to get along, but you know as well as anybody at this table that it will probably never happen. A snowball's got a better chance in Hell. You also know as well as I do that Chase *would* do a rush job just to fuck Cyrus without really fucking him." She paused and looked at Chase. "Don't look at me like that. You know I ain't lying. Now, anybody else want a *real* drink? To Hell with this goddamned snooty-ass wine." She signaled for the waiter.

Bliss looked at Chase, who was looking at Dee like he was holding back a frown. Dee was looking back at him with subtle defiance. A glance at J.T. and Corey told Bliss they were watching the whole thing like a tennis match. She frowned herself. *Maybe it's time I really get to the bottom of this situation with Cyrus and Chase.*

The waiter arrived and took their drink orders. Chase had his Rémy, Dee had a double Grey Goose, and J.T. and Corey selected Hennessey. *Fuck it,* Bliss thought. *Since they're all drinking like men— Dee included—I'll have a shot of Patrón. Maybe the conversation is gonna call for it anyway.*

Chase was sitting with his arms folded across his chest, not quite staring daggers at Dee. He leaned forward suddenly. "Can I get a minute, Dee?" He stood up, and Dee looked surprised—amused, but surprised.

"Uh-oh. I think I pissed off the boss, y'all. He wants to see me outside."

Bliss looked up at him, and Dee was right: Chase was tight, staring a hole through her. "Right now, Delia. I'm not playin' with you."

Some of the amusement left her face when she realized how serious he was. Her mouth formed into a perfect circle, which she hid with her hand, in a flustered little feminine gesture. Then she did the absurd and started to search around under the table with her feet.

Chase looked at her like she was crazy. "Two minutes, Delia." He ran his hand over Bliss's shoulder and walked out of the restaurant. Bliss saw him reappear by the entrance and look at his watch.

"Shit, J.T. Kick my shoe over here. He's not fucking around," Dee said, slipping her feet into her Prada pumps and looking at Bliss apologetically. "Guess this wasn't a good day to run my mouth, honey. Be right back." She stood up, straightened her dress, and wiggled out of the room, turning several appreciative heads.

Bliss crossed her legs and shrugged out of the jacket that matched her dress. Corey and J.T. tried not to let approval register in their faces, but they failed. Bliss smiled at them and picked up her Patrón. She tossed it back and grimaced a little but then gestured to the waiter for another one. "You may want to keep them coming," she said to his retreating back, and then she looked at Corey. "All right, Corey, so what's the deal with Chase and Cyrus? Please fill me in."

Corey lifted his glass and drank half his Hennessey. He shrugged and smiled sadly. "Some people just can't get along, Bliss. Cyrus and Chase never have."

Bliss looked at J.T. for a better answer.

"Talk to Chase, sweetheart, not to us. Trust me," J.T. said and sipped his drink.

Bliss looked out the window. Chase had his back to her and had placed his body so the only thing she could see of Dee were her gesturing hands. Bliss looked at them and spoke in a low voice. "What's the big deal? I know what he's doing. He's out there telling Dee that she better keep her mouth shut about him and Cyrus, right? I'm not stupid. I know what Cyrus does. Chase told me that himself. He also told me he does stuff for Cyrus. So what's up? Is Chase a drug dealer too? He better not be."

Corey knocked off the rest of his drink. "Naw, Chase ain't into that, Bliss."

She looked from him to J.T. "Then what the hell *does* he do for him?"

J.T. shrugged. "You know…stuff, like helpin' him open his club and shit like that."

Bliss sucked her teeth. "He didn't need that horrible-ass Charger to help him open the club."

J.T. raised his hands. "I have no idea what you're talking about, pretty lady." He dropped his hands and picked up his glass. "Perhaps you should holler at Chase about that."

Bliss watched Dee and Chase walk back into the restaurant. A moment later, they were seated at the table.

Chase put his hand on Bliss's knee and smiled. "Sorry about that. These knuckleheads treat you okay?"

Bliss sat back in her seat and stared at him. "Chase, I want to know what's going on with you and Cyrus."

To his credit, he didn't even look at anybody else; his eyes stayed on hers. "There won't be *anything* going on between me and Cyrus in a minute." He took her hand in his and kissed her fingers. "That's why I wanted to sit down and talk some stuff over with the people at this table. Everybody that matters to me is at this table right now, Bliss, and we got a couple decisions to make regarding Cyrus."

Bliss sighed in frustration. "No, Chase. There's something you're not telling me, and I am not going to be involved in any decisions about anything until you bring me out of the dark. I want to know what the major issue is between you and your brother." She pushed away from the table and grabbed her jacket. "I mean it, Chase…or I leave here walking."

Chase listened attentively to her small tirade, still holding her hand and looking in her eyes. He exhaled in resignation, but he didn't lose his patience. "Okay, Bliss. Whatever you want." He turned his head and addressed everyone else. "Bliss wants to know, so I'm gonna tell her. Y'all know I can't do that here, so let's go."

Corey's mouth was open, J.T. was frowning, and Dee was toying with her glass.

"Um…Chase, you sure you want to do that, man?" J.T. asked.

"I know what I'm doin', J.T."

They stared at each other, and then J.T. stood up. "I have no doubt you *think* you do. I put my money on you every time. Let's go," he said. He took his wallet out and left money on the table for the drinks.

They left the restaurant and stood in a little group outside.

"How you gonna make us leave before we eat, Chase? I been drinkin'. I'm hungry," Corey complained.

"Just follow me back to my place. Matter of fact, you ride with J.T. and Dee, since you been drinkin'. I'll make sure you get fed." He turned to Dee. "Do you mind?"

Dee smiled and took out her cell phone. "I got the food. See you there."

Chase held the door for Bliss to get into his Porsche.

"I could have done that, Chase."

He smiled at her and hit the road. "You don't have to compete with Dee, Bliss. She's one of my dearest friends, but I'm gonna marry you one day very soon, if you'll let me."

She couldn't help but smile, even though she was slightly pissed at him. "Is that so?"

He nodded and made a left, smiling his boyish smile. "Yeah. Just tell me when. Tomorrow's good for me. I love you, Bliss."

She giggled into her hand. If he hadn't been driving, she would have crawled into his lap right then and there and covered his face in kisses. Chase made her heart beat fast. "I love you, too, Chase. I'm not gonna marry you though...not right now anyway."

His smile slipped a little. "Why not?"

She put her hand on his thigh, and he sighed. "You know why, baby. Don't even try to act like you don't. There are things you're leaving unsaid. I don't think you're being honest with me." She said the words, and they were true, but all the same, she let her hand creep a little higher on his thigh, and Chase didn't try to move it. She felt his muscles flex as he stepped on the brake to stop at a light, and just like that, she wanted him so bad it became a deep, sudden ache.

He glanced at her. "I'm always honest with you, Bliss. I've never lied to you, and I never plan to. That's not the way I want it to be between us—ever."

Bliss searched his face. She didn't believe he was lying. She *knew* he wasn't, but she asked anyway. "So you'll never just lie to me then, huh?" She let her fingernails trail lightly over the inside of his thigh, and she knew he felt it through the thin fabric of his trousers. His lips parted and he frowned a little, and Bliss smiled. "Would you?"

"No, no, Bliss. I wouldn't *just* lie to you. If I lied to you, I'd have a really good reason."

Okay. Maybe that's good enough, she thought. She continued to let her fingers work their magic as she asked, "Would you ever just not tell me something? You know, like it might be better that I don't know some things about you?"

He blinked and exhaled a shuddery little breath. He bit his bottom lip, then answered her. "Yeah, I would, Bliss. Nobody knows everything about everybody...no matter how close they are. There's probably things I'll never know about *you*—maybe things I don't want to know. Sometimes not knowing things is the way to go."

There was nothing Bliss could say to argue with what he'd said. He was right, but she didn't really want him to be, so she decided to torture him. She put her hand on him and gave him a squeeze, though it wasn't really necessary because he was already like steel. He made a sound that was somewhere between a growl and a moan.

Chase took his eyes off the road and looked at her for a second. "If you keep that up, I'm pullin' this car over, and I'm gonna let you have it, girl—right here in this car, right here in broad daylight, and I won't give a damn who see's us. I'm serious, Bliss."

She laughed and let him go. "I'm sorry."

He smiled. "No you're not. I could still pull over. You know you want me to."

Bliss wouldn't have liked anything more, and she knew he meant what he said. Chase was crazy, and she loved him for it. Their relationship was very heavy on the physical; they couldn't keep their hands off each other and made love at every opportunity. But it was just as heavy emotionally. Every time Chase touched her, she felt *loved.* He didn't just have sex with her. Instead, he made love to her every single time, even if it was just a quickie in the shower before they went to work. Bliss loved him dearly, and she couldn't imagine her life without him. He was very quickly *becoming* her life. "I love you, Chase," she said again.

He smiled that boyish smile, and it lit his handsome face up. "And I love *you*, Bliss." He kissed her quick, then turned back to the road. They didn't talk much until they got to his place.

Chase pulled his Porsche into the garage, and J.T. pulled his Range Rover in right after him.

"Damn. Thought I'd get a chance to feel you up in the elevator." He smiled, but Bliss could tell his disappointment was real…and so was hers.

"I'll let you feel me up later," Bliss said, looking over her shoulder. Everyone was piling out of J.T.'s ride. She turned back, and Chase was kissing her. Bliss put her hands on his chest to hold him back, but he stopped kissing her just as quickly as he started.

He opened his door and smiled at her. "Come on, sweetheart. I'm gonna tell you some stuff you *really* don't want to hear."

Bliss felt a tingle that wasn't quite dread at that one.

Chase watched her face and saw that look. He squeezed her hand gently. "Don't worry. I'll give it to you easy."

They got out of the car, and everyone rode the elevator up together.

Dee took off her jacket and started taking plates out of the cabinet like she'd been there 1,000 times. Bliss pushed back an instinctive stab of jealousy. "Bliss, you come on and help me set the table. The food will be here soon. J.T., you and lazy-ass Corey start pouring drinks. And Chase, you need to open your mouth and start talkin', honey."

Chase gave her a look. "You can't order me around in my own house, Dee." He disappeared into the bedroom.

J.T. and Corey set about bringing drinks to the table, Dee picked up a stack of plates, and Bliss picked up the silverware.

"Chase loves you, you know," Dee said, looking at her thought-fully.

Bliss tried on a smile that felt awkward on her lips; Dee made her nervous. "Yeah. Chase is wonderful. I couldn't ask for a better man. I love him too."

They walked into the dining area and started to set the table. Bliss was surprised when Dee touched her arm. "Did you rehearse what you'd say to me, honey? That was a real brisk answer, and you may have meant it, but your delivery sucked."

Bliss's head went back, but not in anger. She didn't know exactly *how* she felt. Caught off guard maybe? She stumbled for something to say. "What?" was all she managed.

Dee put her hands on her hips and smiled at her. "I only bite when I'm provoked, Bliss. You see me as some kind of threat, don't you? You probably think I want your man. Isn't that true, honey?"

Well, since she brought it up…"I don't know. I hope not."

Dee laughed good and deep, from her diaphragm. "I'm not gonna lie to you. There was a time that I actually entertained the notion. As you know, Chase is fairly easy to fall in love with. We went back and forward with our flirting and teasing, but nothin' ever came of it, and I know why. That has never been the role Chase wants me to play in his life. It ain't what he needs me for. Chase is very deliberate in everything he does. He doesn't do things on a whim, and he rarely does things he regrets."

Bliss nodded. "I'm learning that."

"I'm no threat, Bliss. I know Chase loves you. I've known him for a long time, and I've *never* seen him act like this. You make him happy, and I don't think I've ever seen him this happy."

Bliss smiled, not sure what to make of Dee's revelations. "I'm glad. He makes me happy too."

Dee looked at her seriously. "Chase is a very complicated man, Bliss."

"I know."

"No you don't, honey. Not yet." She shrugged. "I just wanted to tell you that things might get hard. We may never be friends, but I'm your ally and not your enemy. If you ever need me, I'm there."

J.T. and Corey picked that moment to return to the table with their bottles of liquor, and J.T. squinted at Dee. "What are you up to, Dee?"

Dee sucked her teeth at him. "Nothing. I was just talking to Bliss. Is that all right with you?"

Corey opened the Rémy Martin. "Depends," he said. "You should let Chase talk for himself."

"I agree," J.T. added, pouring Hennessey.

Chase emerged from the bedroom, back to casual, in jeans and a T-shirt, just in time to answer the door. "Food's here," he said absently. He took the food and paid the delivery person, and they all sat down. Chase looked at Bliss for a long time, and then he leaned forward in his seat and took her hand. "All right, Bliss. Here goes. I'm gonna tell you the story of me and Cyrus…pretty much. Of course, it's just *my* side of the story, and there are always two sides to everything. Cyrus might not see it exactly the way I do." He paused to sip his drink, then looked back at her with his beautiful cognac eyes. He looked sad and a bit tired.

Bliss glanced around. Corey was busy eating, like he was absorbing himself in his food to keep from hearing what Chase was about to say. Dee was pushing her food around on her plate, hardly eating at all, and J.T. had both elbows on the table, sipping his Hennessey and studying Chase. Bliss sat back in her chair, but she didn't let go of his hand. "Go ahead. I'm listening."

Chase took a deep breath and started talking. "Me and Cyrus have *never* gotten along, Bliss. I think Cyrus hated my ass at first sight."

"Cyrus don't hate Chase," Corey interjected.

"I think he does. Eat your food and let the man talk, Corey," J.T. said quietly.

"Anyway, like I said, Cyrus never liked me—and I got news for you, Corey. He ain't all that crazy about you, either, so don't get too comfortable." He turned back to Bliss. "My mother had three sons by three different men, and none of us knew our fathers. I think Cyrus is resentful of that, but I'm not into psychotherapy. I'm not feeling Cyrus because he's been a bastard to me all of my life. He used to beat my ass or do something mean to me *every day* when I was little. He was mean to Corey, too, but I'd usually take Corey's ass-whippin's for him so Cyrus would leave him alone."

Bliss rubbed her hand over his. "I'm sorry, baby. I didn't know."

He smiled wryly. "You're not supposed to cry over spilled milk, Bliss, and I hardly ever do. I will say this though. I believe when you suffer trauma and have terrible experiences when you're very young, you store that shit inside you somewhere, and it makes you into the person you become—good or bad." He finished his drink and poured another, and then he poured one for Bliss. "Go ahead and drink up. You'll probably need it for this next part."

Corey stopped eating and let his fork clank noisily onto his plate. "Don't start talkin' about Mama, Chase. For real. I ain't feelin' that at all."

Chase stared at him for a moment, not unkindly. "Then you need to go to another room, Corey."

"Ain't no other room in this place. You live in a fuckin' loft," Corey mumbled and then fell silent.

Chase stared at him a little longer, and then he picked up where he left off. "Cyrus is fifteen years older than me. He started selling drugs somewhere in his late teens, early twenties. Him and his boys did some kind of hostile takeover on some old-school turf, and they started a war. When the smoke cleared, I was cryin' in the schoolyard, with Corey next to me, and I was holdin' our dead mother's head in my lap. A bastard named Maceo shot her in the temple right in front of us. One more reason to hate Cyrus, right?"

Bliss shook her head and squeezed his hand. "God, Chase." She looked at Corey, who had turned his attention out the window. "You guys have been through so much. I'm sorry." Bliss was horrified. A story like that was beyond the pale for her. She couldn't even *begin* to imagine what it must have been like for those little boys. Chase sipped his drink, and Bliss finally picked up her own. While it was shocking as hell to hear it all happened to the man she loved, she was not too naïve to know that things like that went down in the world of drugs. It was always tit for tat. "So what happened to that guy? What was his name? Maceo?" she asked, drinking deeply from her glass.

Chase laughed and turned to Dee. "Let me get one of your smokes, Dee," he said and finished his drink. He immediately poured another one.

"You aimin' to get pissy, Chase?" J.T. asked with his eyebrow in the air.

Chase lit a cigarette and Dee got up to get an ashtray. Chase smiled. "Relax. I'll nurse this one. Besides, I'm in my own house with my woman, my brother, and my two closest friends. One of y'all will cover me up when I pass out. It *takes* liquor to talk about this shit. Bliss, you wanted to know what happened to Maceo?"

"Yeah...and you can pour me another one while you're at it."

Chase obliged, then inhaled deeply and blew the smoke out slow. "They found Maceo four years later, stretched out in the parking lot at Roosevelt Field with his throat cut."

Bliss felt a tingle at the nape of her neck. "Oh my God! Who did it? Was it Cyrus?"

Chase smiled around his cigarette. "I'm sure it wasn't Cyrus."

"What makes you so sure? Maceo *did* kill your mother—Cyrus's mother."

"Yeah, he did, but it don't matter to me who took care of Maceo. What matters is the fact that he's no longer here. I'm good with that, Bliss. Anyway, after my mother died, Cyrus took care of me and Corey. Don't get me wrong...I'm grateful he did. I even tried to make him like me. I did stuff for him—illegal stuff—but he *still* didn't like me. He just used me." He put the cigarette out and stood up. He walked to the window with his drink. "He's *still* tryin' to use me. That's what all this shit is about. There's certain shit I'm not doin'. I'm done takin' shit off Cyrus. He's puttin' a lot of pressure on me to do somethin' I really don't want to do."

Bliss got up and went to him. "What is it he wants you to do?"

He looked down at her with sad eyes, but Bliss loved the way he squared his shoulders and cocked his head. She even loved the way he curled his fists and how the veins stood out in his forearms. "He got into a beef with some guy in Brooklyn. Big-time drug dealer on the come-up named Wolf."

"That was why he got shot?"

Chase nodded. "That's *exactly* why he got shot."

Bliss frowned. "Well, what does he want you to *do*? Shoot Wolf?"

Chase laughed dryly. "Something like that."

Bliss's mouth dropped open. *What the hell is this? What kind of maniac is Cyrus? Doesn't he care about Chase—his own brother—at all? Shit, would Chase actually do it?* She closed her mouth, put her hand to her forehead, and shut her eyes. She literally felt like she was reeling. *What kind of man is Cyrus?*

Chase touched her arm. "Bliss?"

Bliss was so angry she was shaking. She opened her eyes and looked at Chase. "What gives Cyrus the *right* to ask you to do something like that?"

Chase was looking at her carefully. "I don't know."

"What are you gonna do, Chase? You're not gonna do something like that...are you?"

Chase stared at her for a second, then put his hands on her waist and kissed her forehead. "No, Bliss. I'm not. I'm not gonna let Cyrus make me kill Wolf. I'm drawin' the line with him at this. Matter of fact, I'm done helpin' Cyrus do anything. Cyrus is on self-destruct, and I don't want to be around when the shit hits the fan...and it will, mark my words. Come back and sit down. We all need to talk."

Bliss let Chase lead her back to the table. She couldn't believe Cyrus actually wanted Chase to *kill* someone. *What kind of shit is that? Why Chase? He's no hit-man...not my Chase.*

Chase looked across the table at J.T. "I'm gonna take your advice, J.T. I'm gonna go for the brass ring. I'm gonna get my ass as far away from Cyrus as I can, before I end up dead or in jail."

J.T. pushed his plate away and tipped his drink at Chase. "Now that's what I'm talkin' 'bout. Let's hear your plan."

"Thank you, Jesus," Dee muttered and lit a cigarette of her own.

Chase held Bliss's hand, but he was looking at Corey. "Corey? Hey, Corey, don't look out the window. Look at me."

Corey sucked his teeth and turned his head Chase's way. "All due respect, Chase, I don't want to hear none of this shit." He pushed his plate away and looked at Chase moodily.

Chase sighed. He got up and took the seat next to Corey, placing his elbows on the table and leaning toward him. "All due respect, Corey, you don't really have a choice. *I'm tired, Corey.* I'm tired of Cyrus. I love him, but I ain't hangin' around for him to ruin my life. I got too much to look forward to. There's too much for me to lose."

Corey stared at him. "What the fuck are you talkin' about, Chase? What do you mean when you say you're gonna get as far away from Cyrus as you can? You leavin', Chase?"

"Looks like I have to, Corey."

Bliss's heart picked up its pace. *Leave? What's he talking about?*

"You can't leave, Chase. What about me? What about Bliss?"

"What about *me*? Corey. You know. You *know*. How could you ask me to stay?"

Corey's bottom lip trembled, and his eyes filled with tears. He shook his head. "*I hate this.*"

"I know you do, Corey. So do I, but I'm about out of options with Cyrus…and I think it would be a good idea if you left with me."

Corey stood up. "You two are never gonna stop this shit, are you? Y'all been fightin' each other my whole life, with me always hangin' in the middle. Y'all been askin' me to choose between y'all my life. *This shit ain't fair, Chase!* Why do you try so hard to protect me from Cyrus anyway? He's my brother, just like you Smoke! What makes you think he'd do somethin' to hurt me?"

Chase shocked Bliss by laughing. "Corey, you gotta be kiddin' me. Are you stupid? Cyrus broke your arm when you were just a kid. I'm gonna say it again, Corey. You *know* the shit Cyrus makes me do. What in the *fuck* would make you think Cyrus wouldn't hurt *you*? I don't need any accolades, Corey, but I been keepin' Cyrus off your ass your *whole life*. I'm keepin' Cyrus off you *now*, Corey. He doesn't mean you any good, little brother. Can't you see this shit the way it really is? This ain't no tug-a-war. It's simple, Corey. *I love you, and Cyrus doesn't!* Wake up and smell the goddamned coffee!"

Bliss was stunned, and even downing the rest of her drink didn't help the shock any. Cyrus's ass should have been in jail for the shit he'd done, and Chase wanted to get away from him so badly that he was ready to just up and leave. She had a sudden deep loathing for Cyrus. He was a fucking tyrant. It seemed like he wanted to destroy Chase and Corey, his own flesh and blood. Cyrus was responsible for some very reprehensible shit in Chase and Corey's lives, and Bliss thought maybe Chase was *right* to leave. She started to weigh the pros and cons of her own situation with Chase while she listened to him talk to his little brother.

"What do you want me to do, Chase?" Corey asked unenthusiastically.

Chase sat back in his chair and looked at Corey with a patient gaze. "Don't be mad at me, Corey. It's for everybody's own good."

"Amen to that," J.T. said.

Corey shot him a dirty look. "Instigator!" he said blackly.

"Brat," J.T. shot back.

J.T. played bartender and freshened drinks. Bliss was tipsy, but she drank anyway. She didn't want to entertain the thought of Chase going away from her. It was all Cyrus's fault, and she suddenly hated him.

Chase looked at Dee. "You've been real quiet," he said with a smile.

Dee, Bliss noted, had been sipping and smoking steadily since they'd sat down—perhaps steeling herself. She smiled back at him and shrugged. "There's nothing for me to say, honey. I've been begging you for years to put some distance between you and Cyrus. Just tell me what you need me to do, and consider it done."

Chase smiled at her. "I love you, Dee."

She smiled back. "You should...but be careful not to make Bliss jealous." She looked at Bliss. "You okay? All this has to be a lot for you to digest."

Bliss nodded. "I'm okay." She looked at Chase. "But I don't want to work for Cyrus anymore."

Chase reclaimed his seat next to her, now that Corey was sufficiently smoothed out. "Good, 'cause that's part of the plan. From now on, you work for me. I'm gonna need you to fill in for Dee."

Dee raised an eyebrow. "For *me*? Why? Where am I going?"

"I'm sending you down to Atlanta with Corey to check some spots out for me. I'm gonna open a club down there—maybe even two—and relocate for a while after they're up and running."

Corey looked disagreeable. "How come you and Bliss can't go to Atlanta? Me and Dee could run shit up here."

"You're good at stuff like that, Corey. You even found Cyrus's club. I need somebody with those kinds of skills in Atlanta."

Corey knew better. "You want me away from Cyrus."

Chase grinned at him. "Yeah…that too."

"What's J.T. gonna do?" Corey asked.

"I'm gonna be my usual flexible self, fillin' gaps wherever I'm needed. It's easy to do that when you own your own company, youngster." J.T. flashed Corey a winning smile and smacked him lightly on the back of the head. "Maybe you'll have one, too, when you grow up."

They finally heated the food up and ate, Corey for the second time. They agreed that Dee and Corey would fly down to Atlanta and start looking the Monday after the club opening. Bliss wanted to give Cyrus two weeks' notice, but Chase said it didn't matter and wasn't necessary; he promised to take responsibility for her leaving, and Cyrus could deal with him if he had a problem with it. He didn't seem to mind taking the brunt of everything, as long as it meant being free from Cyrus.

It was after midnight when their little meeting finally broke up. Bliss got into Chase's bed with him, and they snuggled close together. She thought she'd be sleepier than she was, after all that liquor they drank, but she was wide awake—and quite content feeling Chase's heartbeat against her back. She loved him—everything about him: they way he looked, the way he smelled, and the way he talked. She smiled and closed her eyes, and the minute she did, Chase whispered in her ear.

"You still up, Bliss?"

Her smile widened into a grin because she knew what his problem was.

He kissed her neck and ran his thumb over her nipple. "Bliss, wake up." He pressed himself against her, and Bliss giggled.

"I'm up, Chase." She laughed. "You are *so* horny!"

He laughed, too, but he moved her leg forward with his and pushed his chest into her back, moving her onto her stomach. Bliss went willingly, and Chase planted a knee on either side of her. "I'm not horny. I'm in love with you. Let me in, and I'll show you."

Bliss parted her thighs for him, and he slid in and curled his fingers around hers.

"Close your legs, Bliss."

She did, and she thought she would die. She loved him, and he loved her—and he was showing her, filling her body and heart with every thrust.

Chase started talking to her. "You comin' with me to Atlanta, Bliss?"

She arched her back, and he went all the way in. "God, yes, Chase. I'd follow you anywhere."

He laughed softly in her ear. "You can't follow me unless you marry me. You gonna marry me, Bliss? Say yes. I need you. Please… say yes," he begged, never stopping what he was doing, plunging into her with his magnificent long stroke.

Bliss started throbbing so hard it brought tears to her eyes. "Yes! Yes, Chase! I will! I promise!"

He kissed her cheek. "Good…and while you're at it, I want you to have my baby, too, Bliss." His breath caught, and he growled real sexy.

Bliss could feel his release when he let go, and it made her happy. She'd known from the moment Chase had lifted his helmet and looked at her with his incredible cognac eyes that she belonged to him. She and Chase were inevitable, and they both knew it. She'd go wherever he went because she couldn't live without him. She rocked with him until he had nothing left to give her, and then he turned over with her in his arms. She loved him so much she felt like crying. She was his.

Chapter 14

"I still don't believe I had to damn near make a fuckin' appointment to see my own brother. This is some very insulting shit, Corey," Cyrus said, walking into his brand new club.

Corey looked at him apologetically. "I'm sure he didn't mean it like that, Cyrus. Don't take it so personal. Chase has been pretty busy. Cut him some slack."

Cyrus looked around. *Yeah, he's been busy, all right.* The club was beautiful and completely ready for the opening the next day. Everything was pristine, polished, and fresh. The bar was stocked with a staggering array of mid- to top-shelf liquor, and the dance floor gleamed. Cyrus nodded his head in pride and satisfaction. "That's what I'm talkin' 'bout. This joint is tight."

Corey looked at him sideways. "Yeah, thanks to Chase. You could give him a compliment once in a while instead of your ass to kiss. Maybe if you showed him a little love from time to time, things wouldn't be as fucked up between y'all as they are."

Cyrus nodded and scratched his goatee. "Yeah, maybe. Unfortunately, that's not why I'm here. I need to let Smoke know he ain't handling his business like he promised."

Corey frowned. "Fuck you talkin' 'bout, Cyrus? The club opens tomorrow, and he did what he promised."

Cyrus had arrived at the club in a Suburban with three big, burly, dudes protecting his ass. He was constantly looking over his shoulder, and he could barely stand the paranoia anymore. He blamed Chase that he had to be so careful. "I'm afraid he didn't, young buck. Wolf is still eatin', shittin', and changin' his clothes, and I got a problem with that 'cause I told Chase to put an end his ass. Wolf shoulda stopped bein' a problem for me *weeks* ago. Meanwhile, he's pickin' my people off one by one. Shit, he even tried to take *me* out. I need to know why this nigga Smoke is draggin' his heels."

Corey looked at him as they reached the office. "I know you're pissed, but be nice, Cyrus."

Cyrus frowned. *This nigga's gotta be kidding.* "Nice? I ain't the crazy, temperamental motherfucker, always flyin' off the handle. *That* would be Smoke, with his razor-wielding ass. You tell *that* nigga to be nice. That boy got a split personality or somethin'."

Corey looked at the floor. "Don't talk about Chase like that. He's our brother, and that ain't right."

Cyrus stared at Corey for a second. "I sure hope you take up for me like that."

Corey shook his head sadly. "Y'all are givin' me a fuckin' ulcer," he said and knocked on the door, rubbing his stomach.

Cyrus deeply resented the fact that he had to knock on the office door at his own club. *That nigga Smoke think he's all that? I'll fuckin' show him,* he thought, knowing he was gonna bend his fingers back.

"Come in."

Corey swung the door open. Chase was seated at the desk going over a floor plan, with Bliss peering over his shoulder. She was dressed down in jeans and a light blue T-shirt, but she was still one helluva nice piece of ass.

She looked startled to see Cyrus and took a step closer to Chase. "Mr. Brown. Hi."

Cyrus smiled at her. "Ms. Riley."

Chase stood up and rolled the floor plans into a tube. "'Sup, Cyrus?" He handed the tube to Bliss. "Could you give us a minute?"

Bliss seemed to be purposely avoiding eye contact. She took the plans and picked up another set of papers. "Call me when you need me," she said and walked out.

"Have a seat, Cyrus. What can I do for you?" Chase said, eyeing him coolly.

Fuck sitting down. Cyrus walked around to Chase's side of the desk. "I think you know what you can do for me."

Chase started smiling, but it wasn't a happy smile. "Don't roll up on me, Cyrus. Sit your ass down like I said," Chase ordered.

Cyrus frowned and made a fist. "What?"

Chase looked at his fist and laughed. "I'm tellin' you, Cyrus, don't come at me like that. If you put your hands on me, I'm gonna defend myself."

Corey stepped between them with his back to Chase. "Just sit down, Cyrus, and stop this crazy shit. Please." He turned his head to Chase. "Calm down, Chase."

Chase looked Corey in the eye. "I am calm, Corey."

But even Cyrus could see he wasn't. He could see the pulse beating in his neck, and there was that wild little light in the corners of his eyes. To make matters worse, he couldn't stop smiling. Cyrus felt a cold chill at the base of his neck. He'd seen that wild little sparkle in his brother's eyes before, accompanied by that ferocious little grin. *Oh shit. Damn.* He took a step back, unconsciously keeping his hands where Chase could see them. Cyrus was mortified that his heart was suddenly slamming in his chest. He narrowed his eyes at Chase. "You look like you want to hurt me, Smoke."

To his credit, Chase took a step back too. "I ain't gonna rule it out. I'm warnin' you, Cyrus, I'm not gonna have you comin' at me like that—grabbin' my collar and shit like you used to and puttin' your hands on me. I told you before, and you need to listen, Cyrus. If you want to talk to me, have a seat and be respectful." Chase sat down in his own chair like it was a throne.

Cyrus sat in the chair across the desk from him, albeit resentfully. He could feel his fury rising, and his fingers itched to choke the shit out of Chase's insolent ass.

Chase threw gas on the fire when he laughed. "Boy, you're mad as hell now, ain't ya, Cyrus?"

Corey shook his head and sat down on the corner of the desk. "Stop, Chase. That's not cool."

But Chase clearly had no intention of stopping. He leaned back in his chair and turned to Cyrus. "What's the matter, Cy? Cat got your tongue? You came in here like you had somethin' to say, so say it."

Cyrus glared at the ungrateful son of a bitch. He wanted to hit him until his hand hurt. He wanted to say some foul shit back to him, but he couldn't seem to get enough spit in his mouth to talk. The reality was that it was time to admit to himself that he was afraid of his little brother. It was that crazy light in his eyes that had his balls shriveling. Maybe he was showing out before, but Cyrus knew better than to push the envelope with Chase's unstable ass when he had that glittery, smiley look about him—the one he always got before he opened a nigga's throat up.

"Go ahead and talk, Cyrus. Stop sitting there looking like you're scared of me, 'cause *that could never be true*. Right, Cyrus?"

"Chase—" Corey said from his perch on the desk.

"I'm not doin' anything, Corey. I'm just waitin' for Cyrus to ask me about Wolf, that's all. Go on, Cyrus. Ask me."

Cyrus cleared his throat. "You can't blame me for askin'. You promised me a long time ago that you would take care of him, and so far you ain't kept your word, 'cause he's still breathin', far as I know."

"Maybe not, but I've done other stuff for you, Cyrus. What about Mooch and Post? They won't be shootin' anybody else."

Cyrus shook his head. "All that shit did was piss Wolf off."

Chase laughed a fucked-up little laugh. "It did? My bad."

"You think this shit is funny? 'Cause it ain't."

Chase stopped smiling. "No, Cyrus, I don't think it's funny. I think this shit is tired. Hell, I think *you're* tired. Don't you have anybody in your goon squad who can grease Wolf for you? How you gonna do the things you do and not have some people lined up for shit like this? Some people to calm shit down when it gets too hot? I ain't seen you with no serious executioners since Herc Mercer."

Cyrus stared at him. Chase was playing games with him, and he didn't appreciate it. It wasn't in Cyrus's nature to take shit off of people, and despite the danger of fucking with Chase, he refused to take it now. "Well, I *had* an executioner—Herc, like you said—but some-damn-body went and *executed* his ass."

Chase returned his stare. "He got what he deserved, Cyrus. He pulled his .45 on me and Corey, aiming to kill us both. Even if he had no murderous intent, he knew he was gonna die when he pulled his gun. *Nobody* pulls a gun on me, Cyrus. I don't play that shit, and everybody knows it."

They stared at each other, and Cyrus could tell by the look in Chase's eye that he was going to have to sing a different song if he wanted Chase to cooperate. "If I let anybody else handle this, it ain't goin' down right. You killed my best boy years ago."

Chase raised an eyebrow. "Well, I didn't do it because I wanted his damn job."

"You're the only one who can do this job, Smoke, and you'll do it better than he ever could. You don't leave a trace."

Chase looked at him for a long time. "I'm not gonna do it, Cyrus."

Cyrus frowned. *What the fuck is this?* "You have to...you said you would."

Chase shook his head slowly. "Negative. I don't *have* to do shit. I changed my mind, Cyrus. I'm done."

Cyrus nodded. *Sure.* He'd heard it all before, and it was nothing but a rehash. He decided to do some rehashing of his own. He looked at Chase, then let his eyes slide, pointedly, toward Corey.

Chase smiled his regular grin, not the one laden with danger. "That's not gonna work this time, Cyrus. Don't even think 'bout threatenin' me with that shit."

Cyrus rubbed his elbow, which was still in a sling. He thought threatening Chase with Corey would ultimately work, but he had to drop it for a moment, because he didn't think Corey would react too well if he *knew* he was a pawn in this game. He had to catch him when he was unsuspecting and thought Cyrus was desperate. The thing was, Cyrus *was* damn close to desperation and Chase—that arrogant fuck—wasn't playing ball. Cyrus changed tactics. "You gotta do somethin', Smoke. Wolf is actin' like Maceo. He's poppin' people at random, tryina get me and Khalid. I'm havin' trouble walkin' down the street."

Chase frowned. "That's funny…you managed to make it here."

"I'm serious, Chase."

Chase smiled. "I know. So am I."

Cyrus stood up. He was running out of approaches with this negro. He scratched his goatee and looked at him, smiling slyly, preparing to play his ace in the hole. "I don't blame you, Smoke. Shit is real hot right now. The cops are still actively pursuing whoever killed Mooch and Post. Maybe it's just a matter of time till they find out who pulled that shit." He said it quietly and purposely greasy so Chase would catch his drift.

Chase was no fool and caught it right away. Chase was like lightning with that fucking razor, and all Cyrus heard was that grim and familiar *whick-whick-whick* before the blade was open and in his hand. Chase didn't get up, but Cyrus took a step back; he had to because that crazy light was back in Chase's eyes.

Corey had a look of shock on his face as he instinctively placed himself between them. "Listen…please stop this shit!"

Chase stood up slowly and expertly twirled the razor between his fingers. That crazy smile joined that crazy light. "You threatening me, Cyrus? You gonna tell the cops about me?" *Whick-whick.* The razor twirled in his hand as Chase came around the desk.

Cyrus stepped back, and Corey stepped back with him.

Chase laughed a sinister, ominous-sounding chuckle, like something straight out of a horror movie. "You go ahead and give me up, Cyrus. Go right ahead, but know that if you do open your mouth about that shit, I *guarantee* it won't be Wolf you'll have to worry about…and he won't have to bother with your ass anymore either."

"What you sayin', Smoke? You gonna kill me?"

"Give me up and you'll find out. Find somebody else to do your dirty work, Cyrus. I'm done with you. We'll open your club tomorrow, and start the separation process. If you ever decide to get your shit together—which I doubt your fool ass will—I'll think about lettin' you back into my life."

Cyrus's mouth had always gotten him into trouble—that and his temper. He got so mad, so quick, he didn't even realize it when the insult poured out of his lips. "You ain't nothin' but a fuckin' *pussy,* Chase," he said venomously and spat over Corey's shoulder.

The wad of warm saliva landed on the collar of Chase's T-shirt, and Chase lost his goddamned mind…but he gave it some thought before he made his move. He threw his razor over his shoulder and came around Corey so quick that neither brother had had time to react. He head-butted Cyrus and re-fractured his nicely healing nose. Chase's left knee connected with Cyrus's groin, and his right fist rammed into his windpipe.

In less than ten seconds, Cyrus was on his way down. Chase grabbed him in a headlock on his way to the floor with his left arm and put his right arm across the back of his neck, then grabbed his chin. Cyrus had no idea Chase was as strong as he was, but that was the way Chase put niggas to sleep. He was signing his name on Cyrus, and Cyrus felt his air cut off and his lights going out.

"I don't need a fuckin' razor, Cyrus. I'll snap your goddamned neck if you ever disrespect me again. You have no idea who you're fuckin' with, do you?"

"Chase! Please, Chase! Let him go! Oh God! Jesus!" Corey wailed, trying to pull his big brothers apart, but Chase was too *strong*.

Chase leaned forward and spoke in his ear. "You're gonna make me kill you, Cyrus," Chase said through his teeth. He pushed Cyrus away from him; he fell hard, but he made sure he rolled away from Chase's crazy ass when he hit the floor.

Cyrus tried desperately to get his breath back as Corey started jabbering. "Chase! Chase, what the fuck, man? You could have killed him. Oh my God! What the fuck—"

"Stop it, Corey. Stop. It's over. His ass is still alive, but I bet he won't be spittin' on me no more. Now calm the fuck down. Everything's gonna be fine."

Cyrus got to his knees, and Corey helped him to his feet. He looked at Chase like he didn't want to know him as Chase folded his razor and put it back in his pocket. "You're fuckin' crazy," he said, still trying to catch his breath.

Chase's eyes sparkled, and he laughed. "If you didn't know it before, now you do. Don't fuck with me, Cyrus. I went easy on you, but you're runnin' out of chances with me. I'll see you tomorrow at nine o'clock. Now get the fuck outta my office."

Cyrus realized a couple of things in that moment, things Chase maybe wasn't aware of. First, he could and would find a way to get rid of Wolf himself. It might end up a lot messier than if Chase did it, but he'd jump that hurdle when he got to it. Second, Chase should have known how much of a vengeful bastard Cyrus was; his little brother should have killed him while he had the chance, because he might not have the opportunity again. *If Chase wants things to be like that between us, so be it. I ain't losin' nothin'. I've hated his ass from the beginning.* Cyrus smiled and wiped the blood off his face. He was good at waging war, and Chase had just started one. He might destroy himself in the process, but Cyrus made up his mind right then and there that *he* would have the last fucking laugh. *Have it you way, motherfucker. Time for me to destroy you.*

Chapter 15

Bliss and Chase had their first real argument over whether or not Bliss should attend the opening of Cyrus's club. Bliss wanted to go because she thought something was going to happen, and she thought there would be less chance of Chase getting involved if she were there. Chase didn't want her to go because he *knew* something was probably going to jump off, and he didn't want to have the added worry of keeping her safe during whatever went down. She didn't quite understand, but Chase knew if anything happened to her, he'd probably say, *"Fuck it,"* and sign off. He would die if something happened to Bliss; it would kill his future, and he'd have nothing left to live for. Part of him had been dead inside for a long time, but Bliss was bringing him back to life. For once in his life, he didn't feel so angry. He didn't want to destroy everything in his path, and he wasn't feeling so furious with the world. Because of Bliss, he was starting to feel like he wasn't the raging, bloodthirsty psychopath he'd always thought himself to be.

Bliss sat on his bed watching him. "I really wish you'd let me go with you, Chase."

From where he stood in front of the mirror, Chase put his brush down and looked at her. "I'll come to your place when it's over, I promise. You don't need to be there, baby, and I'm not gonna argue about it anymore."

"You really think something's gonna happen, don't you?" she asked, looking worried.

Chase stood in front of her and touched her hair. "Stop worryin', Bliss. Everything's gonna be okay."

She curled her fingers around his. "How can I stop worrying when you obviously think it's too dangerous for me to be there? Don't you think I worry about *you?*"

Chase smiled at her. "Don't worry about me. I can take care of myself. You oughtta know that by now."

Bliss frowned. "You think Wolf might try something with Cyrus tonight?"

"I think it's a real strong possibility, if he keeps his ear to the ground like he's supposed to."

"Oh God. I don't want you to go, Chase. Just stay here with me. I've got a really bad feeling about this."

Chase understood her trepidation because he felt it too. There was some little nagging feeling that something was about to happen, a thread of unease. He sat down next to her. "I *have* to go, Bliss."

She shook her head. "Uh-uh. No you don't. If I don't have to be there, neither do you. You don't owe Cyrus anything, so let him open his own damn club, Chase. You've helped him enough."

He didn't say anything.

"You just want to be there to protect Corey if anything goes down, right? I know that's what it is, even if you don't say so. But I've got a better idea. Just call Corey and tell him not to go. Even better, cancel the shit altogether."

But it was a little late for that. Chase held his tongue and put his shoes on, his black Uptowns.

This wasn't lost on Bliss, who felt like he was ignoring her. She looked at the shoes, then back up to his face. "Think you might have to run?"

He nodded. "Yeah, I just might." He stood and got his keys. "Let's go."

Bliss reluctantly followed him out to the elevator and down to the garage. She looked at him with a tight smile. "Which car are you taking?"

Chase picked up his helmet and handed her one. "I'm not takin' a car."

Bliss took the helmet and walked over to the Ducati.

"No…the other one." He pointed to the black Kawasaki, and he could see the dread in Bliss's eyes. "You really *do* think something's gonna happen, don't you?"

Chase got on the bike and leaned it down for her. Bliss got on without another word and he took her home, finding a generous amount of solace in being that close to her. Something was going to happen, all right. He felt it deep in his bones, and Chase's hunches were seldom wrong. Chase parked his bike in front of Bliss's building and took out his cell phone. He tried Corey at home and on his cell, but he only got voicemail both times. He even tried Cyrus and got the same thing.

Bliss stood on the curb, holding her helmet in her hands, watching him. "Chase?"

He put his phone back in his pocket. "It's too late," he said in resignation. Whatever was meant to be had already been set in motion, and the course of events was irrevocable. He got off his bike and pulled Bliss into his arms, kissing her soft and long. Then he pulled away, trying to keep his true feelings out of his eyes, though he knew that was impossible. "No matter what happens, look for me. I'm coming right back to you the minute it's over."

She put her arms around his neck and kissed him hard.

He gently broke the kiss and pushed her back. He smiled a little. "I gotta go now, Bliss. I'll be back."

Her eyes were huge when she looked at him. "I'm scared for you, Chase. Promise me you'll be careful."

He smiled for real. "Bliss…I'm not goin' off to fight lions. I'm only goin' to open a club. Besides, God don't want me. I'll be back."

"Don't say things like that, baby. He does." She kissed him and touched his face. "I love you."

"I love you too." He got back on his bike and put his helmet on. "Go upstairs, Bliss. I'll call you when I get there."

Bliss was being clingy, but so was he. He knew if he didn't take off, he wasn't going to be able to pull himself away from her.

Bliss hugged him again and turned to go.

When she was safely inside, Chase put his visor down and took off.

When he got to the club, people were milling around behind the velvet ropes, talking excitedly and waiting to get in. Chase went past all of them and turned his bike into the alley. He lifted his visor and went in the back way, through a fire door near the kitchen and employee facilities.

Chase's dread and misgivings had grown into a *bona fide* case of the jumps, and he'd never learned how to abide that feeling well. It launched him into a mode of self-preservation...and of protector. He took his helmet off and went in search of Corey. He found him down in front near the hostess, and he was hugely relieved to see Corey keeping company with J.T. rather than Cyrus. He walked up to them and gave J.T. dap.

"What's up, Chase? Where's Bliss?"

Chase put a hand on both their shoulders and walked them back to the office. He closed the door and put his helmet on his desk.

"Where's Bliss?" Corey repeated.

Chase went to the safe and looked over his shoulder at him. "I told her not to come."

Corey sat down. "Why? And she listened to you?"

Chase took a strongbox out of the safe and glanced at Corey. "Yeah. I managed to convince her. Is Dee here?"

"Nah. Dee's at Cream," J.T. said, frowning because he knew what was in the box. "You all right, Chase?"

Chase opened the box and looked up at him. "No, I'm not all right. I got a bad feelin' about this, J.T. Corey, you got your gun on you?"

Corey was frowning. "Course I do. What's wrong, Chase? You think Wolf might move on us tonight?"

"I'm almost sure he will. Think about it. It's the perfect opportunity. Wolf still owes Cyrus for that shit him and Khalid pulled, and he owes me, too, for takin' out Mooch and Post. Maybe he feels like he can kill two birds with one stone, but little does he know, I ain't goin' out like that."

J.T. reached into the box and took out a .45 that rivaled Herc Mercer's trusty old pal. "Me neither," he said, making sure it was loaded.

Chase smiled. J.T. was two different people just as much as he was—ride or die. He put up his usual argument. "You ain't got to be in this, J.T."

J.T. smiled and tucked his gun away. "Nonsense. It's invigorating."

"This shit is my fault," Chase said. He took another razor out of the box, along with two long silver chains, the kind bikers put their keys and wallets on, only a little longer.

"How is it your fault?" Corey asked, looking at the chains with great interest.

Chase had been wearing gloves since before he got on his bike, so he wasn't worried about prints. If he was anything, he was meticulous. He took the razor he always carried out of his pocket and clipped the chain onto the D-ring at the end of the handle. "It's my fault because I should have killed Wolf's ass when this shit first happened instead of trying to have a power struggle with Cyrus. I don't know why I fought him so hard for anyway. It always comes back to Cyrus getting his way. Let's face it…he's gonna get his way tonight, too, 'cause I ain't lettin' us live our lives lookin' over our shoulders. Better just to erase the problem."

Corey raised both eyebrows. "You goin' after him tonight, Chase?"

"Only if he steps to me…or you or J.T. I don't really want to do it here. It's way too public—too many people."

J.T. was watching him with his arms folded across his chest. Chase was wearing a brand new pair of black Levi's and a black Dior shirt. Chase never tucked his shirt in unless he was wearing a suit. He lifted his shirt tail and clipped a chain onto each of his front belt loops, then he put the razors in his back pockets. Both Corey and

J.T. were looking at him curiously.

"What the fuck are you doin', Chase?" Corey asked.

Chase shrugged. "It's insurance. I just want to make sure these razors don't get too far away—in case somebody jumps me or somethin'."

J.T. smiled. "That's nice, but can you do tricks?"

Chase smiled back. "Yeah. I can do tricks, all right."

J.T. rubbed his hands together. "Do some tonight. I can't wait to see 'em."

Corey turned around and stared at him. "You're one sick fuck, J.T."

J.T. shrugged. "Maybe I am."

Chase ignored both of them. He took a .32 out of the box, checked it, and put the box back in the safe. "Where's Cyrus?"

Corey laughed. "In the VIP room with his entourage, biggin' himself up to anyone who'll lend a fuckin' ear."

Chase nodded. "Maybe that's the best place for him to be, and with any luck, that's where he'll stay. Hopefully, nothin' will happen at all."

Corey took out his own gun and checked it. "What makes you so sure Wolf is gonna come here?"

"I told you before, Corey…it's a hunch."

"You gonna go talk to Cyrus?" J.T. asked.

"You think I should?" Chase thought back to his last meeting with Cyrus. The fool spat on him! He still couldn't believe that shit. Chase had been two seconds from snapping his neck. The only thing that saved him was the fact that he was his brother. He had absolutely no desire to look at Cyrus ever again. Bliss was right when she said the only reason he was here at all was to protect Corey.

"I don't think you should tell Cyrus shit. If Wolf and his pals *do* show up, you should lock him in the VIP room with Cyrus and his crew and let the best man win," J.T. interjected.

"Sounds like a plan." Chase walked over to Corey and put his hand on his shoulder. He loved his little brother to death and always had, even if he was better at showing it than saying it. "I love you,

Corey. Stay close to me tonight okay?"

Corey looked startled at first, but then he laughed. "I love you, too, Chase. I ain't no punk, though, and I can handle myself."

"I never called you one. Just don't argue with me, Corey, and do like I asked you to."

Corey shook his head. "You *always* treat me like a damn little kid, Chase. In case you hadn't noticed, we ain't walked home from no schoolyards in years."

"I don't think this is a good time to raise up, youngster," J.T. said.

Corey narrowed his eyes at him. "Mind your business, J.T."

J.T. smiled. "I *am*."

Corey looked at Chase resentfully.

"Fuck, Corey, just humor me," Chase said.

Corey shrugged. "Fine. Consider me your goddamned shadow."

"Thank you. Now, if y'all are ready, let's go. We'll sit at the bar and watch who drifts in and out of this place."

******

An hour went by, then another. Though Chase hadn't called in any favors to any of the many celebrities he knew, asking them to make an appearance, more than a few showed up to show Cyrus some love, through Chase. At the end of the second hour, Chase stood up and stretched. Cyrus's club opening was a success, even if he didn't think enough of Chase to at least pop his head out of the VIP room. Chase didn't really give a shit. The club could fall to ruin the very next day for all he cared. He'd done his job, and the rest was Cyrus's problem.

Still, Cyrus's blatant disrespect for him bothered him a lot more than he cared to admit. He was spitting in his face by holing up in the VIP room like that, and Chase was tired of waiting his ass out. He drank the rest of his Pellegrino, but it didn't do anything to put out the small flames of anger he felt for his brother, and his radar was still up. He turned away from the bar.

"Where you goin', Chase?" J.T. asked. He'd been watching him like a hawk since the night started.

Chase smiled to himself. J.T. always had his back, and he always cared where his head was at. He looked over at Corey, who had his back to him, trying to talk to some honey. Chase didn't think either one of his brothers would hold him down like J.T. Cyrus wouldn't because he didn't give a shit, and Corey probably wouldn't because he was so used to Chase holding *him* down like steel that he probably didn't even know how. Chase looked back at J.T. "I'm gonna go holler at Cyrus and find out why he ain't showin' his face."

J.T. shook his head. "I don't know why you keep lookin' for somethin' he ain't never gonna give you, Chase."

Chase stared at him. "I ain't lookin' for shit. I just want to know why he's bein' rude."

J.T. sighed. He looked like he was thinking about saying something slick, but given Chase's current mood, he wasn't sure that would be the way to go. "You want me to come with you?"

"Nah, that's okay. You stay here with Corey."

J.T. nodded. "Don't be too long, or I'm comin' up. I got my own qualms about this shit."

Chase walked out of the bar area and through an alcove to his right. He went up the spiral staircase to the VIP room, looking everywhere at once. The music in the club was so loud that he couldn't hear shit, and it was giving him a headache. He turned left and entered the VIP room. Somewhere in the back of his mind, it registered that he hadn't called Bliss, but that would have to wait. Chase had a feeling what he'd been waiting for all night was just around the corner.

It was off the chain up there, and it was no wonder Cyrus hadn't brought his ass downstairs. It looked like Cyrus had his whole crew up there partying hard and drinking champagne straight out the bottle. Cyrus and Khalid were holding court in one of the big round booths, smoking trees, with women hanging on their arms and wannabe hustlers hanging on their every word.

Chase looked around. Everyone in the room seemed to be over their fucking limit—some more than others. There was even a brother in the corner getting a blowjob like he was in his bedroom.

Chase walked over to Cyrus's table and stood there staring at him.

Cyrus was so high that he didn't even see him at first, not until Khalid hit him in the shoulder and nodded in Chase's direction.

Chase smirked at him and nodded. "Cyrus."

Cyrus laughed, grabbed a bottle of champagne off the table, and started pushing his way out of the booth. He finally made it, and Chase stepped back. Cyrus was one drink away from being totally fucked up, and Chase was disgusted.

"Cyrus, look at you. You twisted back man."

Cyrus swigged out the bottle. "Yeah, I am. You give a great party, Smoke, and I'm grateful, but if you want to talk to me, you gotta follow me to the head. I gotta get rid of some of this liquor."

Chase was so surprised by the compliment and the thanks that he followed Cyrus into the bathroom without a second thought. He watched Cyrus as he set the champagne on the counter and turned his back to him to use the urinal. "Glad you're satisfied, Cyrus. You get any weird feelings about tonight?" Chase asked, running his thumb along the scar under his jaw. He shook his head, watching Cyrus, and answered his own question. "Never mind. You're probably too fucked up to notice."

Cyrus flushed the urinal and fixed his clothes. He turned and looked at Chase in exasperation. "Why you gotta say shit like that, Smoke? You always say shit to piss me off. I was *tryin'* to be nice. I wasn't tryina fuck with you. I didn't bring up the fact that I should be walkin' a mile in your ass right now for breakin' my nose—twice— now did I?"

Chase looked at him grimly. "No, Cyrus, you didn't."

Cyrus washed his hands and retrieved his champagne bottle. He swayed a bit. "Good. Then shut the fuck up."

Just as Cyrus was turning the bottle up again, there was a thunderous *crash* from the VIP room. They both dropped into crouches, sending the champagne bottle crashing to the floor and exploding into shards. Cyrus pulled his gun out as Chase made his way to the door, still in a crouch. He cracked it open and saw that people were screaming, and there was the unmistakable sound and stench of gunfire. "Shit!"

Chase muttered.

Cyrus started for the door, and Chase stood up to his full height. He stood between Cyrus and the door and put his hand on his chest. "You can't go out there like that! You'll get yourself killed. Gimme your gun...I know you got another one."

"Fuck *you*," Cyrus said. Panic was working its way into his eyes, delayed because he was high.

Chase snatched his gun out of his hand, without saying anything else. He gave Cyrus a dark look. "I can get you out of here, stupid."

A bullet punched through the door near Chase's right shoulder. It zinged through the air and shattered the mirror.

"Don't fuckin' move! I'll send somebody back to get you." Chase went out the door with Cyrus's nine in his hand, almost duck walking. There was a man directly in front of him, firing into the crowd with his back to Chase. Chase gave him a quick once-over. He didn't know the guy, and it was time for the shooter to go down. Chase thought of using his razor, but the gun was already in his hand. He walked right up to him, stuck his gun behind his right ear, and pulled the trigger.

The man's brains exited through his left temple and splashed his boy, who was standing next to him, reloading.

"Joe!? Oh shit, man!" was all he had a chance to say before Chase grabbed him in a headlock and pulled him back toward the bathroom. Chase tucked Cyrus's gun into his waistband and pulled out his razor. He flicked it open and held it in front of his captive's face.

The hostage immediately started mewling and trying to fight.

"I see you know who I am. Wolf send you?"

He was fighting so hard that he almost broke free.

Chase tucked his lips in and cut the man's right ear off with one swipe of the blade. "Stop fightin', or I'll cut your fuckin' throat.. Is Wolf here?"

"Noooooo! Jesus Christ!"

"How many of you motherfuckers are here?"

He developed a case of lockjaw again, and Chase opened his scalp up.

"*Jesus*! Ten! There's ten of us! *Please, man*!"

"Fuck you," Chase said and cut his throat. He pushed him away and let him fall like yesterday's garbage. Chase didn't want his face exposed, so when he walked into the VIP room, he snatched a cap off a guy fleeing toward the stairs and put it on his own head. The whole place was a mess. Some people were already shot up, some were still shooting, and others were crushing each other trying to get down the spiral staircase.

Chase spotted Khalid, who was blazing his gun and bleeding profusely from a shoulder wound. He caught one dude in the head, and the guy went down. Chase made his way over to the fire exit and threw the door open. He started pushing people through, knowing others would follow and free up the stairway.

When he turned around, Khalid was right next to him. "Where the hell is Cyrus?"

"In the bathroom."

"What's he doin'? Takin' a fuckin' shit?" Khalid asked harshly.

Chase shrugged and stepped away. "Go figure. I'm checkin' for Corey. Go get him." Chase hurried down into the pandemonium that was the main floor. People were running and breaking out. The party was over. Chase got to the middle of the floor and did a 360. *Okay. There ain't any shootin' going on down here.* As soon as he thought it, a shot rang out, followed by a chorus of screams, and Chase turned in time to see J.T. step away from a man going down slow, holding his chest. Chase didn't see Corey anywhere, so he made his way over to J.T., who'd put some distance between himself and the man on the floor. "Where's Corey, J.T.?"

"I'm not real sure, but the cops are most likely on their way. We need to be ghostin', Chase...NOW!"

Cyrus came down the stairs with Khalid right behind him, holding his hurt shoulder.

"I'm checkin' the office, and then we're out. Do a quick search and meet me in the alley."

"Done," J.T. said. He turned on his heel and started scanning for Corey.

Chase went as unobtrusively as he could to the office. There was no sign of Corey. He exited the club through the door by the kitchen and came out by his bike. Chase heard the blow even before it connected, and he almost turned into it. Something really hard caught him in the side of the head. He staggered and went down to his left knee, fighting the urge to hold his head in his hands. Chase's hand went instinctively to his razor and flicked it open. The small noise was loud in the relative quiet of the alley.

"Quick! Put his head out!" someone whispered furiously.

Two of them? Chase staggered back to his feet and whirled around, not caring if he fell or not, but buying time for him to get his other razor out.

Someone grabbed him in a bear hug—a big dude—pinning his arms down.

What the fuck are they doing? They should have just shot me. It woulda worked out better for them than this is going to, Chase thought of his attackers. He grinned—hell, he *laughed*—and slammed his foot into big boy's unsuspecting knee.

The huge man brayed in pain as his knee extended far beyond a healthy range of motion. This caused him to relax his grip, but he still had Chase across the chest.

Chase brought his own arms up, his hands holding the razors with their blades pointed outward. In one swift motion, he brought his arms down forcefully and dug them deep into big boy's wrists.

Blood flew everywhere as the big boy screamed in pain and surprise, "He cut my fuckin' wrists! You crazy bastard!"

Chase pushed himself away from him and pivoted to reverse his position. He brought his blade up and caught him in the soft, vulnerable meat just under the shelf of his jaw. Chase drove the blade an inch into the flesh and dragged it down brutally through his jugular. When the man's dying heart spurted the blood through the hole in his neck in great, gruesome bursts, Chase spun away, missing the worst of the shower as the big man thudded to the pavement.

His partner was shaken, standing there with his mouth hanging open and his gun shaking in his hand.

Chase was vaguely aware that he was grinning like a lunatic. He advanced on the dead man's friend with a razor in each hand. The temporary survivor shook the willies enough to fire his gun, but his aim was shaky, and Chase was already ducking. The bullet ricocheted off the brick wall behind them, and Chase felt a distant hot pain in the back of his left calf. Chase popped back up in front of him like a spring-loaded psychopath. His left hand plunged the razor into the man's belly and drew it across his body as his right hand slashed his throat. Again Chase twisted out of the spray, but he stumbled and fell in the process. He tried to get to his feet quickly, but the world twirled around him, violently, and spun away. Chase dropped to one knee again and put his throbbing head in his hands.

After a couple of seconds, he managed to make it to his feet, but he teetered and stumbled dangerously to his right, slamming into the side of his bike and knocking it over off its kickstand. His equilibrium was all fucked up. Something dripped into his eye, and he wiped it away with the heel of his hand. It took him almost a full minute to realize that it wasn't sweat, but blood: *his* blood.

His vision began doubling up. *Oh shit! I'm hurt!* He was pissed, because getting hurt was usually reserved for his adversaries. *What'd that nigga hit me with?* Chase crouched against the wall and made himself a smaller target. He looked over at the last guy he'd greased. His intestines were hanging out of his body like some kind of jam-covered party streamers. He saw the gory scene clearly, but when he blinked and looked again, the image doubled, and he knew he was in trouble.

Two blurry sets of legs turned into the alley, and Chase put his hand on Cyrus's gun. If it was somebody looking for trouble, they might find it, even if it was in the form of a blast instead of a razor strike.

"Smoke? You out here?"

Relief washed over Chase when he recognized his little brother's voice. He was glad Corey and J.T. were there, but he was even gladder to know that Corey was okay.

"Corey…" he said. It came out in a whisper that he was sure they couldn't hear.

J.T. stepped over the guy whose guts were hanging out. "Look at *this* shit. He's gotta be here somewhere. Walk careful. Try not to step in the blood, Corey."

"Where you want me to walk, Cyrus? On the fuckin' wall like Spiderman?"

Chase pushed himself to his feet and they stopped talking, drawing their hands reflexively to their weapons. "It's...it's me," Chase squeezed out between the waves of pain in his head. "It's Chase. I'm...I'm here."

The two hurried over to him. Corey looked very worried, and J.T. wasn't exactly the picture of calm. Instinctively, they moved to carry him out, each of them taking one of his arms over his shoulder.

"Wait a minute," Chase said, before he paused and tried to gather his thoughts. They seemed to be doubling over like his vision. "Where's your car, J.T.?"

"I didn't bring it. I rode with Corey. Where are you hurt, Chase?"

Chase reflexively shook his head and was instantly sorry he'd made the simple gesture because Corey and J.T. became four people, then six. His head throbbed, and his knees turned to water. "My head. He hit me in my head. J.T., you gotta take my bike. Get it out of the alley. Corey, you drive." He hoped he was making sense, but his tongue felt thick. "Take me home. I gotta go."

"Screw home. I'm takin' you to the hospital," J.T. said, flatly.

"No!" Chase said, having a hard time pulling his tongue down from the roof of his mouth. *Shit! Am I dying?* If he was, he couldn't say he didn't deserve it. "Home," he said again, and then everything went black.

Chapter 16

When Chase failed to call Bliss by eleven thirty, she put her clothes back on and headed to his place. She'd called his cell so many times that his voicemail was full, even though she was sure he'd turned his phone off. Bliss *never* got Chase's voicemail more than once, and he usually called her right back. She was so worried about him that she couldn't be still. When she got to his place, she let herself into his loft with her key and sat at the breakfast bar, watching the elevator, but she didn't have enough patience to do that for long.

She got up and went to the bedroom. The shirt he'd been wearing earlier was still on the bed. Bliss took her own blouse off and put on Chase's shirt. It smelled like him, and she inhaled deeply as she closed her eyes and pulled the collar up. Bliss had only known Chase for three months, but he'd already left an indelible mark on her heart. She loved him strong and hard, and if he left her, it would be the end of her.

She climbed into his bed with her clothes—and some of his—on. She put her head on his pillow and pulled the covers up. Silent tears ran down her face. *Where is he? Why won't he call me back?* She curled into a ball and started praying for him—praying for *them*.

She was starting to drift off when she heard the garage door going up, and Bliss was on her feet at once. She ran into the next room and stood by the breakfast bar with her heart slamming in her chest.

The garage door went back down right away, but it took the elevator so long to get upstairs that she was about to press the button to go down herself, just when the door slid open. Bliss was totally unprepared for what lay behind those doors. It pushed the breath out of her body and made her so lightheaded that she thought she might pass out. She backed up with her hands over her mouth to hold the scream in.

Corey and J.T. had Chase between them, his arms over their shoulders and hanging back limply. Their arms were under his knees, holding him off the floor in a sitting position. It was obvious he couldn't walk. His head was lolled back so far that she could clearly see the scar under his jaw, and his face was turned away. He was unconscious, too, but the worst part was all the blood.

Most of it was dry, a putrid rusty brown color, but some of it was still bright red and moist. It was like some abstract painter had a bucket of it, dipped his brush, and just started splashing Chase like a goddamned canvas. It looked like he'd been *wrestling* in it. It was on his shirt, his pants, his gloves...even grimed into the bottoms of his goddamned sneakers! There were chains hanging off his jeans that hadn't been there earlier, and Bliss wondered briefly what they were.

Bliss, J.T., and Corey stared at each other silently for a moment before Corey said, "Uh..." for lack of anything else to say. It wasn't the best thing to utter, but it broke everyone's paralysis.

J.T. actually smiled at Bliss. "I'm not gonna fill your head up with bullshit, Bliss. Could you step aside, please, and let us put him in his room? Once we put him down, I'll come back and talk to you. You got my word on that, girl."

Bliss nodded with her hands still over her mouth.

J.T. smiled again. "Maybe you can make us some coffee? I got a feeling we'll be up all night."

Bliss nodded and stared at Chase as they brought him past her, with Corey avoiding her eyes. He had blood in his hair and down the left side of his face. His eyes were slightly open, revealing the crisp, whiskey-colored irises. The one on the right was surrounded by white, but the one on the left was completely bloodshot. Bliss gasped involuntarily as she watched them take her lover into the bedroom. *What happened to him?* It was obvious he'd been hit in the head, but all that blood! *Was he shot? Is all that blood even his? It can't be! Oh my God...is he...dead? Damn close to it? Who did this to my Chase?* The questions raged on in her head, but she knew it would be a minute before she got any answers. She sat on the sectional and put her face in her hands for a moment to calm herself. She went back to what she'd been doing earlier: praying for him—praying and trying to tamp down her anger. She was angry at him for going to that stupid opening in the first place and for getting hurt like she was afraid he would. She was angry at J.T. and Corey for bringing him home instead of taking him to a hospital, where he so obviously belonged. She stood up, so scared and angry she couldn't stop shaking. *Fuck sitting here, and fuck getting coffee like a good little woman! I'm going back there to see what the hell's going on, and I am calling a fucking ambulance.*

"Take care of his clothes, Corey...and run a bath. I'll be right back," J.T. said, stepping out of the room just as Bliss was going in. He gave her a charming smile and slipped an arm around her shoulders, efficiently turning her in the other direction. Bliss tried to look over her shoulder into the bedroom, but J.T. kept her moving and seated her at the breakfast bar. He leaned on it and looked her in the eye. "You okay?"

She wanted to hit him. *What the hell kind of question is that?* She was shaken up, and she stood up to tell him so. "What do you think, J.T.? What happened to Chase? Why isn't he in the hospital? Why did you bring him back here and leave him in his room with Dr. Corey?"

J.T. laughed and started making coffee. "Dr. Corey? That's funny," he said, shaking his head.

Bliss came around the counter at him. "That's *not* funny, J.T. He could be in there dying! He's got a goddamned head wound! What are you and Corey, stupid? You're not supposed to be moving someone with a head wound around like that!" She stomped her foot and pushed him. "You get your ass in there and take him to the hospital. *Right now, J.T.!*" she screamed at him.

J.T. looked at her calmly. "Sit down, Bliss. If you calm down, I'll talk to you, but otherwise, I'm not saying a word. I've been aggravated enough for one evening." He stared at her until she complied, even though she did it with major attitude. J.T. sat beside her and looked at her sympathetically. "I know you're upset, Bliss, but we've got a situation here. Before he passed out, Chase told us to take him home, so that's what we did." He paused. "I think it makes sense."

Bliss frowned. "What are you not telling me, J.T.?"

He shrugged. "Nothing. Tonight was a bad night. Wolf sent his boys to Cyrus's club to take us out, and we didn't let them."

Bliss rolled her eyes at him as she put the coffee on. "Looks like they almost took Chase out. Where were you and Corey when they did this to him?"

"We were handling our business, Bliss, and Chase was handling his. I can guarantee you that blow to his head was a rare and extremely lucky thing for them." J.T. was looking at her steadily, but Bliss was still frowning.

"What are those chains on his jeans?"

J.T. frowned and smiled at the same time. "What chains, Bliss?"

Bliss turned her head and looked at him sideways. "Okay, J.T. I guess it would be stupid of me to assume all that blood is his, right?"

J.T. shrugged and eyed her gently. "I don't know, Bliss"

They stared at each other for a long moment. Bliss wasn't stupid. There *was* one thing she could give all of them credit for, especially Chase. She could not remember any lies. She took a deep breath and stood up, letting it out slowly, and tears filled her eyes. "Oh," she said quietly.

J.T. was watching her like she might flip out any minute. "It is what it is, Bliss. Looks like you've got to make a decision."

Bliss caught a flashback of Chase looking down at her and asking—no, *daring* her—to jump of the cliff with him. She smiled through her tears and shook her head. "There's no decision to make, J.T. If I left him, I'd die…and so would he. *I can't.* That's out of the question." She folded her arms across her chest and sighed shakily. "How bad is it? Did he hurt somebody tonight?"

J.T. shrugged again. "I have no idea. We weren't together all night, and at one point I got a little busy."

She nodded. It was very close to what she'd figured he'd say, and she looked at him knowingly. "You're not gonna give him up, are you? Even to me?"

He smiled at her. "Never in this lifetime, Bliss. He's been my best friend since we were eight years old."

Bliss was touched, but there was a lot of shit going on. "I can understand and respect that, J.T. Let me ask you a question you *can* answer. Did *you* hurt anybody tonight?"

J.T. laughed and shook his head. "Don't, Bliss. You know I'm gonna plead the Fifth on that one."

"What are you guys, gangsters?"

He laughed again and went to the coffeemaker. "Nope. We're just businessmen. Cyrus though? Maybe."

Bliss frowned. "Where *is* Cyrus?"

J.T. shrugged his broad shoulders again. "Don't know, don't care. I'm sure we'll be hearing from his stupid ass shortly though."

Bliss sat back down. "This is all his fault, isn't it?"

J.T. nodded. "Yes, yes it is."

"I think I hate him."

He laughed and poured coffee. "Join the club, darlin'. We all hate Cyrus—well, everybody except for Corey."

As if he'd heard his name, Corey came out of the bedroom carrying a package tightly wrapped in duct tape under his arm. "I got everything, J.T. He's ready for the tub."

J.T. stood up. "Did he wake up?"

Corey shook his head, looking worried. "Kinda, but not really. He sort of opened his eyes and was movin' around a little, but he went right back out."

Bliss raised an eyebrow. Those fools could sit here fucking around if they wanted to, but she wasn't about to have Chase lying there with no help. *Fuck them and whatever they had to say about it.* She went to her bag and took out her cell phone.

Corey came across the room real fast, holding his hand out to stop her. "Whoa! Whoa, Mama! Who you callin'? Put the phone down, Bliss."

When he reached for her phone, Bliss held it away from her and put her hand on his chest. "Don't you come at me, Corey! You two are not doing anything! You can't just let him lie there like that. He needs a doctor…and I fucking know one." She looked at J.T. "I'm calling Tasha. It's our blind luck that she's a neurologist. One of you is gonna go get her, and I'm gonna go in there and take care of my man. *I'm* making *this* decision, and I don't want to hear shit about it."

Corey frowned up. "*You* make the decision? You sound like his wife or somethin'."

Bliss smirked at him. "Yeah, well, get used to it, Corey…because I *will* be."

J.T. laughed and clapped his hands. "Now that's what I'm talkin' about. *Ride or die, Bliss!* Make the call, and I'll go get your girl."

Bliss called Tasha, whose only complaint was that she was pulled out of sleep in the middle of the night. J.T. left to get her, and Bliss and Corey went together to Chase's bedroom.

When they got there, Chase wasn't in his bed. They glanced at each other and followed the path he'd left with one bloody footprint; it led to the bathroom. They found him on the floor of the shower, kneeling with his hands against the wall. The cold water was on full blast, raining down on him. Chase's teeth were chattering, and blood swirled down the drain from a wound on his calf.

Bliss stepped into the shower, fully clothed, without a second thought, and turned the hot water on until the water was warm. She got on her knees next to him and put her arm around his shoulders. "Baby, it's me. It's Bliss."

He opened his eyes and smiled at her. "Hey, baby."

Bliss smiled back and kissed his cheek. "I got you, Chase. Don't worry, it's gonna be okay. Can you stand up?"

He closed his eyes and frowned, then he stood, slowly, never taking his hands away from the wall. "I'm okay. I can't let go of the wall, though, 'cause the room is spinning."

Bliss let go of him long enough to push her hair out of her eyes. "Okay. You hold on to the wall and I'll clean you up. You think you can handle that, or do you want Corey to step in here and help us?"

He frowned and blinked. "He's in here?" He started to turn around, but that would have meant letting go of the wall. "Get outta here, Corey," he said. There was a smile in his voice that didn't quite make it to his lips.

"Fuck *that!* I'm makin' popcorn. You all right, Chase?"

"No, but I'm not unconscious."

"That's a start. Holler if you need me," Corey said before he stepped out of the bathroom and left them alone.

Bliss started to soap him up. "I called Tasha. J.T. is going to get her."

He smiled at her. "You did that for me?"

She squatted to wash his calf and took a moment to look at the wound. It was a really bad graze, but it was obvious it had been made by a bullet. Bliss sucked her teeth. "There's not very much I wouldn't do for you, Chase." She paused to look at him. "You better not bring your ass back in here shot and knocked out ever again though. I'm not playing with you!" she shouted at him.

Chase took one hand off the wall and reached for hers. "Bliss…"

She was crying again. She knocked his hand away and kept doing what she was doing. "*No*, Chase. There's nothing you can say to me right now to keep me from being mad at you, so don't even try. Just be quiet." She stood back up and put her hands on his face. "Bend over so I can look at that gash in your head."

Chase looked at her for a moment, then did as he was told.

Bliss cleaned and inspected it as best as she could. She was gentle, but she knew it had to hurt, even if Chase didn't let on like it did. She got him out of the shower and into the bedroom and dried him off. Working together, they managed to get him dressed in a pair of comfortable pajama bottoms.

Bliss took her soaked clothes off and put on one of his T-shirts and a pair of his sweat pants. She was brushing her hair when Corey knocked on the door.

"Hey…Tasha's here."

"Okay!" Bliss called back. She pulled a T-shirt carefully over Chase's head.

"What's this for?"

Bliss smiled. "That's for Tasha."

Chase looked at her funny. "She's a doctor, Bliss."

"She's a *woman*, Chase, and I don't want her looking at you like that. You're real cute, you know…and she already told me more than once how fine you are."

He laughed. "Yeah? Right now I'm not."

"Still cute as hell to me." She kissed his forehead and went to the door.

Tasha walked in with J.T. and Corey in tow. She was carrying a small Prada train case. "Hey, Bliss. Has he passed out again since he woke up?"

Bliss shook her head. "No. I gave him a shower. Maybe that kept him up?"

Tasha sat on the bed and opened her case. "I doubt it." She took out a small pen light and smiled at Chase. "How you doin', slugger? Feel okay? Gotta throw up? Do you know who I am?"

Chase leaned back against the pillows and looked at her. "Yeah, you're Tasha. I don't think I'm missin' anything, but you are a little blurry."

She got up and shined her light in his eyes. "Damn. Whoever hit you didn't mean for you to get up. You better be glad your head is so hard." She stepped back, squirted hand sanitizer on her hands, then slipped on rubber gloves. She thoroughly examined his skull, looking in his eyes again and also in his ears. She looked at the wound and went into her case. "I'm gonna have to close that up. Hope you're not squeamish."

Chase smiled. "Nope. I wouldn't say I am."

Tasha smirked and picked up her case. "I figured as much. Let's go in the kitchen, and I'll sew you up." Once everything was set up in the kitchen like a makeshift doctor's office, Tasha cleaned his wound properly and shot lydacaine into his scalp.

J.T. winced. "Damn, Chase. You want a drink?"

Tasha laughed and threaded her little curved needle. "He can't have one. I'm gonna give him something for the pain that's gonna put him out."

Chase shook his head slowly. "That's okay. I don't want it."

Tasha looked at him sternly. "Well, too bad, cause you're taking it. Why don't you want it? You plan on runnin' out and gettin' back at whoever it was that parted your scalp?"

Chase looked at the floor. "I ain't gotta worry about him."

Tasha looked at him for a moment, then turned to J.T. "*Okay.* I'll take a double of whatever you were gonna give him." She took her time and sewed him up, while Bliss and Corey sat at the breakfast bar and J.T. leaned over Chase and watched her handiwork with a great deal of interest. She finished with a flourish and winked at J.T.

"Nice work, Doc," he said, smiling at her.

Tasha smiled back and looked him over. "Thanks, but that's not the best I can do."

J.T. returned the look. "I'll just bet it's not. You flirtin' with me, Tasha?"

"I'm tryin'."

Corey got up impatiently and raised the leg on Chase's pants. "Well, before y'all get your freak on, could you take a look at this?"

Tasha rolled her eyes at Corey, but she looked at Chase's leg. "Damn, negro! You managed to get yourself shot too?"

"It's just a graze."

She looked at him at him seriously. "Yeah, but it almost wasn't." She cleaned it and dressed it and then gave him a shot of antibiotics.

"Thanks, Tasha," Chase said as she gave him another shot—a painkiller.

She looked at him dubiously with her hand on her hip. "You're a lucky guy, Chase. You could have gotten yourself killed tonight."

Chase blinked at her, and his mouth dropped open a little. "What did you just do?" He slumped in his seat like somebody had hit him.

Bliss got up and went to him and put her hands on his face.

Tasha looked unfazed. "I just gave you something for the pain, that's all."

Chase stood up suddenly, knocking Bliss's hands away. He teetered a little, and J.T. grabbed him and held him steady.

"Honey, what's wrong?" Bliss asked, surprised by his reaction and the panic on his face.

For once, Chase ignored her. He turned his head and talked to Tasha. "Don't think I don't appreciate your help, Tasha. I do. I just wish you could have waited on that. I don't need to be feeling like this right now."

J.T. patted his back. "It's okay, Chase. Me and Corey ain't goin' nowhere. You got time to get yourself together."

Tasha looked at Bliss. "You want me to stay? He's got a pretty nasty concussion. Whether I stay or not, I want to see him in my office in the morning."

Bliss nodded. "Yeah, if you can stay, that'd be great. I'm sorry, Tasha."

Tasha smiled at her. "Fuck sorry. I'm your friend. Take your man to bed and watch him. You see anything strange, hear any strange breathing, you holler, okay?"

"Thanks, Tasha." Chase slurred, but he walked to the bedroom under his own power.

Bliss got him settled into bed with two pillows under his head. She snuggled in close to him and closed her eyes.

Chase startled her when he spoke because she thought he was asleep. "I'm sorry for this, Bliss. I'm really sorry."

She turned over on her back and looked at him in the moonlight. He was frowning hard. She touched his face. "What happened tonight, Chase?"

"I...I can't tell you. It was something I don't want to think about, but I'm sorry to you, Bliss, and I couldn't really stop it from happening."

Bliss frowned. He *could have* stopped it. He didn't have to go. He could have stayed right there with her, and she told him as much.

Chase held her close, and she didn't pull away. She couldn't have if she'd wanted to. "I *had* to go, Bliss. I know you don't understand, and I don't really expect you to…" He sounded like he was drifting off, but he was talking, and Bliss wanted to hear what he had to say.

"You didn't have to do whatever it was that you did tonight, Chase." She said it quietly, with a great amount of reproach in her voice.

Chase put his face very close to hers, like he was trying hard to see her in the dark. He said her name with a sigh and put his cheek to hers. "I had to do that, too, Bliss. I *had* to. They were gonna kill me, and I couldn't let that happen, could I? I had to save myself, Bliss. I had to save me for *you*. I had to save me for *us*."

Bliss frowned, but she held him tighter. "I don't know what you did, and I don't really want to know. You better stop this nonsense though. We can't change what already happened, but you damned sure can stop doing whatever it is that you do."

"It's not that easy, Bliss."

Bliss sat up, and he sat up with her. She reached over and flicked on the light. She looked him in the eye. "Do you love me like you say you do, Chase?"

He frowned. "Of course I do. How could you question that?"

She put her hand on his cheek. "I'm not, baby, but I've got a feeling you've got a side to you that I never want to see. What were those chains on your jeans, Chase? Sweetheart, I'm looking at you now, and sure, you've got a pretty good gash in your scalp and a decent-sized wound on your leg, but Chase…neither one of those injuries justifies all that blood you had on you—neither one of them."

He tried to turn his face away, but Bliss wouldn't let him. He stayed where she kept him, but he cast his eyes down and wouldn't look at her.

She remembered the way he'd looked when he came in—all that blood—and she shuddered. Bliss felt delayed hysteria trying to creep in and pushed it back. "I don't think you just got in a fight, Chase."

He wouldn't look at her and wouldn't comment.

"Are the police looking for you? Do they have a reason to?"

"I doubt it," he said quietly. He looked at her, and his eyes were tremendously sad. "You gonna walk away now, Bliss?"

Bliss smiled in spite of the horror of the night. "It's a little late for that. I don't want to live without you."

He smiled. "You still gonna marry me? You promised, you know."

Bliss smiled back at him. "I don't have a choice. I'm in love with you...in spite of all this."

He kissed her with a soft, sweet kiss. "I love you, Bliss."

"I love you, too, but you've got to make me a promise, Chase."

He kissed her again. "I'll promise you anything, Bliss."

She kissed him back, but she looked at him skeptically. "I want you to mean it, Chase."

He smiled. It wasn't really a happy smile but was more like a resigned one. "If you haven't noticed by now, I mean just about everything I do."

Bliss shook her head. "Not when it comes to Cyrus. You're too torn when it comes to him. Chase, *why*? All this shit is his fault. I know he's your brother and you love him as such, but you're going to have to mean what you said. We have to get away from him. Cyrus is a destroyer, Chase. One thing I know to be true is that you two don't get along, yet you're always doing something for him. What the hell does Cyrus ever do for you? You're either always upset after you see him, or else you're fighting him. *Leave him alone, baby!* He's like poison to you. You have to promise me that you'll do what you said and step away from him."

Chase stared at her for a long time that Bliss almost shook him to see if he was still conscious. He finally sighed heavily and piled the pillows up. Chase leaned back against them and looked at her. "I promise you, Bliss, but I've gotta warn you." He took her hand and held it tight. "A lot of things happened tonight—bad, story-at-eleven kinds of things. If there are reprisals, I might not have a choice but to answer them, and not because of Cyrus or Corey or even my own ego, but because I have to stay safe." He looked into her eyes. "Do you understand what I'm sayin' to you, Bliss? I *want* to do what I need to do to make you happy, but I need you to know that there are a lot of extenuating circumstances that might require me to go back on my word. I told you before that I'll never lie to you unless it's an absolute necessity, so I'm letting you know now, just in case this shit spirals out of control."

"It's already out of control, Chase. Look at you! I thought you were *dead* when they brought you in here." Her voice was rising, and tears slipped down her cheeks.

Chase pulled her to him and she straddled his lap, facing him. He rubbed her back and whispered in her ear, "It's okay, baby. I'm right here…and I'm fine."

She leaned back and looked at him. "What if you weren't, Chase? *What am I supposed to do without you?*"

He smiled his boyish smile at her and wiped the tears off her cheeks with her thumbs. "I'll do my best to make sure you never find out." He kissed her, and when he pulled away, he had a mischievous sparkle in his eyes.

Bliss frowned. "What?"

"Since I gotta keep my promise, you gotta keep yours."

She smiled at him coyly, knowing exactly what he was talking about, but deciding to play dumb. "Yeah? What promise is that, Chase?"

Chase ran his hands up her thighs and let them come to rest on her hips.

Bliss raised an eyebrow and smiled. She had no idea what was in that last shot Tasha gave him or how bad his head was still hurting, but she knew neither one of them had any effect on his libido. She didn't think he should be thinking about making love under the influence of injury and all that medication, and she didn't want him hurt any more than he already was, but when she tried to get up, he held her where she was.

Chase smiled at her. "Where you goin', Bliss? I was talkin' to you."

"I'm listening, baby, but I don't think it's a good idea for you to get too physical just yet."

Chase laughed and moved against her, causing a ripple of goose bumps to break out on her skin as he put his arms lovingly around her neck "I ain't too hurt for that."

Bliss giggled and kissed him quick. She was so glad he was okay. "I do love you."

"I know you do, and I hope you know how much I love you." He paused just long enough to slip his pants down and get in. Bliss sighed and started to move with him, and Chase smiled. "I could spend the rest of my life right here, Bliss—right here, just loving you. Would you mind? Would you let me?"

Bliss loved the feel of him. "You know I would. I love you, Chase. I can't help myself."

He laughed lewdly. "Why would you want to? You feel this? *This* is bliss, baby."

Bliss blushed and closed her eyes. When she opened them, Chase was looking at her as serious as she'd ever seen him look.

"I can't help myself either. Keep your promise, Bliss. Marry me."

There was no fight left in her. She was done dodging him and evading the issue. "When?"

"Saturday after next. We'll go away and get married somewhere almost as pretty as you."

Bliss nodded. She didn't care where they made their vows. Wherever it was, she'd be there with him by her side, and she'd be ecstatic. "Okay, Chase."

He kissed her and turned her over on her back. "I'm serious, Bliss. Saturday after next, somewhere nice. Don't say okay. Say *yes*."

Bliss wrapped her legs around him as he wore down the absolute last of her reservations. How could she possibly go through the rest of her life without ever being with Chase? It was too much to ask. It was impossible. Her body started to hum. "Yes. Yes I'll be there. I'll be your wife. I will. I promise, Chase!"

Chase was sliding into her deliciously. "Good. We'll get your ring day after tomorrow." He covered her mouth with his, and they came together. It was sweet and tender, full of love and passion. Chase held her close and whispered words of love in her ear, and both of them fell asleep in each other's arms, not thinking of the horrors of the night, but of the promise of love in their future.

G STREET CHRONICLES
A NEW URBAN DYNASTY
WWW.GSTREETCHRONICLES.COM

Chapter 17

Cyrus couldn't believe the shit had gone down like that. It was a fucking disaster, and it was all over the fucking news—even in the goddamned paper! He'd managed to dodge them so far, but the cops were looking for him hard because he owned the club where all hell broke loose. Cyrus smirked and swirled his Hennessey. The irony of having ultimately named the club Eternal wasn't lost on him. He should have named that shit Five Fuckin' Minutes since that was as long as it lasted. He sipped his Hennessey slow. It was hair of the dog. He was so hung over, he felt like there was a tiny man with a hammer inside of his head. The Hennessey was helping a little, but he still felt sick.

Cyrus looked over at Khalid. He knew he didn't really have a choice than to be where they were. They had to go somewhere out of the heat, so they were currently at Khalid's sister's house in Staten Island. Khalid was sprawled on the couch, looking like he was getting sick from that shot to the shoulder.

His sister Khadijah was trying to clean the wound. It wasn't bleeding like it had been, but it still looked nasty. She bandaged it and stood up. "That's the best I can do. There's a bullet in there, and I'm not 'bout to dig my fingers in there to find it. It'll do more harm than good. When the hell is your friend gonna get here?"

Cyrus shrugged. "Hopefully soon."

He'd sent one of his boys to fetch a dude named Monty, who'd served in Iraq as a medic and was pretty good at picking bullets out of niggas. They'd used him many times before with no casualties.

Khadijah sucked her teeth. "You don't seem too concerned."

Cyrus sipped his drink and looked out the window. "Everything's gonna be fine. You think I could get somethin' to eat?"

She sucked her teeth again. "If you want something delivered, be my guest, but I ain't cookin' for you, Cyrus. I'd rather die."

He looked over his shoulder at her. "No need for all that. Mind your manners, Khadijah."

She rolled her eyes at him. "You're in *my* house. I think you need to mind *yours*."

Cyrus watched her walk out of the room, mad like it was all *his* fault. He turned his drink up and finished it. It *wasn't* his fault! *It's fuckin' Chase's fault! All of it! This is just one more thing to hate his ass for!* If his hard-headed ass had only greased Wolf when he told him to, none of this shit would have happened. This was becoming common with Chase, instead of doing what he was *supposed* to, that nigga had done what he *wanted* to and let enough time pass for Wolf to come after Cyrus. Did he kill him then? *No.* That clown killed Mooch and Post. Of course, it was for get-back, but all he'd succeeded in doing by taking out them niggas was making the situation worse.

The killing spree at the club last night was worse still. That was Wolf's brother with his guts splashed across that alley, and that was one of his top enforcers with his wrists split. Cyrus frowned and scratched his chin. He was *still* trying to figure out how Chase had managed that one. He heard through the grapevine that nigga looked like he'd committed suicide.

The doorbell rang, and Khalid opened his eyes. "Who the fuck is that?" he whispered gruffly, reaching down in the cushions for his gun.

Cyrus put a hand on his arm to restrain him. "Chill, man. It's probably Monty…or maybe it's Corey." He'd left Corey's tired ass a voicemail telling him where to find him, even though he didn't seem to give enough of a fuck about him to look for him in the first place.

When Cyrus had asked him where *he* was, Corey had shucked and jived him at first, then admitted he was at Chase's place, holed up with him. "Fuck them both," Cyrus had said. "Fuck 'em hard for not even comin' to see about me." Cyrus smiled. He knew how to lay it on extra thick when he had to. He could slather on more guilt than a Jewish grandmother, and he always managed to make Corey's ass fold right up. Chase used to fold pretty easy himself, but now he refused to bend, and that was the main problem that was causing all this shit.

Khadijah walked back into the room with Corey and—surprise, surprise!—J.T. and Chase. "Your little brothers are here to pull your fat out of the fire…again," she said sternly.

Cyrus looked at her sharply. "I'm tired of tellin' you about that mouth of yours, Khadijah."

Khalid sat up painfully. "Leave her alone, Cy. She didn't have to let us in here."

Cyrus looked at Corey, singling him out on purpose. "Nice of you to come, Corey. 'Course, if I'd been shot, I'd probably be dead by now waitin' on your sorry black ass."

Corey looked at the floor, but J.T. rubbed his chin thoughtfully and sat down next to Khalid. "I don't know about that, Cyrus." He looked Khalid up and down comically. "This nigger's shot, and he's still livin'. How long do you think he might stay that way with no doctor, huh?"

Cyrus looked at J.T. darkly. He hated J.T. with a passion.

J.T. stared back just as dark because he hated Cyrus just as much, if not more. "You gonna let him get septic shock and die just because you care too much about your own ass to save your boy? That's some fucked-up, selfish, shit, Cyrus."

"Well…we didn't take Chase to the hospital," Corey chimed in quietly.

Cyrus's eyebrow went up. *Didn't take him to the hospital?* He bit back a smile. *Did Chase—the almighty Smoke—almost get his wings clipped?* He looked over at Chase, whose actual appearance hadn't sunk in yet. Chase was standing very quietly in the corner with his arms folded across his chest, dressed in his "work clothes," black from head to toe. He was even sporting a black Yankees cap and a really nice, really dark pair of shades.

"What happened to you?"

Chase took off his shades and his cap. There was blood in the white of one eye and a nice little line of stitches in his scalp. "I got hit in the head."

Cyrus had very rarely seen Chase hurt, so he was understandably a little shocked. But he also found it hilarious. It was all he could do to keep from laughing with satisfaction. Good for his ass. "I know whoever did that paid for that shit."

Chase smiled a cold little grin. "He bled out."

Cyrus poured himself another drink. "I believe you." He took a sip of his drink and looked at Chase with that same dark look he'd given J.T. "Anyway, I'm not supposed to be talkin' to you. What the *fuck* could you possibly want? Did you come here to try and kick my ass again?"

Chase laughed dangerously, but his eyes refused to smile. "I didn't *try* to kick your ass, Cyrus. I *did* kick your ass. For the record, I really don't want see to your helpless wannabe gangster ass, either."

Cyrus's mouth flew open, and he started spewing venom. *Who did this nigga think he was fuckin' with?* "Wannabe gangster? You ungrateful little shit! Who you raisin' up to? If it wasn't for me, who knows what would have happened to your crazy ass! What do I get from you? Disrespect and insubordination. I shoulda smothered your ass while you were still in your fuckin' crib! All you've ever given me has been grief and more grief—for your whole damn life. You've *always* been difficult. You never just fell in line. All this shit is your fault! You call me helpless? Well, I guess I am, 'cause I don't get any damn help from *you*, do I? Look at the fuckin' mess you made, you worthless son of a bitch!"

Chase was looking down with his lips tucked in. Cyrus knew he'd hurt him, because he refused to make eye contact. *Go ahead and cry, you little bitch.*

Corey stepped in front of Cyrus and put his hand on his arm. "Hey,

Cyrus, don't do this. Chase came to help you."

Cyrus sneered and swigged down the rest of his drink. "Help me? He ain't *been* helpin' me. You want to help me *now*? After all this shit? Well, fuck you, Smoke! Take your help and go fuck yourself."

"Wait a minute, Cy," Khalid said from the couch.

"Fuck him. We don't need his ass."

"Cyrus, stop," Corey said.

"I ain't gotta kiss his high-handed ass, Corey, and I can say whatever I want. I was damned near grown when you niggas *met* me. What you gonna do, Smoke? Pull your razor out on me? Go ahead, 'cause if you ever step to me again, I'm gonna put a bullet in your goddamned forehead."

Chase's head popped up, and his eyes twinkled. He was smiling.

Corey's eyes pleaded with his brother. "Cut it out, Cyrus. You must be drunk. Stop this shit."

Cyrus noticed that J.T. had retreated to stand at Chase's elbow. Yeah, maybe he *was* a little drunk, but he had a fucking reason to be. He was furious at Chase for letting that shit get out of hand. He looked at Chase with his glittering eyes and icy grin, and then he put his glass down and pulled his gun out of his waistband. "I meant what I said, Smoke. You can stand there and glitter and shine all you like, but you come at me to kick my ass and I ain't fightin' your crazy ass. I'm puttin' a hole in you."

Chase didn't move a muscle, but he never stopped smiling.

"Put the gun away, Cyrus," J.T. said in a low voice.

"*Please* put the gun away," Corey echoed.

Cyrus looked at Khalid, who was watching him like he was holding his breath and cautiously shaking his head slowly from left to right. Cyrus touched his nose; that shit would never be the same, thanks to Chase. He hated his punk ass. He always had, and there was no need to pretend it was something it wasn't. He didn't put his gun away but held it with the business end pointed toward the floor and poured himself another drink. He sipped it and looked back at his little brother. "So what do you want, Chase?" Cyrus was far from stupid. Chase was so angry at him that he was almost shaking.

That smile had become quivery, but he hadn't moved an inch. Cyrus smiled. Chase was showing amazing self-control. If he hadn't been, Cyrus would have been on the floor trying to keep his blood in his body from the first moment he started talking shit. A frown had replaced the glittery look in his eyes, though, and he seemed to be looking everywhere at once. Chase flexed his hands, and Cyrus raised his gun, knowing he was fucking up bad. *Nobody* pulled a gun on Chase; that was the very reason he'd killed Herc Mercer.

Chase surprised him when he laughed and started pulling his gloves up on his hands. "I don't believe your stupid, careless ass just pulled a gun on me, Cyrus." Chase pulled the zipper up on his jacket. It was too warm for it, but he always wore on when he greased someone. "First, you talk to me like I'm a fuckin' animal and then you show your weapon. You know how I feel about that shit."

"Oh God, Chase. Please let it go! Cyrus just ain't thinkin' straight. Let's just go take care of Wolf like you came here to do," Corey pleaded.

"Nah, I don't think that's how this is gonna play out, Corey." He turned his attention back to his gun-wielding brother. "You really pullin' a damn gun on *me*, Cyrus?" Chase asked again before he started toward Cyrus from where he'd been standing just inside the living room.

Cyrus raised his gun and leveled it. "One more step, Smoke, and I'm pullin' the trigger."

Chase stopped where he was and smiled at him; it was a crazy smile. "You really gonna shoot me, Cyrus?"

Cyrus didn't answer. He just kept his gun level and picked up the Hennessey bottle. He took a swig and winced at the burn. "I don't really *want* to, Chase, but I think we're entering the phase of our relationship where I just fuckin' might."

"Cyrus, please stop!" Corey was begging now.

Cyrus turned on Corey. "You know…you're an irritating little motherfucker, Corey. Stop beggin' us to get along okay? The shit ain't gonna happen." Cyrus was aware that he was starting to slur his words, but he took a short swig of Hennessey anyway. *Fuck it now.*

The liquor burned as it went down, but it boosted his bravery. Cyrus pointed his gun from Chase to Corey. "You're pushin' your luck with me, too, you closed-mouth little bastard. You can get some too."

Hurt and disbelief washed over Corey's face, as Chase stepped in front of him and pushed Corey firmly behind him.

"What's the matter with you, Cyrus?" Chase demanded.

Cyrus resented even the sound of his brother's voice. "Shut up!" he said and pulled the trigger of his nine.

The bullet hit Chase dead center in the chest, the force of it knocking him backward into Corey.

"Oh my God," J.T. said in a very quiet voice as he rushed at Cyrus and grabbed the gun out of his hand. J.T. had it pointed at him before Cyrus could finish blinking. "Chase?" he called out to his friend.

Chase had taken Corey down with him, and Corey started bawling as he held Chase in his arms and tried to check for him. "Oh no! God no! Cyrus, what did you do? What did you fuckin' do to our brother, man?"

"Oh shit, Cy! What the fuck, man?" This came from Khalid in a raspy, injured voice.

Khadijah appeared in the doorway, shocked into speechlessness, with her mouth hanging open.

"Chase! Holler at me, or I'm gonna blow this nigger away! You all right?" J.T. yelled.

Chase's face was contorted in pain, and he was clutching the front of his jacket in both fists like he was going to rip it off. His breath was whistling in and out like he was having an asthma attack.

Cyrus watched Chase as he pushed away from Corey and struggled to his knees. He was unmoved. He lackadaisically took another swig out of the bottle and sat down next to Khalid, not really caring that J.T. now had his own gun pointed at him. He didn't know what everyone was so upset about. Everyone there knew how Chase usually handled his business.

Chase made it to his knees, unzipped his jacket, and pulled his T-shirt up. He looked down at the bullet embedded in the Kevlar, with a total look of shock on his face.

Cyrus smiled; he was about 99.9 percent certain Chase would be wearing a vest. He'd been hoping there was some small chance he wasn't, but it *was* there.

"Oh thank God!" Corey said and helped Chase to his feet.

Chase held the vest away from his chest like it was hot. He was standing, but he couldn't get his breath back. He dropped back to his knees against his will and hugged his chest.

Cyrus smirked. *That shit must've really hurt. Good.*

Corey hovered over him indecisively.

"Don't stand over him like that, Corey. He just got the wind knocked out of him, that's all. He'll be all right in a minute," Cyrus said.

Khalid looked at Cyrus and shook his head.

Cyrus shrugged. *Whatever.*

"If I were you, I wouldn't be sittin' there lookin' so unconcerned. I might be thinkin' about tryin' to get my ass anywhere Chase is *not* right about now."

Cyrus had to think that maybe it was a good idea.

Chase gasped loudly and finally got up under his own power. He pointed his finger at Cyrus. "I can't believe you took it there, Cyrus."

Cyrus stood up and shrugged again. "You took it there first."

"That's a lie."

Cyrus was a little shocked when Chase didn't come at him. In fact, he wouldn't even look at him. He just brushed past Khadijah and left the apartment, and he didn't even slam the door on his way out.

J.T. clicked the safety on and handed him his gun. "You reap what you sow, Cyrus."

"You can shut up, too, J.T."

Corey moved to leave with J.T.

"Where you goin', Corey?" When he asked the question, Cyrus received the most malignant look he'd ever gotten from his youngest brother.

"Chase was right about you, Cyrus," said Corey as he walked out right behind Chase.

Khalid looked at Cyrus like he'd just thrown a major piece of his machinery. "That shit was wrong, Cy…and damn stupid."

Cyrus took another swig of Hennessey. "I know," he said, and then he sat back on the sofa with Khalid and waited for Monty to come.

G STREET CHRONICLES
~A NEW URBAN DYNASTY~

WWW.GSTREETCHRONICLES.COM

Chapter 18

Chase's chest was on fire. He thought it would have subsided by now, and in a way it had. It wasn't a bright, hot, pain anymore; it had ebbed into a dull burn. He frowned. It felt like...like he'd been shot in the fucking chest.

Whenever Chase went on a run to take someone out—someone like Wolf—he usually wore a Kevlar vest, because he knew people like Wolf usually weren't alone when he snuffed them. People like Wolf usually had at least two enforcers watching their asses real hard. Sometimes that made it difficult to get in, but Chase was tenacious, and he always found a way. It was a good thing he'd worn the vest this time, or else he'd have been pushing up daisies.

He winced, and not just from the pain. He knew a shot like that would leave one hell of a bruise, and he wasn't in a big hurry to find out what Bliss was going to say about that. He was going back on his word to her already, but he was doing it for a damned good reason—and that reason wasn't Cyrus.

In spite of his issues with Cyrus, he was still going to take Wolf out. After all, he'd never lived his life looking over his shoulder, and he damned sure wasn't going to have Bliss, Corey, and J.T. looking over theirs. He'd done enough damage at the club—and especially in that alley—to make Wolf feel the need to exact some serious retribution.

Chase was not about to lie in the cut and wait till he was ambushed. He wasn't going to give Wolf time to plot and scheme. Instead, he'd find Wolf's sorry ass and take him out ASAP. *Tonight*, he thought. *Tonight I'll finally take the head off the monster.*

Chase was currently in his Charger with J.T. and Corey, parked on Central Avenue, waiting for Baby Hustle to show his ass up. He had found him earlier and told him to keep his ear to the ground for Wolf's whereabouts, which Baby was keen to do for a little more drug money and a few more promises of protection.

"I don't fuckin' believe Cyrus shot you like that," Corey said from the backseat.

Considering it was about the tenth time Chase had heard that shit, he sighed heavily and rubbed his chest, tired of hearing about it. "Let it go, Corey. Just let it go."

But Corey was like a dog with a bone. "I can't, Chase. Cyrus would have shot *me* if you hadn't stepped in the way, and I ain't wearin' no vest. He must hate us. He wanted to *kill* us."

J.T. drummed his fingers on the steering wheel. "Y'all know what I think? I think maybe Cyrus hates everybody, Cyrus included."

"Well, I'm done with him either way. I ain't tryin' to worry about my own brother looking to grease me," Corey said.

"Speakin' of brothers greasin' brothers," J.T. started, looking at Chase curiously, "Cyrus has got to be the only nigger in the world left livin' after pullin' a gun on you. Why'd you walk away, Chase? Just because he *is* your brother?"

"This ain't over, J.T. Don't sleep on me. I'm tryin' to be good about it and respect our dead mother's memory, but it's not forgiven or forgotten. Remember, Cain killed Abel, and those two were brothers. If I don't hurry and get away from him, he's gonna make me kill his ass. Like I said before, he must have forgotten who he's fuckin' with."

J.T. nodded, and Corey kept silent. "I ain't mad at ya, Chase," J.T. said.

Chase wasn't mad at him either. He knew if Cyrus had really hurt him, J.T. would have blown his ass away. "Good. Since you ain't mad, what are you doin' next Saturday?"

"I got a clean slate. What's up?"

Chase turned his head, and that hurt like a bitch too. "What about you, Corey?"

"If you need me, I'm free."

"Well, I do, Corey. I need both of you, 'cause I'm marryin' Bliss."

J.T. grinned at him. "Wow! That's what's hot."

"Get the fuck outta here!" Corey said, like Chase was yanking his chain. "You sure you've known Bliss long enough to wife her?"

Chase smiled. "I've been wantin' to wife her since I splashed her skirt, Corey."

"Damn, that's deep. We'll be wherever you need us to be. And congrats, man," J.T. said.

"Yeah, that's real nice, Chase. I'm happy for y'all."

Chase looked out the window. "Thanks. I'll give you the details later. Here comes Baby."

Baby pedaled toward them—a grown man on a little kid's bike that he probably stole—and stopped at Chase's window.

Chase got out of the car and leaned with his back against the door. Baby got off his bike. "Hey, Smoke."

"Hey, Baby. What you got for me?"

Baby Hustle put one hand on his hip and scratched his chin. He looked at Chase with serious eyes. "I guess it sort of goes without sayin' that Wolf knows you lookin' for him, Smoke."

"Yeah, that's true. You seen him?"

"Saw him more than once. He's lookin' for you, too, you know."

"Kinda figured that."

"I saw the news. That was some shit, Smoke."

Chase shrugged. "Shit happens, Baby. Where's the last place you saw him?"

Baby looked a little uncomfortable with the question. He looked at his feet and ran a hand over his mouth.

Chase raised an eyebrow. Baby seemed a little stuck, and Chase was not above dangling the money he'd brought for him like a carrot.

The clock was ticking, and he needed Baby to spit it out. "You okay, Baby? Where's he at?"

Baby tore his eyes away from his feet and looked at Chase. "Well, you know I got a baby sister named Vida, right?"

Chase nodded; he knew Baby's sister.

Baby squinted through his disloyalty. "Well, Wolf is cheatin' on his wife with my baby sister. I ain't gonna tell you where they at unless you promise me you won't kill her too."

Chase looked at him sideways. "It ain't your sister I'm interested in, Baby."

Baby looked at him for a long moment, then sighed. "Okay. They're holed up at Vida's place. He'll probably be there all night. He had two niggas with him earlier, parked outside in a Yukon, but I ain't seen 'em for two hours. I ain't see nobody but Wolf and Vida go inside." He gave Chase an address on Evergreen Avenue.

Chase nodded, picturing the houses and the layout of the street in his head. "Thanks, Baby," He reached into his pocket and handed him a knot of cash. "I promise not to kill your sister, Baby."

Baby looked at the cash. "You good to me, Smoke."

Chase nodded. "You earn it. See you later, Baby." Chase watched him get on his little circus bike and ride away. Then he got back into the car and looked at J.T. "It seems fairly simple. Nigga's either that stupid or that fuckin' arrogant. He's at Baby's sister's house, layin' up. Seems like his dumb ass even sent his protection home."

"Bad move," J.T. said. "What's the address?"

They drove over to Evergreen Avenue and past the house, keeping with the normal flow of traffic.

"Did you get it?" J.T. asked, pulling over in the next block.

"Got it," Chase answered. He pulled the cuffs of his sleeves down over the tops of his gloves and put his shades back on. "Park in the middle of the next block, J.T. Corey, you stay in the backseat. Don't you get out of this car, you hear me?"

"I hear you" Corey answered laconically and slouched down in his seat.

Chase looked back at J.T. "If it seems like I'm takin' too long, pull out and start circling. I'll flag you down when you're comin' through. If you see or hear a lot of shots bein' fired by a lot of people, don't stop. Just keep goin'…and tell Bliss I love her."

"I got you," J.T. said.

"Be careful, Chase. In and out," Corey added.

Chase turned his head and smiled at his little brother. "That's why they call me Smoke, Corey. See you soon."

Chase stepped out of the car, pulled his cap down, and put his hands in his pockets. He walked fast, though not overly so, keeping close to the shadows, away from the street lamps. It was ten thirty, so it was truly night, which made him a lot more comfortable. There were people out, but nobody seemed to be checking for him. Chase, as usual, was looking everywhere at once, and his mind was working overtime.

The houses were two- and three-family homes. He wasn't worried about getting in; rather, he was worried about getting *out*. Vida lived on the second floor, which he thought might present a problem. Chase had literally jumped from a second floor on more than a few occasions without causing major damage, but it always left a few marks, and on this occasion, he was *already* hurt. He wasn't trying to kill himself. Bearing this in mind, he knew his most likely way out would be back through the front door.

He looked around quickly and went up the stoop. He knew from Baby that Vida's door was on the left. Chase slipped his tools out of his back pocket and quickly picked the lock on the storm door. He pulled it open slowly, hoping like hell it didn't squeak. He didn't need much room—just enough to get in—and to his relief, the door stayed silent. He picked the bottom lock on the front door easily and then went for the one on the top. It came open easily, but with an audible *click*. Chase froze and listened, waiting a full thirty seconds before he proceeded.

Chase stepped into the small foyer soundlessly. He fixed the storm door so it wouldn't lock behind him then pushed the front door almost closed. Chase started up the long flight of stairs in front of him. He got to the top without making a sound, but there he was faced with yet another door. He opened the top lock quickly and silently and pushed the door open slowly, expecting and finding a safety chain. Chase started grinning slow; he couldn't help himself. *I got a tool for this!* Chase took out a small retractable hook and took the chain off. He slipped his tools back into his pocket, and tucked his lips in to stop grinning.

When he stepped into the apartment, he put his back against the wall, surveying the room. Wolf and Vida were obviously having a romantic evening. There were candles everywhere, and rose petals were strewn across the room. There was a gold platter of half-eaten chocolate-covered strawberries, half a bottle of champagne, and two empty glasses on the coffee table.

Chase moved into the room, letting his eyes adjust to the candle-light. He cocked his head in the direction of a small sound he heard coming from his right. He smiled, knowing he hadn't been mistaken. The bedsprings were singing…*loud.* Wolf was tearin' Vida's ass up! Chase walked over to the open bedroom door and took his razor out. He peeked in and couldn't believe his luck. Both their backs were to him because Wolf had Vida up on her knees, letting her have it dog-gie style. Chase opened his razor and stepped into the room.

Wolf and Vida never stopped fucking; they didn't even hear him. Chase took his shades off and put them in his pocket. He pushed his cap back so Wolf could see his face and stood next to him to his right. Chase was grinning. "Nothin' like dyin' in a nice piece of ass, huh, Wolf?"

Wolf's eyes flew open, and he stopped mid stroke. "Oh shit. Oh shit! Smoke!"

Vida turned her head and started screaming.

Chase started laughing. "*Stop fucking!*" Chase yelled at him. He pushed Vida away from Wolf with his knee and grabbed Wolf's considerable manhood with his left hand.

Vida scrambled away from them and pressed herself into the headboard, screaming in short bursts, like she was too damned scared to let out a full-blown shriek.

Chase's right hand came up brutally under Wolf's balls. Candle-light glimmered briefly on the ultra-sharp blade of his razor before it separated Wolf from his engorged genitalia. Wolf howled as Chase threw his severed penis across the room. It hit the wall with a small *thud* and fell to the floor. Blood spurted from the place it had been, soaking the sheets. Vida was still doing that choked screaming until Chase clipped her under the chin, still holding his razor. "Shut up, Vida," he said as her lights went out.

Wolf, meanwhile, had fallen off the bed, onto his back, his hands clutching for something that was no longer a part of him. He stopped screaming and started making great gasping, whooping sounds— sounds of absolute shock and terror.

Chase leaned over him, careful to avoid the warm crimson spray. "Hey, aren't you married?" he asked curiously.

"F-fuck you, Smoke!" Wolf stuttered.

Chase slashed his right Achilles' tendon. "Wrong answer! I asked you if you are married. It's a simple yes-or-no question, motherfuck-er!"

Wolf burst into tears. "Please, man. Pl-please don't—"

"Fuck you. Answer me!" He slashed his other tendon.

Wolf screamed through his tears. "Yes! Yes! *Please!*"

Chase laughed like he'd just heard the world's funniest joke. "Well, your cheatin' ass just earned a scarlet letter!" he yelled and slashed a capital A in the man's chest.

"You're fuckin' *crazy*!" Wolf screamed.

Chase nodded, grinning maniacally. "You goddamned right! Die, you troublesome motherfucker!" Chase stuck his razor behind Wolf's ear and dragged it deeply across his carotid artery. Blood gushed out in a red-hot deluge, spurting and spraying with each remaining pump of Wolf's heart. Chase didn't remove his razor until it dug into Wolf's collarbone. He wiped the blood on the bed sheet and sprinted out the door and down the stairs.

He was so full of adrenaline that his ears were humming. He took the stairs two at a time and raced out the front door, making himself a blur. Chase sprinted through oncoming traffic and into the next block. He slowed to a trot, and J.T. threw the passenger door open.

Chase got into the car, and J.T. pulled smoothly into traffic.

"He gone?" J.T. asked.

Chase's smile was gone; he was coming down. "He's a fuckin' memory. I don't feel good. Take me home, J.T." Chase stripped his gloves off, and Corey put his hand on his shoulder. Chase sighed heavily and put his hand over Corey's. "I'm sorry, Corey. I'm a really bad person."

"You're my brother, Chase."

Chase blinked and nodded. "That doesn't change the fact that I'm a bad person who does atrocious things—but I guess that doesn't matter as long as Wolf is dead, right?" Chase wasn't mad when neither one of them answered him.

They drove back to Chase's loft in relative silence, only stopping to get rid of Chase's bloody gloves and his jacket. J.T. parked Chase's Charger in the garage and took Corey home in his own vehicle.

Chase rode the elevator up to his loft and stopped in the kitchen for a bottle of water. He felt terrible. His head hurt, his chest hurt, and he was tired as hell. More than that, he had to wonder, *Who the fuck was that guy who snuffed Wolf? Do I even know him?* Chase was not going to kid himself about the level of violence he'd displayed. It was gruesome and horrendous. Wolf may not have been a poster child for goodness, but no one deserved to die that hard or that terrified. Chase had lost control and tortured him. Chase's brow creased with a worried frown. *Who the fuck is living in my head? This shit is scary.* He knew *that* was what Cyrus didn't understand about him.

Chase took his clothes off and got into the shower as thoughts of his big brother wandered across his mind. Cyrus didn't understand that after Chase went past a certain point, there was no going back. When Cyrus shot him, it took absolutely everything he had not to slice him to shreds, brother or not. In doing that, Cyrus had literally taken his life into his own hands, and Chase was angry enough that he could have killed him that very day—just as angry as he was when he took that menacing blade to Wolf and carved the hell outta him.

In the throes of killing Wolf, Chase had felt a strong physical release—like letting steam out of a pressure cooker. It was almost orgasmic. He'd felt better immediately and wondered why he hadn't done it sooner. Chase shook his head and winced. He'd *liked* it.

"I'm a sick fuck. I *am* crazy. God help me." He said it out loud, but he couldn't bring himself to admit contrition, at least not to himself. He didn't give two shits about Wolf, and that fucker deserved to be greased, though maybe not like that.

Chase got out of the shower and dried off. He moved to the mirror and looked at his chest. He had a very serious bruise, just like he expected he would from the force of that bullet against the life-saving Kevlar. Since it wasn't going to disappear in the next five minutes, he had to wonder what Bliss was going to say when she saw it. She'd freak out, but he wasn't going to lie to her.

He went into the bedroom. Bliss was in his bed, lying on her side with her back to him. As horrible as he was, he still loved her with all his heart. It wasn't infatuation, and it wasn't a crush. He couldn't even begin to describe what he felt for her. Looking at her like that, with her hair fanned across the pillow and one small, honey-colored shoulder peeking out from the sheet, smoothed him out. He slipped into bed behind her and put his hand on her shapely hip. "You asleep, Bliss?" he asked, knowing she wasn't.

Bliss was an extremely light sleeper, but she didn't answer him. In fact, she didn't even move.

He kissed her shoulder. "You mad at me, Bliss?"

Still nothing—just the steady rise and fall of her breathing.

"Bliss? Come on. Don't do me like that. Be mad, but *please* talk to me."

No response.

Chase tucked his lips in and looked away from her. "You don't want to talk to me, Bliss? All right." Chase was bent out of shape by it, but he wasn't really tripping because at least she was there in his bed—*their* bed. He got up to give her space to be mad at him like she had every right to be. He went out to the kitchen in his boxers and bare feet and took a beer out of the fridge. Chase took the cap off the bottle and turned it up. He drank half of it and rubbed his hand across his lips. Chase wished Bliss wasn't freezing him out, because he needed to be close to her.

He picked up the bottle of pain pills Tasha had left for him and threw them in the garbage, deciding that he deserved every ounce of pain and that he'd suffer through it like a man. He left his unfinished beer on the counter and went and sat on the sectional with his face in his hands.

Even though he was upset, he wore a smile. He was a peculiar man. Yes, he got shot by his own brother and had just mutilated a guy to death, but what really upset him most was that Bliss wouldn't talk to him. Her silence was fucking him up, but he still needed to give her some space.

"Chase?"

He took his hands down, and there she was, standing right in front of him. It wasn't like Chase at all to let someone get that close to him without him knowing it. Now, it was his turn not to answer *her* because he couldn't. Chase leaned forward with his elbows on his knees and clasped his hands in front of him. He closed his eyes against the completely unwelcome sting of tears. Chase wasn't a crybaby, but he *was* emotional, and as his mother used to say, "a little high strung." The events of the day had taken their toll on him.

Bliss sat next to him, as close as she could get. She put her fingers in his hair, mindful of his stitches, and kissed his cheek. "I'm sorry, baby. I didn't know you needed me like this. What happened? What's wrong?"

He looked at the floor until he felt the water in his eyes dry up.

"Chase? Baby, tell me. Talk to me. I'm here," Bliss coaxed. Her fingers left his hair and rubbed his back.

He wanted to say something salty to her for ignoring him, but he couldn't. He could never talk to Bliss like that, and Chase didn't want to argue with her. He just wanted to love her and for her to love him back. He smiled a little softer and put his hand on her knee. "It's nothing. I just had a really bad day."

Bliss grew very still. She stopped rubbing his back and stood up, looking at his chest warily. "What happened to you? How'd you get that?"

He smiled sadly. "Cyrus shot me."

Bliss was horrified. "*He what?* Oh my God, Chase! How come you're not dead? You should be dead from that!"

Chase looked at her unhappily. Once again, he had brought her to the brink of hysteria. "I was wearing a vest, Bliss."

"*What?* I mean, thank God you were, but what were you doing wearin' a vest, Chase? Why do you even *have* one?"

"I have my reasons," he said quietly, folding his arms across his chest. He felt the conversation he'd been dreading bearing down on him like a freight train.

She narrowed her eyes at him and folded her arms across her chest too. "Reasons? What reasons, Chase? Tell me, because I really think I need to know."

They stared at each other, but he didn't answer her.

"What else happened today?"

He looked her in the eyes; he couldn't lie to her. "I can't…I just can't tell you."

Bliss took two steps away from him, and Chase noticed her trying to put distance between them. "This is all about that guy Wolf, isn't it? What's going on with him? Is he looking for you?"

"Not anymore. Wolf's dead," he said flatly.

Bliss seemed shocked. "*Really?* Did you have anything to do with that?"

Chase didn't answer her, and he couldn't bring himself to maintain eye contact. She took another step away from him—something else he noticed—but he didn't open his mouth. Bliss looked at him like she was afraid of him, and that broke his heart. He'd die before he hurt Bliss.

"*Who are you, Chase?*" she asked, looking at him in disbelief, rubbing her temples. "I mean you're this sweet, romantic, wonderful person to me…but…but I'd have to be blind and stupid not to wonder if you're also not somebody totally different—somebody I don't know at all. *Who the hell are you, Chase?*"

He reached out to touch her, but Bliss stepped away from him. *That hurt*. He disregarded her move and reached for her again, and she darted away from him like he had a contagious disease. Chase frowned. "What's the matter, Bliss? You don't want me to touch you? You scared of me? Don't say you're scared of me, Bliss. Please." Chase wasn't one to beg anyone, let alone a woman, but if Bliss wanted him crying and on his knees, that was what he would do to keep her. She was staring at him with extra wide eyes. He took a step toward her, but while she didn't retreat, she looked like she was ready to run if he came any closer. "Bliss! Please, baby," he said, struggling to keep his voice calm. "It's me. I'm just me…Chase. That's who I am, the man who loves you."

She looked at him like she was searching his eyes for the truth. He took another step toward her, and she bolted away from him and ran into the bedroom.

Oh God! This can't be happening! He didn't mean to run after her, but that was exactly what he did. "Bliss!"

She ran into the bathroom and tried to slam the door in his face, but he grabbed the knob.

"Stop, Bliss! You act like I'm gonna hurt you! Bliss, please. Stop! *Please*!" Chase was yelling at her and acting aggressive, and when he caught himself and realized it, he cautiously backed away. He could hear her crying—because of him—and it ripped his heart out. Chase leaned with his back against the dresser and waited for her. It was time for a time-out. Things were escalating out of control. He waited for her for twenty minutes, until she stopped sobbing.

Bliss cracked the door open, and they stared at each other. Her eyes were red, and her face was puffy from crying, but he was so glad she'd come out of there that it was almost irrational.

"You ready to talk?" Chase asked in a very tentative voice. He was afraid to move, fearing she'd bolt back in the bathroom.

She wiped the tears off her face with the heel of her hand. "Yes," she said with a weak smile.

That's at least a good sign. "Okay," he said and pushed away from the dresser. He stood there indecisively. "Are you gonna come over here, or do you want me to come over there?"

She started crying again, but she was still smiling. She wiggled her finger at him. "You come here."

"Okay." He walked over to her, and she opened the door all the way.

She put her arms around his neck and kissed him like she loved him. "This thing between us is bigger than we are, Chase. You know that, don't you?"

"I know. I love you more than anything, Bliss. You're not gonna leave me are you? I'll do anything you say. Just please don't go."

She smiled at him. "I love you too. I can't go anywhere. Seems like we're meant to be, Chase. Come here."

He frowned and stepped into the bathroom with her.

Bliss handed him a white plastic stick off the counter. "I *have* to marry you next Saturday. We made a baby."

She caught him off guard and knocked him for a loop with that one, and his mouth dropped open. "Oh shit, Bliss," he said softly, his voice filled with wonder and surprise. He wanted it and meant for it to happen. It had been his aim. He was just shocked it had happened so quickly. "Are you serious?" His heart was beating fast; this was monumental.

Bliss smiled and raised his hand, holding the pregnancy test up to his face. "Look at it."

He did, and she was. "Oh shit, Bliss," he said again.

Bliss couldn't stop herself from smiling at him. "Is that all you can say? Are you happy?"

He smiled and raised an eyebrow. "Are you gonna marry me? *Really* marry me?"

She nodded, smiling and crying at the same time. "Uh-huh. I can't wait."

He kissed her slow and tender, with all the love he had in his heart. "Yeah, I'm happy, Bliss—real happy."

G STREET CHRONICLES
A NEW URBAN DYNASTY
WWW.GSTREETCHRONICLES.COM

Chapter 19

"I told you that negro was gonna get you pregnant, didn't I? It was all in his eyes, Bliss. You could smell it on his damned breath. I knew it," Tasha said, grinning. She sat across from Bliss eating pancakes and turkey sausage, while Bliss nursed dry toast and weak tea.

Bliss didn't answer her right away, because she was trying real hard to keep from throwing up.

Tasha kept smiling and eating. "Yep, I told you. Chase came up in here with his fine ass and his charmingly boyish swagger and knocked your ass down, and then he knocked your ass up. I knew you needed a condom for his ass—no pills, no shots, no foam. You needed a goddamned *barrier method* for that fertile brother." She leaned forward and pointed her fork at Bliss. "Your mother's gonna kill you...and your daddy's gonna kill Chase."

Bliss drank some of her tea. "Nobody's killing anybody. Everything's gonna be fine." She was still dressed in her robe, and she should have been ready an hour ago. They were in St. Lucia, and Chase and Bliss were getting married the next day, and they'd all flown down the prior afternoon. Bliss's parents had arrived very late the night before, along with her sister and brother, and she only had about a half-hour before they were supposed to meet for a late brunch. Bliss frowned at Tasha. "Why are you eating all that now? You won't even be hungry when you get there."

Tasha ate the last of her sausage and licked syrup off her fingers. "I had the munchies. I'll have 'em again at brunch."

Bliss smiled and shook her head. "You better stop blazin' trees. You're gonna get fat."

Tasha looked pointedly at Bliss's midsection. "Not before you do."

"Later for you, Tash."

They shared a laugh and then settled back in their chairs.

Tasha smiled and looked at her a long time. "You look happy, Bliss."

Bliss laughed. "That's because I am."

"Good. In that case, I'm happy for you, but…" She trailed off and looked at the closed bedroom door. They were in Bliss and Chase's suite, and he was in there getting dressed.

Bliss frowned, not feeling where the conversation was going. She pushed her engagement ring up on her finger and blinked at Tasha. "What? Go ahead and tell me what you want me to hear, but go easy on my husband. I'm serious, Tasha."

Tasha sucked her teeth. "Listen to you! *Go easy on my husband.* Girl, he ain't your husband yet. Right now he's your baby's daddy. Lighten up! This is just me—Tasha—and we talk shit to each other, remember? You're my girl, Bliss, and I would never try to ruin your big day for you. Although I do have to admit that I'm a little jealous—*not hating*. Never hating, just jealous." She leaned forward and lowered her voice to a whisper. "Do you really know what you're getting into? As much as I like Chase, he got some real gangster shit about him. Don't ignore that just 'cause you love him, Bliss. That shit ain't play-play. *That shit is real.*"

Bliss sighed. "Come on, Tash—"

Tasha leaned even closer and grabbed her hand. "Listen, Bliss…I stitched Chase's head up myself. I saw his X-rays. Whoever hit him in his head like that wasn't his goddamned friend. They were tryin' to hurt him real bad. A little to the left, and they would have. His brother is a drug dealer whose club was *on the news* gettin' shot—"

Bliss held her hands up. "I know about all that stuff. We talked about it, *all of it*. This is *our* decision, and none of that other stuff matters. The only thing that does matter is that we love each other... and we're having a baby."

Chase walked in the bedroom looking handsome in a cream Prada shirt and a pair of jeans. "Hey, Tasha. What's up?"

Tasha gave him the once-over. "You look nice, but Bliss's mother is gonna make you tuck your shirt in."

Chase sat next to Bliss and kissed her quick. "Yeah, well, speaking of Bliss's mother, you could use a little Visine to keep her off you." He smiled when he said it, so Tasha wasn't offended.

She got up and came around the table. "Your ass wasn't complainin' when I was sewin' your head up." She put a hand under his chin and looked into his eyes. "Very nice. The hemorrhaging cleared up nicely," she said in her doctor-like voice. "You're a fast healer," she noticed, since she'd only taken the stitches out a couple days earlier.

"Thanks to you."

She shrugged and picked up her bag. "Anytime, but keep you gangster shit to a minimum please."

Chase's eyes twinkled. "I'm no gangster, Tasha. That was Cyrus's beef, not mine."

She smiled at him knowingly. "I'll bet you got a bridge you want to sell me too. Y'all better hurry up. This brunch is for you, you know. See you downstairs." She threw some shades on and slammed out the door.

Chase laughed and stood up, shaking his head.

Bliss stood too.

"Tasha is bananas. She was tryin' to convince you not to marry me, wasn't she?"

Bliss smiled and put her arms around his waist. "No, not really. She was just a little concerned that maybe I don't know what I'm getting myself into, marrying a gangster."

Chase frowned. "I'm not a gangster, Bliss. I'm a businessman."

She patted his cheek. "Yeah. I'm pretty sure most so-called gangsters see themselves that way."

Chase blinked hard and raised his eyebrows. "So what you sayin', Bliss? *I told you,* I'm not a gangster. Every business I own is legitimate. I run 'em straight, and I pay taxes and bills just like everybody else. I ain't no drug dealer like Cyrus."

Bliss looked at him warily. There *was* that one thing still between them. "Okay, baby. Let me ask you a question or two then. Why did you come home all bloody like that the day you got hit in the head, and what were you doing the day Cyrus shot you?"

Chase wouldn't look at her. He smiled and gently stepped out of her arms. "You know I can't tell you, Bliss."

She stared at him. "Why not? I'm about to become your *wife*. I'm not just your girlfriend anymore."

"Yeah. *Wife.* That's the operative word. It's my job to protect you, Bliss…and our baby. I'm not tellin' you 'cause I don't really think you need to know. The less you know, the better, at least while I finish disentangling myself from Cyrus. When I'm done, I promise you, Bliss, I'll be done…unless I just can't go another way."

Bliss looked him in the eye. "I already know, Chase," she said.

Chase looked at her like he was holding his breath, and maybe he was. This was serious. "You already know what, Bliss?"

Bliss looked at Chase looking back at her. If someone had told her what she *knew* was true about Chase, she wouldn't have believed them, even though all the pieces fit. She'd turned everything over in her mind. She'd made her deduction on Sunday morning, reading the paper in bed, with Chase sound asleep beside her. It was an epiphany. She'd finally put her finger on what she couldn't quite put her finger on, and it hit her right between the eyes like a sledgehammer. She shook her head slowly. "I don't think you're a gangster, Chase. I think you're something else."

He spread his feet and folded his arms across his chest. "What am I, Bliss?"

She looked at him with his head cocked to the side and his jaw set defiantly so she could see the scar underneath. Ice glistened in his eyes. Still, there was that boyishness about him, because his hands were tucked under his arms, and he couldn't be still. His body swayed slightly, and he shifted from one foot to the other. Bliss gave him a small smile, and his eyebrows went up. "Don't be like that with me, Chase. I don't want anything to be between us, baby—not even this...especially not this. I'd never tell on you, Chase, and I'll never leave you. I *love* you." Bliss knew exactly where she stood in Chase's heart. She knew she *owned* it. There was nothing she could even begin to think of that he wouldn't do for her. He'd move mountains to keep her happy. She knew it bothered him deeply whenever they argued, and if she decided to walk away from him, it would seriously fuck him up. She knew Chase was marrying her because he was so in love with her that it was almost a physical ache when he couldn't be with her. She knew exactly how he felt, because she felt the same way about him. She touched his hand, and Chase dropped his funky little posture immediately, but he looked away from her, even as his fingers curled around hers.

"I never thought I'd meet you, Bliss. I would have done everything different if I had known you were waitin' for me. I swear to God I would have."

Bliss nodded. "I know, baby. I believe you." She put her hand on his face. "Chase, look at me."

He closed his eyes and turned his face away. "I can't. Don't ask me to."

She put her arms around him, and he put his around her and held her tight. "Chase...Cyrus makes you kill people for him, doesn't he?"

"Yes."

She wasn't shocked because she already knew it was true. "That's why you're always fighting with him, isn't it?"

He nodded. "Yes."

"You hurt a few people that night at Cyrus's opening, didn't you, baby?"

He took a deep breath. "Yes."

"What about Wolf? Did you do that?"

He didn't answer that right away. The story had been in the paper for two days, and it was a gruesome tale. "Yes. Yes, Bliss. Please don't ask me any more questions. Please."

She put a hand on either side of his face and made him look at her. "We can't take back what's already happened, but we can always try to do better. No more, Chase. No more."

He nodded, and that was good enough for her—at least for the moment.

"Good," Bliss said. She undid the belt to her robe and let it fall to the floor, smiling at him. "Now show me how much you love me."

They were an hour late to their own brunch.

Chapter 20

Chase couldn't believe it was all for real. It was the best thing that had ever happened to him, but he kept waiting for the rug to be snatched from under him. He convinced himself that things couldn't possibly be that perfect, even if it was only for this one moment in time. Chase had wanted something small and intimate—and technically, it still was, he supposed—but thanks to the former Bliss Riley, fifty people had shown up to watch him marry his bride in the sand.

Bliss had been his wife for four hours. Night had fallen, and Chase thought their little party would have thinned out by now, but every single guest was still there, dancing, eating, and drinking under their big tent on the beach. Finally, though, he found a moment to himself and retreated from the epicenter of the party.

He took off his tie and his jacket to his white linen Armani suit and draped them over the back of a chair. He took a glass of champagne from a passing waiter, sat down by himself, and watched Bliss dance with Corey. Chase sat back in his chair and undid the first two buttons of his shirt. He smiled and sipped his champagne. Bliss looked beautiful. Corey was swirling her around in her simple Vera Wang gown. She had flowers in her hair, and she was smiling at Corey like he was her new best friend. Chase couldn't wait to be alone with her. A hand fell on his shoulder, and he looked up. Bliss's father was standing over him, smiling.

"Can I sit with you, son, or do you want to be alone?"

Chase laughed and sat up in his seat. "I definitely don't. Come on and have a seat."

Lewis Riley sat down next to his brand new son-in-law and gave him a look. "You know, when Bliss called us last week, the very last thing I expected to hear was that she was getting married today. I was very surprised."

Chase smiled. "Why's that?"

"'Cause from what I understand, you two haven't been dating that long."

Chase frowned thoughtfully. "To tell you the truth, Mr. Riley, I, uh…I don't think me and Bliss really *dated*. I mean, we went out and stuff, but dated? Nah, not us."

Lewis frowned. "What does that mean?"

Chase smiled and leaned toward him. He looked him in the eye. "It means we didn't have time for all that dating stuff. We were too busy falling in love and tryin' to get *here*, where we are right now." Chase looked at him seriously. "Mr. Riley, I loved Bliss the minute I saw her. I put the idea of us gettin' married out there to her a week after I met her. The only thing that would have stopped me from marryin' Bliss was a flat-out refusal from her. I'm a lucky man, though, because she loves me as much as I love her." Chase couldn't seem to stop smiling, but for once, it wasn't for a bad reason.

Lewis tilted his head to the side and raised an eyebrow. "Nobody wants to tell me, but I picked it out of the air that Bliss is pregnant. Is that true?"

Chase nodded, still smiling. "Yeah, it's true. I did it, and it wasn't a mistake. *We love each other,* Mr. Riley. You can relax."

Lewis Riley stared at the handsome, brash young man and made his own evaluation. Finally, he smiled at Chase and extended his hand. "Well, all right then. I guess you've told me everything I wanted to hear. I like you, son…and please, call me Lewis."

Chase shook his hand just as Corey brought Bliss back and plopped her in his lap. "Your wife is wearin' me out, bro. Your turn."

Lewis stood up and pulled Bliss off Chase's lap, smiling. "I'll take this one with your permission."

Chase nodded. "You got it."

Bliss planted a kiss on him first. "Gotta dance with my daddy! Be right back."

Corey sat down next to Chase and sighed. "I'm happy for you and Bliss, Chase."

Chase looked over at his brother and smiled. He thought he'd never speak on it. Some things you didn't have to say out loud, but there it was. "Thanks, Corey."

"You're welcome, 'cause I almost stepped to her when she showed up late to that interview."

Chase sipped his champagne. "I know."

Corey looked at him carefully. "Then I guess I don't have to say anything else."

"Not a word. I've always known you had a crush on Bliss."

Corey smiled, and it was a little woeful. "Maybe, but I'm glad you got some happiness, Chase. I know how dark it's been for you. I love you, man."

Chase smiled and grabbed the back of his neck affectionately. "I love you, too, Corey. Don't come sniffin' 'round my wife, though, or I'll have to beat your ass."

Corey laughed. "Don't worry, Chase. I'd never even think about doin' you greasy like that. Cyrus, maybe, but not me. Speaking of Cyrus—"

Chase sat back in his chair and rolled his eyes in exasperation. "I *wasn't,* Corey, and don't be bringin' him up. If you notice, he wasn't invited. I don't want to think about his ass, especially not *today."*

Corey leaned forward. "Yeah, but Chase, Cyrus has been blowin' my phone up since we left town. He been callin' you too?"

Chase felt himself getting angry, and he leaned forward too. "I really wouldn't know. I got married today, Corey. I wasn't tryin' to take a call from Cyrus in the middle of the ceremony."

"He's gonna be real pissed that he ain't here, Chase."

Chase laughed. "That nigga shot me in the chest, Corey. He didn't want to come."

Corey shrugged with one shoulder, looking at Chase like he was scared to voice his opinion, but he did it anyway. "He didn't really shoot you, Chase. He was drunk, and you had a vest on, so—"

Chase laughed again. "He *did* shoot me, Corey. *He did!* How can you sit there and say he didn't? You were there! Matter of fact, he would have shot *you* if I hadn't stepped in front of you, and like you said, you wasn't wearin' no vest."

"Yeah, but Chase, Cyrus was—"

Chase banged his fist on the table. "*No, Corey!*" He yelled at him and instantly regretted it—not just because of the look on Corey's face, but also because everything in his immediate vicinity came to a screeching halt. Bliss stopped dancing with her father, people turned to look, and even J.T., Tasha, and Dee gawked at him from halfway across the room. He brought his shit down 1,000 at once. Chase put his hand on Corey's shoulder and spoke into his ear. "I don't want to hear Cyrus's name again until we get back to New York. Do you understand me, Corey? I mean it."

Corey looked at the floor. "But—"

"I mean it, Corey."

Corey nodded reluctantly. "Okay, Chase. I'm sorry. It's just—"

"I know, Corey, I know. It's gonna be okay. Just stop it now. For me, all right?"

"You got it."

Chase rubbed his shoulder. "Good. All right, then." He gave Corey's shoulder a squeeze and walked out of the tent to smooth himself out. He knew Corey's only intention had been to keep them together or at least talking, but Cyrus was the last person he wanted to think about on his wedding day.

Cyrus. That nigga had shot him like he was a dog on the street. If he hadn't been wearing that Kevlar, he would have been dead. Cyrus had meant to kill him. After everything they'd gone through together—good and bad, right or wrong—he couldn't believe Cyrus wanted to kill his own brother. Cyrus clearly would have no problem killing Corey either. His brothers, yet he didn't give a fuck about them.

Chase had always suspected it, and now he knew for sure. Nothing says, *"Fuck you"* like a bullet in the chest. Chase smiled cynically, put his hands in his pockets, and started walking in the sand.

He hadn't wanted to think about Cyrus. He'd pushed him out of his mind every time he'd popped up since the day he'd shot him. With everything else going on, he'd managed to do that pretty well—until Corey unexpectedly brought that nigga up right in the middle of his wedding reception. Chase was pretty sure Cyrus had blown his phone up too. He'd called him every day—sometimes two or three times a day—and Chase always let that shit go straight to voicemail. He had absolutely no desire to talk to Cyrus. He was still trying to decide on the way he'd hold him in his heart. For the life of him, he couldn't understand why he still loved Cyrus at all or even cared about what he thought, especially since Cyrus had done so many things to make him justifiably hate his ass—things that made him want to smoke his ass.

Chase heard something behind him and turned around sharply. Bliss was running across the sand, holding up the front of her wedding dress so she wouldn't trip over it. He frowned and closed the distance between them. "Hey, Bliss! What are you doing out here running in the sand? You can't be doin' that."

She was a little winded, but it didn't stop her from talking. "I was worried about you! Why did you just run out of there like that? Are you okay?"

"I didn't *run* out of there. I just came out here to get some air."

"What happened between you and Corey?"

Chase shrugged indifferently. "Nothin'. He started talkin' about Cyrus, and he wouldn't shut up. Not today, Bliss. Cyrus has no place here, even in conversation."

Bliss touched his face. "I'm sorry, baby. I really am."

He smiled at her. "It's okay. It really doesn't matter. Nothing really matters except what goes on in this little circle we made—you, me, and whoever is in here," he said, touching her flat stomach.

She smiled at him. "Don't forget about Uncle Corey."

He laughed. "Yeah, Uncle Corey too."

"You say the sweetest things, Chase."

He looked down at her standing there, still a bit breathless with flowers in her hair, looking beautiful in her wedding dress. She was the prettiest girl he'd ever seen, and she was his. God had let him have this one, but he wondered what he'd have to pay for it. Whatever it was, the price tag would come later, if it came at all. There was always the hope that He would just let Chase have that one blessing on the house. Maybe Bliss would be his first freebie. But regardless, at that moment, he was just grateful.

Chase pulled Bliss into his arms and kissed his bride with a sweet, smoldering kiss that quickly turned into a raging inferno. There was so much passion between them. Chase wanted to slip into her right there on that beach. He ran his hands over the soft fabric of her gown, wanting to tear it away and get at her even softer skin. His fingers found her breasts as Bliss's hand slipped into his pants.

He took his lips away from hers, but not too far. "I think we should stop. We got a tent full of people not so far away."

"I don't care, Chase."

He knew the look in her eye, and he wanted to please her. He smiled at her and took her hand. "Time to ditch the party."

Bliss grinned at him like he was a bad boy. "We can't do that."

"Yes we *can*."

They walked back to the tent, and Chase picked up his half-empty glass and grabbed a fork off the nearest table, clinking against the glass to get everyone's attention. He stepped on the platform where the deejay was and made his request and then he spoke into the mike. "Me and Bliss would like to thank y'all for comin' so far to help us celebrate our marriage. It's getting late, and I'm dyin' to be alone with my wife." The crowd snickered and cheered, and Chase smiled. "That's right. That's why we're leaving. We got music, we got food, and we got plenty of liquor, so y'all keep partying and sendin' us your blessings until it all runs out. We're gonna dance with y'all one more time!"

He stepped down from the platform and took Bliss into his arms as Mint Condition started singing "Pretty Brown Eyes." Chase was a good dancer, and so was Bliss. He twirled her around the room much better than Corey had. Their guests clapped and shouted their approval. Chase dipped her near the end of the song and came back up kissing her. They stopped dancing and stood right in the middle of the floor, kissing like no one else was there. Everyone started clapping again.

Chase stepped away from her but kept holding her hand. "Okay. That's all you get to see. We'll see you in the morning."

They left quickly, and Chase picked her up when they got out of the elevator.

"Chase, you don't have to do that." Bliss giggled.

"Sure I do. The key card's in my pocket."

Bliss opened the door, and Chase carried her into the bedroom. He put Bliss on the bed, unbuttoned his shirt, and took off his pants. Bliss made a move to take her dress off, but Chase stopped her. He pushed her dress up and slid her panties off. Bliss looked at him strangely when he put them in his shirt pocket. Chase put his hands on her knees and parted her thighs. "It's a memento. You save your dress, and I'll save your panties."

Bliss laughed. "You are so bad, Chase. I love it!"

He kissed the inside of her thigh, and she trembled. Chase raised an eyebrow. "You like that?"

"Oh yes," she answered with a shudder.

"Then you'll really like this," he whispered and put his mouth on the most tender part of her body. Bliss cried out, and when she arched her back, Chase put his hands underneath her and had a vivid flashback of licking the top off her ice cream. He worked on her just like that—like she was the sweetest thing he'd ever tasted.

Bliss put her hands in his hair as her hips moved in rhythm with his tongue. Her texture changed as she did that little screamy thing she always did when she came. He felt the softest part of her throbbing against his mouth, and the feel of it was so erotic he got chills and shuddered himself. He had to have her; he simply couldn't wait any longer.

Chase moaned when he slid into her. She was so soft, hot, and slippery it took his breath away. He had one knee on either side of her, and he gasped when she brought her legs together. It was a smooth and exquisite pleasure. He wasn't stroking her like he usually did; instead, it was a sweetly spicy, slow grind. He didn't want to stop. He could have made love to her for hours.

Bliss shifted and parted her thighs, allowing Chase to slip in even further. She gripped his biceps and brought her hips up, grinding as hard as she could. They stared into each other's eyes. Small, passionate sounds that weren't quite words rushed breathlessly through their lips. Bliss's hands dropped to his ass and pulled him in, making him drop the grind and start pumping. Bliss bore down on him and sucked him in like a vacuum.

She screamed his name, and all Chase's muscles weakened at once, as all the blood in his body seemed to drop to one place. He pounded into her helplessly as his arms trembled and Bliss rained down on him, squeezing her body around him, warm and slick.

He dropped his head and came hard, taking great pleasure in every thrust, relishing the fact that Bliss was his wife and he was filling her up with himself and loving her like he'd never loved another person. Chase kissed her long and deep, and just when he thought he was spent, they started all over again.

Chapter 21

If he could have turned back the hands of time, Cyrus might have thought about doing a lot of things differently. He never would have opened that godforsaken club, and he never would have asked—let alone damned near begged—Chase to kill Wolf. If time were retractable, he wouldn't have to worry about Chase greasing Wolf because he never would have fucked with him in the first place. The sad fact is that you couldn't go back. It's very rare that anybody gets a do-over, and Cyrus thought that was too damn bad.

At the moment, he had a lot to think about. For one thing, it was looking very seriously like Khalid might die. That fuck J.T. had been right, as much as Cyrus hated to admit it. Cyrus knew he should have at least dropped Khalid at a hospital, even if he couldn't stay with him. Unfortunately, that was not what happened. Khadijah told Cyrus she would call the police on him if he didn't get the fuck out her apartment after he shot Chase. Cyrus had called her bluff, and she'd called 911. Cyrus got the fuck out of there quick, thanks to that crazy bitch.

From what he could gather, Khadijah had let Monty take a look at Khalid at his own insistence. Khadijah didn't want to get the cops involved, so she'd relented, against her better judgment. Monty got the bullet out, but two days later, Khalid's shoulder was running pus, and he had a fever of 104.

Khadijah didn't actually take him to the hospital until *another* two days later, when she could no longer stand the stench from the wound. Cyrus had taken his chances and poked his head out long enough to go check for him at the hospital. The nigga's skin had a serious gray tinge to it. He was in the ICU hooked up to four different machines, with a drip in each arm. It didn't look good for his boy.

Cyrus was in deep trouble. He had so many people looking for him that he was afraid to make a move. Naturally, the cops were still looking for him because of the nightmare at the club. That was bad, but Cyrus was used to evading the law, and he was good at it. The truly horrible thing he had to deal with was avoiding Fabian Gregory.

When Cyrus and Khalid hit Wolf's drug spot, they'd done it with no idea that Wolf and Fabian had ties. There was no way on God's green Earth that Cyrus would have knowingly fucked with Fabian, even indirectly. Fabian was based in Coney Island, and he had that shit on lock. He also sold ecstasy, crystal meth, heroin, and coke to all the good white folks from Gravesend to Dyker Heights.

Fabian was obviously the reason Wolf had upped his drug game to include the heroin and ecstasy Cyrus and Khalid had stepped to him about in the first place. Fabian was a true Teflon kingpin: *Nobody* fucked with him on the street. Only the Mafia rose up, and that was only occasionally because Fabian usually kept them satisfied with a cut. Fabian had run his game so long that the NYPD had grown tired of trying to knock him. He was even fucking the Feds up at every turn.

After the shoot-'em-up at Eternal, Cyrus laid low and put his ear to the ground. When Khadijah threw his ass out, Cyrus cashed in a favor with his old boy Rome's cousin Freddie out in Canarsie. Freddie let Cyrus hole up in his basement for two grand in cash and three grand in coke. *Some fucking favor.*

Cyrus tried to reach out and get a hold of Chase and Corey, but it was like those two assholes had fallen off the planet. He couldn't find them anywhere, and no one had seen them. Corey's phone rang and then went to voicemail, but Chase's went *straight* to voicemail.

He was shocked when he was watching the news a day later and heard the story about the gruesome murder of drug dealer Warren "Wolf" Jenkins. The reporter didn't go into great detail, but she said the body was horribly mutilated, and the police had no leads as to who the suspected killer might be. Cyrus wasn't worried about them finding Smoke: That was the one thing about Chase he put all his confidence in. Chase was thorough, and he didn't leave a trace.

The news of Wolf's demise had Cyrus ecstatic at first. It had taken Chase long enough to grease that fool. But his delight didn't last long, and he had to cut his happy dance short when he found out about Wolf's tie to Fabian Gregory. One of his foot soldiers came by to bring him some money and the bad news—a kid named Darryl that everybody referred to as Swing. Swing handed Cyrus $10,000 and told him Wolf was Fabian's son and that Chase had fucked up royally.

"How can that be?" Cyrus had wondered aloud. The time difference made no sense. Fabian would have had to have been a very young father, screwing pretty early in life. Then Cyrus thought about it again and understood exactly how could it *could* be true. Swing had informed Cyrus that Fabian was "scouring the streets" for his ass. He knew Khalid and Cyrus were behind the death of his child, and he'd put the word out that he wanted them both dead on sight.

Khalid was in the hospital, probably dying, and the end of it all, Cyrus would most likely be dead too. For once, he honestly couldn't see a way out. Cyrus wasn't that afraid of dying, but he had a score to settle before he did. *All of this is Chase's fault. He's just an arrogant lunatic who refuses to listen—a stubborn, defiant, ungrateful bastard who fucked my life up just by being fucking born.* He hated Chase with the blackest part of his black heart.

Chase had signed Cyrus's death certificate by killing Wolf, and Cyrus had a feeling Chase probably knew Wolf was Fabian's son when he killed him. He was certain Chase was probably trying to get rid of Cyrus without having to do the deed himself. If Cyrus had to die over this shit, he wasn't going quietly. Chase had fucked his life up, and payback would be a real bitch. *It's time for that nigga to take his medicine for his bad judgment.*

Cyrus's cell phone rang just as he finished getting dressed. He looked at it and smiled malignantly: It was soft-ass Corey. Cyrus took his time answering it but picked it up before it went to voicemail. "Hey, Corey!" he said, his voice dripping with false good cheer.

There was a heartbeat of silence and then Corey answered, "Um... hey, Cyrus. Where you at?"

Cyrus laughed humorlessly. "I got an even better question, Corey. Where the fuck you been for almost three weeks?"

There was a pause from Corey that was so long, Cyrus thought he'd hung up.

"Your punk ass still there?" he asked.

Corey sighed heavily. "Yeah, I'm still here, Cyrus. I didn't call you so you could ream me out. You need to chill with that shit, Cyrus—for real."

Cyrus frowned and gripped the phone harder. "Who you talkin' to, Corey? You raisin' up?"

"Nah, nah, Cyrus. I don't raise up. You treat me bad enough. Raisin' up would just make it worse, wouldn't it?"

Cyrus smiled. "Well, you see where it almost got Chase. I wouldn't advise it."

Corey sighed again. "You want to get somethin' to eat? I kind of need to talk to you."

"About what? About how you always disappear with Chase and leave my ass swingin' in the wind?" Cyrus could almost see Corey shaking his head.

"Nobody left you swingin' in the wind, Cyrus."

"No? Then why am I *here by myself*, Corey?"

There was one last stagnant break in conversation before Corey asked again, "You want to get somethin' to eat or not?"

Cyrus raised an eyebrow. *No, this little nigga didn't just put some bass in his voice.* Cyrus was suddenly real eager to see him. He was going to put his foot in his ass. "Yeah, sure, Corey. Sounds good."

"Okay, then meet me at—"

Cyrus cut him off. "I ain't meetin' you nowhere. If you want to break bread with me, you're gonna have to come get me."

"Damn, Cyrus. The streets are hot like *that?*"

"Hotter than that, Corey," Cyrus said and gave him the address.

******

Corey didn't show his late ass up until dusk. He blew his horn, and Cyrus came out with a serious attitude. He was already mad at his brother, and him showing up late just fanned the flames of his discontentment. Cyrus ran his eyes over the block before he decided it was safe and got in. He let Corey have it as soon as the door was closed. "You're fuckin' late, Corey. You don't ask somebody for their time, then show up late. What the fuck is wrong with you?"

Corey, to his surprise, looked at him sideways. "What the fuck is wrong with *you*, Cyrus? Why you comin' at me like that? All I wanted to do was talk to you and try to get somethin' to eat. You gotta make a big fuckin' deal outta every little thing."

Cyrus's jaw dropped in shock. "*What?*"

He wasn't used to Corey talking to him like that. Corey usually took low on every level with him, just to keep the peace. "You heard me, Cyrus. That's all you do—bitch and moan just like a goddamned woman. I'm tired of that shit. From now on, I ain't interested in hearin' all that, unless I'm gonna be gettin' some ass when it's over."

Cyrus stared at Corey, driving the Lexus *his* money had bought, with his face screwed up. "You been spendin' a little too much time with Chase."

Corey shrugged. "Whatever, Cyrus."

Cyrus's eyebrow went back up. "Whatever? I ain't lettin' you talk to me like that, Corey "

Corey stopped at the light and turned his head Cyrus's way. "What are you gonna do, Cyrus? Shoot me?"

Cyrus smiled at him tightly. "Keep it up, Corey, and I just might. Where the hell you been?"

"I was out of the country."

Cyrus smirked. "Doin' what?"

Corey shrugged. "Nothin'. Chillin'."

Cyrus couldn't believe he was talking to Corey. The boy's newfound backbone and nonchalance was unsettling. *What the hell does he mean, he was chillin'? He was somewhere chilling and doing nothing while I been up here tryina fend for my damn himself? Fuck that!* "You got some balls on you, Corey. Was Chase with you?"

Again came that sideways look from Corey. "Why you askin' about Chase? What do you care?"

Cyrus smiled. "He's my brother, Corey."

Corey chuckled dryly. "You don't care about Chase, Cyrus, brother or not. You never did. You shot him! I can still see that shit in my head. That was one of the most fucked-up things I ever saw in my life. Chase might forgive you, but I never will—not *ever.*"

Cyrus stared out the window, then looked back at Corey. He was even starting to sound like Chase, whining for no reason. *I don't need this shit right now,* he thought, scowling at his baby brother. "You'll never forgive me for that, huh? Boy, you and Chase just love to get up on your goddamned soapboxes, don't you? I wasn't really tryin' to shoot him. I was just tryin' to make him shut up."

"Yeah...shut up forever."

Cyrus smiled. *Maybe.* "I knew he was wearin' that vest."

"You did not! You know he don't *always* roll like that. *I* didn't even know."

Cyrus smirked. At the time, he really hadn't cared one way or the other. He still didn't. "Lucky guess?"

Corey turned his head and looked at him. "That's fucked up. You played Russian roulette with his life, Cyrus. Your own brother's life! And you woulda shot me too. You don't care about us! You're a piece of shit, Cyrus, and I don't think I can stomach eating with your sorry self-entitled ass. I'm takin' you home."

Cyrus laughed. "I can't go home, stupid! I got people after me, thanks to that fuckin' dickhead, Smoke."

It was Corey's turn to laugh, and he did—loud and long. "Who started all this shit, Cyrus? *You* did—you and Khalid. I hope they do come and get you! I really hope they do because that's what you deserve." Corey pulled over suddenly and unlocked the doors. "Now get the fuck outta my car, Cyrus! Get out right now!"

Cyrus was way past furious, but he was making an effort to control his temper. He'd already made up his mind about Corey, but there were some things he wanted to know. They stared at each other: Corey was so mad he was breathless, and Cyrus was so mad he was...*smiling*.

"I didn't know you felt that way about me, Corey."

A brief look of comical shock passed over Corey's face. "And I didn't know *you* felt that way about *us*. You were gonna kill your own brothers, Cyrus. I don't think we can ever make that right. Get outta my car."

Cyrus grinned thoughtfully and rubbed his chin. *Time to put the hurt on Chase's ass for real. Time to break that fuckin' monkey's heart.* His eyes twinkled merrily. If he could have stepped outside of himself at that moment, he would have seen that he looked very much like an older version of Chase, about to fly off into one of his murderous rages. "Is that all you wanted to say to me, Corey?"

Corey nodded. "Yeah, that's it. Get out."

"Fratricide is what they call it," Cyrus said pointedly, reaching under his T-shirt like he was about to scratch an itch.

Corey frowned. "*Fratricide?* What the fuck are you talkin' about, Cyrus?"

"Fratricide, Corey," Cyrus said patiently, "is when you kill your own brother." He pulled his nine out and pointed it at Corey.

Corey didn't even look scared. Instead, he looked resigned and angry. He shook his head. "I ain't scared to die, Cyrus. Life with you has been Hell on Earth anyway. But I hope you know that if you kill me—or even if he finds out you drew your damned piece on me—Chase is gonna kill *you*. You sure you want to die like that?"

Cyrus smiled and shrugged. "It doesn't really matter. Nothin' really does, not to me anyway. You and Chase turned your backs on me just when I needed you most. You niggas left me hangin' in my darkest hour. That's some shit *I* can't forgive, Corey."

Corey looked at him like he knew it would be pointless to even try to change his mind. He looked extremely sad, yet Cyrus had never seen such a stoic look of acceptance on such a young face. In a very twisted way, he was almost proud of him. "I'll say it again. Ain't nobody leave you hangin', Cyrus. We came right back."

Cyrus raised an eyebrow. "Right back from where?"

Corey looked at him steadily and smiled a glittery little smile of his own. "I'll never tell, so you might as well kill me. Chase is happy now. Just leave him alone."

"What the fuck does that mean?"

"Pull the trigger, Cyrus," Corey said quietly and then shook his head. "Mama is probably rollin' over in her grave."

Cyrus laughed. *If he only knew.* "Your mother was a piece of shit, Corey. You didn't know her like I did. Maybe you can ask her about it when you see her."

Corey looked at him with revulsion. "Why do you keep talkin'? Just pull the trigger, you mean, selfish bastard."

Cyrus laughed and shot him in the space between his eyebrows. The sound was very loud in the small space, and Cyrus watched with a mixture of curiosity and distaste as his baby brother's brains flew out the back of his head and dripped down the window behind him. "So you *did* have more than straw in your head, huh, Corey?" *So Chase was happy?* He looked at Corey and smiled, knowing he wouldn't be for long.

Chapter 22

Bliss was having a late dinner with Chase in his office at Cream when Dee walked in without knocking and closed the door behind her. "Chase, I'm sorry, but I think we got a problem." She looked at Bliss apologetically as Chase stood up and tossed his napkin on top of his plate.

"What kind of problem?"

Dee took a deep breath and came a little further into the room, wringing her hands.

Bliss stood, too, suddenly scared—especially when Dee's eyes filled up with water. Dee was not a woman who was easily ruffled.

"Chase, the cops are outside. They want to talk to you."

Chase's eyebrows went up, and he took a step back. "What do they want?"

There was a sharp knock, and J.T. stepped into the room. He was visibly upset, but he was calm. "Chase, we got a couple detectives by the bar waitin' to speak to you."

Chase rubbed at the scar under his jaw. "That's what Dee said. They lookin for *me*?"

Bliss put her hand over her mouth. "Oh God!"

Chase put his arm around her.

"No, I don't think so. They didn't roll up, Chase. They came in real quiet and respectful."

Chase's head went back a little. "Aw shit, J.T. What do you think they want?"

J.T. shrugged, though not with indifference. "I don't know. Sounds like bad news to me."

Chase kissed Bliss's forehead and looked in her eyes. "If they take me out of here, you go stay with Dee until everything works out. She knows where I keep all my documents. I still got stuff for you to sign. *Sign it immediately*. If something happens to me, you and Corey get everything, except what already has Dee's and J.T.'s names on it."

What the hell is he talking about, if something happens to him? "You mean…if they arrest you?"

He nodded. "Be quiet, baby. Don't talk. Don't say anything without our lawyer." He turned to Dee. "Send them in and then call Stan Markowitz and get him on standby."

Dee nodded and disappeared.

"Stan is our lawyer?" Bliss asked.

Chase nodded. "That's right. Everybody relax," Chase said and leaned against the corner of his desk.

Dee came back half a minute later with two big cops, one black and one Hispanic. They stepped in and looked around appreciatively, and Chase folded his arms across his chest. The black one spoke. "Good evening, sir. Are you Chase Brown?"

"Yes I am."

The cop looked at Bliss and J.T. "Family?"

Chase nodded. "My wife and my best friend."

The detective nodded at them and pushed on. "I'm Detective Gibson, and this is Detective Silva. Do you know Corey Brown?"

Chase bounced off the desk like it was on fire.

Bliss was instantly at his side. She glanced at the other cop who tucked his lips in and looked away.

Dee returned to the room and stood near J.T. "What happened to Corey?"

Gibson pressed on. "You *do* know him?"

When Chase started shaking, it terrified Bliss. She knew it was bad. She tried to put her arms around his waist, but Chase pushed her away and walked right up to Gibson.

"He's my little brother. *What happened to Corey?!"* he screamed at him.

Gibson put a firm hand on Chase's arm and looked at him like he'd rather be anywhere but there, giving him this horrible news. "Mr. Brown, I'm sorry, but we are here to inform you that your brother, Corey Brown, was found—"

Before the officer could finish, Chase went into what Bliss first thought was a swoon, like he might pass out.

"Oh God! *Corey!"* he said, his voice mournful and full of sorrow. He dropped to his knees with his hands over his face.

Bliss went down with him, her arms wrapped around him protectively.

"Oh God. Not Corey," he wailed.

"Mr. Brown?" Gibson called his name with audible sympathy.

"What happened?" J.T. asked.

"Corey Brown was found in his car on Avenue D with a single gunshot wound to the head."

Dee gasped, and J.T. shook his head.

"Oh no," Bliss whispered.

Chase had grown still.

"Mr. Brown, your brother was taken to Brookdale Hospital. We need someone to come and ID the body," Detective Silva said.

"Could you give us a minute?" J.T. asked.

Gibson nodded. "We'll be outside. We have a few questions."

They left the room, and Chase removed his hands from his face. Bliss thought he was crying, but he wasn't. He stood and pulled her to her feet. His eyes were full of misery, and a muscle clenched angrily in his jaw. "Let's go. Dee, could you stay here and hold things down?"

Dee nodded through her tears. "Whatever you need. Chase, I'm so sorry."

Chase nodded grimly. "Not as sorry as whoever killed Corey is gonna be."

"Chase what are you gonna do?" Bliss asked. *This can't be*

happening, she thought. She put her hand to her face and brushed away her own tears.

Chase put his arm around her and gave her a squeeze. "Don't get upset, Bliss. You stay here with Dee, and I'll be back as soon as I can. Come on, J.T."

When he turned to go, Bliss grabbed his arm. "I'm going with you."

He looked down at her like he was weighing the pros and cons in his head. He finally nodded and took her hand. "Okay."

They left the office and followed Gibson and Silva in J.T.'s Range Rover to Brookdale Hospital.

Bliss watched Chase silently the whole time, waiting for him to fall apart. Other than his initial reaction, Chase had been extraordinarily calm, as if he'd retreated to some deep, dark place inside of himself. Bliss knew how much Chase loved Corey. His grief had to be enormous, but so far he was holding it in. She was *very* worried about him, and she didn't like what he'd said about whoever killed Corey being sorry.

They reached the hospital and followed the detectives down to the morgue. Chase held Bliss's hand and walked slightly ahead of her, with J.T. at her side. Gibson ushered them into a small room with a monitor, and Silva joined them shortly and folded his arms across his chest. "It'll just be a moment," he said.

They stood in silence and waited. A few moments later, the monitor turned white, and Corey's handsome face appeared. It was swollen, and there was a hole right between his eyes.

A small choked sound escaped from Chase as he put his hand over his mouth and turned his face away. He shook his head in disbelief.

"Is this your brother, Mr. Brown?"

Chase nodded. Tears spilled over and ran down his face, and Bliss's heart went out to him. "Yeah. Yeah, that's him." His voice was a whisper.

J.T. put his hand on Chase's shoulder, and Chase shrugged it off, but J.T. didn't seem offended.

Bliss was afraid to touch him. She looked back at the screen. *Poor*

Corey. Who could do such a thing?

Chase looked at the screen again and walked out of the room with the cops following right behind him.

Bliss looked at J.T., who was also staring at the screen. He put his hand out and touched it. "Damn, youngster."

Bliss left the room in search of Chase. She stopped short when she found him down the hall talking to Gibson and Silva. She didn't know what to do, so she just waited for them to finish as J.T. came out of the room and dropped an arm over her shoulders. Chase waved them away.

"Come on, Bliss," J.T. said.

Bliss felt sick as she followed J.T. out of the hospital and back to the car. Corey was dead, and it all seemed surreal. *Corey...*

J.T. opened the door for her and helped her in. He stood there looking down at her with hurt eyes. "Um..." he said and choked up. "You okay?" Before Bliss could answer him, he broke down, sobbing harshly. He folded his arms on the hood of the car and buried his face into them.

Bliss jumped out and put her hand on his broad shoulder. There were no words she could console him with. In fact, there was nothing she could do for anybody—Corey least of all. Bliss was crying, too, for she'd also loved him. She watched J.T. cry for Corey like his heart was broken.

Chase touched her shoulder. "I got him, Bliss."

Bliss stepped out of the way and wrung her hands helplessly.

Tears were running steadily down Chase's face as his hand replaced Bliss's on J.T.'s back. "*Jayson,* come on, man," Chase said in a soothing voice, using his name that Bliss had almost forgotten about.

J.T. straightened up, pulled his handkerchief out of his pocket, and wiped his face with it. Then he blew his nose and returned it to his pocket. His voice trembled at first but then grew stronger. "Well...I guess that's that."

"No it ain't. Let's go," Chase said in a low voice. He got in the backseat with Bliss as J.T. started driving.

Sabrina A. Eubanks

"Where are we goin'?" J.T. tossed over his shoulder.

"Home," Chase answered. Then he turned to Bliss and took both of her hands in his. The tears were still coming, but he acted as if they weren't there at all. "Bliss, sweetheart, you have to listen to me. I know we talked about certain things before we got married, and I know I made certain promises, but, baby, this is different. Somebody took my baby brother away from me tonight. You have to understand that I can't just let that shit stand. Somebody killed Corey, Bliss, and they ain't gonna be walkin' around like that don't mean shit—like it's all right."

Bliss didn't say anything at first. She studied her husband's face and examined his tears. He was crying for Corey, of course, but he was also crying because he was angry. She slid over to him and put her arms around him. She kissed his wet cheeks, and he hugged her back. "I loved Corey too. I'm so sorry. I can imagine how you must feel if I feel so bad. I'm your wife, Chase, for better or for worse. I understand what you're saying, but I'm not gonna give you my permission to go lookin' for revenge and gettin' yourself shot too."

Chase looked so hurt and grief stricken in that moment. He narrowed his eyes in his sorrow and shook his head, but then he smiled through his tears. "Okay, Bliss, but I really didn't ask you for it."

Bliss wasn't mad at him. He was her *husband,* and she understood him. He ran his fingers through her hair. "When we get home, I'm gonna have to make a run, sweetheart—me and J.T. I don't want you to be alone, because I don't know what's goin' on, so I'm gonna ask Dee to come stay with you until I get back."

"Okay. Whatever you think is best, Chase."

Chase made the call, and they rode the rest of the way in silence. When they got home, Chase went to the bedroom to change his clothes. Bliss followed him and sat on the bed, watching him. He pulled on his black jeans, put on his black Uptowns, paused, and put on a vest.

Bliss shook her head.

Chase looked at her, but only smiled a little and didn't say anything.

Then he slipped on a black T-shirt and pulled on his driving gloves.

"You're gonna shoot someone tonight, aren't you, Chase?"

Chase laughed, and his eyes sparkled dangerously. "No, honey. I usually don't shoot people." Chase took a flat wooden box off the top closet shelf and opened it. From it, he withdrew a silver-handled straight razor and put it in his pocket.

Bliss put a shocked hand over her mouth. "Jesus, Chase! You're scaring me."

He smiled at her with that bone-chilling glint in his eyes. "I know. I'm scarin' me too."

Bliss shuddered. She'd never seen that side of Chase, and she never wanted to see it again. She put an unconsciously sheltering hand over her stomach.

Chase looked alarmed. "You okay, Bliss?"

"I'm fine, but I don't like this at all."

Chase looked at her. "Me neither, but I gotta go, baby. Dee should be here real soon. You want me to stay till she comes?"

"No. Just get this over with and hurry back."

"Okay." He reached into the closet and took a .32 out of the pocket of a suit jacket and handed it to her. "If anybody comes around here with an unfamiliar face—and I mean anybody—you shoot his ass without askin' questions and then call the police."

Bliss nodded, even though she could never imagine herself doing something like that. "Whatever you say, Chase."

Chase frowned at her. "No, Bliss. Don't just dismiss me like that. *Do it.*"

She blinked back tears. "Okay, Chase."

His face softened. "Don't cry. I'm sorry, but please do it."

"*I said all right!*" she yelled at him.

He walked over to her and kissed her. "I love you, Bliss."

"I love you too."

They walked back out into the living room, and J.T. stood up. "You ready?"

"Yeah, let's go. Bliss, I'll be back as soon as I can."

She nodded.

Chase kissed her again and left with J.T.

Bliss went into the bedroom and put the gun Chase had given her on the dresser and changed into a pair of shorts and one of Chase's T-shirts. She went back out to the kitchen, barefoot, and got a glass of water. She put the kettle on for tea and sat at the breakfast bar. Corey was dead, and her husband was going to kill whoever did it with a straight razor, and she knew it. She couldn't really blame Chase; everybody loved Corey.

The elevator started to rise, startling her. Bliss got up and looked through the peephole. She frowned and opened the door before the bell rang. "Cyrus? What are you doing here?" she asked.

Cyrus looked her over slow and smiled sunnily. "Better question, Ms. Riley, is what are *you* doing here?" He pushed his way in and closed the door.

Chapter 23

So this is why Chase has been so difficult? I should have known. Nothing can fuck a man up more than a pretty woman. Cyrus chuckled to himself and shook his head as he locked the door.

Bliss took a step back as he took one toward her. She looked uncertain.

Cyrus smiled at her. "You didn't answer my question, Ms. Riley. What are you doin' in Chase's apartment, barefoot and wearin' his shirt? You his girlfriend now?"

Bliss stared at him with enormous, almost scared brown eyes. "Um...no. No, I'm not."

Cyrus frowned. "Then what you doin' chillin' in his spot, wearin' his shit? Is he here?" Cyrus rolled up on her, and she backed away. A sparkle caught his eye.

"Cyrus, I don't know what—"

Cyrus laughed, not quite wrapping his mind around what he was looking at.

Bliss realized what had caught his attention and put her left hand in her pocket.

"Is that a *wedding ring* you're tryin' to hide from me, Ms. Riley?"

"Why are you here, Cyrus?"

He grinned and grabbed her arm. "Never mind me. Let me see your hand!" He pulled on her forearm and wrenched her hand out of her pocket. Bliss shrieked like he was killing her, and he just laughed, ogling at all the pretty diamonds that made up her ring. "Son of a bitch! You married him, didn't you?"

Bliss looked at him with those huge eyes, like she was afraid to move. Her mouth started trembling, and he could see in her eyes that her mind was racing. She put her hand out to keep him from coming any further. "Do you know about Corey, Cyrus? Is that why you're here?"

He laughed real low. "Of course I know about Corey. I killed him myself."

Bliss's skin paled as all the blood rushed to her head. "Oh no! You killed Corey?" she asked in high-pitched, terrified disbelief.

Cyrus nodded. "Oh yeah. I did it with this!" he said and pulled his nine out of his waistband with a flourish.

Bliss started screaming and ran toward the bedroom.

Cyrus caught her by the T-shirt and gave her a backhand across the face. "Shut up! Stop that screamin' and come tell me about the wedding! I must have misplaced my fuckin' invitation!" Bliss kept screaming, so he slapped her again, busting her lip this time. He threw her down on the sectional and pointed his gun at her. "You need to calm the fuck down before you end up like Corey."

Bliss had blood dripping down her chin. She wiped at her wounded mouth with her fingers and stared at the bright red blood for a moment. Her eyes narrowed in fury. "Chase is gonna fuck you up!" she spat at the monster.

Cyrus sat down next to her and smiled. He'd been tired, but he was suddenly invigorated, like he could tap dance to China. The police were looking for him, Fabian was looking for him, Khalid had gotten his last rites, and he'd killed his own brother. He wasn't about to go back to prison 'cause he knew that shit sucked. There was nowhere for him to go but down. However else this shit ended, he knew he was going to die and that Chase was going to be the one to kill him. But he'd have his say first, maybe raise his last bit of ruckus before Chase's crazy ass silenced him forever.

Bliss was whimpering now, and Cyrus wasn't above hitting her again. He didn't hold women in the same high esteem as Chase and Corey did, and he had his reasons for that. Cyrus slid toward her, and Bliss pressed herself into the sectional, making herself seem even smaller than she actually was. Cyrus leaned toward her. "You scared of me, Bliss? I *can* call you Bliss now that were family, right? You shouldn't be half as afraid of me as you need to be of that crazy, unstable motherfucker you married."

Bliss bristled, even though she was terrified. "Don't you talk about my husband like that! How dare you! Maybe you're the crazy, unstable motherfucker," she hissed at him.

Cyrus laughed. *That shit's funnier than she knows.* "You know what, Bliss? Maybe we're *both* crazy…and I just may really prove to be a real *motherfucker* after all. Why don't you tell me about this marriage shit that I somehow managed to miss."

"You better get out of here before Chase gets back. He's going to kill you for murdering Corey."

Cyrus shrugged. "Yeah, yeah, yeah…and he's gonna fuck me up for hittin' you. So what? You think I'm scared of him? You think I give a fuck what that psycho does?"

The doorbell rang, and Cyrus's eyebrows went up.

"Who the fuck is that? You expectin' company?" He shot up and went to the intercom and buzzed in whoever was there, never taking his gun off of his sister-in-law. Cyrus scratched his chin and looked thoughtful. "Hmm…let me think like Chase. Corey was killed tonight. He's taken J.T. and run out to kill whoever did it, only he's got his new wife at home. He doesn't want to leave her alone, not knowing the full situation, so he needs a babysitter to look after you. Corey's too busy occupying a slot at the morgue, so he couldn't ask him. Who else does he trust?" He walked to the elevator as it trundled up. "Good ol' Dee!" he reasoned and laughed as the door slid open.

Dee was inside talking on her cell phone. When she saw Cyrus her eyes grew wide with surprise and then narrowed in fright when they caught sight of his gun and Bliss's busted lip and bloody nose.

"Hey, Dee! Who you talkin' to?"

Dee stared at Cyrus and spoke calmly into her phone. "Yes, Chase, that was Cyrus. It looks like he's been beating on your wife. He's got a gun, and he seems a little undecided about who he wants to shoot first. Get here as soon as you can." She hung up and put her phone in her bag as she looked at Cyrus with steely eyes. "You're in a lot of trouble, buster."

Cyrus frowned at her. Dee was another one he'd always hated. She'd always treated Chase like he was God come down from the mountain. "Shut up, bitch, and get over there with Bliss, before I knock your teeth out." He went to the bar and took out the Hennessey. Cyrus sat across from them and opened it up, and Dee looked disgusted when he started swigging from the bottle. "Oh, Dee, I didn't get the chance to tell you the news."

"What news is that, Cyrus?"

Cyrus gestured to Bliss with the bottle. "Go ahead and tell her, Bliss."

Bliss looked at Dee with shocked eyes. "Cyrus killed Corey!" she announced in loud indignation.

Dee's mouth dropped open, and her strong front faltered as her eyes filled with tears. "Cyrus! No! *Why?*"

Cyrus smiled a dark little smile. "He told me to get out of his car. You know, Corey had entirely too much mouth on him at the end."

"Chase is going to kill you, Cyrus."

Cyrus nodded and took another swig from the bottle. "Yeah, I know, but before he does, I got somethin' to say to him that will ruin his life the same way he ruined mine."

"What are you talking about, Cyrus?" Dee asked like she was tired of him.

"Chase painted me into a very nasty corner when he waited so long to kill Wolf instead of doing it when I asked him to. He fucked me over, and now it's either go to jail or die. I been to jail, Delia, and I *did not* have a good time there. All this shit is Chase's fault. He was supposed to be holdin' me down...but instead, he was chasing Bliss." He gave Bliss a black look and weighed the gun in his hand. "Now that I put it that way, maybe all this shit is *your* fault. I should smash your pretty little face for that."

Bliss slid real close to Dee, and Dee put her arm around her. "Haven't you done that already? Leave her alone, Cyrus. You're already in enough trouble."

Cyrus took another swig and laughed comically. "You're right, Dee. Wouldn't want to have Chase *mutilate* me before he cuts my throat just because he's extra pissed, would I?"

There was no answer from either one of them. They both just stared at him in disbelief, like he was a lunatic.

Cyrus drank more liquor; he wasn't drunk enough. As brave as he was, he was still a bit of a coward. He didn't actually want to *feel it* when Chase pulled his razor through his flesh, and he thought a couple more would do the trick. He turned the bottle up again and looked at the frightened women huddled together. He had no *real* beef with them, and any he did have, he blamed Chase for anyway.

Still, they were sitting there looking at him like they hated him, as they should have. He'd done plenty of damage to plenty of lives, but he wasn't finished. His life was over, and he was sure it was all because of Chase. Cyrus frowned, and his thoughts began to get muddy. He stood up and swayed a little, and he considered it a good thing. He still knew what he was doing, but he'd just crossed the line into the altered state of feeling no pain. He walked over to Bliss and looked down at her.

She shrank away from him.

"You and Chase happy, Bliss?"

She looked at him like she thought he was joking. "What?"

"You heard me. I asked if you and Chase are happy." He spoke to her like she was slow.

Bliss gave him a defiant look and turned her head.

Insolence. Just like Chase. He couldn't stand that disrespectful shit. He grabbed her by the hair, snatching her out of Dee's arms, and threw her to the floor.

Dee sprang off the couch and started pummeling him with her fists. "Get off of her! Stop it, Cyrus!" she screamed at him as she scratched and clawed and yanked, trying to pull him off Bliss.

Cyrus started laughing. One of his hands was double wrapped in

Bliss's hair. He could feel strands snapping as she struggled against him and clawed at his hand, trying to get away. He found their attack a bit interesting, but he couldn't deal with them both at the same time, especially with his gun still in his left hand. Cyrus rammed his shoulder into Dee, knocking her away, then turned the gun around and smashed her in the face with it. He hit her twice, as hard as he could, and Dee dropped to the floor.

Bliss was screaming her head off, and she kept attacking him with her hands, still trying to get away.

Cyrus pulled her to her feet by her hair and threw her back on the sectional. She wouldn't stop screaming, so Cyrus punched her in the jaw hard enough to hurt his knuckles.

Bliss reverted to silence and stared at him with huge eyes.

"See what you made me do? All you had to do was answer one simple question. Jesus Christ!" He looked down at Dee and saw that she had a pretty decent gash in her forehead. He left her where she was and picked up her purse. Cyrus found her cigarettes, took one, and lit it with her lighter. He reclaimed his seat and turned the Hennessey up again. Cyrus stared at Bliss and smoked his cigarette, dusting the ashes on Chase's blond hardwood floor. Just as he finished, he heard the garage door going up. Cyrus sighed and stood up, grinding the cigarette butt into Chase's beautiful floor with his heel. He smiled at Bliss sadly. "Guess it's time to holler at my boy."

Chapter 24

They were a half-block away when Chase raised the door to the garage. He was having a hard time digesting the events of the day. Somebody had killed Corey, and the streets were coming up cold, without anybody laying claim to Corey's death. Baby didn't even know. And to make matters worse, now he had to deal with more of Cyrus's bullshit. *That asshole probably popped out of his hidey-hole and went damn crazy when he heard about Corey.* Chase also figured Cyrus blamed him for the whole thing. That didn't matter—he was used to it—but if Cyrus had put his hands on Bliss, Chase was going to snap his neck, and that was a promise.

Chase turned to J.T. when he pulled into the garage. "Park the car and then go up in the elevator. I'm gonna take the fire stairs that come up in the kitchen. I don't know what's up with him, but if Cyrus is in there wildin' out, we'll be coming at him from two different sides."

"Sounds good to me," J.T. said and finished parking the Charger.

They got out, and Chase looked across the car roof at his boy. "This is turning into the worst day of my life."

J.T. nodded. "I know."

Chase ran his thumb along the scar under his jaw. "He's probably got his nine. If he comes at you, just shoot him. You good with that, J.T.?"

J.T. nodded and took his own gun out. "No problem at all, Chase."

Chase looked at the floor and grimaced. He looked back at J.T. with sadness born of resignation. He already knew how it was gonna go down. "I'm going to kill my brother, ain't I?"

J.T. nodded. "Yeah, Chase. I'd say that's more than likely."

Chase had known for most of his life it would come to this, but he'd always held on to the hope that maybe—just maybe—it wouldn't have to happen that way. It was horrible, and he didn't want to do it, even if Cyrus *had* put his hands on Bliss.

J.T. looked at him long and hard. "I see *you* have a problem with it though."

Chase sighed and ran a hand over his mouth. "I've got a million problems with it, J.T."

J.T. studied his face. "I know, but something tells me you won't feel that way when this is over."

Chase frowned. "Why not?"

J.T. smiled a tight mirthless smile. "I got a feeling Cyrus has a bit of a death wish. He doesn't want to face whatever's out there waitin' on him, so he's takin' the cowardly way out and lettin' you put him out of every-damn-body's misery, his own included. He's always blamed you for everything that didn't go his way, and he wants to blame you for this too. I also got a feelin' he's gonna go the same way you greased all those fuckers for him. He's gonna force your hand and *make* you do it."

They stared at each other for a moment before Chase turned and started toward the door. "I hate this," he said it to himself, inadvertently loud enough for his friend to hear him.

"I know," J.T. replied, always ride or die.

Chase heard the elevator slide open as he entered the door to the fire stairs. It was the last place on Earth he wanted to be, but Bliss was in there, and he loved her. The sad thing was that he somehow loved Cyrus too. He felt that nasty sting of tears again, but he fought them back. If J.T. was right, he'd probably need them for later.

He stopped at the top of the stairs, listening for the elevator to grind to a halt and trying to get his emotions to their lowest level. He knew from experience that he had less chance of totally losing control if he started with a blank slate. He had to be on E if he didn't want to veer into that psychotic state of bloodlust that kept his razor so busy before the deed was actually done. Chase put his hand on the doorknob and frowned worriedly. There was something very seriously wrong with him, and he was painfully aware of that fact. If the night ended with him killing Cyrus, maybe it would finally be over, because there would be no reason for Smoke to even exist without Cyrus to push Chase to it. The elevator slid open, and Chase opened the fire door as quietly as he could and stepped into the kitchen.

Cyrus had his gun pointed toward J.T., and J.T. was doing the same. "Where's my punk-ass, so-called brother, J.T.?"

Chase closed the door behind him and put his hands in his pockets. "I'm right here, Cyrus." He took in the situation very quickly: Bliss was cowering in a corner of the sofa with blood all over her face, looking like she'd been in a street fight; Dee was unconscious on the floor- bleeding from a head wound; and Cyrus was obviously stark raving mad and damn near three sheets to the wind.

Cyrus whirled around to face Chase, still pointing his gun. He was grinning, and it froze Chase's heart because the grin reminded him of himself. "Good! Come on over here, Chase. I got a lot of shit to say to you."

Chase looked first at the gun, then at Cyrus. He started walking toward him very slowly. "What are you doing here, Cyrus? What made you come into my home and put your hands on my wife? What made you do this to Dee? What's wrong with you, Cyrus?"

Cyrus kept grinning, but his eyes turned serious. "Stop walkin', Chase. Take your hands out of your pockets."

Chase kept walking, but he took his hands out of his pockets. "Fuck you, Cyrus. I'm checkin' on my wife."

J.T. kept his gun pointed toward Cyrus, while Chase crossed the room to Bliss. She leapt off the sofa and ran to him. He closed his arms around her and kissed her swollen lips.

"Are you all right?"

She was hysterical, crying and babbling almost incoherently, clutching at him, then holding him tight.

Chase kissed her forehead and rubbed her back. "Stop, honey. Calm down. I'm here. Nobody's gonna hurt you anymore." He touched her belly lightly. "Is the baby okay?"

She nodded and wiped her tears away. "Yeah, I think so."

"Baby? What fuckin' baby? She's pregnant? Oh *Jesus Christ.* Fuck y'all with this happily-ever-after bullshit!" Cyrus bellowed.

"Shut up, Cyrus, before I shoot you," J.T. said in a low voice.

Dee stirred and sat up slowly, holding her head. She groaned softly, and Chase went to her. "Dee, you all right?"

There was a scary moment when she looked at him like she didn't know him, but then her eyes cleared and she seemed to gather her wits. She looked at Cyrus and got a burst of adrenaline, but she tried to get up too fast and went back down.

Cyrus sucked his teeth. "Get up. I didn't hurt you that bad."

Chase shot him a look and helped her to the couch.

"Back up, Cyrus. Step away," J.T. said in that same low voice, cluing Chase in to the fact that Cyrus was coming toward him and giving him time to straighten up and take his razor out of his pocket.

Bliss made a small, frightened sound and covered her eyes.

"Relax. I just want a drink," Cyrus said. He picked up the Hennessey and turned it up.

Chase looked at him in genuine puzzlement. "Cyrus, what's the matter with you? Why are you drinkin' like that? Is it because of Corey?"

Cyrus shrugged a little. "What about Corey?"

Chase blinked real hard. It seemed like Cyrus didn't know, and he'd have to be the one to tell him. Before he could open his mouth to break the news, though, Dee opened hers.

"He knows, Chase."

Chase looked at Dee and then swung his head back to Cyrus. "Yeah?"

Bliss ran up on him with that hysterical clutching, pointing an accusing finger at Cyrus. "That bastard did it! He told me he did it! He killed Corey!"

"He told me too," Dee said quietly.

Chase was still looking at Cyrus. Cyrus took one last drink and recapped the bottle. He smiled at Chase—a horrendously sinister grin. A funny thing happened in that moment. Chase realized that Cyrus was just as crazy as he was, because he was grinning back at Cyrus with the same diabolical grin himself. Chase pushed Bliss away from him as gently as he could and opened his razor.

Some of the light fell out of Cyrus's eyes, but he held his grin. "I guess it all comes down to this, huh, Smoke?"

Chase felt his blood boiling in his veins. He felt like his eyes were open too wide. His heart was racing. He laughed, even though he didn't mean to. He meant to scream, because what he'd just heard was too far to the left of reality to be true. He didn't think his voice would tremble when he spoke, but it did. "You killed my little brother, Cyrus?"

Cyrus nodded vigorously and licked his lips like what he was about to say tasted really good. "Well, yeah, Chase. I sure did. I blew his brains out and watched them drip down the window of the car I bought him with my own money."

Chase twirled the razor in his hand, and it played its familiar song: *whick-whick-whick.* "What did you kill Corey for, Cyrus?" Chase's voice was a dry, harsh whisper, like the heat from his rage had absorbed all the moisture from his throat.

"Corey waited until his last hour on Earth to grow a backbone. I liked him a lot better without one. He was raisin' up a lot like you, so I popped him." Chase took two steps toward him, but Cyrus just casually sat at the breakfast bar. "I also did it because I knew you'd kill me for it," he admitted, suddenly looking very tired.

Chase stopped in his tracks "What?"

J.T. had said Cyrus would force his hand. He *couldn't* let him live. He'd taken Corey from him and put his hands on Bliss. Yet he was hesitating and he knew it. In his heart, he didn't want to kill Cyrus. He was his fucking brother.

"You heard me. My life's a wrap. It's prison or the cemetery for me, thanks to you. I ain't going back to jail and if I gotta die...I think this is the way it was meant for me to go. Do me two favors before you cut my throat, though, Smoke."

Chase narrowed his eyes. "What?"

"Send everybody outta here. I don't want to die in front of an audience."

Chase laughed and shook his head. "What else?"

Cyrus looked him in the eye. "Let me tell you a story."

They stared at each other, and Chase wondered what he was talking about. *A story? What the hell kind of story could Cyrus possibly tell me? Fuck a story!*

Chase spoke to J.T. without taking his eyes off Cyrus. "J.T., take Bliss and Dee down to the garage. I'll call you when I'm done up here—either that or come back when you hear the screamin' stop."

"Oh God, Chase! No!" Bliss started crying, and Dee grabbed her and went to J.T.

"You got this?" J.T. asked.

Chase nodded. "I got it."

"All right then," he said, and he guided the women downstairs.

Cyrus smiled at Chase. It had none of the bravado and craziness of his recent grinning; this one was one of the saddest smiles Chase had ever seen. "Ready for your story?"

Chase sat on the arm of the sofa a safe distance away from him. "No, but I'll let you have your last request, Cyrus."

"Thanks. I'm about to tell you exactly why I've had such a love-hate relationship with you for your entire life. I think it's only fair to warn you, though, that it may make you crazier than you already are. You *do* know you're crazy, don't you?"

Chase nodded and pulled his gloves up on his hands, still holding his razor. "Yeah, I know." He looked at Cyrus and knew his eyes were glittering. "Go ahead, Cyrus. Shatter me."

"Why are you crying?"

Chase hadn't even realized he was, but he didn't bother to wipe the tears away. "I don't want to kill you, Cyrus."

"Why not? I deserve it."

"Yeah, you do, but you're my brother."

Cyrus shook his head. "Corey was your brother, Chase. You and me got a different type of relation."

Chase's heart tripped over itself, and he frowned. "Fuck you talkin' about, Cyrus?"

Cyrus stared at him, but he seemed a bit removed, as if he was looking into the past. It was a moment before he spoke again. "You know, I got almost fifteen years on you, Chase. Things were really different before you was born. My life with Mama wasn't the same as yours or Corey's. Neither of y'all even knew Mama until she'd halfway gotten her shit together."

Chase had no idea where he was going with his story, but he wasn't gonna sit there and let Cyrus talk shit about his mother. His mother was sacred; she'd died in his arms. "Don't talk about Mama, Cyrus. I mean it. I ain't gonna allow it."

Cyrus kept going like Chase hadn't said anything at all. "When Mama was fourteen, she met a nigga named Wendell Baxter. He was twenty-six years old, fuckin' around with a little girl like that. Wendell didn't give a shit how young she was. He just wanted to know if she could turn a trick. Wendell found our mother, Francie, fresh off a bus from St. Louis at the Port Authority. She'd run away from home because her father was touching her in places he shouldn't have, and nobody believed her. Wendell got her and turned her little young ass right on out."

Chase stared at Cyrus. "You're a fuckin' liar, Cyrus. Mama wasn't no hooker."

"She *was,* Chase. I'm tellin' the truth. Why do you think we don't have any family? We *do*. We just don't know 'em because of the way Francie handled her business. Can I go on?"

Chase shook his head, but Cyrus kept talking.

"Francie got pregnant with me pretty quick. I don't even think she really knew who my father was, but she blamed it on Wendell, and he didn't argue her down since he might have been. After all, he was her pimp. She had me when she was fifteen."

Chase put his fingers on his temples. "Shut up, Cyrus. It's not true."

Cyrus smiled that sad smile. "It is true—every word. I remember being real young—like five or six—and all types of men coming in and out of our apartment, usin' Francie and leavin'. Sometimes I'd wake up in the middle of the night and see and hear Wendell beatin' her ass. He did that on the regular. I remember those days real well, 'cause that was right before Francie had what I like to call her 'breakdown' and turned into another motherfucker on me overnight."

Chase twirled the razor in his hand, getting angrier by the second. He watched Cyrus carefully and knew in his heart he was probably telling the truth—or at least the truth as he believed it to be. "What breakdown? Mama ain't never had no breakdown."

Cyrus sighed and leaned forward. He looked at Chase with a great deal of patience and went on. "Breakdown is just a better way of sayin' Francie got strung out on heroin and stopped givin' a shit about anything that was important, including me."

Chase stood up and put his hands over his ears. "Shut up, Cyrus!"

Cyrus didn't bat an eye. He just talked louder. "Take your hands down, Chase! You need to hear this shit. I know it hurts, but you gotta be a man and listen, okay?"

Chase took his hands down. His lips trembled. "Mama wasn't no dope addict."

Cyrus's sad smile returned. "*She was*, Chase. Don't you remember all the needle marks on her?"

Chase *did not* want to hear it. He narrowed his eyes at Cyrus. "Mama was a diabetic."

Cyrus actually laughed. "Come on, Chase! Diabetics have equipment—boxes of syringes, alcohol pads, and guess what…insulin! They have to keep the insulin in the fridge, Chase. You never seen none of that shit in Francie's house. She was a heroin abuser for eight years, and the only reason she quit was because she got pregnant with *you*."

Chase shook his head in disbelief and returned to his seat. "Mama used heroin while she was pregnant with me?"

Cyrus nodded. "Until she was pregnant enough to show, and then she found Jesus."

Chase stared at him. "Are you telling me this because you think that's what made me the way I am? 'Cause she took heroin when she was pregnant with me?"

Cyrus shook his head, and then he smiled. "Nah. This is the reason I think you're the way you are. I don't believe Francie was wrapped too tight. She did a lot of crazy shit, and she had a lot of flaws. Francie used to talk to herself so loud I'd think she was singin' or somethin'. She'd hurt herself too. She'd burn her fingers with a cigarette lighter, cut her thighs with a razor, and shit like that. Sometimes she'd just slap herself. I used to watch her with my mouth hangin' open. I used to think maybe it was the heroin, but I ain't never seen another addict act quite like that."

Chase felt cold. *Oh my God. I am crazy...because of my mama? Crazy does run in families.* He shuddered and closed his eyes. "Jesus, Cyrus. Please stop." But Cyrus was right. He didn't *want* to hear it, but he *needed* to know.

"That was light shit, Chase. Now I'm gonna tell you somethin' that's *really* gonna fuck you up. This is the part that may make you crazier. It's the reason why I love you, but I hate the day you were born. If you want, you can go ahead and kill me after this, but know that it wasn't my fault."

Chase stood back up. "Take it to the grave, Cyrus. I don't want to hear any more." Chase felt like he didn't even know Francie. This person Cyrus was talking about was not his mother. He looked at Cyrus coldly. He wanted to cut his throat so he'd just shut the fuck up, the lying bastard.

"Francie was a hooker for a long time, and she didn't just do it to keep Wendell happy or for the money. She was probably just as addicted to sex as she was to heroin. Business dried up when she started lookin' like what she was. Wendell used to try and force her to kick, and she'd always go right back. When I was twelve, I had a real good friend named Russell. Mama sent me to get cigarettes, and while I was gone, she fucked Russell in my bed. She did shit like that sometimes, but usually not when she was on heroin by itself. That only happened when she mixed it with other stuff, even if it was just liquor. I woke up one night, and she was on me like a jockey—"

Chase dropped his razor and covered his head with his arms. He fell to his knees, screaming. "I don't wanna hear any more! *Please, Cyrus! Don't tell me that! I don't want to know that!*"

Cyrus sat there and watched him scream. He made no attempt to go for Chase's razor.

Chase took his arms down and backed away from him. He stopped screaming, but tears were coursing down his cheeks so hard he could barely see.

Cyrus smiled at him. "It's the worst thing in the world, isn't it, Chase? It's a deep, dark, greasy, slimy secret—somethin' to make you finish goin' crazy, right?"

"You're a liar, Cyrus!" Chase screamed at him.

Cyrus laughed softly. "Yeah, maybe, but not about this. Francie wouldn't come in my room often, but she came. I can't think of a another man she had anything to do with during that time. If she did sleep with somebody else, I didn't see him. So that makes me a little more than your brother, Chase, doesn't it?"

Chase snatched his razor up off the floor and leapt at Cyrus like a lion on a gazelle. He knocked him off the stool at the breakfast bar and brought his razor down. It slid across Cyrus's cheek, exposing blood and torn flesh.

Cyrus screamed laughter.

"Shut up! Shut up, you fuckin' lying bastard! I'll kill you! I'll kill you! I'll kill you!" Chase slashed at him furiously and blood few hitting the walls, spraying the furniture, coating Chase like paint. He was screaming at the top of his lungs, slashing at Cyrus until his arm was tired. Then he finally got up, exhausted, crying, and shaking uncontrollably. Chase crawled to the farthest corner of the room and dropped his razor. He curled himself into a ball and was still.

Epilogue

Chase stood by the window with his hands in his pockets, watching the snow fall. It was Christmas Eve, and he would have thought all that peace on Earth, goodwill toward men stuff would have sent him in a downward spiral, right back to the blackness he'd stayed in for two months after Cyrus "died." But surprisingly, he wasn't upset. Instead, he was happy—happy and grateful. The corners of his handsome mouth turned up into a small smile of contentment. He'd finally found happiness; he'd found Bliss. He'd asked her once if she could live up to her name, and she had...ten times over.

Chase thought Bliss would bounce after what went down between him and Cyrus, and he would have understood if she had. It was awfully heavy stuff to deal with, too heavy for Chase himself to handle. He remembered that night a lot more vividly than he cared to. J.T. had put Bliss and Dee in a cab to Dee's place, and he'd come back upstairs after the screaming stopped—only it was Chase's screaming and not Cyrus's. *His* screaming had stopped *way* before Chase's. J.T. just silently picked Chase up in a fireman's carry and put him to bed. When Chase woke up much, much, later, the place was pristine, Cyrus was gone forever, and his wife was in his bed.

Chase and J.T. never spoke about that evening. There was really no need to. They'd been friends for a long time, and they loved each other like brothers, but Chase didn't want J.T. to know what Cyrus had told him before he took his life. There was only one person in the world he'd told about that, and that was Bliss. He only told her because she had a right to know; she was his wife, and she was pregnant with his baby. She listened to the whole sordid story without judgment, and when he was finished, she looked him in the eye and told him she loved him—for better or for worse—and she meant it.

Chase turned his head and looked at her. She looked happy too. They'd traded up, gotten rid of the loft, and bought a chic and stylish apartment on the Upper West Side. Right now, they had a full house: Bliss's parents, her brother and sister and their families, Tasha, J.T., and Dee. To Chase's surprise, Dee had brought a date. Not so much to his surprise, J.T. and Tasha were seeing each other, without claiming they were actually seeing each other.

Bliss caught his eye from across the room. She smiled at him warmly and made her way across the room to him and handed him one of their babies; she gave him Corey and kept Hope to herself. Chase looked down at his son and missed his baby brother poignantly. Losing Corey hurt him deeply every day. He guessed that was Cyrus's legacy to him—to make him hurt forever. Funny…he didn't miss Cyrus at all. He didn't even miss him enough to ask J.T. what he did with the body, and he didn't really care. Cyrus was gone, and he was free.

Bliss smiled up at him, and she was like the sun. "What are you thinking about, standing over here by yourself, being so quiet?"

Chase kissed the top of Corey's head and smiled back. "I was thinkin' about how much I love you and our kids, just standin' here being grateful. I don't have to go searchin' for happiness anymore 'cause I got it right here. Thanks, Bliss."

Bliss kissed him, and their babies giggled and squealed. "You don't have to thank me for loving you, Chase. I'm your wife. I always will."

Chase smiled. "Merry Christmas, Bliss."

"Merry Christmas."

He kissed his wife, appreciating her for what and who she was. She'd shown him that there was always light after darkness—that there was hope and love…and Bliss.

G STREET CHRONICLES

~ PRESENTS ~

Lies, deceit and murder ran rampant throughout the city of Atlanta. Real and his lady, Constance, were living in the lap of luxury, with fancy cars, expensive clothes and a million dollar home until someone close to them alerted the feds to their illegal activity.

At the blink of an eye their perfect life was turned upside down. Just as Real was sorting things out on the home front, the head of Miami's most powerful Cartel gave him an ultimatum that would eventually force him back into the life he had swore off forever. Knowing this lifestyle would surely put Constance in danger, he made plans to send her away until the score was settled but things spiraled out of control. Now Real and Constance are in a fight for survival where friends become enemies and murder is essential. Atlanta's underworld to Miami's most affluent community—no stone was left unturned as Real fought to keep Constance safe while attempting to regain control of the lifestyle he once would kill for.

From the city of Atlanta to the cell block of Georgia's most dangerous prison, life under the City Lights would never be the same.

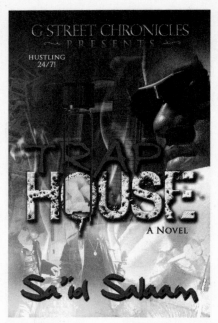

Trap House is an unflinching account of the goings on of an Atlanta drug den and the lives of those who frequent it. Its cast of characters include the Notorious P.I.G., the proprietor of the house, who uses his power to satisfy his licentious fetishes. Of his customers, there's Wanda, an exotic dancer who loathes P.I.G., but only tolerates him because he has the best dope in town. Wanda's boyfriend Mike is the owner of an upscale strip club, as well as a full time pimp.

Tiffany and Marcus are the teenage couple who began frequenting the Trap House after snorting a few lines at a party. Can their love for each other withstand the demands of their fledging addiction, or will it tear them apart?

P.I.G.'s wife Blast, doorman Earl and a host of other colorful characters round out the inhabitants of the Trap House.

Trap House is the bastard child of real life and the author's vivid imagination. Its author, Sa'id Salaam, paints a graphic portrait of the inner-workings of an under-world. He takes you so close you can almost hear the sizzle of the cocaine as it's smoked—almost smell the putrid aroma of crack as it's exhaled. Yet for all the grit and grime, Trap House has the audacity to be a love story. Through the sordid sex and brutality is an underlying tale of redemption and self empowerment. Trap House drives home the reality that everyone is a slave to something.

Who's your master?

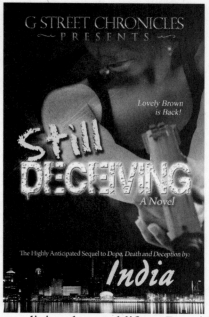

G STREET CHRONICLES
~ PRESENTS ~

Lovely Brown
is Back!

Still
DECEIVING

A Novel

The Highly Anticipated Sequel to *Dope, Death and Deception* by:

India

Lovely Brown was living the good life as Detroit's top drug dealer, operating under the alias LB. Everything was going smooth until her father Lucifer escaped from prison, ready to return to the throne and destroy anyone in his path, including Lovely. While running for her life, she was also being investigated by the Feds and simultaneously set-up for the murder of her mafia connects' nephew. This resulted in a ONE MILLION DOLLAR bounty being placed on her head. Achieving the impossible, Lovely managed to escape unscathed.

Now, five years after she left all the Dope, Death and Deception behind and she's finally living a normal life, things get complicated. Issues from her past come right to her front door. Once again Lovely finds herself in a bad situation with her back against the wall—looking sideways at everyone in her corner. Lies have been told and love has been tested.

Just when she thought things were over, it looks as if someone is Still Deceiving!

WELCOME TO THE JUNGLE!!

The King, raised in the hood with his family, saw a lot of suffering. He witnessed death and destruction within his own family—poverty and desperation of his own people. Instead of being part of the problem, he became part of the solution and rose to the top of his game. In his mind… it was survival.

After an encounter with a brilliant scientist, King began to plot something so huge, that no one would see it coming or be able to stop the cycle…not even the police.

Mz. Robinson's
Love, Lies & Lust Series

Mz. Robinson

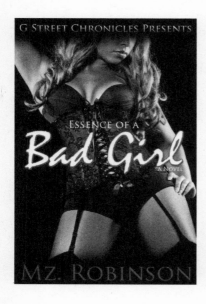

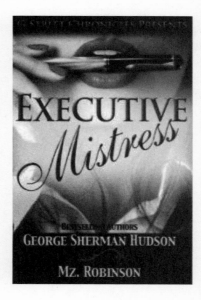

Please join our G Street Chronicles Fan Page on Facebook
and
follow us on Twitter.

Your feedback is important to us.
Let us know what you think about our books.
fans@gstreetchronicles.com

To keep up with the latest from G Street Chronicles,
email us and we'll add you to our mailing list.
fans@gstreetchronicles.com